Who am I...?

    She woke alone in the dark, face–down on the floor and with dirt in her mouth. The first thing she felt was the pain, like a hundred needles sliding deep within her right side and stomach; the second was heat, searing her skin from behind and singeing the hair on her arms. There was no time to wonder where she was or how she'd gotten here. Instinct sent her hands forward, making them search for something to grab onto. She found a chair and a table and hauled herself to her knees, then managed to lurch upright. In the short span of seconds it had taken her to stand, the darkness had become lit by a fierce red glow...

Coming in 2001 from DarkTales Publications...

The Asylum Volume 2: The Violent Ward
More tales of madness edited by Victor Heck

Cold Comfort
Stories by Nancy Kilpatrick

Six–Inch Spikes
Stories by Edo van Belkom

Harlan
A novel by David Whitman

A Flock of Crows is Called a Murder
A novel by Jim Viscosi

Faust: Love of the Damned
A screenplay by David Quinn

True Tales of the Scarlet Sponge
A novella by Wayne Allen Sallee

The Shaman Cycle Series
Novels by Adam Niswander

and more...

www.darktales.com

To: Gak —
Please stay away
from anything
resembling
one of
those...

DEAD TIMES
YVONNE NAVARRO

Earthquake
Things!!!

Love Yvonne

DarkTales Publications

Kansas City, Missouri • Chicago, Illinois
2000

DEADTIMES by Yvonne Navarro.
Copyright © 2000 by Yvonne Navarro.
All Rights Reserved.
For information contact Darktales Publications.

Published in the United States by:

Darktales Publications
P.O. Box 675
Grandview, Missouri, 64030

ISBN 0-9672029-5-7

PRINTED IN THE UNITED STATES OF AMERICA

ACKNOWLEDGMENTS

Thanks to Martin Cochran and Jeff Osier for reading through the original manuscript, and to Wayne Edwards of Merrimack Books for publishing Chapter Three in *Palace Corbie 6*, Chapter Six in *Palace Corbie 7*, and Chapter Seven in *Palace Corbie 8*. Special thanks to Debra Salata for lending her expertise to Chapters Four and Five, and also to my mother for offering some of her historical knowledge. As for Linda Schroyer...I've never forgotten how she saved several troubled documents from oblivion, destruction, or outdated equipment. A lot of time and research went into this project: its writing and final composition has outlived four computers and more than as many addresses...almost as many as the character in these pages!

In loving memory of

Rochelle Yvonne Holmes
April 7, 1973 - July 2, 1973

and all the wonderful
things that might have been.

You are not forgotten.

PROLOGUE
The Early 1700s

he Indians were screaming in the night.

Crouched between a couple of man-sized boulders around which he had stuffed dried brush and tumbleweeds, Daniel Johnson wished he could chance a quick drink from his waterskin and thought longingly of the lush, green forests on the east coast. The people there were soft and placid and knew nothing about the harshness of life in this arid western wasteland. They moaned about the cold and the winter and having to dry and store food to make it through the long, dark months; let them come out here, Johnson thought with a scowl, where people spend entire lives just making sure their families have water and shelter from the blistering sun. Let them come out here and learn about *dying*.

Eight feet in front of his hiding place, a young Hopi warrior lay dead, his battered spear fallen from his slack grip. His eyes were full of blood as they stared at the night sky, his spirit gone on to greet whatever great thing he'd been taught to believe waited beyond this world. Thirteen hours earlier Johnson had talked and traded animal pelts with him, and he could still remember the suspicion with which the man, destined to be the next leader of his tribe, regarded the trapper. A lot of that was attributable to the fact that Johnson's eyes kept straying to the group of women grinding flour off to the side—one young maiden, in particular—but death had come not from Johnson, but from a band of Navajo raiders. Their battle cries still filled the village as the men fought their enemies and the thirsty sand soaked up the redskins' blood.

Johnson shifted carefully and parted the brush, quickly checking over his shoulder to make sure he was still undetected. While the Hopi looked as though they were occupied by the surprise Navajo attack, it was not unlikely that a scout could be creeping along the outskirts of the village to make sure other raiders weren't coming to join the force already devastating their ranks. It was time to make his move; things were starting to wind down and if he waited any longer he risked the battle coming to an end. The attack was as unexpected to him as it had been to the village; he had to use it to his advantage while he could.

His target was only a few yards away, a small hut of sewn skins that was deceptively dark. Johnson knew it wasn't empty—he'd seen the four women run inside at the onset of the raid, watched the light of the fire pit abruptly go out as they smothered the flames and draped moistened hides over it to minimize the smoke. Knowledge from his earlier visit told him that two of the women were warriors' wives—the most dangerous of the group—the third was the medicine man's wife, and the fourth, the one Daniel Johnson wanted for his own, was the holy man's unmarried daughter.

Heart pounding, Johnson gave up his protected space and sprinted for the hut. Most of the fighting had centered at the other end of the village where the food supplies were stored, and the last of the warriors on both sides, exhausted and bleeding from too many injuries to count, shrieked unintelligible curses at each other amid wildly flickering flames and the clouds of dust kicked up by their scuffling. Once he was in the dubious safety of the hut's shadow, Johnson crawled on his belly around to the front and quickly put a flame to the entrance flap. The outside hides were oiled and caught without much resistance; soon a finger of fire licked up the seam of the doorway, raising a babble of frenzied voices inside. In the few seconds it took him to scurry around to the far side, the squaws inside were already using a hunting knife to cut their way free.

Johnson's guess that the first one through would be the youngest was right on the mark, and he was ready when she clambered out of the opening. With her attention focused on her footing, she barely had a chance to yell when he grabbed her. Johnson was a big man, and with his free hand, the trapper grabbed one of the support poles that balanced the hut, then twisted hard. The whole thing tilted sideways amid the screams of the women still inside; his captive's cries added to the chaos as several of the Hopi braves spotted the collapsing hut and rushed towards it, their gazes trained on the burning entrance flap instead of the trapper and the struggling young woman behind it. Johnson slapped a hand over the girl's mouth and dragged her into the cover of boulders and scrub. She kicked at him like a wildcat, trying to bite and claw, and he finally had to belt her across the jaw so they could make their escape.

✳   ✳   ✳

"Here," he said carefully. "Drink." He pushed the tin cup toward the squaw's parched lips, but she only glared at him, then turned her head. Johnson scowled but held his tongue; what good would it do to rant at the woman? None—in fact, he'd learned that the more he yelled, the less cooperative she was apt to be. Two days in the desert and one along the mountainside—Christ, she *had* to be weakening. Of course, she was a Hopi and more used to the dryer climes, and God only knew what tricks she could use to get water that he, despite his store of wilderness knowledge, had never discovered. She certainly looked just as lovely as she had the first time Johnson had seen her in the Indian village...the same instant that he'd known he had to have her for his own.

It had been an odd thing. The decision and implementation had both been unconscious and instinctive. No advance planning or scheming; just the absolute certainty that if he spent the rest of his natural days trying, he would have this woman for his own or die. And so here she was, sitting across the tiny fire in the campsite with her hands and ankles firmly tied and a furious expression on her face. The twin circlets of hair that had caught his eye in the village were tangled and slipping apart and her cheeks and neck were layered in sand and mountain dust, but to his eyes the Indian maiden was no less beautiful. She had a pixie-like face with a broad, slightly flat nose and the dusty coloring of full-blooded Hopi ancestry; Johnson felt he could look into those deep, dark eyes for the rest of his life without ever tiring of the sight. Of course, that same life would be a whole lot happier if she could at least come to accept him. This seemed like it was going to be more of a problem than he'd anticipated.

She finally ate on the sixth day, cleaning up the small quarter of rabbit and—he was so relieved he nearly hugged her—washing it down with a small glass of stream water. His smile of approval was met with a cold stare, but he fancied it wasn't so piercing as before—after all, he was a pretty good cook and he had a way with wild herbs. Things eased up a little between the two of them and he was gratified to note that he no longer felt like she might throw dirt in his eyes and make a run for it every time he leaned over to help her stand. That she was still tied or had no idea where they were might have something to do with it, but at least the notion that she might be warming a bit toward him gave him a feeling of having accomplished something.

✳ ✳ ✳

Eleven days out of the village and away from the desert, Johnson got lax and took a small spear in the shoulder.

He didn't know if it was the girl's crazy medicine man father or a band of tribal warriors, but he barely got himself and the girl out with the skin still attached to his head. There was also a good chance that the attack had come from one of the roving bands of Navajo, but he wasn't going to stick around and find out. He was a dead man if they got caught either way, and if it was Navajo the girl was a goner, too. *That* he could never allow.

They rode hard for three days, twisting through mountain passes and dense forest until Johnson was sure the hunting party tracking them couldn't follow. They doubled back over streams and left false trails, started fires and putting them out to make it look like they had camped when in reality he'd barely dismounted before going in a different direction. The stone head of the spear was hardly bigger than an arrowhead, but it was buried in the meaty part of his shoulder the entire time, festering and making Daniel feverish, feeding him a constant diet of pain to keep him awake and on his guard. Still not convinced they had lost their pursuers, he kept pushing onward. As they forced their horses along a high path somewhere in the midst of the mountains that separated the sweeps of desert from the lush greenery of the central part of the country, they got caught in a sudden snowstorm and his horse stumbled; poorly balanced, his head spinning with infection, Daniel tilted sideways and fell out of the saddle.

✳ ✳ ✳

When he woke, the first thing Daniel saw were branches, woven together over his head to make a sturdy shelter. He was warmly wrapped in hides, but when he tried to sit up the agony in his shoulder nearly made him gray out. He heard something unintelligible and turned his head; the Indian maiden, obviously free of her bonds, sat beside him in the lean–to, her black eyes regarding him solemnly before pushing him back down. He was in far too much pain to protest and at this point it no longer mattered—if she was going to kill him or flee, she'd passed on both opportunities. He glanced out the open end of the shelter with a frown. Outside the storm still raged; that alone could give her reason to wait…well, there was nothing he could do but wait and see.

The storm did not let up. They had a decent amount of dried meat and the Hopi maiden kept a small fire tended. She would not let Daniel do anything but lie there as she periodically checked the wound in his shoulder. The first time she removed the makeshift bandage, he was shocked to see it slowly healing and his bewildered look brought the first ghost of a smile to her lips that he'd seen. As he questioned her in broken, ill–pronounced Hopi, her response was to reach beneath the furs and hold up the blood–stained spearhead. When her mouth twisted and she said something too fast for him to understand, her meaning was still clear: *Navajo.*

Daniel's recovery was swift and they rode out as soon as he was able to withstand the cold temperatures and the bumpy gait of the horses across the mountains. It wasn't long before the air began to warm and the last of the snow flurries disappeared and turned into a cold, clean mist that smelled forest–sweet and coated their faces and continually astonished the young Hopi woman. As the miles behind them began to number in the hundreds, the Hopi girl's dangerous father faded into the past like the memory of a weak star at dawn.

Watching her and listening to her laugh in the morning fog, Daniel wondered what on Earth she was going to think of the East Coast rains.

✺   ✺   ✺

Daniel never knew the name given to her by her tribe. By the time they made it to the well–populated east and settled in a small town he remembered from his travels, he had begun to call her Rose simply because he liked the name and she seemed to accept it. The town was called Feldman's Creek and sat at the bend of a river at the base of the Adirondack Mountains; Daniel would have liked to go deeper into the rich forests, but now he had a wife—of sorts—and needed to be closer to civilization. While he still made a living by trapping and selling skins and hides, now he did it from no farther away than a four–week trek; unwilling to leave her alone for so long, Johnson's days of cross–country journeys came to a halt. With his woman lying next to him at night and the wild and slightly oily scent of her hip–length black hair filling his senses, the once–wild trapper never missed his former lifestyle.

As they have a way of doing, the years passed. Daniel and Rose kept to themselves and the people of Feldman's Creek generally let them be. They weren't much on redskins and mixed couples but their opinions went unvoiced. Daniel Johnson was a big man and it didn't seem wise to cross him; his woman seldom spoke and never came to town alone.

✳ ✳ ✳

Rose's labor pains started on a frigid winter morning in January slightly more than six years after she had been stolen from her family. Daniel Johnson was not prepared.

The child was coming early, and he paced the cabin, brought heated water and towels, and worried as the hours went by but nothing happened. Too late Daniel realized his mistake; his familiarity was in killing animals, not birthing them, and his assumption that his experience with nature would see them through this was the most foolish thing he'd ever believed. The idea of traveling to town in search of a midwife came far too late for him to leave Rose unattended. Thirty–six hours after her first ache, on a cold, moonswept night, Rose bore Daniel a daughter with features much like her own and Daniel's lighter coloring.

Daniel caught the baby girl as she came into the world amid a dangerous rush of blood and pain. Moving quickly, he wrapped his daughter against the winter chill and placed her in Rose's arms, gratified to see the pain on Rose's dusky face change to pleasure. His knowledge was limited, but he did remember that there were womanly things like afterbirth to be dealt with; but when he went back to the end of the bed he found Rose lying in a spreading pool of scarlet. "Oh, Rose," he said helplessly. He wanted to scream in frustration, but couldn't because he might frighten her; instead he knotted his fists behind his back tight enough to bruise his work–roughened fingers.

"I have no more pain," she said, and she smiled tenderly at their daughter. Watching the play of emotions across her face, he had no way of knowing that she was thinking of her proud father, and how he would have killed the child because it was a halfbreed born of the cursed union between a white man and a red woman. All because of hate and pride…how silly. She looked up at Daniel and held out the baby. "For you," Rose said softly. He hesitated, then took the baby from her hands.

Then she died.

✳ ✳ ✳

Daniel named his baby daughter Mae, after his mother. Although he didn't much remember the woman, it seemed like the thing to do and the name was pretty enough. He missed Rose terribly—the truth was, he'd never known another woman—and buried her in a small, snow–laden plot behind his cabin that he marked with a cross—to the consternation of the townspeople, most of whom had considered Rose a heathen. As before, their protests went unvoiced.

He had no idea how to raise a newborn, much less a girlchild. Daniel kept her for as long as he could, but eventually was forced to board Mae with a widow in the slowly growing town. He brought her hand–hewn toys and flowers on awkward visits between trapping trips that began to lengthen into the cross–country expeditions with which he had been so familiar in earlier years. He loved her fiercely but saw her less and less; she never knew it, but she reminded Daniel too much of her mother.

When Mae Johnson was seventeen, she saw her father for the last time. His hair was white and his face deeply lined from the harsh mountain seasons, but he was still healthy and strong, too much so to explain why he never returned from his last trapping expedition. The seasons went full circle, and when the second spring and summer had passed, she and the rest of the townspeople accepted that her father was gone for good and probably dead. Mae grieved deeply for her father although they had never been close.

On the night she finally gave up hope, Mae sat in a rocking chair on the front porch of the house that had been her home for most of her life and thought about how it was a bitter thing that a woman, even a daughter, should wait so futilely on a man.

She never married.

※   ※   ※

Two thousand miles away, an embittered Hopi snakepriest still dwelled on his failure to catch the white man who had stolen his only daughter. This last year had been the most miserable in his existence; his wife, the final member of his family, had died of a fever from tainted meat, and he had buried her wasted body within the sands of a cold, midnight desert. Had his beautiful daughter not been stolen nearly a quarter century earlier, he would have been warm and secure within her household, probably amid a horde of grandchildren. Instead, he was old and alone and would remain that way for the rest of his life.

Hungering anew for vengeance, he set a curse upon the man who had kidnapped his daughter so long ago, appealing in song to the darker spirits that this man, and anyone of his blood, might suffer for all time. He did not tax the spirit world heavily and his request was deceptively simple: he asked only that all born of the white thief's blood should live a long and lonely life, as he had, never knowing for long the worldly love of another nor the spiritual peace within.

It was an ill-planned plea, and one which unknowingly cursed his only granddaughter—a child gifted with his own dark talents, and whom he would have loved in the face of the loss of his family, white-man father or not, since both his other sons had been killed by the brutal Navajo.

Across the width of a continent, his dark curse had devastating results on a child he never knew existed.

CHAPTER I
1825

er name was Mae Johnson, and as folks around her part of the Adirondack Mountains were apt to say, she was just about as old as the hills or, more reasonably, at least as ancient as the oak tree on Farmer Mollows' back barn acre. She took secret pleasure in never telling any of the nosy youth that now comprised the townsfolk that she remembered not only Noah Crain, who had owned the property before that smartass Mollows, but Jonathan Geiss, who had *planted* that very tree the same year—her twentieth—she first came to this area. Anyone who saw Mae now, and how parts of her thin, cracked skin didn't seem to carry blood anymore, felt certain she was pushing one hundred, though no one had a clue as to her true age.

But the years rolled on, and somewhere around her hundred–and–tenth birthday, or as close as she could recall, Mae knew her final time was almost at hand. And she was ready; a good thirty years earlier she'd decided that she fancied living on God's green earth a good deal more than most. Too many old folks got tired after all that time, but not her—no, sir.

Mae's hair was knotted into a heavy bun and she took it down with shaking fingers and combed it out. Her knuckles were bent and twisted with arthritis, but she worked it carefully into a thick braid that fell all the way to her hips—not something usually seen on an elderly woman, even deep in the mountains. Dark, iron gray too, a nice color, though maybe a little dry on the ends. She'd been cultivating this head of hair for the last twenty years or so—things didn't grow as fast as they used to—but she was ready now, and she tottered around her ramshackle cabin as quickly as her unsteady legs would allow, setting things in place and mentally preparing herself.

Mae had moved here from farther east not long after her father had disappeared, and living in the mountains and among these superstitious folk for nearly a century had taught her more than a few things that God–fearing Christians might or might not want to know. These same things seemed to just naturally *take* to her while bypassing all those men and women who broke their backs trying to feed their families from the rock–infested earth of the Adirondacks. It was time she used that learning, as well as all that questionable…*talent* to accomplish something tangible. No one, not even the Bible thumpers who screeched from the pulpits every Sunday, knew what waited on the other side, and Mae Johnson had stopped being adventuresome when a hungry forest had swallowed her only family member. She'd been shy and cautious instead, and while she'd been courted all the way into her seventies, she'd never married. Now she regretted that stubborn decision; a whole lot of things, including her present attitude, might have been different had there been a field full of great–grandchildren romping outside. While it was clearly too late to do anything about the years past, this time she wasn't going to miss her chance.

Another thing she'd been tending was that tabby cat, Jezebel. The feline was probably fifteen years old—pretty elderly for a country farm cat—and *smart!* That cat had to know what her part was going to be in the scheme of things—why else would she have gifted Mae with her only litter of eight perfectly formed kittens, mostly female, so late in her feline life?

Finally, everything was ready, and so close to the end that Mae could feel her heart already trying to stutter to a stop. Instinct made her want to climb into bed and rest, but she knew better; instead, Mae sat at the scarred old table, spit on the stem of a handmade tallow candle and lit it. Then she pulled the heavy braid of hair forward and over her left shoulder, feeling its coarse texture and thinking briefly back to a time when its color had been Indian black, presumably like her mother's. She swallowed stiffly around the fear trying to edge up her throat, reached back with a sharp knife, and cut the rope of hair cleanly at her nape. The dark plait fell heavily onto her lap, and save for one small feather that she quickly clipped from the tied end, she picked it up and placed it carefully on the table in front of her, shaping it into a curved line with an end on each side of her arms. Her head, suddenly freed of weight after so many years, felt light and unsure. Time froze in the flame of the sizzling fat candle as the tiny spot of light reached toward the ceiling, oblivious to the chill draft that prodded the back of Mae's thin shoulders.

From the pocket of her apron the old woman pulled a small straight razor, the most prized possession of the one beau she'd almost broken down and married some seventy years ago; as luck would have it, he'd been fairly young when his left eye had gone blood red and he'd keeled over at the chopping block one winter's day. After all this time the blade was slightly tarnished, but its sharp edge still gleamed in the mellow light and she drew in a cool breath, knowing intuitively as she felt the cold air roll over her toothless gums that if she didn't hurry, that breath was one of not many left.

Quickly she snicked the flesh at the tip of her right forefinger, not deep, just enough to gain a small, crimson flow. The left hand was harder; she'd always been partial to her left hand and her right fingers didn't want to hold the razor properly. Besides that, the small cut had pained her worse than expected and it was harder doing the second cut when she knew what was coming. But finally it was done and her age–thin blood dripped miserly from both fingertips onto each end of the elongated semi–circle of hair on the table. With both forefingers at the same time, she wrote her name in blood within the curve of the braid, making a double signature that was quite a feat of coordination. Then she wrote *his* name, the way she'd learned it from folklore books and whispered old women's tales. The instant she spelled out the last letter on the table's surface, she felt the change in the room around her.

Jezebel and her litter must have felt it too, and the cat sat up and hissed nastily while her kits whimpered and tried to burrow underneath their mother's belly, looking for safety rather than suckle. The cat's yellow–flecked eyes reflected the candle's glow with a nightshine all her own.

The old cabin seemed to draw in and around its occupants, holding them nervous prisoners within its walls. The air went cold first, then hot, then cold again—like going in and out of a cook-warmed kitchen on a bitter January day. Abruptly Jezebel went silent, and the only sound was Mae's breathing, each inhalation more like a struggling gasp. Occasionally one of the kittens mewled, but the mother cat ignored the cry, staring at the woman instead.

After a five-minute span that felt like hours, *he* finally came, to sit across from Mae, silent and dangerous, as he listened to her proposal. In another ten minutes—such a short time!—they reached an agreement and Mae rose from the table, razor in hand. Her soul quailed at what she was about to do, but she was an old woman and her mind was too made up to change now, especially after nearly two decades of planning. *He* stayed at the table, watching, his long, delicate fingers twining about each other in rapt anticipation. Once he reached a thin finger forward and dipped it into the drops of blood smeared within the circlet of hair on the tabletop, then brought the finger to his lips and slowly licked the blood from it. His tongue was black and overly long.

Mae stepped toward Jezebel, her pulse fluttering. The cat gazed up at her, silent, not bothering to run, as if knowing all along what its purpose in life had been. The old woman bent and picked up the animal with one hand, feeling the feline heart beating strongly beneath the soft, warm fur. She swallowed and pressed Jezebel close as her stomach knotted in on itself. Pet in hand, she turned back to the table and faced her visitor. She desperately wanted to close her eyes, but she needed to see.

In spite of the agony, Jezebel did not scream.

When Mae lifted her gaze from the first of her handiwork, his smile was hideous, showing teeth the likes of which she had never imagined. At first there was only the hint of pleasure, a small turning up of the corner of the mouth, but with each small butchering his enjoyment grew, and so did that unspeakable grin.

White female.

Black female.

White and white, twin females.

I'm a farm woman, Mae told herself numbly, *an old farm woman at that*. Heaven knew she'd slaughtered and gutted enough animals in her time for food—pigs, calves, goats and chickens—not to mention the numbers of rats and gophers and such that she'd done away with over the years, using everything from a pitchfork to an old pistol. But heaven had nothing to do with this.

With each final, plaintive screech of a kitten Mae felt the loss of a little more of her soul. *He* felt it too, she knew. And he'd like nothing better than for her to fall over and die before the last of the kittens was offered up—a forfeit. He'd have her and would be under no obligation to deliver.

Black male and white male, exact opposites in every marking.

The runt of the litter, a white kitten so tiny its sex was undetermined.

The final female, white and strong, fighting and clawing to the end.

Mae indulged in a small, hidden blast of triumph at the final killing when she saw that his smirk had dimmed slightly at her ability to finish. Still, she felt drained and dirty; cat blood splattered her clothes and the rickety kitchen furniture in vivid patterns made black by the candle's flickering light. The room smelled like copper ore fresh from one of the mountains' brutal mines. Droplets of animal blood dotted his face and hands and puddles covered the table. His fingers moved constantly, drawing strange, wet patterns around the now-soaked braid.

"You will sit," he said. She didn't want to, yet she had no choice. She obeyed, her skin crawling in disgust at the wetness that soaked through her dress to the backs of her legs.

She winced at his sudden, ferocious smile. "I will give you what you have given me," he burbled happily. "No more, no less."

Mae found her voice. "No cheating," she rasped fearfully. "I've heard of your ways and how you like to twist things about. I've given you everything you required."

"Yes," he said solemnly. "You have. You will die by sunrise." He gave a cheery smile at the look on her pale face and shrugged. "But you already knew that—which is why you called me to begin with, right?" When she finally nodded, he continued. "The one you're finishing now will count as the first—now, now! No interrupting!" He leaned toward her and she wished she could slide away. "You would have been wiser to use a younger cat, but then sometimes things just happen the way they happen, isn't that so?" He slid his hands gleefully into the mess on the table, like a child playing with mud paints. "But the bargain's been sealed and I'll not cheat you. In each case you'll have control over your destiny—however limited that may be—in much the same way anyone else would. Choose what you will."

He brought his dripping hands up and drew four thick streaks from the bottom of his eyes to his chin.

"In the end, Mae Johnson, you're *mine*."

✳ ✳ ✳

He was gone. The cabin stank of dead animals and rotting flesh and she had only a few hours to live. Mae forced her tired limbs to move; she would not have her neighbors find her in a few days covered with gore and rotting amid the wreck of her one-room home. There would be no end to the gossip that would fly among the townsfolk if they found her with nine butchered cats.

She gathered the bodies, still pliable but caked with both dried and tacky blood, and dropped them into a burlap sack. Their pitiful, lifeless eyes condemned her and she set her jaw against the guilt that wanted to flow through her veins like a million-fingered living thing. The sack was pathetically light— Jezebel had not been a large cat—but digging a hole out by the barn was another thing. It'd been years since she'd done more with a shovel than poke at a weed in the garden, and in the end the grave was less than two feet deep.

There was still no rest; she pumped and hauled water until she thought her arms would break before she had enough to sop up all the blood and bits of flesh that speckled the floor and furniture. Her empty stomach felt squeamish and her head pounded, and she thought resentfully that a body ought to be able to spend her last couple of hours feeling decent, not poorly. With the burning of her stained dress and a cold sponge bath her chores were done at last, and she finally had a chance to wrap herself in a threadbare blanket, sit and gaze around the small cabin—shack, really—that had been her home for these last fifty years or so. It still stank of copper, though she'd done all she could to eliminate it.

Now Mae rocked and thought about the stars that were fading from the sky one by one; with dawn only an hour away, she wondered how long it would be before that smartass Samuel Mollows came nosing around and found her—or would it be Miz Berlina instead? What would they think of the smell permeating the room and, finally, what *really* happened to Miz Berlina's husband eighteen years ago?

There were so *many* great things on this Earth, so many things to think and learn about that it was no wonder she was loathe to let it go, even though she'd had so much more time than most. *He'd* said she'd be able to choose her destiny, and that much she believed. But there were other questions, just as monumental, such as how long in between, and where? And how old at each beginning? Her nerves twanged uneasily—she'd given him far too much leeway! He *had* said that she'd know what she was doing each time, enough to keep going, a smidgeon of self still remembered. All those questions remained unanswered, but no time was left to figure them out. And even though she'd been a teacher in her early years, had she ever *really* been that bright to begin with? Even her adopted mother had sometimes doubted that Mae would ever have more than a fool's share of common sense.

And at the end of this first one, after all the pain and work and being tired and alone at the end, Mae still didn't want to let it go.

※　　　　※　　　　※

Miz Berlina stopped by two days later and found Mae Johnson sitting in her dilapidated rocking chair with her eyes still open.

Before she went for the sheriff, Miz Berlina held her nose closed and went through the little shack, taking anything she figured to be of value, reasoning that the sheriff would claim it for himself or to pay for the burial anyway. She tried to close Mae's eyes but they wouldn't shut, as though the corpse was still straining to see into the world from which her spirit had fled. It was taxing, the feeling of being watched by the dead as Miz Berlina carefully checked all the drawers and under the bed. And the *smell!* She didn't see any blood and Mae looked as if she'd gone real peaceful-like, just sitting there in her chair. But by damn if it didn't smell like a rotting old slaughterhouse! In an ancient wooden box under the bed, Miz Berlina at last found a yellowed lace handkerchief, something she'd never seen Mae use before, so she slipped it in her pocket and finally went for the sheriff.

In her own home later that afternoon, Anne Hawkins Berlina washed the musty smell from the hanky and wrapped it around a few flowers picked fresh from the side of her cabin. At dusk she slipped into the woods behind her property, walking diagonally some three hundred paces. There she knelt beside a hidden grave and, smiling, placed the flowers at its head.

Eighteen years earlier Errol Berlina, her husband of twenty–seven years, had cheated on her twice. The first time, she forgave him. The second time she cleaved the back of his head with his own axe and simply told everyone he'd run off. The whole town knew he had a wandering eye and had shamed her once, and no one ever doubted it.

Except maybe Mae.

CHAPTER ii
1691

he awoke from the blackout—a condition with which she would become familiar over the coming years—in a too-soft bed with something heavy pressing on her stomach, heaving itself up and down with nauseating regularity. On the heels of that came the immediate realization that she did not feel well at all; in fact, she decided, as soon as she got whatever this thing was off of her belly, she would throw up.

She struggled out from under the weight and almost fell off the bed when the heaviness flung itself away in one quick move. The "heaviness" turned out to be a woman in a long, dark dress, still fairly young but prematurely wrinkled, her mouth an "O" of shock, her face blotched and streaked with tears, chest heaving.

"Mam," she heard herself croak, "what's wrong?" She tried to sit up but found the body unwilling and weak. Looking down, she managed to focus on her own pitifully thin wrists and fingers pulling at the bedcovers.

"Thank you, Lord, for bringing my only child back! It's a miracle, it is! A miracle!" The woman ran back to the bedside and pushed her against the pillows, if the lumpy things behind her head could be called that. "My sweet Rachel, you've been spared! And here I was, sending your husband after the parson for your last rites." She peered close into Rachel's eyes. "How are you feeling, child? It's been almost a week since you last opened your eyes."

"It has?"

"'Tis true! We thought you were gone for good, we did. Your man will be joyful, that's a fact. And him most times sitting down by the barn all silent and won't speak to a soul." The other woman fussed about, tightening and tucking in the bedcovers, then brought a damp rag to wipe Rachel's forehead. "Can you eat? Surely you can try a little broth. I'll fetch it now." She hurried to the door, then stopped and turned back. "Oh, Rachel, I thought I'd lost you for sure. I can't believe you've been spared! Lord, I'm so grateful!"

For a moment Rachel thought her mother was going to sink to the wooden floor, clasp her hands and begin to pray; instead the woman turned and left the room, pulling a curtain shut behind her. The entire scene had hardly lasted two minutes, yet she was exhausted. She dragged at the bedcovers and finally managed to hoist them enough to look under—Jesus, what a pathetic sight! *The girl must have been sick for weeks*, she thought, then amended her thinking. I *must have been sick, not* her. I *am* her now. *I* am *her and my name…* Rachel.

✻   ✻   ✻

The body was weak all right, but by God it was also young, surely no older than sixteen. Sickness had shrunk it to probably ninety pounds or so and left her with little strength, but there was still enough to fuel her curiosity and let her push aside the bedcovers and hike up the long, rough cotton gown she wore. In doing so she found childish legs with knobby knees and bony ankles, and not much in the way of a chest, either—but then she guessed a sick teenager wouldn't have much of one anyway. There was no mirror in the room, but fine brown hair that hadn't been washed in a while hung over her shoulders and down to her waist, and her fingers could feel arched brows and a somewhat short nose, though that really didn't help with a mental picture. She ran her tongue around the inside of her mouth; it was sore and she could swear a couple of her teeth were loose. Probably the result of the disease with which she'd obviously been stricken. Had she caught smallpox? Or consumption?

Rachel stared at her surroundings. Memory gave her a little, but there were chunks missing, like big black clouds in her mind. She knew, for instance, that the woman in the other part of the house was her mother, but she recalled only bits from this girl's past, those nasty clouds popping up again to muck it all up. She sighed; she was way too tired and sick to force her rusty memory into action. She'd just have to watch herself and keep her mouth shut. A lot, she was sure, would come naturally.

The room was dark and smelled bad, a stench of sour illness and used linens. It was large enough to hold the double bed in which she again struggled to sit upright, plus a plain mahogany wardrobe and washstand that supported a porcelain bowl holding dirty water and damp rags. The reason everything was so dim, she saw, was that the glass from the sole window had been removed and the opening covered with oilcloth, thick with dust and dead flies. Rachel thought it would have been better to let in the insects rather than block the light and fresh air, and she wanted desperately to get out of this bed. Her poor backside felt raw and covered with sores, but she doubted she could walk even if she did manage to get on her feet. She was considering the effort anyway when she felt a low vibration as the front door of the house opened and closed, then heard excited voices rise from beyond the curtain—really little more than a pretty scrap of material hung for privacy. She jumped as the curtain was yanked aside and a huge, menacing figure barrelled into the room and stomped to the bedside to glower at her. Reflex made her yank the quilt up to her chin, though the nightgown she wore was high-necked and buttoned tight.

"You girl! What say you for thyself?" The man's voice sounded like thunder in her ears, so used to the quiet these past weeks. Rachel winced and fought the disrespectful urge to cover her ears. Her mother was right on the man's heels, followed by a husky man she instantly knew was her husband. Primed for her death, his expression was stunned and happy; her heart warmed a little.

"Please, Reverend Parris, don't shout so! The child is still ill—she just woke a few minutes ago. Can't you see how pale she is?"

"Aye, I can see, all right. I see a child of the Devil, I do! Brought back from the dead, yanked from the Good Lord's embrace by some impish play of Satan!" The preacher was so close Rachel could smell his breath—like burned venison—as he spit the words at her. That and the unwashed smell of his heavy black clothes pressed into her nostrils, try as she might to breathe only through her mouth. Her stomach roiled threateningly.

"Oh no, that's not it at all! Why, it's clear she wasn't dead at all, just heavily sleeping while my own silly panic made me think she was gone for good." Her mother's voice was strong and confident, and Rachel saw a flicker of hesitation gain ground in the reverend's stern eyes. He stared at her, his gaze turning curious.

"Well, perhaps," he said, then bent towards her again. "How do you feel, girl?" The proper words came automatically. "Not very well, sir."

"Hmph. I should expect not, after being sick all this time. It seems to me that you being alive at all is miracle enough," he said, glaring at her mother, who raised her chin stubbornly, "without you showing a quick recovery to boot." He jammed his hat onto his head. "I'll be going on now, Mary Esty." Rachel's mother held the curtain for him as he stepped through. "But I will be keeping a *close* eye on this family, I promise. God speed."

✵   ✵   ✵

Her husband John was a handsome man a good fifteen years older than her, a man whose hard life had left him firm–jawed and a bit worn around the edges. His sternness, however, was a world apart from the granite disposition of Reverend Parris, and it was easy for her to detect the softening in his brown eyes when he looked at her and feel the gentleness in his hands as he helped her to her feet and held her shaking form as her mother grabbed at the opportunity to whip clean linens onto the bed. "Rachel, I think it's foolish for you to be on your feet. It will only hinder your recovery, or worse, bring the fever back on you."

"I just wanted to get off my aching backside," she panted. John's stubbled cheeks pinkened and she couldn't help smiling. Acquiescing to his worry, she agreed to get back in bed, but only after her mother had helped her to the sick-pot in the corner. The two women waited until John left the room, then lifted the lid and Rachel carefully sat down. The smell, combined with the discovery that she was bleeding—apparently her menses—made her retch painfully. Abruptly the room swam in crafty circles, trying to make her fall off the disgusting pot. *Fine*, she thought, *I'd like nothing better than to get off this filthy thing*, and she tipped obligingly sideways into her mother's sturdy arms. Mary's outcry quickly brought John and together they carried Rachel back to the bed and wiped her clean. She found herself blushing deeply at her husband's eyes on her bare skin in the daylight and was relieved when the emergency bathing was over.

✵   ✵   ✵

Exhausted, Rachel slept deeply for a little while, though overall she rested poorly that evening, tossing and turning and finding new aches and pains with nearly every movement. The worst of the hurt came from her stomach and privates; those parts felt raw and split, as if her insides were ready to spill from her body in a bloody heap. Sometime that night she came full awake and heard the murmur of voices from beyond the closed curtain. Her room was cool and dark, lit only by the tiny light of a small candle and the minuscule glow filtering through the material covering the door. Seen in this twilight it was almost comforting, like an old photograph that spoke of happier times, with the candle's gentle glow spilling over the hand sewn quilt and tatted doilies scattered here and there about the room. She smiled to herself in the dark; she'd have to watch those odd memories and make sure they didn't escape her mind. The voices in the other room rose slightly and she automatically strained to hear.

"I don't know what to say, John. She hasn't even asked." Her mother's voice, trembling with worry.

"Why not? Has her memory become that addled by the childbed fever? How could she not know?"

Childbed fever? Rachel thought. Did I have a child?

Her mother's voice again. "I—I don't know. I've never heard of such a thing, but my experience is limited. What I've seen about childbirth has only been in Topsfield and here in Salem Village, though the good Lord knows there's been plenty of that."

No wonder my insides feel so beaten, Rachel thought wildly. Her heart began hammering madly. I *did* have a child, I did! "John! John, please!"

Rachel's hoarse cry brought him on the run. "What is it? What's the matter? Are you hurting?" He stood by the bed anxiously. Carrying another candle, Mary followed him.

"The baby! Where is the baby—why isn't it here, by me, where it belongs? I want my baby!" Maternal instinct crashed over her, giving her a stolen strength that propelled her off the high mattress and onto her feet. "Where—"

"Rachel, no! John, catch her—she mustn't—" The hysteria in her mother's voice made Rachel even more determined to get out of this room and find the infant they were keeping from her. Why would they do that? What kind of people were they? She stared at them in horror and disbelief as her husband's solid arms pushed her back onto the bed.

"What are you doing?" she screeched. Her hands flailed at his grim face. "Let me go! Let me—*you*!" She pointed an accusing finger at her mother. "What have you done with my child? Where is it?" Mary's face went pale with shock.

"Rachel, stop it! Stop it, girl—don't you know what you're saying? Don't you remember?" John was panting now, the exertion of fighting Rachel's uncanny energy beginning to tell. Sweat stood out on his brow.

She tried to claw him, only to find that her fingernails were soft and bent double before they could do any harm. Hissing in frustration, she pummeled him with her small fists. "You beasts, you've stolen my child! Devils!" She found herself wrapped in John's embrace, a bear hug that forced most of her struggles to a halt. Her breath was wheezing painfully in and out of her lungs and he began to rock her back and forth.

"Rachel, my sweet, I'm sorry," he murmured, his lips against her hair. Her clenched fingers were trapped between her own collarbone and his shoulder, and she felt something wet drop onto her knuckles. She tried to turn her head and see what it was, but found herself still held tight. She thought she felt a tremor in the broad chest that pressed against hers, a vibration that might have been a sob.

"Oh, Rachel, you really can't remember?" He sounded so miserable and his arms tightened about her as dread filled her throat. She suddenly found his hold comforting.

"Our child was born dead."

※ ※ ※

Rachel's recovery was slow; she had lost an appalling amount of blood and was tired and weak, and though the spirit was ready to go, it was forced to wait for the thin slip of a thing in which it was encased to catch up. She felt the loss of the unseen child—a girl—more than she would have expected, and Mary and John often found her staring into space, her eyes filled with longing. Her arms ached to feel the warm weight of a baby and sometimes, though her milk-filled breasts pain her a little less each day, she imagined she could actually *smell* the infant, a soft, soapy scent unlike any other on this earth. Her outburst was costly and meant another week before she could make it any farther than the small pot, and two more before she managed to step outside the bedroom and see what was beyond the curtain.

While the frequent memory flashes helped, Rachel still wasn't prepared for the rest of the house. The close, dark bedroom had led her to belief the family was poor, but she couldn't have been more wrong. Her husband was not only a farmer but a constable of Salem Village—a double source of income. The furnishings in the small house were simple but elegant, and Rachel felt quite comfortable there. She still rose late in the morning, and often she could hear the voices of callers in the early hours, stopping by to chat with her mother, leaving sweet-smelling offerings of food and warm wishes. Except for the bittersweet ache in her heart for a child she would never see, it would have been a pleasing existence.

But time passed and the loss within her dulled and grew hazy. As her body healed, Rachel began to think that perhaps they could have another child, to replace the one she could not remember carrying within her womb. Her health improved, nurtured by the care of her mother and husband and the gentle sameness of the days in Salem Village as Christ's Even approached and the chilled fall days blew into bitter winter. Mary brought her a fine linen material and Rachel, working with old but never forgotten skills, worked it carefully into a shirt for John which she hid away in the cedar chest.

Her past life brought more knowledge to Rachel's fingers; woodcarving, a mountain hobby that had been taught to her by Daniel Johnson and one which had often amused her, although the man himself was now no more than an old ghost in her mind. Her battered body was still fragile and she wrapped heavily before venturing into the small woods behind the house on a rare occasion when she was left alone. There she found a piece of raw oak to suit her purpose, carried it back to the cabin and wrapped it in burlap; it, too, she hid in the cedar chest, a place set aside for her personal possessions. Inside were many treasures and she dug through them carefully, eager to learn as much as she could about Rachel's past through familiar association. One of her most pleasing discoveries was a beautiful lace dress and a small veil, and she surrendered to the urge to pull it out, holding it in front of her and gazing into the oval mirror John had brought home so she could mark her health's progress by the pallor of her cheeks. It had been difficult to hide her surprise at the first glimpse of her own face, but easy to let John believe her reaction was due to the shock of seeing the damage her illness had caused.

But she was used to being Rachel now. While the borrowed body was a bit small, it was by no means plain. Washed and shining, her chestnut–colored hair framed her face and spilled over the white lace wedding gown in her trembling fingers; her deep brown eyes misted at the renewed memory of the forgotten occasion…

"Do you, John Willard, take Rachel Esty to be your wife? Do you promise to be faithful to her in good times and in bad, in sickness and in health, to love her and cherish her all the days of your life and until death do you part?"

"I do." John, looking handsome and strong in his Sunday best suit, healthy face scrubbed clean and pink under a fresh hair trim, his hat held contritely in one hand.

Reverend Samuel Parris, turning his hard eyes on her now. The only mar on her wedding day—those eyes had always made her wither inside. "And do you, Rachel Mary Esty, take John Willard to be your husband? Do you promise to be faithful to him in good times and in bad, in sickness and in health, to love, honor and obey him all the days of your life? And until death do you part?"

Her voice in the chapel, clear and for once loud enough to be heard. "I do."

The rest of the ceremony a blur, only the minister's final, still stern words sticking in her mind:

"Before the Good Lord and the good people of Salem Village in the year of our Lord 1690, I now pronounce you man and wife."

Given that memory, and the fact that she had carried a child full term and almost fully recovered from the resulting fever, she thought she finally knew what year it was.

1691.

She'd never expected to go *backwards*.

✻   ✻   ✻

Christ's Eve. It was a cruel and relentless winter, with no sign of respite from the steadily falling snow and bitter cold winds laying drifts ten to fifteen feet high against the sturdy house. The sound of tree branches racking under the white weight in the surrounding forest could be heard all through the village and dogs gone wild with cold and starvation preyed upon what small animals they could catch and robbed the villagers' traps at every opportunity. Sheltered to some degree inside their homes, the people of Salem Village had adopted a hermit–like existence, born not only of the hellish winter but out of fear of the smallpox that struck its victims at random.

The house held a chill almost all the time. Though built well by John's own hands, even the thick walls were hard–put to keep out the brutal temperatures and drafts. To that was added the constant dimness; John had long ago shuttered all the windows against the weather, and it seemed as if the poor man's hands, split and bleeding from constant wood chopping, would never heal. But the fire was cheerful and at least the parlor and kitchen were warm most of the time, the parlor having a small fireplace and the kitchen fires going sunrise to sundown. Rachel and Mary tried to stay lighthearted, if only for John's sake when he stumbled in from the frozen world outside.

On this day, however, Rachel's spritely nature was sincere—tomorrow was Christmas! Up to her elbows in flour, Rachel kneaded bread dough in the kitchen, her hands deep into the stickiness, carefully working it back and forth. She could hear her mother in the low cellar, banging things about in her search for raisins.

"Ah! Here they are—ouch! Curse this mess! Rachel, for goodness sake, why don't you and John clean out this cellar? It's beyond me how you find a thing down here amidst all this clutter."

"We will, Mam. Perhaps in the spring when it's warmer," she answered, turning the heavy mass carefully in the bowl. She would add the raisins now and let the dough rise around them. By midday it would be ready to bake, provided she could keep it in a fairly warm spot. "Have you got the raisins?"

"Here," her mother puffed. "I tell you, those steps are hard on a body. I'll start plucking." This morning John had delighted Rachel by arriving with a freshly killed turkey. Mary dragged it up on the work board and began pulling out the tail feathers.

"Oh, save those!" Rachel said. "I can use them."

Her mother looked at her oddly and turned a few feathers in her hand. "Whatever would you do with them?"

"I don't know," Rachel said, concentrating more on the raisins she was gently working into the dough. "Maybe I can work them into a wall hanging. That would be nice." There, she was finished. She covered the mass with a damp towel and rinsed her hands in the washbowl.

"A what?"

"A wall hanging, Mam," she said. "Since you're working on the turkey, I think I'll start the cranberries." Rachel reached for a fresh bowl.

"You mean like…needlepoint?"

She'd been thinking of the feather weaving that her father had taught her and Rachel's legs almost gave out as she realized what she'd done. She struggled to keep the crockery bowl from slipping from her fingers and set it quickly on the counter before she dropped it. "Uh, no…more like weaving. It's when you make leftover material into a decoration." She glanced at her mother's puzzled face furtively. "Like a quilt, only for the wall rather than the bed, or sometimes a window. A tapestry."

"I don't understand. We've paintings for the walls, why would we hang sewing upon them? And where did you learn this weaving or whatever it is? Who told you about it?" Mary frowned. "I don't believe I've ever heard of such a thing. Using feathers sounds like something the Indians would do."

"I can't recall. It's just something I remember from somewhere," Rachel said desperately. Better to say that than to make up some elaborate lie and get trapped in it sometime in the future when she didn't expect it. Her mother was looking at her again, her furrowed brows showing her doubt. "Really, I can't remember. It must be the sickness." Nervousness made Rachel nearly slam her wooden spoon down on the work board. "Can we please talk of other things? It angers me when I can't remember things before the loss of the baby." Her hands were shaking badly now, and the damned cranberries were rolling everywhere. Grabbing at them only seemed to spread them further, and she felt like smashing them all with the spoon. How could she have been so stupid?

Mary came up behind her. "I'm sorry, truly I am. I didn't know it upset you so. And I'm sure your memory will improve as time goes on." She squeezed Rachel's shoulders affectionately, then went back to the turkey. "Where should I put the feathers?" Apparently she had accepted the explanation, though in retrospect it seemed like utter nonsense, even to Rachel.

She glanced at her mother as Mary struggled to yank the feathers from the bird. For the most part, they were crushed and slimy. "Let's just put them with the rest of the trash. They're really not in the best of shape, and I suppose they would look silly hanging on the wall, anyway."

Her mother looked up from her task. "If you like, I can try to be more careful."

"That's all right, really," Rachel said with a shrug. "Now that we've talked about it, I don't think I can remember how to fashion it together anyway." She smiled encouragingly, so her mother wouldn't suspect she was lying.

"As you wish." Mary continued her work silently, plucking the bird and placing the waste in an old canvas feed sack at her feet. For the quickest of moments, Rachel saw her mother shudder, as if her daughter's words had brought a chill across the back of her neck that couldn't be explained by the draft from the fireplace damper.

Weaving, indeed. There wasn't a chance in this life that her mother had believed her.

※   ※   ※

On Christmas Day the weather broke, but what should have been a blessing was nearly a curse instead. Melting snow became slippery and treacherous for those who ventured out to visit relatives, and many found themselves floundering through small drifts that had once been frozen hard enough to hold their weight. John was a bundle of nerves on their way to church, listening constantly for the sliding sound of meltdown from the trees that towered overhead and yanking his wife and mother–in–law aside more than once at the sound of a snapping twig. He tried to think of another route to the chapel, but nothing else was any less dangerous than the normal road followed by most of the townspeople. When they finally arrived at the chapel, Mary could see their own relief mirrored on the faces of the others as they rested and waited for Reverend Parris to begin his sermon. It was clear by the way a few kept nervously glancing out the small windows that many already dreaded the trip home.

Rachel looked around the room, seeing familiar faces and drawing names to fit them from the rusty places in her mind, as she had every Sunday since her illness. Now she could remember most of the people here, though she worried constantly that someone would start a conversation with her and she might not be able to recognize the person. Next to her, John sat straight and still, eyes half–closed, perhaps deep in prayer.

Off to Rachel's left and up one pew, she saw a young girl watching John with an openly greedy look on her thin features. Rachel was studying the child with interest, wondering who she was and why she stared so boldly at John, when the lass raised her eyes and their gazes locked. Rachel was astounded at the hostility she sensed in that glare—not only did she know of nothing which could have caused it, nothing in her thoughts helped her place the girl's identity. She frowned and was about to ask John when the man sitting next to the girl turned and cuffed her smartly, then bent and muttered in her ear. Throwing a last, murderous look in Rachel's direction, she flounced on the bench and faced forward. In that instant Rachel recognized the man as Thomas Putnam, another constable in the Village who worked with her husband when the need arose. The girl who had looked so brazenly at John must be his only daughter, Ann. On the other side of Ann sat the girl's mother—also named Ann. Relief filled Rachel that, finally, her memories were coming more smoothly and she momentarily forgot the girl's animosity as Reverend Parris entered through the back door and marched up to the pulpit. Sudden nervousness made her hands tremble; since the day she'd awoke from her illness, the thought of speaking directly with him had terrified her. She felt as if he might know something, as though his piercing eyes could stab right into her mind and pluck out the secrets of her past life for all to examine…impossible, of course. Painful childhood recollections flickered in her mind and she glanced to her left and right, seeing a stern village man standing stiffly at the start of each of the three aisles, newly cut switches in hand, ready to deliver a stinging blow to those caught sleeping during the sermon. She pulled her collar closer around her neck; God only knew who could sleep in this chill.

W<small>HAM</small>!

Both Rachel and Mary flinched as the Reverend Parris's fist suddenly crashed against the surface of the podium. Gasps escaped around the room from many of the startled women and the room rustled with the noise of shifting people. A child in the back began to cry and Rachel could hear the mother desperately trying to quiet it.

"People of Salem Village, behold!

"For a virgin shall be with child and shall bring forth a son, and she shalt call his name Jesus—!" WHAM! Another thunderous crack on the podium's wooden top reverberated through the church and the townspeople jumped anew. "For He shall save his people from all their sins!"

Reverend Parris began to stride across the width of the pulpit, punctuating every third or fourth step with another whack at the banister.

"And when the child JESUS was born—"

WHAM!

"—behold there came three wise men from the east—"

WHAM!

"—saying 'Where is He that hast been born KING—"

WHAM!

"—of the Jews? For we have followed His Light—"

WHAM!

"—and have come to worship Him!'"

With each of Reverend Parris's blows, the child in the rear of the church became more terrified, its cries finally elevating into screams.

"WOMAN, remove that infant!" the Reverend bellowed. From where she sat, Rachel could see that he had grabbed the front rail so hard that his knuckles were white; he seemed about to leap over. *Some Christmas*, she thought morosely. John had come out of his reverie and shocked faces surrounded them; there were surely no sleeping children in this church today. Even the men holding the whipping sticks were frowning, though it had always seemed to Rachel that they enjoyed their job immensely. The chilliness in the room increased as the woman almost ran out the door, her baby clutched protectively in her arms.

At the front, Reverend Parris smiled crookedly. *The man is sick*, Rachel thought suddenly, *terribly,* terribly *sick. He should have never been allowed to preach to a single soul, much less a whole town. There is a deep evil in him and this town will rue the day they let him into their lives.*

The sermon went on, if not joyous at least a bit calmer, but Rachel couldn't explain the dread she suddenly felt.

✹ ✹ ✹

As they threaded their way from the pew to head home, John found Thomas Putnam waiting to speak with him. They shook hands and Thomas addressed himself to Mary and Rachel with a respectful nod. "Begging your pardon, ladies. Would you mind if I spoke with John for a moment?" Shivering, the women returned to their seats and waited as the two men spoke out of earshot. Rachel noticed that Mrs. Putnam and the girl also still waited, the child once more sending unmistakably malicious glances toward Rachel. Rachel ignored her and turned instead to look at her husband, watching him for a minute and wondering at the feelings of affection she felt. Was it simply that she was used to him? How could it be anything else, since although they shared the same bed every night, he hadn't put a hand on her—intimate or otherwise. She was beginning to wonder how she had gotten pregnant in the first place; she surely couldn't remember and John seemed ill-inclined to demonstrate. Disgruntled at the direction her thoughts had taken in the small church, Rachel turned back to her mother and they huddled together, trying to keep their warmth against the chapel's now open entryway.

Off to the side, John looked at Thomas Putnam in confusion. "I'm sorry, Thomas. I don't really understand. What's that?"

"It's my daughter Ann, John." Putnam fumbled with his hat and finally jammed it under his arm so he could rub his freezing fingers together. "I can't for the life of me figure out what's got into her—she's nearly uncontrollable these days. And when she sees you, it's worse." He glanced to where his youngster sat scowling at Rachel, then frowned. "For awhile it seemed she'd be all right, but now that you're back—"

"Back? What do you mean?" John was becoming more puzzled by the moment.

"It's just that when you didn't come into the village for so long, what with Rachel being down with fever, Ann seemed to forget about this wild idea of hers. I thought maybe it was gone for good. Since it isn't, I wondered if you might have some suggestions as to what I should say to her, to bring her back to her right mind."

"What wild idea?"

Thomas looked at John in amazement. "You mean she's never said anything?" John shook his head and Putnam sighed. "Upon my mother's grave, now the girl's taken to lying on top of everything else. She said that…well, there's no sense in bothering you with the weight of our family's problems, that's for sure. I'm sorry to have bothered you." He started to leave, but John touched his jacket.

"You're not troubling me at all, Thomas, you should know that. We've been acquainted for a long time. If you'll only share your problem with me, perhaps I can help or at least offer an idea or two."

Thomas hesitated, then his expression crumpled into helplessness. "My daughter fancies herself in love with you, and claims that you've spoken to her about it." He stared down at his shoes. "She even claims that while your wife was ill, you said you would marry her when Rachel finally died."

John was dumbfounded. "Thomas, your daughter's only eleven years old! Why would she say such things?"

"She's just turned twelve, and I've no idea what's gotten into her, except that she prattles and carries on, and has even taken to having fits on the floor, much to her mother's horror. My wife seems convinced it's simply some sort of spell the girl's going through because she's starting to become a woman and that it will all pass." Putnam's face was as despairing as it was embarrassed. "I'm telling you, it's about to drive me mad! I can't get a moment's rest in my own house, what with fits one day and lies the next, and all the while my wife does nothing but make excuses for the chit!"

"Maybe it would help if you explain to your daughter that you spoke to me, yet say nothing about our knowledge of her lies," John suggested. "Simply tell her that as it turns out, I'm very happy that Rachel is well, and it's obvious I'm very much in love with my wife. Tell her I talked of little else." John thought for a moment. "Lay the blame on me, if you like. Tell your daughter I didn't mention her at all and that it appears I've forgotten any conversation between her and I entirely."

Putnam looked doubtful. "Seems to me that would do nothing but cause more tantrums and ravings."

John shook his head. "I don't think so—at least not for long. She'll surely be furious, but I think once she recovers from her anger she'll turn her attention to other things more befitting a twelve-year-old. Besides, how long is the attention span of a child anyway? I think she'll forget all this nonsense soon enough."

Thomas looked back at his daughter, noting her defiant posture in the pew. The cold didn't seem to affect her, yet his wife sat shivering visibly on the wooden seat. "I hope you're right, John. I'm so tired of this behavior I'm tempted to tie her at the whipping post and thrash her good. Perhaps that would teach her to act like a proper young lady instead of a brat—though it surely wouldn't set well with her mother." He looked at John gratefully. "Thank you for listening to another's man's problems, John, especially on Christmas Day. You've a good heart."

Seeing the girl watching him as her father returned, John was disturbed by the expression on her face and barely stopped himself from glowering at her. It was hard for him to believe her parents would endure such irritation, but it was best on his part to ignore her and he decided to say nothing as he escorted his wife and mother-in-law back to their house. Still, he wondered if the best thing for young Ann Putnam really wouldn't be a good thrashing.

✳   ✳   ✳

Rachel felt the first true excitement since her illness; with the chore of attending Reverend Parris's hellfire sermon behind them, her small family could now give full attention to enjoying the holiday. Since most of the meal had been started the day before and the remainder placed on the fire that morning, the greatest part of the day's work was behind them. John had hung the turkey above the fire immediately upon their return; now it was roasted to an appetizing brown, steadily emitting cheerful sizzling sounds as grease dripped onto the hot wood below. Between the break in the weather and the constant cooking fires over the last two days, the house was pleasantly warm and Rachel and her mother put the finishing touches on the afternoon's meal with their sleeves unseasonably rolled above their elbows. Once, as she was bending to pull the spider skillet from the fire, she felt John's eyes on her. When she looked up, Rachel found his gaze not on her face, as she had expected, but on the swell of her breasts above the few buttons she had unfastened because of the heat. His face reddened as he realized he had been caught and he quickly pulled on his coat and mumbled a few words about more firewood. With the slam of the door, Rachel smiled and wondered if tonight she would finally find out how she and John had made a baby the previous year.

The sun was low in the sky when dinner was finally served. John seemed truly surprised at the food on the table; Mary was likewise a little overwhelmed, and Rachel had a dim memory of leaner years in the village's past. The small family bowed their heads and listened as John gave a sincere prayer of thanks for the Lord's generosity before eagerly serving up the meal.

"I've never tasted a bird cooked like this," John said around a mouthful of stuffing and boiled onions. "To be truthful, I didn't even know you could cook this well, Rachel."

Uneasiness stirred in her belly and Rachel wondered if she had made a mistake by preparing such an elaborate meal. At the time she'd thought herself using the same knowledge available to any other woman in the colonies and learned from her mother as well. Mary had certainly not said otherwise.

But her husband smiled easily and raised a spoonful of cranberries. "Be careful, or you'll spoil me and I'll expect a setting like this every night!" He chuckled at his own joke. "Is there any more cornbread?"

Rachel passed the bread over the array of succotash, sweet potatoes and onions. She *had* cooked too much; they'd have to eat themselves sick or the food would be tainted in a few days. Only yesterday she'd thrown week–old fish into the snow outside as her mother complained. Thank God a stray cat had sped from behind the house and snatched it away before Mary's protests had turned argumentative. Mary had suggested it could have been seasoned to disguise the strong smell, but the methods of food storage in the colonies left much to be desired and Rachel had known the fish was spoiled and would likely make them ill. It was yet another reason for her mother to think her odd since her recovery from childbed fever—a sickness Rachel also knew was an infection caused by her body's inability to rid itself of all of the afterbirth. Her appetite diminished by her nervous thoughts, she pushed her food away and went to fetch the syllabub, apple crumb and Indian Pudding. Her good mood returned at John's expression when he saw the desserts, and she marveled that he could find room for a helping of each plus three full cups of the creamy, spiked syllabub. As she sipped her own, she had to admit it would be easy to "force" another cup down; Mary smiled but limited her own to only a half–helping.

The remains of the meal were finally cleared and set away as darkness settled over the small household, and they gathered quietly around the fire, resting and appreciating the company and the warmth of the bright flames. After a time, Rachel excused herself and went to the bedroom, where she lifted the gifts she had made from the cedar chest. She touched each lovingly and longed for Christmas paper and bows, but such things were not available to her. Carefully hiding the treasures beneath her apron, she returned to the parlor.

"John, I have a Christmas gift for you," she said somewhat shyly. He looked up in surprise when she handed him the shirt. Since her illness, the surprises that came from Rachel seemed endless, and he examined it thoughtfully. He looked over at Mary and saw his puzzled expression mirrored on his mother–in–law's face.

"It's very handsome, Rachel," he said finally. And indeed it was, with fine, careful stitching around the cuffs and collar, and a pocket on each side. He studied her face, and decided to keep his true thoughts to himself. "Thank you. I'll wear it to church on Sundays." He passed it over to Mary, who ran her fingers over the meticulous needlework with a small frown and passed it back.

Not noticing her mother's furrowed brow, Rachel reached beneath the apron of her skirt and brought out her mother's gift. Mary's fingers closed around it in disbelief and John gasped.

"Daughter, how could you have paid for something so fine? Wherever did you get this?" she asked in amazement as she turned the intricately carved angel in her hands. She peered at the angel's face, seeing each painstaking detail and touched the delicately shaped wings. John rose to stand behind Mary and inspect the gift over her shoulder.

Rachel laughed, delighted that she had pleased her mother so much. "I didn't *buy* it, I made it! I've been working on it for a long time. I hope you like it."

Her husband was watching her carefully. "You made this, Rachel? How?"

"I carved it, of course. Out of a piece of wood from the forest." For the second time that evening, anxiety twisted in her; it seemed John was always looking at her like that, with that strange expression of bewilderment. Was she making that many blunders? Better to find out now before things got worse. "Is something wrong?" she asked with a boldness she didn't feel. When he didn't answer, she turned to Mary. "Mam? I asked if there was something wrong?" She knelt in front of her mother's chair, where the woman still held the angel somewhat reverently. "Or is it that you don't like it?"

Her mother's eyes raised from the polished wood. "Oh no, Rachel, of course I do! It's a wonderful gift, really it is." She hesitated. "It's just that...well..." She glanced at John and saw her own concern unspoken in his eyes, as well as his decision to remain silent.

"It's just that I—we never knew you could carve wood." Her gaze touched on the shirt John still held. "It always seemed you took after me, with my own skills so lacking for talent. And neither of us knew that you could turn a thread so well."

✳   ✳   ✳

With the passing of the new year, things calmed down. Rachel explained away her woodcarving ability and new–found skills at sewing by saying she had taught herself both, with patience and a lot of practice, learning one and simply improving upon the other. Her husband and mother accepted the lie, though privately neither understood how this could have been possible, since Rachel was only occasionally left alone. While it was true that John was gone for much of the day, Mary remained to care for Rachel and help with the heavier household chores, though she thought she might return to her hometown of Topsfield when the weather changed in the spring.

The bitter winter returned with a force even more brutal in the beginning of January. The snow piled upon the small village, burying traps and freezing smaller farm animals, sometimes caving in barn rooftops already weakened by the pre–holiday drifts. The men, working frantically at repairs in the freezing temperatures, often came home with chilblains and more than a few fingers and toes were lost to the hardship of farm life by the beginning of February. But while it was a hard existence it was not without its small pleasures, the greatest of which Rachel found to be her home life. She took immense pleasure and comfort in her mother's companionship during the day and while she longed for warm weather as much as anyone, it disappointed her to know that the season drew near when Mary would depart.

With the new year also came the renewal of intimacy between Rachel and John. Although her former existence as Mae Johnson seemed as far away as the moon, and while she may have been tempted a time or two back then, she had never been with a man. Thus the wedding bed was something new to Rachel, and having heard whispered comments from other wives and how they dreaded what they called their "wifely duties," she was understandably hesitant the night John decided she was recovered enough from the fever to make love again. Her husband took her reaction to be shyness, a personality trait which had been unknown to Rachel before the birth of their child. In fact, it had been Rachel's boldness in pursuing *him* that had captured his attention in the first place and finally pushed him to court her. Although he wasn't complaining, now it seemed he would have to get used to a whole new woman. He had loved the woman he had married, of course, but reluctantly admitted—but only to himself—that he found the "new" demure Rachel more appealing.

Rachel was delighted when she discovered her husband to be a considerate and knowledgeable lover. While she could recall the day she and John had married, try as she might their encounter on the night of their wedding eluded her memory searches, and she was completely unprepared for the feelings he invoked in her. Wrapped in the warmth of the featherbed and pillows (new ones, by God, she had reticked those right away!), she surrendered to John as he gently touched her just so there, and then there. She relaxed and responded—something else John found different; the "old" Rachel may have been bold in the chase, but she'd been a Puritan at heart and in the marriage bed. Toward the end of their lovemaking her eyes opened in surprise as she climaxed.

Perhaps it was the new depth of feelings within the small family that pulled them all so tightly together.

Or maybe it was simply the overhang of unknown disaster.

✺   ✺   ✺

The horror began on Friday, the twenty–ninth of February.

John was so excited he could barely stand still; he kept striding around the room and twirling his arms around like some piece of wind–blown rope—it was clear that he was full of the fire Reverend Parris was spreading amongst the townspeople.

"We've taken Sarah Good to the jail! They've accused her of being a witch, of using witchcraft and performing sorceries and such, and of tormenting children in the village." John's chest was puffed up and his shoulders were squared, so pleased was he with himself. "I myself was one of the constables who arrested her!"

Mary held her tongue and continued chopping potatoes at the worktable, but Rachel frowned. For once her memory of Salem Village's residents served her well and without hesitation. "Sarah Good? Isn't she that pitiful beggar woman who wanders around the village? It's a wonder she hasn't frozen by this time. The poor old thing is unwell in her head, that's all." She stared at her husband in astonishment. "How could anyone think that addled thing is a witch? Why, the biggest sin she commits is that pipe she smokes up under the Reverend's nose!"

John was silent for a moment, then he shrugged as his festive mood faded a bit. "Well, she's been arrested, that's for sure, and she's waiting to be examined tomorrow. A man's been sent to fetch both Judge Hawthorn and Judge Corwin to oversee the examination and make sure things are handled right."

Rachel turned away, stirring the food in the cook pot hanging above the fire. "I still don't see how that harmless, poor old woman could bewitch anybody."

Her task completed, Mary wiped her hands and looked up. "Who are her accusers?"

John sat and with relief began pulling off his boots and wet stockings. "Let's see…I believe it's Sarah Biger and Elizabeth Hubbard. Oh, and Thomas Putnam's daughter, Ann."

Rachel's heart quickened for a moment and she quietly drew in her breath. History lessons a hundred years old stirred in the deepest recesses of her brain, names and sluggish facts that Rachel knew instinctively would be utterly useless, even if she could remember them correctly. For a moment she felt totally helpless. "Isn't she the girl who's been causing so much trouble in chapel lately?" she managed at last.

John grinned. Obviously, his wife's memory was finally improving. "Why, yes!" He twisted his head to look up at her, his face earnest, and Rachel's heart sank as she realized he truly believed all this. "And listen, remember Christmas Day, in the church? Her father came to me and told me he was having quite a time with her, that she was having what he called 'fits' and tantrums. This would explain all that, Rachel. It's clear that the child *has* been bewitched, perhaps by this very woman." He opened his mouth, then stopped; he could think of no good reason to mention the girl's ridiculous notions regarding him, although if she could tell her father such a falsity, perhaps…he put it out of his mind.

"Well, I think it's all nothing but stories," Rachel said flatly. "I can't for the life of me see how that pathetic old creature could hurt anyone or anything. All she does is wander around and ask for food. She's just *hungry*, that's all. Maybe

I'll even go to the hearing tomorrow and say so!"

John was on his feet faster than Rachel had time to react, giving her a hard shake of the shoulders before pushing her roughly down onto the kitchen bench. "You'll do no such thing, or so help me I'll take a switch to your backside!" Before Rachel had a chance to snap out a reply, he continued, even angrier than before. "Don't test me, Rachel, or so help me God, I'll do it!"

Suddenly afraid he would strike her daughter right then, Mary touched his arm timidly. "Oh no, please! She meant no harm, John!"

Rachel's anger fled for the moment. "Don't you see, John?" she pleaded. "An innocent woman has been jailed because of nothing but vicious lies." She hesitated a moment, then plunged on. "She may even die—what if they do that? We can't just stand by and watch—we must at least *say* something to—"

"Die? Pah!" John dismissed her with a wave of his hand. "She's just a beggarwoman. Why in God's name would they kill her? Besides, if she's innocent, as you believe, they'll find that out and release her, I'm sure."

✳   ✳   ✳

Sarah Good, they soon discovered, was still being held, but not alone. In fact, the building which housed the jail had never known such a full house as now—every room held occupants to overflowing, some four or five to a cell in the small, dungeon–like quarters. Not built for that capacity, the squalor was unspeakable; women and men huddled in corners, on benches, with little or no heat during the last of that bitter winter, with meager, tainted food and frozen water as their only sustenance. By the beginning of May, well over a dozen people were still jailed.

Rachel and John weren't speaking. Caught in the crossfire of the emotions building within the suddenly too–small house, Mary longed for Topsfield and her own home, where she could get away from this grim village and go back to a normal existence, one where you needn't avoid your neighbors and worry over every word that passed your tongue. And God help you if you were careless! She wanted desperately to depart but was terrified that her leaving would draw attention and be blown into something more sinister by folks with whom she'd barely passed the time of day. Besides, if she left with John walking about the house in perpetual stubborn silence, who would control her daughter? She had never known Rachel to express such strong, vocal feelings about anything, yet it was getting increasingly difficult to keep the young woman from speaking out against those who had not only originally condemned the poor souls being detained, but who found more "witches" every day. Mary herself was inclined neither way—but John, apparently, had simply decided that since they were being held on common belief, they must therefore be guilty. Perhaps he knew better than Rachel and Mary, for being a constable he was required to attend most of the trials and had himself arrested the first suspects. Yet nothing on this earth seemed to convince Rachel that the accusations were anything more than wild imaginings. The nightly arguments between her daughter and son–in–law had finally ceased, though Mary thought she would have preferred those to the resentful silence which ultimately pervaded the house because of the unyielding beliefs of each.

Yet now, as she did every morning, her daughter sat at the small window, periodically wiping away the moisture and fearfully staring out at the town while waiting for John to return for the night.

"Rachel," she began, then stopped. She did not want to hurt the girl's feelings nor risk a quarrel, but something had to be said.

"Yes, Mam?" Rachel did not turn around; she seemed content to sit like this for an hour or more each day around the time of John's return, yet each time she saw him finally approach she rose and busied herself with chores so he wouldn't know how worried she'd been.

Mary sucked in her breath and spoke again. "Why do you wait like that, then pretend you don't care when John arrives. He would be gratified to see how you worry after him." Such a small start, Mary thought ruefully.

Rachel turned on the chair to face her, but it was a moment before she finally answered. "Because he is angry with me, I suppose. And because I do not believe as he does that these people are witches, or are bewitching others." She looked out the window again, seeing her own sad face mirrored in the pitted glass. "I'm afraid I've lost his affection because of it."

Mary went to stand behind Rachel's chair and her fingers reached to smooth the thick brown hair that Rachel had taken to leaving unbound while in the privacy of the home. She had often combed it when Rachel was a child and had seen John's eyes follow Rachel longingly about the room in the evenings. Yet they might as well be sleeping in different counties for all they touched or spoke. "No, I don't think so. He still loves you very much." Rachel glanced at her quickly and looked away. Mary continued, her voice serious.

"Listen to me, Rachel. I think he fears for your safety, and I also think that if the two of you can go beyond the pigheadedness that keeps you from speaking to one another, you'll see that I speak the truth. He's your *husband*, Rachel. Can't you at least listen before you cut him short and close your ears?"

"It's John who closes his *mind!*" Rachel insisted. Her fists bunched the fabric of her apron. "I hear him but he can't see beyond the end of the accusers' pointing fingers!"

"If you would let him talk without interruption, maybe he would do the same for you."

"I doubt it," Rachel replied. She looked down at her clutching fingers and forced them to relax. When *was* the last time she and John had talked, rather than argued? She couldn't say.

Perhaps it *was* time to try.

※   ※   ※

Mary had been asleep on her small bed in the corner for over an hour and after some time spent staring into the fire, John and Rachel retired to their bedroom, still not speaking, nor, as had been the case for several weeks, touching. Rachel watched him surreptitiously as they climbed into bed and knew they could not continue like this. Instead of presenting her back, her fingers brushed his arm before he could reach to blow out the candle and he looked back at her in surprise. A pulse beat slowly in her throat. "John, it's true that we have different opinions, but it's a sad thing that because we believe differently our home should be split like this."

His work–roughened fingers picked nervously at the bedcovers and when he spoke, his voice was hoarse with feeling. "Rachel, my love, don't you know that it's your safety I'm afraid for the most? Your mother's, also." He paused for her answering argument and when she sat quietly, he grabbed at the opportunity to go on. "I thought at first those people were guilty, but now I'm not so sure. They accuse *anybody*. Last week Rebecca Nurse was charged—for God's sake, the woman is bedridden!" He clenched the covers in his hands, twisting them almost savagely. "I'm *afraid*, Rachel. We should all be afraid. Yesterday they issued a warrant for the arrest of the Reverend George Burroughs. This morning men set out for Maine to bring him back for trial."

"Who are the accusers?" Rachel asked. "Is it still Ann Putnam and her friends?"

"Yes. And the stories grow each day, unbelievable tales the likes of which I've never heard! Rachel, you must not, not *ever* let them hear you defending someone who has been charged, or even recently accused. Because of your illness you haven't been in Salem Village often over the last year, and luckily no one has asked for your testimony on their behalf."

She stared at him in astonishment. "John! What if someone needed my testimony to help them? How could I in good conscience refuse?"

"Rachel, don't you understand? *No one* is going free, *no one* is being released—at least, no one who claims to be innocent. Only those who confess gain a reprieve. And I know in my soul that these confessions are nothing but lies for people to regain their freedom, although being guilty costs them all their possessions. Yet who can blame them? These people aren't witches—most are simply old or, Gold help us, have had an argument or cause to make the witch–bitches angry with them in the past. It's a constant wonder to me that the judges can't see this, though maybe they are blinded by the fact that the girls' own parents are defending them and expanding the insane tales they tell."

"What do they say? What could possibly be said about a man such as Reverend Burroughs? He has done no one harm—he hasn't even lived here for years."

John got out of bed and stepped to the washstand. Talking about this had made him flush with anger and sweat spotted his forehead despite the chilly room. He rinsed his face with the cold water in the basin. "As if the man didn't suffer enough at the time, Reverend Burroughs has gained further misfortune from the deaths of both his wives. Besides bewitchment, they've accused him of murder."

"Murder!"

"Yes, and also of torturing Ann Putnam and Mercy Lewis, and tempting them to write their names in the Devil's book. They claim he said he can raise the Devil."

"This is nonsense!" Rachel cried. "Why don't the fathers of these girls switch them until they learn better than to bear false witness?"

"Because they color their stories with biblical quotes and back one another in the courtroom. And remember, in many cases their own parents are adding more details to the testimony." He shook his head and slid beneath the covers once more. "It's really amazing. When I was a child, my mother used to tell me stories about the theater in England. It's obvious these girls should be put on a ship and sent back there!

"Do you understand now why I've badgered you all these weeks? It's not at all that I believe these poor people are in league with the Devil, but that disbelief—at least outspoken—can be damning. Please, Rachel. I would never try to force you to do something against your will, so disbelieve if that is your inclination. But there is great danger in vocalizing your opinion and I'm begging you to keep silent or, God forbid, we might find ourselves among the ranks of the accused."

There wasn't much she could say in reply; all her arguments flew in the face of the danger in which they would be placed if she spoke her mind in defense of someone else. Yet it was so *hard* to keep quiet when she knew that each and every person who was arrested was innocent, and this knowledge would be all the more damaging if, more to the heart, a friend or neighbor pleaded for their help. All Rachel could do was curse her own memories and hope it never happened.

✳   ✳   ✳

Toward the middle of May, Mary decided it was time to return to Topsfield. The weather was still cold, but clear and warming more each day; she judged by the end of the month the temperatures would be comfortable and the roads dry enough for a wagon; John could take her then. Winter had done its best to extend an ugly hand beyond its normal grip, and as a result they were just now beginning to feel spring–like warmth in mid–afternoon; mornings and nights were still bitter and damp and likely to show sharp icicles reaching from the roof outside. Mary often thought of the poor souls locked in the jail and what cruelties they must be suffering. She had hoped they would be released long ago, but such was not the case and, in fact, Ann Foster had died in jail, partially from the foul weather but mostly, Mary was sure, from ill treatment. She wanted desperately to leave this cursed village, yet she feared also for her daughter and son–in–law's welfare. While they believed Mary's departure would be construed as the normal return of a mother to her own home after a daughter's illness, Rachel and John wanted to return to Topsfield with her but were afraid to do so lest they appear to be fleeing witches. They would have to stay.

Nearly packed for the journey, Mary's sense of foreboding and panic escalated at the end of the month, when the judges announced that Bridget Bishop's formal death warrant would be signed on June eighth and the convicted woman would be hanged on June tenth. Rachel appeared to want Mary to leave even more than the older woman herself, though her mother knew it was safety that concerned her daughter now. Incredibly, the number of accused now numbered well over seventy and was still climbing; no one, it seemed, was safe. Although the people being accused ranged around several counties and included Topsfield, Rachel still clung to the hope that Mary would be safer in her well–known hometown than she was here in Salem Village. It was with this optimism that Rachel helped fill Mary's chest with belongings the Monday before Bridget Bishop's threatened execution, praying as she and Mary worked that the townspeople wouldn't go through with such an atrocity, and knowing in her heart that they would. At least, Rachel thought, let the deed wait until they were well into the midst of their journey. No one in the small household was inclined to view the execution.

But her hopeful thoughts of Mary being at least somewhat secure were smashed when John finally made it home that evening after yet another of the endless meetings at the town hall. When he had realized the lengths to which the townsfolk appeared to be taking their witch hunt after he had been required to make yet another arrest—his tenth—he had forbade Rachel and Mary to attend any more meetings, afraid that just their presence would prompt a sudden fit from one of those hellish girls. In the back of his thoughts, he still privately worried over Thomas Putnam's words about how Ann had fancied herself in love with him and how she and John would be together after Rachel died. Since Rachel and Mary were forbidden to attend the meetings or visit Salem Village any more than was absolutely necessary, they relied on John for news of the townsfolk, and slowly they began to realize that most of the time John hung to the back of the meetings and tried to remain as inconspicuous as possible— especially where the Putnam family was concerned. While it gnawed at him that his behavior might prove dangerous, he still managed to be unavailable most of the times when a constable was needed. Still, when John came home that night, Rachel could tell by his eyes that he brought bad news. Afraid to ask, she said nothing and instead helped him with his jacket and boots, then set a cup of mulled cider on the table to warm him. For a time, the three of them sat at the table in silence, the women watching John stare at his cup, though he did not drink. When he finally spoke, his words were brutal in spite of the forced gentleness of his voice.

"We cannot leave for Topsfield on Tuesday morning."

Mary gasped and Rachel's mouth was a circle of shock. "But it's not safe in this horrible place!" Rachel cried. "We must take Mam home!"

John looked at them helplessly. "I know, I know! If I could, we'd leave Monday morning and not even stop there—not until we reached Boston, or beyond! But we can't, not now. At the meeting tonight, Judge Hawthorn told all in attendance that the execution on Thursday would be the telling evidence of even more people in the village who are witches but remain undiscovered. He said that the impending execution of Bridge would cause many to flee, and it would be obvious that those who fled were witches themselves, running for their lives." He was gripping his cup so hard that his fingernails were half red, half white; afraid he'd crack the pottery, he released it and held onto the edge of the table instead. "Don't you see? It's a certainty that if we leave now, even just to take Mary home, they'll swear it's incriminating evidence. At the very least, they'll accuse Mary."

"But in all probability, they'll charge all of us."

✳   ✳   ✳

Talking yet another chance—it seemed lately he challenged fate at every turn—John instructed Rachel and Mary to stay away from Salem Village on the day of the execution. They had all been in town for supplies on Tuesday when the death warrant was read, and he could still hear the words in his mind, where they hung filthy in their injustice:

"*...indicted and arraigned upon five several indictments for using, practicing, and exercising on the nineteenth day of April last past and divers other days and times before and after, certain acts of witchcraft in and upon the bodies of Abigail Williams, Ann Putnam, junior, Mercy Lewis, Mary Wolcott, and Elizabeth Hubbard, of Salem Village...whereby their bodies were hurt, afflicted, pined, consumed, wasted, and tormented...*

"*To which indictments the said Bridget Bishop pleaded Not Guilty, and for trial thereof put herself upon God and her country; whereupon she was found Guilty of the felonies and witchcrafts, whereof she stood indicted, and sentence of death accordingly passed against her as the law directs...*

"*...safely conduct the said Bridget Bishop...to the place of execution, and there cause her to be hanged by the neck until she be dead...*"

As a constable of Salem Village, John was required not only to attend Bridget Bishop's execution, but help preside over it. Afraid he would be asked to actually place the rope around the terrified woman's neck, he pretended difficulties with the horses until another man finally picked the horse on which the woman would be seated and John managed to place himself at the other end of the crowd milling about the square and rumbling with impatience. Roughly tied in place atop a nervous mount, Bridget, tears streaming down her dusty face, pleaded her innocence to the crowd while her husband Edward ran among the townsfolk crying for help in saving his wife. Unnoticed by most, John glowered from his place near the stables and was not surprised when Judge Corwin, who sat on a viewing bench at the front of the crowd, ordered two constables to place Edward Bishop under arrest for consorting with a convicted witch. As they dragged Edward away from the square, his raw cries of farewell to Bridget brought a burning to John's eyes.

Even caught as he was by Edward Bishop's misery, John's gaze followed the constables as they forced Edward into the town square. John was sickened far beyond any emotion he had previously thought possible. What manner of evil flourished here to make Salem's townsfolk determined to murder innocent people on trumped–up charges of witchcraft and sorcery? If this continued, no one would be left unaccused—perhaps even his own family. He wondered if Edward would end up as his wife was today, up there on the gallows—

Th–Thump!

He had lost track of the proceedings, and John found himself staring in horror across the top of the crowd at Bridget Bishop's shoes, the scuffed black leather and silver buckles now adorning a cooling, twitching corpse. He heard the crowd murmur then begin to applaud, and felt bile rise bitter in his throat.

It was the tenth of June, 1692. The first witch had been hanged.

✳   ✳   ✳

Rachel watched her husband pace the width of the parlor. He hadn't been the same since the hanging in June, but now, almost a month later, she found her patience with his worry wearing despite the realization that they were all getting on one another's nerves. The house seemed to have gotten smaller as each day passed and Mary's frustration grew. Before snapping at her mother or husband, Rachel would grind her teeth and pinch her own flesh beneath the white apron she wore; thankfully her senses returned each time with the pain, along with the knowledge that these times were hard on everyone and they all had to endure the same tension. Still, the skin of her upper thighs was mottled with tiny black and blue bruises.

And tonight was the worst yet. Sharply tuned to her husband's feelings, she could see a deeper course of trouble in the set of John's shoulders and feel it in the way the sturdy floor vibrated with every agitated step he took. She and Mary worked together on a new quilt for the bedroom, the tedious stitching making their necks and eyes ache. Finally Rachel could wait no longer.

"John, please! I can't stand to see you like this. Tell us what's wrong." Rachel dropped her section of the quilt in frustration. Grateful for some respite from the tiresome stitches, Mary let her hands rest on her lap. Rachel's tone made her nearly as nervous as her son–in–law's unceasing movement. John's restless stride hesitated, then resumed without an answer.

"John, listen to me."

He seemed to only partially hear her as he finally stopped before the fire, the embers now barely glowing. "I should fetch more wood," he said dully.

Rachel joined him before the fireplace. When he still refused to talk, she tugged impatiently on his arm. "John, if you don't tell me what's going on, I'll—" She paused, not sure of a suitable threat. The most likely idea came almost instantly. "I'll go into the village myself and find out."

His turn was so sudden she would have lost her balance and tumbled into the ashes had he not fiercely grabbed her shoulders. "No! You will *not!* You mustn't go anywhere near Salem Village, do you hear?" He released her and gestured at Mary, who perched fearfully on the rocking chair. "Nor should you—we must all stay as close to the house as possible. And it's safer if we speak little, or even not at all, to those who live on the farms around us." His eyes were dark recesses as he stared at each of the women. Fear deepened the creases in his forehead and made dark shadows shift beneath his eyes and in the hollows of his face.

Recovering from the shock of his outburst, Rachel again touched him. "Why, John? You've said little the last couple of days. What's going on there?"

"It's a vile place filled with people gone mad with murder!" John stumbled and Rachel encircled his waist and helped him to the table bench. He sat and ran trembling fingers through his hair, then made a strangled sound. Her heart tried to skip a beat as she realized he was actually *crying*. "Oh God, forgive us all!"

She needn't have asked, but she knew her mother expected it. Still, Rachel could hardly manage her whispered question. "What are they doing, John?"

Mary's hands covered her mouth, holding back any sound; they itched to cover her ears instead, to protect herself from things she knew she didn't want to know. She could feel the guilt that fed on her son-in-law as though it were an evil dog skulking behind her own chair.

"They read the bans today. They plan to execute five more women next Monday—*five!*" He sobbed, not even trying to conceal his fears. "I arrested four of those women, Rachel, and now those four women are going to die. What black thing has captured the hearts of men in this county? If I hadn't arrested them, maybe they'd be free today—perhaps they would have escaped to relatives living somewhere else. Jesus forgive me…what have I *done?*"

Rachel squeezed his shoulders, knowing it was small comfort. "There was nothing you could have done," she said, brushing his sweat-soaked hair back from his eyes. "If you hadn't arrested them, another constable would have. The judges would simply have sent someone else. Look at me." She pulled his chin around, her brown eyes earnest. "This is not your fault, John Willard, not at all. All of this would have happened anyway, despite anything you could have done." The tenseness in his shoulders seemed to ease, though she knew he'd never be fully convinced. Still, she would do the best she could.

"If I had just talked to them—"

"No," Rachel interrupted. "I'll hear no more of it." She looked at her mother for confirmation and was gratified to see a supporting nod. "We must worry for ourselves now, protect our backs and do our best to survive."

Mary, her eyes wide with fright, came to stand next to her and reached for Rachel's hand. Rachel took it and in turn clasped John's with her other. "For those unfortunates who will die at the hands of these madmen," Mary said softly, "we can only pray."

And pray they did, standing before the dying embers of the fire, heads down and eyes closed as each made their silent entreaties.

None saw the pallid, jealous face at the window.

✺ ✺ ✺

Ann Putnam ran back through the field the way she'd come, the sugar cakes falling from her basket, unnoticed in her rage. How sweet, she thought bitterly. Such a tidy little family—all standing before the fireplace, praying together. She should have never agreed to her mother's request that she bring the Willard family the sweet cakes—should have, in fact, thrown a fit at the very mention of John Willard's name. Instead she had jumped at the opportunity to see him. But what she had seen was not the burdened, unhappy man of whom her father spoke, no indeed! Rather there had been a husband and his wife (who was no doubt working diligently at getting with child again) and mother–in–law, gathered cozily in their home, comforting each other in troubled times.

"Bah!" she spat. "I'll fix him, and good." The girl, a too–thin twelve–year– old who showed no signs of filling out, smiled nastily to herself. *Perhaps*, she thought, *I'll accuse them all of being witches*. She dropped her basket on the front porch and scuffed at the grayed wood beneath her feet. The harsh winter had taken its toll; a piece of it splintered and she dug at it viciously with the toe of her shoe. No, then John might hang, and she couldn't have that. Damnation! She'd had no idea his wife had recovered so fully—the woman not only looked more than well, was petitely beautiful. As for herself, Ann could never hope to look like Rachel Willard, not in a hundred years.

But if Rachel was out of the way—and her mother, of course—then John would look to someone for comfort. And being a fairly young man and having a hint of Ann's interest, John Willard might even look for a new wife, possibly right away.

"Ann, is that you?" Her mother's voice rang impatiently in Ann's ears.

"Yes, mother. Coming."

But she would think about it first. And, she decided, she would talk to him. She was sly but not stupid; the possibility that he might hate her forever if she caused his wife and mother–in–law to hang had not escaped her.

"Ann Putnam, you get in this house this instant! I need help with this spinning wheel, and I need it right now!"

"I'm *coming*." She opened the door and stepped inside, her thoughts working furiously. Yes, she decided, but this would take a little planning.

After all, John Willard and his family were more than mere sport.

✳   ✳   ✳

The Willard family could not avoid church. To do so would cause unwanted attention, and John would sooner cut off his arm than invite suspicious eyes upon his wife or Mary. As they seated themselves, Mary and Rachel bowed their heads respectfully, but John's skin crawled unexpectedly from the sensation of *eyes* and he glanced cautiously around, nervously searching the inside of the church.

Reverend Samuel Parris stood rigidly behind the lectern at the front, and when John met his gaze he knew immediately the source of his feeling of being watched. Parris was openly scrutinizing each and every person in attendance, and mistrust was clear on the preacher's face. No doubt the man was just itching to find another victim among the parish who could be denounced as a witch or as being in league with the Devil himself. John pulled his gaze away, barely hiding his distaste. And although Reverend Parris had turned his head to study others in the room, John still had that ugly, disconcerting sensation of being spied upon, as though someone were examining him, hair by hair. He peered around again, trying to be inconspicuous yet unable to shake the annoying sense of—

There, two pews up in the usual place, sat the Putnam family. He should have known it would be that exasperating and now dangerous girl again. Right now she had twisted herself around on the bench with her right elbow hanging insolently over its back. The fingers of her left hand sassily twirled a lock of hair that had escaped from her bonnet, in total disregard for her whereabouts. He met her stare and frowned, yet she seemed delighted that he had discovered her indiscretion and for a moment he thought she'd actually giggle out loud. Irritated, he turned his attention to his prayer book and ignored her, although the memory of that stare plagued him throughout the sermon. *How*, he asked himself, *could a child of such young years have such treacherous fervor in her eyes?*

If there was no comfort in the sermon, it was surely sincere. The words blazed righteously from Reverend Parris's mouth, seeking and finding every person in the chapel, leaving no soul untouched or at peace.

"Yea, though we walk through the valley of the shadow of death, we will fear no evil—*none!* The people of Salem Village have banded together to drive from amongst us those who useth divination, or enchantments, or charmers, or those who consult with familiar spirits or practice necromancy. Those, good people, who consort with devils—*witches!*" He pulled his ruler from the lectern and stepped down to the banister. The folks in the front pew winced visibly and pulled back, huddling together.

"And the Lord said, 'Thou shalt not suffer a witch to live.' It is here with the Lord's authority, here in this chapel and by His Divine Word, that I command that all the people of Salem Village—not just the few who live within the village limits, but *all*—attend the executions this nineteenth of July and bear witness to God's harsh punishment upon those who dare not confess and ask forgiveness for their sins!"

The church suddenly filled with muffled noise and John clenched his fists around his hat and prayer book. *Damn!* He had especially wanted to keep Rachel and Mary away from the hangings, yet now he had no choice but to bring them into Salem Village...and he had no doubt that the man's intense observation had noted his family's presence for Sunday service. *Damn!* he thought again. Better to have avoided the service altogether and pleaded illness—even to have purposely injured himself in his farm chores for an excuse. Now it was too late for even the most panicked tactic. Besides that, he could feel that silly little Putnam girl looking at him again, and he glowered at her openly this time; he had more pressing things to worry about and no time for her adolescent infatuation.

Ann Putnam's eyes widened appreciably when she saw the expression on

John Willard's face, and she wondered briefly what he had done that morning to put him in such a foul mood. She had a moment's uncertainty about what she planned to do after church, and almost told her father she'd reconsidered the whole thing. But she glanced at John again, this time not so obviously, and decided she would indeed go through with her plans—he was such a fine, handsome man! Even from where she sat some fifteen feet away, she could see the clear blue of his eyes and the broadness of his shoulders. Yes, she surely would appreciate a man such as him coming home to her each night.

Calmer now, Reverend Parris droned on, more talk and lessons about the evils of witchcraft and how it was treason to God and country. His words drifted in and out of John's attention, weaving around the problem he faced of keeping himself and his family safe. The close of the sermon brought his focus rudely back to the church.

"—and they shall stone them and their blood shall be upon them. For them that do these things are an abomination to the Lord and his people, and the Lord thy God shall drive them out! Good people of Salem Village, my own servant now resides in jail, and there she shall stay for her evil ways!" He gripped the sides of the lectern tightly. "Or perhaps she will hang—and if she consorts with the Devil, so she should!" The preacher's voice rose to a half-scream. "Again I say to you, *thou shall not suffer a witch to live!*"

John barely had time to think *hypocrite!* before the pastor slapped his Bible shut and strode from the chapel. Instead of going through the rear door as was his usual custom, Parris went straight down the center aisle, subjecting all to his accusing glare. He finally stopped at the back so he could bid goodbye to all who had attended—a sure way of not missing anyone in the time it took him to go around outside from the back to the front. His switch bearers—unnecessary since the frightened children had stayed very much awake—stepped aside in confusion. While none too pleased herself, Rachel had to smile a little when she heard a few people in the pews around her groan under their breaths.

Since there was no avoiding it, the Willard family waited resolutely in the line exiting the church for their turn at small talk with Reverend Parris. A memory returned to Rachel as she waited between John and Mary, shivering in a building where the warmth had bled away over the last few months: the chapel, full of people and bright sunshine as it had been only last summer. The townsfolk had been relaxed and content then, listening to the sermon and talking about the lessons cheerfully at its end. She realized with a start that her belly had been big with child at the time and tried desperately to expand on the image, to really *feel* the mystery baby that she had carried, but the memory floated away, suffocated by the dreary, burdened churchgoers around her and their fearful murmurs. She pulled her shawl closer around her shoulders; though it was the second week into July, the small building was perpetually chilly and damp. She knew the farmers prayed for rain to feed the crops that were drying up, but God knew they'd all take chills if it rained in these cool temperatures.

When it was their turn to speak with the parson, Rachel was dismayed to find she was a little more nervous than expected. Following the crowd of people toward the door brought them closer and closer to Parris and they could hear some of the harsh questions the reverend was directing to the unprepared people. Rachel placed her hand on Mary's arm and felt the older woman tremble, then willed herself to be calm and silent for her mother's sake, and to stop betraying her tenseness by biting at her lower lip. It was not at all comforting to see the muscle ticking in John's jaw as he stepped up to greet the preacher.

"Ah, John and Rachel, how nice to see you. And Goodwife Esty." Parris's smile was all the more hideous for its insincerity. "We seldom see the family in Salem Village, John. Why is that?"

Rachel answered before John's hesitation could cause suspicion. "No doubt it's my doing, Reverend." John frowned but Rachel continued quickly, touching a gentle hand to her husband's arm. "John is so very patient with me. Isn't he, mother?" She glanced at Mary, who nodded automatically. "I'm afraid I haven't fully recovered from my illness and the loss of our child." She rarely spoke of the baby and prayed the parson wouldn't notice the startled glances of her family.

Reverend Parris glowered at Rachel. "But it's been almost a year. Surely you're well by now."

She smiled sadly. "For the most part, yes. But there are times that I still feel so poorly I can barely tend to the household chores." Her voice dropped to a whisper and Parris was forced to lean forward to hear. "And the loss of our daughter still weighs heavy on my thoughts."

Although Parris appeared to accept her explanation, Rachel could see in his eyes that he was not convinced and she forced herself not to squint when his expression darkened. "I expect you would have been better served to take comfort from the Lord by attending His church. In any event, I'm sure you've recovered enough to attend the purging ceremony next Monday." He looked at each of them in turn and Rachel was relieved to see that John had recovered from her reference to their child's death. "I meant what I said at the sermon about *all* attending."

"Oh, yes," Rachel agreed sweetly. "We'll be there. Good day, Reverend."

She and Mary curtsied slightly and moved away as John shook hands with the preacher, struggling to disguise his growing hostility. *Purging ceremony, indeed!* While his face was outwardly serene, John's mind boiled. *Purging ceremony! Why doesn't he just call it what it is?* he railed to himself. *Why doesn't he just call it* murder? Realizing that he was getting more upset by the minute, he hurried his family past the others who milled about the front of the church sharing hushed, eager speculation. The previous year, the Willards had been a very outgoing and well-liked family and had looked forward to the after-church socializing; now the main topic of conversation was the upcoming executions and they had no desire to stop and talk.

"John! John, wait up!"

Disappointed at the delay, John paused. When he saw who had called out, he cursed under his breath for the third time that day as Thomas Putnam trotted up and pulled his hat off to the women. "Good morning to you! I hope you're all well?" He smiled broadly, but John thought he detected something nasty hiding behind that false, happy grin. Once the two men had been close friends, but the witch hunts of the past months had caused an irreparable tear in their relationship. Though John had believed in the guilt of the accused in the beginning, even then he had thought Thomas took too much pleasure in the arrests of the so-called witches, and as the months passed, his doubt turned to dislike as Thomas seemed to enjoy more and more their terror and cries for mercy.

Still, John doffed his cap politely. "And a good morning to you, Thomas." He indicated Rachel and Mary. "We're very well, thank you. And you?" He knew his responses sounded stiff, but he couldn't help it. He'd had his fill today of play acting with the Reverend Parris; he had little patience to spare for the gleeful Thomas Putnam.

"Fine, just fine." The merriness deserted Putnam abruptly and he addressed the woman. "Ladies, I'm sorry to ask, but would you excuse us for a few minutes?" At Rachel's glance, John looked highly displeased but to refuse would have been an insult; he had no choice but to nod his agreement.

"Of course," said Rachel. She struggled to keep the worry from her face as she noted her husband's irritable expression. "Mother, let's go look at the garden the parson's wife has planted against the side of the church." She tugged Mary quickly away, not letting her curtsy to Putnam. In her view, the man was a weasel who preyed on other peoples' misfortune, and she'd not give him that much respect.

Rachel's move was not lost on Putnam and his eyes narrowed as he watched the two women walk away. Then he blinked and all traces of annoyance disappeared before he lifted his gaze to John, who looked longingly after his wife and mother-in-law. "John, do you remember how I spoke to you before about my daughter, Ann?" he asked.

Reluctantly, John nodded. *Her again*, he thought angrily. His face was placid, but he was mentally switching the child's backside. Never a patient man with those he disliked, John's temper was stretching to its limits. "Yes, I remember," he managed.

Thomas shifted his feet, suddenly unsure of himself. "She begs to speak with you privately." At John's look of disbelief, Putnam rushed on. "She tells me that she thinks she can—cleanse herself of what she calls her attachment to you, if only you will grant her a few moments alone to explain her bold behavior. Her mother and I would step outside later tonight if you would come by—"

"Bold behavior!" John exploded. "In*deed!*" Only pure will kept him from grabbing Thomas Putnam by the jacket and shaking him. "Are you mad? To think that a grown man of thirty-three years would speak of such a thing to a girl of that age without a chaperone is preposterous in itself." In spite of the fierce control he was exerting, John couldn't keep himself from stepping toward Thomas, and felt Putnam deserved every bit of the fear that sprang to his eyes. "Especially, *Mister* Putnam, a child who screams 'bewitchment!' at the slightest provocation and throws fits, and whose own parents do nothing to control her!" His voice was escalating and he struggled to bring it back to a normal pitch before he drew attention to himself.

John's insult of his parental duties made Putnam's cheeks go red. "The child is having a hard time of it! She has been beset upon and needs indulgence," he snapped.

"Indulgence, my arse. The only thing that has *beset* your daughter is a sense of power from your lack of discipline." Now the two men were standing eye to eye, though Thomas Putnam had no intention of matching muscles with the substantially larger John Willard. "You misjudge me, Putnam, if you think I would set myself up by going anywhere near your little—" John stumbled at his words, then spat them out in spite of their crudeness. "—witch–bitch!" Putnam's furious face went from red to white and John turned with the intention of leaving the fool where he stood, then stopped to give him a final bit of advice.

"Be warned, Putnam. If your daughter dares to come within reaching distance of me or my family, I promise you I'll switch her backside bloody in your stead!"

✳   ✳   ✳

In her room, Ann Putnam beat on her feather pillow and screamed unintelligible sounds into her coverlet. *How dare he! Switch my backside, will he!* She ripped viciously at the pillow with her fingernails and feathers instantly spilled from the tear and began drifting around the room. Screeching again, she swiped at the floating whiteness, then grabbed a porcelain figurine from the bed table and hurled it against the wall, where it exploded into a dozen sharp fragments. It made no difference to her that the little statue had been her grandmother's in England. *Damn him to hell—I'll fix him! I'll see to John Willard, all right, and to his pretty little whore of a wife besides!* With another howl she began yanking the drawers from the bureau and heaving them onto the floor.

In the front room, her mother winced at the sound of breaking glass but did nothing. She had given up trying to control Ann several months ago; it was much easier and quieter to simply back her daughter when the need arose and wait for all the trouble to pass. Surely within a few months this witchery business, and Ann's involvement in it, would be over. She had thought that by helping her daughter testify against those who were being accused she could hurry the process and push the lives of the Putnam family back toward normalcy, though in truth she now regretted being caught in the midst of it all. Never had she intended for anyone to die, and guilt was a constant, heavy companion now, along with a nagging but unspoken question about her little Ann's sanity. At her daughter's next scream of rage, the older Ann Putnam clapped her hands over her ears and cowered on her rocking chair. Wherever had the girl gotten the idea that John Willard could be forced to put aside his wife? Beyond the silent moments when she doubted her daughter's sanity were those times when she thought that Willard was right and a good beating was exactly what Ann needed most, though her husband would surely do exactly that to *her* if he discovered she felt that way.

DeadTimes

*   *   *

On the morning of the executions the Willard household was a powder keg of emotions. The three of them had talked for hours since the Sunday sermon, searching for a believable reason to excuse their attendance in the village, but every suggestion crumbled in the face of the Reverend Parris's anger and the possibility that the man might come to the house afterwards and discover that all three had been capable of attending but had purposely defied his edict. Rachel, especially, begged John to stay at home, saying that if it came down to it she'd throw herself down the cellar stairs so that she might break something and give the family the excuse they needed. Though she knew it was a silly, empty idea even as she uttered the words, John's furious eyes silenced any further suggestions.

In the end, because they must, they attended.

Early that morning the rain the farmers had been praying for finally came, rolling in with massive thunderheads and unseasonably cold winds. At midday the downpour finally ceased and, fearing their wagon would slide off the road in the mud and lose a wheel, the three walked to Salem Village beneath a chilly, sprinkling rain. Wagon accidents were common and dangerous on mud-covered roads and John had no intention of risking injury even in their desire to avoid the village.

The judges, afraid that some of the accused women might become hysterical at the sight of their lifeless counterparts, had ordered the gallows in the square expanded so that all five women might be hanged at one time. Benches had been set up for the judges and witnesses; others had brought along their own small seats for themselves or their family. Children laughed and ran to and from in the muck while several women sat with each other working on quilts beneath the porches that lined the square. Even in the nasty drizzle the gathering had all the atmosphere of a town party.

The condemned women were shackled together beneath the line of gallows, gaping frantically about. Of the five, John most guiltily remembered Sarah Good, the first to be accused back in February and whose arrest he had personally supervised. Now he saw her for what she was: an older woman whose family—a husband and four-year-old daughter—had little or no resources and whose only oddity was, as Rachel had pointed out, that she smoked a pipe and begged for a few extra pence. He felt sick as he realized that the bedridden Rebecca Nurse was also among those to be, as Reverend Parris had put it, "purged." Unable to sit on a horse or stand without assistance, the elderly woman had been tied by ropes beneath her armpits to the crosspiece of the gallows; she hung there like some pathetic hunting trophy, her useless legs dangling as she swayed back and forth. Cruel children darted forward again and again to push her and laugh at her twirling figure; more than frightened, she seemed indignant at this incredible humiliation.

Thomas Putnam stood before the women, prodding them back to full attention with a staff when they began to sob, striking them outright if they became unruly or tried to call out to someone in the crowd. Obviously he intended that today's doomed prisoners would be better behaved than had Bridget Bishop last month. The man's eyes caught John's across the mass of folk gathering for the show and John felt his temper climb as Putnam glared at him hatefully and spat on the ground. A special section had been built for the informers, a box of sorts within which sat Ann Putnam, Mrs. Putnam and seven or eight other young women dressed in their finest, most of them Ann's young friends. Seeing them, especially Thomas's daughter, brought bitterness to John's mouth; instinctively he knew she was the worst of the lot.

Rachel and Mary huddled on either side of John, each clinging to an arm. Rachel was horrified by the happy, festival-like activities—women laughing and sewing while the children played and indulged themselves with sweets, the men standing about, talking and smoking—surely she and her family, with their sad, shocked faces, must stand out among this truculent crowd! Yet she could not help her dazed expression, and knew her mother and John could call up pleasant appearances right now about as easily as they could fly on the imagined brooms of the condemned witches. Looking around carefully, Rachel saw a few more joyless men and women scattered in the growing crowd, though fewer than she would have hoped; most she recognized as belonging to the families of the women about to be hanged. Some, upon catching her gaze, hurriedly rearranged their features into bland cheerfulness, but Rachel found little comfort in knowing that she and her loved ones had companionship in their fear.

The crowd was now tightly packed and it surged forward; the Willards found themselves forced to move toward the platform by the pressure of the people behind them. The horses carrying the other four women were being moved to where the ropes waited, ominous in their intent. Rebecca Nurse still dangled in place like some ill-used marionette hung on uneven strings, and John could see Ann Putnam in the informers' box, her eyes glittering as the ropes were dragged over the heads of the condemned. Her head swiveled and John saw the girl as she recognized Rachel. Ann's thin face distorted with loathing; though she had no idea that Ann's gaze had fastened upon her face, John felt Rachel shiver slightly beside him.

On the platform, ropes now circled the throats of all five women. From their position below, the scene was almost ethereal—the women appeared no more than dark, dripping shadows backdropped by the swirling gray of the rainsoaked clouds. To John the whole thing seemed hellish, like a nightmare gone mad and from which he must soon awaken or lose his own sanity. The noise of the jittery crowd drowned out the words of Judge Corwin as he stood upon the platform steps and read the death warrants, the people clamoring in their haste to see the now slack ropes jerk tight with the weight of human flesh.

John knew the magistrate had spoken his final words, yet even the sound of the crowd's gasp failed to mask the shockingly familiar noise of a falling body that John remembered from the first execution. He staggered and Rachel grabbed his arm to steady him as his chest constricted when he saw Sarah Wilds' body spasm violently, then hang still. Her face, thankfully, had turned to the back of the gallows with the tightening of the noose. Though transfixed by the horror taking place above him, the sight of the witch–bitches in the informers' box sneaked into his mind. He wished to God the judges had ordered the prisoners' faces covered.

Th–Thump!
Th–Thump!

He moaned as the mount was pulled out from under the next woman. Sarah Good's body convulsed in time with the frail Rebecca Nurse as two men who had climbed on the crosspiece above chopped through the ropes supporting her shoulders. As she fell and strangled, one man gave the rope around her neck a pull that sent the old woman's corpse on a macabre twirl. On the platform, Susanna Martin began to scream hoarsely, while Elizabeth How, the last woman John had arrested, stood as if paralyzed, staring blankly over the heads of a crowd that now clamored for more. In that accursed informers' section in the front, Ann Putnam and Mary Wolcott were smiling and clapping with delight as they made excited comments to the others seated around them. John's heart was beating so loudly it seemed to cover the noise of the people as fury built inside him, smothering common sense. Leaving an astonished Rachel and Mary, he began to claw his way toward the gallows. Although he was yelling, no one seemed to notice him.

Th–Thump!

Quickly, so the judges' ears would not be bothered further by her screams, one of the constables smacked the rump of the horse supporting Susanna Martin, sending the young woman into eternity just as John reached the front of the crowd and stumbled. He knew that Rachel and Mary were struggling along behind him, shouting frantically for him to stop, but he could no more check the rage within him than he could stop the rain from falling. Regaining his footing, he ran to the side of the mount bearing Elizabeth How, realizing with a shudder that as she sat there she was monotonously reciting the twenty–third psalm, too softly for anyone else to hear.

"Tell me," he cried out, "is this a witch? This woman who sits here about to die and reciting one of the Lord's own psalms?" A pause rolled slowly back through the crowd. To his left, a furious Ann Putnam had risen to her feet, along with her mother and the rest of the informers.

"It's a lie!" Ann screeched. "She recites not the Lord's words at all, but changes them to lies that fall upon the ears of good people such as us!" Her mind was boiling—first he embarrassed her to her father, now he was insulting her credibility to the townsfolk—how *dare* he?

John whirled to face the informers' box, then stepped forward, his face scarlet. For a moment, Ann thought he might leap over the wooden railing and slap her, and she yanked her face out of range, her mouth dropping open. She felt her mother's hands clutch at her, trying to pull her to safety, as John Willard jabbed a forefinger in their direction.

"Hang *them*!" John cried. "There are the *true* criminals of this county!" He whirled back to the crowd and spread his hands pleadingly. From the corner of his eye he could see Elizabeth How looking at him, and the sudden hope in her eyes was enough to break his heart. He waved at the four bodies above them, knowing that he would never forget this close–up of their swinging, strangled bluish faces. "Can't you see that these poor, dead women are nothing but their *victims*?"

In the box, Ann Putnam was nearly out of control. "GET HIM!" she shrieked. "He's a witch, too! He torments me!"

But though some grumbled angrily at John's outburst, no one in the crowd heard Ann or seemed to notice her words. Behind her, Mrs. Putnam grabbed her daughter's hair and gave it a painful yank. "Stop it!" she hissed. "You're too obvious—we'll see that he gets his due later!" After another yank and a hard, unseen pinch, the younger Ann finally quieted, although she sat upon the wooden bench digging her fingernails into the wood until they bled.

TH–THUMP!

Seeking to end this spectacle, a constable jerked on the reins of the horse beneath Elizabeth as Thomas Putnam and another man scrambled toward John. From their place in the crowd, a horrified Rachel and Mary could do nothing but watch as John grabbed at the woman's feet in a wild attempt to lift her body above the rope's deathgrip. He knew even as his arms pushed at her calves that it was too late. Crying openly, he managed to heft her weight above shoulder level, but her eyes were already bulging and leaking blood, lifeless in a face that had gone plum–colored. More blood seeped above the rope where it had buried itself in the skin of her snapped neck, and knowing it was a lost fight, John didn't resist as Putnam and the other two constables forced him back into the crowd. Propelled forward, John nearly fell into Rachel's arms. He could hear people muttering angrily around him, but one old man stepped forward to help him to his feet.

"Giles," John gasped. "How are you?" In other circumstances it would have been humorous—here was a man asking politely after another while still half on the ground. Giles Cory clapped him on the back and smiled after he pulled John up, a friendly gesture, but John strained to hear the old man's frantic whisper.

"Run, John! Your actions here today were brave but foolhardy, and as soon as they get their wits about them they'll see that your skepticism condemns you. Unless you want to swing like the woman you tried to save, take your family and get out of this bedamned village!"

John stared at the old man in sudden terror and his warning to Rachel of so many months ago suddenly surfaced in his mind. "They would accuse us because I question this slaughter?" It was an asinine question and he knew it.

"Shhh! Keep your voice down! And yes, you know they will. In their eyes a man who disbelieves is a sure suspect—especially a lawman." The elderly man's intelligent eyes were bright with moisture in his wrinkled face. "Take your women to safety, John, or they'll hang beside you."

"You shouldn't even be speaking with me now." John's hoarse voice could barely be heard.

Turning to leave, Cory shook his head sadly. "I'm a dead man anyway, my friend. The witch–bitches already whisper of Martha and I." He raised his head slightly. "I won't leave Salem Village. My land and my property are here and before God I'll stand to try and keep it." Another two seconds and he'd blended into the surrounding hostile faces.

Not us, thought John, jamming on his hat stoically. *No piece of ground is worth our lives.*

※ ※ ※

They left that night, packing the wagon with whatever food and necessities would fit, yet trying to keep the load light for speed. Knowing the constables would think them foolish enough to travel to Topsfield, John decide the safest choice would be to head for Boston.

He wanted to leave a candle burning so the house would look occupied if someone prowled by that night, but he was too afraid it would be knocked over by one of the mice that scampered about the place when no one was home; he settled instead for a good–sized fire on the hearth. Their single milking cow would slow their speed far too much, so just before dark John drove her out to pasture, hoping that one of the neighbors would take pity on her in a couple of days and milk her. The chickens could fend for themselves. *But what about us?* John wondered grimly. *Can we fend for ourselves? Can we find somewhere to live in peace?* With barely a light in the house or barn, and hardly an animal to be heard in the dusk, the sturdy house looked sad and lonely as they climbed aboard the wagon and headed out.

Hoping for anonymity, John kept their pace normal, as though they were nothing more than a family gone to visit relatives. Despite their careful, measured pace, four days out the right rear wheel cracked in half and the wagon's back end nearly shattered as it went down. Forced to stop for nearly three more days, they huddled around a small fire at night, Rachel and Mary jumping at every noise while John grimly worked at repairs.

On the eighth day they finally got the wagon fixed and started off again, this time trying to pick up speed and widen the too–short distance between them and Salem Village. Exhausted, they stopped for camp and slept fitfully, dreaming of swinging black shadows against gray skies and the creak of weight–bearing wood.

John woke to the gleam of firearms and the righteously pleased face of Thomas Putnam and four newly appointed Salem Village constables.

※ ※ ※

All three were accused. On August second the court levied seven indictments against John, with six girls and Mrs. Putnam stepping forward to testify. Throughout the trial he protested his innocence and damned himself repeatedly by declaring his own judges the murderers of the six who had already died.

Even their final decree that he would hang on August nineteenth failed to silence his contempt of the witchhunters.

Since Mary Esty of Topsfield was lesser known in the village, fewer indictments were made. Charged mostly with consorting with witches, the normally reticent woman sealed her fate by spitting at Judge Hawthorn when he asked her to confess and name her daughter and son–in–law as accomplices so that the Village of Salem could punish them that much quicker. Red–faced by the insult, Hawthorn would have put her on the gallows that afternoon had she not been a woman.

Mary would be executed on September twenty–second.

✳ ✳ ✳

"All rise for the Honorable Judge Corwin. The people's court of Salem Village is now in session. On this day, the seventeenth of August, year of our Lord 1692, we as witnesses attest to the trial of Rachel Mary Willard, alias Esty, charged with consorting with Satan, practicing sorcery and other detestable arts, and tormenting and afflicting Ann Putnam, Ann Putnam, junior, and Sarah Bibber, attending witches' sabbats and maintaining one of the Devil's familiars." The cryer turned toward Rachel where she stood, shackled to a banister in the meeting house. "How do you plead, Rachel Willard?"

Hungry, chewed over by insects and badly in need of a washing, Rachel still raised her head high to the court. "Not guilty." Judge Corwin looked at her scornfully, but when she met his eyes he quickly averted his gaze. *Perhaps,* she thought in disgust, *his own conscience preys on him.*

The trial, a farce from the beginning, proceeded.

She knew already that she would hang, and although she loved life and had only lived in this time for slightly more than a year, Rachel no longer felt any desire to stay in this wretched place—especially if the only two people she loved were also going to die. While she did not, *would* not, confess—which, as everyone knew, was the only way to gain a reprieve—she did little to benefit her own case, realizing early that without a confession, nothing short of pregnancy—and she wasn't—would help anyway. Malnourished and near exhaustion, she spent most of the time leaning on the railing and simply listening to the lies of her accusers. Since most of what was said were simple truths that were twisted to fit the occasion, it would be hard to make her denials heard when so many stood against her.

Sarah Bibber, a woman with whom Rachel was not acquainted, stepped forward to give her statement. While they were imprisoned, no doubt the house and their belongings had been closely inspected by many, and in the weeks following the arrests Sarah must have learned of or perhaps found the angel Rachel had carved for her mother at Christmas. "And she took a piece of wood from the forest and bewitched it, so that it came out in the form of a carved figure. Most who see this statue see an angel, but because she afflicts me and attempts to turn me to Satan, I see it in its truly wicked form—that of a demon."

DeadTimes

"My daughter returned from the Willard farm in such a state that I had to lock her in her room until the Devil's influence passed from her," Ann Putnam told the court. "She was horribly afflicted and things were flying about her room and breaking against the wall of their own accord. She was screaming in pain and said she was being pinched and bitten by something unseen."

At this point, Judge Corwin sat up and called on the younger Ann Putnam to step forward.

"Do you have marks from this attack?" he asked. "*Bite* marks?"

"Your honor, the bite marks have healed themselves miraculously in time for the trial today," the Putnam girl declared, casting another accusatory glance in Rachel's direction. "But I do still bear pinch marks upon both my arms." At this she raised her sleeve, showing small black and blue bruises above both elbows.

But Judge Corwin was not yet convinced. "But why would the accused pinch you, Miss Putnam?"

"Because I witnessed the sabbat she and her husband and mother held the very day that I visited their farm."

"Oh? And what was your reason for calling upon the Willard family in the first place?"

"I was sent by my mother to deliver sweet cakes," Ann said smugly. From her seat, Mrs. Putnam nodded. "This was done in return for some kindness John Willard had done for my father—a kindness no doubt meant to bring ill effects in the future."

Reverend Parris, up to now sitting silently at the front of the room, rose and stepped forward. "As this accusation seems to deal particularly with God's divine realm, may I beg your honor's permission to ask the witness a few questions?"

Corwin sat back, happy to turn the floor to someone else for a change. "By all means, Reverend."

"And what was it, Miss Putnam, that you witnessed at the Willard farm on the day you visited, and how were you able to witness this?"

The girl never hesitated. "I came up to the door and knocked. There is a window close to the door, and when no one answered my knock I stepped to it and looked through." She folded her hands primly on her lap. "There I saw the three of them—Rachel and John Willard and Mary Esty—standing in front of the fireplace and entertaining the Devil."

"That's a lie!" Rachel finally cried from where she stood. "I remember that day well, and we prayed to God together to deliver us from the evil that has beset Salem Village!"

Reverend Parris ignored Rachel and chose to direct another question to the girl. "And how do you know they called upon Satan and not, as the accused witch claims, prayed to the good Lord Himself?"

"Why, because," Ann's eyes were wide and innocent, and for a moment Rachel fancied she could see the lies taking shape in the vicious gleam of the young girl's eyes, "as they prayed, the dead embers on the hearth came to life and grew to flames without the touch of a human hand. And her familiar came from the barn in the form of a female cat and began scratching at my ankles, punishing me for witnessing their ceremony."

Rachel pulled at her shackles angrily, causing Corwin and the preacher to look her way in alarm. Having their attention, she though she might as well get the most out of it. There were a few things the people of Salem Village might find interesting about this lying little vixen, and Rachel's voice carried loud and clear.

"Do you think that I don't know, Ann Putnam, that you lusted shamelessly after my husband? Did you think he would not confide in me?" The murmurs of those in the room increased and as the girl's face drained white, many turned mistrustful and speculative eyes upon her. From his seat, Thomas Putnam's mouth dropped open as Rachel's gaze searched him out. "And don't you realize that John told me of your father's attempt to arrange a private meeting between you and John, a meeting my husband refused to attend? *Harlot!*"

The younger Ann Putnam had planned to go into fits immediately if Rachel Willard had dared speak to her, but she was too shocked to remember the idea. She had never dreamed the man would admit to his wife that he had been approached by her father, and Ann's face was an incriminating shade of crimson. She seemed too frozen with humiliation to offer a defense to Rachel's countered accusations, although the people in the meeting house who had come to witness Rachel's trial were now muttering among themselves, beginning, finally, to doubt the validity of the charges.

Then Reverend Parris's zealous voice boomed above them all.

"The woman returned from the dead!"

The resulting silence told better than anything that Ann Putnam was no longer alone in her astonishment and that the court's attention had been drawn back to Rachel.

"Yes!" From the emotion apparent in his voice, Parris might have been standing in the pulpit on Sunday, preaching fire and brimstone to the terrified members of his parish. "I tell you, good people, the most vile of witches stands before your eyes today. I well remember that day and the feeling in my heart"—here he thumped his chest for emphasis—"that all was not right in the Willard household."

Stunned, Rachel could only stand and listen to the man's words. If only he knew how close he had come to the truth!

Reverend Parris turned to face the townsfolk in the court, addressing spectators and jury alike. "I was summoned to their home last midsummer by her husband—a man who, as you all know, has also been tried and condemned as a witch—to perform the last rites for his wife." The preacher's eyes blazed with triumph as his head swiveled toward Rachel. "Her own mother had sent John Willard on the errand, after tending to the girl—or I should say, woman—who wasted away not only from more than two weeks of childbed fever, but the grievous weight of a stillborn child. Yet when I arrived, sorrowed but ready to do my Godly duty, I found Rachel Willard not only very much alive, but awake and speaking."

He's not the only one who remembers, Rachel thought sourly. She still recalled her fear upon her first sight of this so–called man of God.

"And I submit to this Holy Tribunal that the child was not stillborn at all!" Here, Rachel gasped in outrage. Had he been within reach, she would have cheerfully buried her fingers in his eyes. "Instead, it is my belief that the soul of that poor, defenseless infant was given up by this witch in unholy sacrifice to Satan!"

Only her fury kept Rachel from collapsing, and her voice rang even above the uproar within the courtroom. The preacher smiled with satisfaction until he realized the crowd was quieting and straining to hear Rachel's statement.

"Your cruelty knows no limits, Reverend!" she cried. "That you would accuse me of such an unspeakable act should shame you in the sight of God. And on the day He judges you for the lies you speak, I'm sure He'll remember the nights I prayed for the soul of my dead daughter and begged again and again for the privilege of carrying another within my body!"

Confusion reigned. Judge Corwin motioned impatiently for the constables to empty the room as conflicting shouts began to escalate. Many felt safe enough among the chaos to voice their true opinions, and amid the accusations of "Child killer!" and "Hang her!" could be heard cries of "She's innocent!" and "Set her free! She's suffered enough!"

When the room was finally bare of all except the county officials, witnesses and Reverend Parris, Thomas Putnam and another constable led Rachel up to stand before Judge Corwin. Nagged by his conscience, he looked at her sadly.

"Save yourself, Rachel Willard. Confess and the court will grant you a reprieve. Otherwise you'll hang."

Rachel could feel the preacher's eyes burning into her back as he waited smugly for her words, hoping for the confession that would make him righteous in the eyes of the town and doom her and the memory of her condemned family to a tainted life in Salem Village for the rest of her years.

She'd die first.

Rachel met Judge Corwin's eyes steadily, feeling almost pity for the surge of guilt she sensed within them. "Like the others hanged by the judgment of Salem Village, I cannot lie and confess to that which I am not." He blinked and for a moment she could almost *see* his anguish building. Her brief feeling of sympathy disappeared and she hoped that of all those involved, this man who would so coldly pass sentence on her and so many others would suffer the most in the years to come for his cowardice. "And what of it, Judge Corwin?" she asked bitterly. "Who will care when I am gone? Certainly not those two people about whom I care the most and who this court has also decided will die. What reason is left for me to live?"

Reverend Parris stepped angrily up to the judge's table. "I think she's—"

"Silence!" Judge Corwin roared suddenly, his face flushing. Unused to such sound from anyone but himself, the preacher's teeth snapped audibly as his mouth closed. "Let her speak! God knows she's been given little enough chance in this courtroom!" Constables and witnesses alike looked at him uneasily. Corwin's face was grim, but his motioned Rachel on. "Speak, then," he directed her. He dreaded her words but felt compelled to hear her out.

Finally able to say her mind, Rachel looked calmly at each of the officials. Her face, much thinner than the previous month, was serene, her eyes clear and accepting. "Hear me then, all of you who would see me and my family hang, and who would murder others beyond me. The history of Salem Village will bear a black mark on the books of this great country for having executed so many innocents upon nothing but the ravings of malicious, hysterical children."

At this she heard Thomas Putnam curse her under his breath, and she turned to face him.

"You, Thomas Putnam, and your wife are beasts, and your child is no better than an animal that kills for sport." He spat at her then, and though Rachel felt the moisture against her cheek she didn't move; her next statement raised chills on the arms of the Putnam family. "Your daughter's name will be written as a murderer throughout time."

"She threatens us with a witch's spell!" Putnam screeched, drawing his hand back to strike.

"Enough!" Corwin stood, his black-robed figure imposing. "Leave the courtroom, Putnam. And I know of your reputation: don't let it reach my ears that you've placed a hand upon this woman—or any other accused of witchery—or I'll have *you* before me on charges!" Rachel could see sweat trickling down the sides of the judge's face from beneath the white wig he wore. "Have you finished, Rachel Willard?"

She nodded, realizing she had stretched to the limit what little compassion he had.

"I ask again, will you not confess."

"I am innocent."

"Then I have no alternative but to sentence you. On September twenty-second, you will hang by the neck until dead."

※ ※ ※

It was a beautiful day and the sun was high and warm on Rachel's face. Though the weather still held summer breezes there had been enough chilly nights to bring a touch of gold to the leaves of the trees that surrounded the square; she saw early pumpkins sitting on porches here and there along the street, ripening slowing from green to deep orange. Wild marigolds still bloomed amid the tufts of long grass flourishing along the houses while fat, overly brave squirrels darted along overhead branches.

She could see all this from her place beneath the sturdy gallows.

Her mother was on her right, closest to the constable who would jerk the horse out from under her and thereby condemn her to die first. The ropes were full, Rachel saw, and more waited—besides herself and her mother, six women and two men were set to die on this day. She tried to smile encouragingly at Mary, but the older woman didn't seem to see, just kept staring out over Salem Village. *Perhaps she sees those things I never will,* Rachel thought. *Perhaps she sees heaven, or even John.*

Dealing with her husband's execution had been more painful and harder to bear than she'd ever imagined. The rumors flew and she learned from another prisoner that a constable had claimed John had asked for and been denied permission to see her before his hanging. It was easy to blame herself for his death, and for the impending demise of her mother. There were so many mistakes she had made, both in speech and action, and perhaps if she hadn't been so disbelieving in the witches and convinced John of her own beliefs, her tiny family would have been able to ride out the witch hunts without incident. Ultimately, she knew better; history, at least this part of it, would play itself out with or without her. She was just another pawn.

The jail was close enough to the square so she had heard John's outcry on the day they executed him; John was not one to be put down quietly and she easily heard his final shout that he loved her.

And too, though muffled by the distance, Rachel had heard the sound of the execution itself.

Today the crowd milled about, a different bunch than those who had been so merry in July. Many were absent, and those who did attend did not seem to be sure they wanted to be there at all; couples kept walking to the edge of the square nervously, as if they had more important chores to do at home and wanted to be about them. Two days earlier Giles Cory had been pressed to death for his refusal to confess and thereby forfeit his small savings and land to the Village; now many eyed the bell weights that had killed him with undisguised revulsion and Rachel hoped this was a sign that the witch hunts were losing momentum. She knew hers was not the only family to be wiped out by this madness, and should she forget, Giles Cory's seventy-year-old widow, Martha, stood on Rachel's left, eyes red-rimmed from crying, yet still holding her chin defiantly high above its deadly necklace of rope.

There was a butterfly feeling of fear in Rachel's stomach. She had no wish to see her mother die.

None other than Thomas Putnam read the bans as a noticeably smaller crowd reluctantly gathered in front of the gallows. No one would meet her gaze who had denied her innocence; only those who had scorned the executions had the courage to look into her eyes. Reflected in those gazes she saw her own helpless rage and regret.

Samuel Wardell was the first to die. In the instant after his body was pulled from his horse, Rachel wished desperately that she could freeze time and return to the life—and death—that should have been hers in another world. She would do anything so that she would not have to see the woman beside her killed, the only woman who had ever been a mother to her.

She stretched her hand out to Mary, trying to touch her one last time. Miraculously, the older woman came out of her daze and smiled gently at Rachel. The horse bearing her whickered softly.

Th–Thump!

And her mother was gone.

Rachel could not bear to look. Fighting a feeling of loss so great it threatened to paralyze her, she spoke instead, her voice hoarse at first, but quickly strengthening and carrying the words from the Bible throughout the square. The townsfolk strained forward to hear the familiar quote.

"'That innocent blood be not shed in thy land, which the Lord thy God giveth thee for an inheritance, or blood will be upon thee.'"

She was rewarded with an unobstructed view of Reverend Parris's pale, furious face as she heard the snap of a riding crop against flesh and felt her horse jerk away.

Th–Thump!

A terrible, choking pain and—

blackout.

CHAPTER III
1943

She woke alone in the dark, face-down on the floor and with dirt in her mouth. The first thing she felt was the pain, like a hundred needles sliding deep within her right side and stomach; the second was heat, searing her skin from behind and singeing the hair on her arms. There was no time to wonder where she was or how she'd gotten here. Instinct sent her hands forward, making them search for something to grab onto. She found a chair and a table and hauled herself to her knees, then managed to lurch upright. In the short span of seconds it had taken her to stand, the darkness had become lit by a fierce red glow.

She was in some kind of tiny room or shack. Fire was spreading rapidly around the walls in her direction and blocking what might have been a door, the flames in a wild race against themselves as they jumped from a mini-inferno that had once been a stuffed chair to a small bed, then onto the side of a rickety wooden chest of drawers. She stumbled, then hissed in fear and rage and pain; she would not die—*again*—in this hell-hole and be roasted like a butchered pig! Smoke swirled in heavy clouds around her head and she thudded back onto her knees, cursing the invisible wasps that were bent on torturing her side. Barely detectable off to her left was a small window with no glass—if she could get there before the ravenous fire, she might be able to escape.

Scrambling forward along the dirt floor, she made it to the window and summoned the strength to hoist herself up, feeling the fire licking at her bare feet and ankles, like the flashes that leapt from a campfire. Jesus, she was tired! And hurting, too. Falling rather than climbing over the sill, she landed on the ground, gasping at the new rush of pain and holding her side, her hands finding the area wet and sticky. She rolled on tough, scrubby grass, putting distance between herself and the flames that were busily consuming the small structure. It was night and except for the fire, she could see no other light; above her the trees parted to show sky but the stars were blocked by roiling clouds of smoke even blacker than the night sky. She could hear voices calling out in the woods; dazed, she wondered who they were and if they were calling for her. She wondered who she was.

"Myra? Honey, you all right?" Suddenly there were hands on her, firm but gentle, a woman's. *Myra must be me,* she thought as she gazed up at the concerned face of a middle-aged black woman. All at once more dark faces surrounded her, silhouetted by the light from the burning pile of wood that had once been her home. The sudden realization that all she owned in this world was being destroyed hit her and she began to cry, hitching and choking as the pain in her side worsened.

"My place!" Her wail as she tried to rise was hoarse and painful; her mouth felt as though someone had spooned soot into it. Hands reached to help from all sides, then unaccountably drew back. A dozen voices with deep southern accents rose in outcry as her legs gave out and she pitched forward once again.

"Mama, look! She's all bloody!"

"She's been cut!"

"Oh, my lordy, who would do such a thing?"

"Must be somebody with no fear, that's for sure!"

"Adam, go get some rags and some water—*clean* water from the well, you hear?"

"Do you think she's gonna die?"

"Hush your mouth, boy! Go with your brother—git!"

A deeper voice. "Looks like she's hurt real bad, Lucy. How—"

Sounds pulsed in and out as she felt the old woman's capable hands pushing her arms away and pulling at the shredded place in the side of her dress, heard her nurse's dismayed, indrawn breath.

"Jesus, Wilson. This is worse than I thought—"

"Shhh! She'll hear you. We'll take—"

Mama Lucy's voice, harsh and suddenly afraid. "Myra, can you hear me? Who did this to you—can you tell me?"

She wanted to answer the insistent question, straining unsuccessfully to focus the garbled, faraway memories of the last hour beyond the pain that coursed through the nerves. "Can't...'member, right...now," she gasped. She fought to clear her raspy throat of the smoke's residue.

A young boy ran up with a small pail and Lucy dipped a hand into the water and held her cupped palm to Myra's lips. "Drink—easy! Not too much at once—"

She inhaled some of the water and choked, her lungs spasming around the liquid and forcing it back out with a croaking cough. The involuntary movement sent a ferocious peal of agony through her belly and her eyes opened wide, then rolled upward as the fire's hellish light dwindled to a small pinpoint that finally winked out.

※   ※   ※

The men from town built her a new shack. Myra didn't know why; she had no money to pay them and only a fleeting notion of what kind of hold she maintained over them. The replacement was a simple one-room affair constructed right next to the one that had burned away; she assumed that meant this was her own land although the constant sight of the charred ground rankled and teased her at every glance.

It had taken nearly two weeks for Mamma Lucy to pull Myra through the worst of it, and not a board or nail was picked up until the men were sure Myra would live and be worth their efforts. Now she sat and healed and watched the men work, thinking and getting used to her new surroundings and to the feel of sleeping on the hard ground despite the homemade quilting in her bad side. She studied the others; she studied herself. She watched her own fingers open and close, appreciating the sinewy movement of working muscles. She'd never had reason to think about it before, but having black skin didn't make her feel any different and she decided she liked it; her skin was a clean, dark ebony, smooth and young, lightening to pink and cream at her palms and the bottoms of her feet. So far she'd seen herself only in the moving reflection of the creek's water during the rare time or two she'd fetched her own water; she couldn't tell much except that she might be pretty and her hair was short and curly and wild. She ran her fingers through it and felt its tangles, but she couldn't remember what to do with it.

For the most part the other folks were avoiding her, either out of respect or fear or both; her injury and the trauma of the fire had taken a bad toll on her memory, and she was doing good to even guess her whereabouts, so the *whys* and *wherefores* were mostly out of reach right now. In the heat of this late Louisiana summer, the men could only do so much and she waited patiently through the week it took for them to finish the shack, the ragged wound in her side and belly slowly healing but yowling anew each morning. Her new place was like all the others she'd seen in the tiny town on the edge of the swamp in the course of her week–long stay with Lucy, roofed with a battered sheet of tin and constructed mostly of pieces of wood foraged from anywhere possible. After a while Myra came to realize with a small shock that this was not her land any more than it was anyone else's. Watching the men nail the stray pieces of board together, it occurred to her how interesting it was that her house was placed so far away from the others. She did not know why, and didn't dare ask.

Myra was lonely. There was so much she wanted to know and re–learn, but how could she do this if no one would speak to her? She knew just enough to get by and to make the townspeople furrow their brows at her hesitant questions, and only so much could be blamed on the fire. Even her own voice sounded foreign—deep for a woman and husky, with an ingrained Cajun drawl so different from anything she'd ever heard that she found it musical and ceaselessly amusing. To make her situation that much stranger, the only one who would talk to her was Mama Lucy, the old woman who had sewn up the gaping wound in her side and stomach with a minimum of conversation, wariness ever–present in her watery eyes. And though Myra hadn't seen the elderly woman in days, it was Mama Lucy's sons who brought Myra meals each day.

The insects were terrible—how would she ever get used to them? Gnats, mosquitoes, muddaubers, constantly flying around her, always trying to stick her somewhere, no doubt lured by the blood–spotted bandages under her dress. It was a good thing that they were almost finished with the shack, she thought irritably, otherwise she might stand up and scream and really give everyone something to be frightened about…that is, if her side weren't still so sore that she could manage only intermittent swats at the vinegar flies and mosquitoes dive–bombing her sweaty skin, and the rusty fly swatter at her side for the meaner horse flies went mostly unused. Myra's fingers were an oddity unto themselves, moving constantly, searching for something still unknown to touch or twist or tie. It was just as well, otherwise she'd be slapping at herself constantly, stretching the scabby lips along the webwork of linen thread across her gut. She couldn't wait to get inside a new shack, no matter how hot, find some netting to block up the window opening and the door, and be away from these damned bugs.

But the bugs were not the worst of what bothered her, no indeed. Dark questions nagged at her constantly—

Who stabbed me?

And why?

—as she watched the townspeople watch her.

Which of you wanted to be my murderer?

Myra looked up to see a small girlchild gazing at her from a distance of about ten feet; she motioned the child to come closer. The little girl took a few hesitant steps and stopped, waiting, poised to run.

"Why are you so afraid?" The child jumped and Myra realized her voice was harsher than she'd intended. She softened it. "No, don't go. Tell me your name."

The child stood as though frozen. "S–Sulu," she stammered. Suddenly her lower lip protruded and she drew herself up in defiance. "And I *ain't* afraid."

Myra smiled for the first time since the night of the burning. "You're not, are you? Well, let us see. Come closer." Sulu hesitated and Myra's voice became demanding once again. "Come!"

The child obeyed. The noises from twenty yards away sputtered then stopped altogether as the men nailing the final boards in place at the shack flagged from their work and looked toward her in apprehension. Myra inspected the child standing before her with interest: grubby face and hands, clear brown eyes, a hundred tiny corn rows in her hair. The smell of breakfast biscuits wafted from the child's shabby clothes. "How old are you, Sulu?" she asked.

"I'm seven," Sulu replied shyly, then she looked down at her toes. Digging into the dust, they showed the girl's nervousness. "But Mama says I'm too small for my age," she admitted suddenly.

Myra felt honored that this little girl, so scared only a moment ago, would share her mother's thoughts. "Well, maybe a little bit," Myra agreed. "But I'm sure you'll grow out just fine." She ran her hand gently over the small head, feeling the tight rows and the mixture of oil and perspiration between them. It had been a long time since she touched a child and doing so made her feel warm inside.

"You really think so?" Sulu's hands clutched at her dirty shift, bunching it up and showing knobby, little–girl knees. There was something odd about one of her hands, a missing middle finger. "Maybe then the others'll stop pickin' on me."

Myra smiled. "You go on home now," she said. "Before your Mama gets worried." She waved the girl off and Sulu trotted away obediently as the men returned to their labor; Myra laughed inwardly at them. Did they think she ate children?

Just around the path Sulu's excited voice floated back through the thick foliage of the ash and cypress trees.

"She blessed me! The Mambo blessed me!"

At the worksite, a man called Lucius drove the final tenpenney in place with a furious stroke.

DeadTimes

✴   ✴   ✴

Myra was resting inside her new shack, enjoying at least a small reprieve from the swamp insects, when the townspeople started arriving. They came in groups of two or three, each person presenting her with one, sometimes two small gifts. Privately bewildered, she greeted each visitor politely and accepted his or her offering with a calm thank–you. They gave her so much more than they realized; with each item returned a little more of Myra's past.

"Here's my best chicken, to give you eggs," offered a tall, bony man with skin so black he might have been cut from coal.

"Sheets, so's you kin be comfortable, Miss Myra." This came from a huskily–built woman who carried a toddler as if he were a second skin. It was the first time anyone had called her "Miss" Myra, though it settled into her cracked recollections with easy familiarity.

A burly young man and his brother lugged forward a cracked formica table and two beat up chairs, another woman came up with a few mismatched dishes and some flatware, a child sent by her ailing mother presented a battered pot and frying pan. Myra was grateful but remained silent, accepting each item as if it were her due although she couldn't imagine why it would be; while it was impossible, she wished she could tell each benefactor how much she was beholden not only for the housewares but for the flash of memory each provided. Her feelings for these simple people grew.

A gangly teenager held out his packet. "Miss Myra, my maw sent these here pieces of cloth, figured you could make some clothes." Pieces ticked into place in her mind, filling yet another gap in the puzzle: the boy's name was Samuel and he lived alone with his mother, Mattie. She had no man and times were hard; they barely got by, yet she sent a gift. Still, Myra squelched the urge to refuse, knowing that to do so would go beyond insult and into a gray area of her mind that had not yet returned.

More of the townsfolk came with their offerings: a middle–aged woman named Janu, whose hair had gone prematurely gray when her husband vanished in the swamp six years previous and left her with eight kids to raise, brought Myra a newly made broom; a man called Marcel, Janu's brother, came with the much longed–for mosquito netting. By sunset her small shack was furnished well enough to be more than comfortable, and others, Myra knew, would continue to bring gifts of game and vegetables and bread.

When the last person had left, Myra sat by her carefully netted window and rested on a new–to–her but thoroughly broken–in rocking chair and listened to the night crickets sing.

The swamp, she had finally come to realize, wasn't just a place or a part of the land tacked onto the southern end of the country in which she'd been born. First of all, Louisiana, as it actually *existed* in 1943, was a pretty big nut to swallow for a woman who'd never given much thought about what America west of the Mississippi River was like beyond the far–fetched tales told by a father who had died more than two and half centuries earlier. While it was true that superstition in the Adirondacks was strong, most—but not *all*, and she sure knew that more than the average farmer—of those old beliefs were nothing but grandfathers' yarns twisted up around spooky night campfires. And yes, she'd been through a whole 'nother set of beliefs, hadn't she, and sometimes she'd wake deep in the hot, damp night and still feel the bite of rough hemp around her throat as a reminder.

But *Louisiana*, ah! This was a different woman altogether, a dark, sultry she–snake who twisted and danced among the people in the swamp with breathy promises and the threat of a hundred ugly deaths if disobeyed.

And with a start, Myra knew.

All those gifts, they weren't really for *her*. They were for what the people of this green and bedeviled swamp believed lived *within* her. That slippery, seductive swamp mistress.

The *loa*.

※　　　※　　　※

What she couldn't grow in the brush–choked dirt behind the shack, Myra dug up in the swamp. Instinct kicked in at last, feeding her hundreds of bits of knowledge each day, everything from knowing where not to put her hands when she was hunting for roots to the proper ingredients of the tiny jujus she was constantly twisting from branches and leaves. But her memory was still like an out–of–reach harlot: besides the always tantalizing question of her would–be murderer, something which never left her thoughts for long, Myra burned to know what kind of a person she had been to bring such fear into the gazes of those in town, people with whom she now longed to sit and talk and learn from. But she was never bored; she hung plants and herbs and roots to dry, then ground them up into fine powders that she stored in the little jars, boxes and bags the townsfolk were constantly bringing her, as if they knew she would have need of such things.

The swamp, Myra discovered, was a mysterious place filled with strange creatures and wildly potent plant life, from mushrooms that could kill a person inside ten minutes to roots that would make a man's heart quicken with desire when combined with certain special words. It hadn't taken her long to come up with a concoction to ward off the biting flies and mosquitoes, and now, boatless, she wandered the marshes for hours each day, watching and listening to the creatures and knowing that something in her spirit could charm even a deadly copperhead right into her hands without harm. She thought at first the constant humidity along the waterways would bother her and though it never did, the general *spookiness* sometimes made her nervous; with all those shadows and rustling leaves and chittering animals, not to mention the 'gators sliding through the water like living gray logs, a woman wouldn't be able to tell if she were being watched or not—and sometimes she felt as if she were, indeed, being spied upon.

Dead Times

Evening would find Myra back at her shack, sitting on the old rocker and longing for company. Better than two months had passed and the people still avoided her, though she'd find their daily offerings of food and what–nots on her porch each evening when she came in from the swamp. Everyone and everything seemed to have its place or purpose—some folks harvested food, others were builders, others were storehouses of old knowledge and advice that she had no way of tapping. What was her place in the scheme of things beyond a few good–luck trinkets and an apparently expert knowledge of swamp survival? But the answer, if there was one, always stayed just out of reach. What, she wondered, would be the thing that jarred the memories free?

✳   ✳   ✳

"I don't have much to offer," said Marcel. "But I figure there's got to be something that I could trade. You jus' name it."

Myra studied the man standing before her and said nothing. He shifted anxiously and his wide eyes glistened with a deep fear that wanted to make him turn and run. Stubbornness and love of his sister forced him to hold his ground.

"Please, Miss Myra," he said. His pleading gaze collapsed and he ended up staring at the ground. "There's eight kids over there and I don't know nothin' about raising that many young'uns."

"I don't know," she finally answered. He looked crushed and her doubt wavered. "But I guess I can try."

It was the first time an adult in the town smiled at her.

✳   ✳   ✳

"Janu," Marcel whispered to his sister. "Can you hear me? I've brought Miss Myra. She's gonna help you."

Janu's lids fluttered open and Myra thought she saw a flash of fear in the woman's watering eyes. She was sick, all right—her brown skin was dry and almost gray, her lips pale and cracked bloody with a fever that wouldn't break; the old acne scars sprinkled across her cheekbones looked as though someone had pocked her skin with black ink. Janu's forehead burned with heat under Myra's gentle palm.

"Leave us," Myra ordered without taking her eyes from the bed. She heard Marcel's reluctant footsteps as he pushed the children from the room and drew a ragged curtain across the doorway. As Myra knelt next to the bed, Janu's harsh attempts to breathe increased. "Don't be scared, Janu," she said soothingly. "I won't hurt you." There was a bowl of clear water and a cloth on the stand next to the bed and Myra soaked the cloth and wiped the woman's face. When Janu seemed calmed, Myra stood and opened the small pouch she'd brought with her, then carefully sorted through its contents at the foot of the bed. There— dried milkweed petals. She swept them up and stepped around the curtain.

"You there," Myra said, pointing at one of the younger boys. She didn't know his name and probably wouldn't have remembered it if someone had told her; there were just too many kids around. This one was about six years old and whip–thin; she was sure he'd be able to find what she needed in no time at all. He looked up at her, his little face nervous, but stepped forward obediently; she put a firm hand on his shoulder.

"I want you to go into the swamp and fetch me a turtle—an *edible* one. You know which ones are, don't you?" He nodded solemnly, his black eyes flicking past her to his mother's sick and shuddering form. "Good. Then go, as fast as you can. And mind you be careful of snakes, you hear?" The last of her words were called out to the boy's back as he scampered through the door on small legs. Myra turned and went back into the bedroom, the curtain all that stood between her and the frightened, mistrustful eyes of Janu's family. There were other faces scattered around the room besides, friends of Janu and Marcel, no doubt come to add their support, and the instant the curtain was drawn the muttering began, arguments tempered here and there by a few weak warnings. Perhaps they thought their presence would intimidate her and Myra laughed aloud purposely, noting with satisfaction the sudden silence from beyond the doorway. She searched her feelings but found no fear.

It took the child a little more than an hour to find and return with the turtle, and in that time Myra planned her moves. At her direction Marcel built a fire outside and boiled up a kettle of water, then brought it into the bedroom with the boy's find, a young, dark brown snapper. She could tell the small boy was proud he'd carried it home without getting bitten and though she said nothing else to show her gratitude, Myra did smile warmly at him. In the bedroom she dipped a small pot of scalding water from the kettle before dropping in the live turtle and holding it under the water with a wooden spoon. The iron kettle held the heat like tar on a hot roof, and Myra began adding things from her pouch by instinct—had she been questioned, she wouldn't have been able to name the ingredients. To finish up the whole thing she added salt and a bit of dried garlic to make the soup palatable, thinking even the sickly would have a hard time swallowing the thick, greenish liquid. In the meantime, Myra brewed a tea of milkweed and hot water and added a spoonful of sugar, coaxing Janu into drinking a little every few minutes until it was gone. By the time the soup was done, Janu's labored breathing was coming a little easier.

"Janu," Myra said firmly as she stood next to the bed and stirred the final ingredient, a heavy, vile–looking red powder, into the soup, "this is going to burn your mouth and throat, but you have to drink it anyway or the fever won't break and you probably won't last the night." Janu's black eyes stared into hers a little too wisely and Myra dreaded the unspoken question but felt compelled to answer.

"I don't know if this will work or not," Myra reluctantly admitted. "I can't promise anything. All we can do is try it and see what happens."

Myra waited, and finally Janu closed her eyes wearily and parted her lips to accept the first dipper of fiery liquid.

* * *

Janu went into spasms, her fever climbing so high that it knotted her muscles until her whole body shook and danced. At dusk Myra called Marcel in to help bathe his sister with cool water; he looked guardedly at the straw and herb charms that were thrust here and there about the room and grimaced at the pungent air as they struggled to keep Janu from twisting onto the floor. Myra accepted the presence of the charms blearily; she did not remember making them during her past hours of keeping watch. His face a study of worry and mistrust, Marcel nevertheless held Janu and watched as Myra forced more of the soup down her patient's throat in between spasms.

Shortly before midnight sweat finally poured from Janu's skin as the fever relinquished its hold. Within an hour the woman slept soundly for the first time in a week.

* * *

It was nearly two more hours before Myra felt confident enough with Janu's progress to step outside the battered little house and think about her own shack and bed, a good fifteen or twenty minutes' hike down the dusty path. A crowd had gathered behind Marcel and even at this late hour most of the townsfolk had turned out, though the children had long since been sent to bed. It was strange to feel their eyes upon her, yet hear no sound or movement, unthinkable that so many would care what she had to say; in a way, even the swamp seemed to be holding its breath with anticipation, unaccountably silent. Myra put one hand against one of the poles supporting the porch overhang with a carefully casual move; all those faces—not at all friendly, either—raised a quick, ugly memory of a crowd in another place and time best forgotten. Experience had taught her to expect noise from so many people, but the folks in this group lowered their eyes and waited for Marcel to speak.

"Your payment?"

Myra saw with a frown that now Marcel truly *was* afraid. It showed in the way the whites of his eyes seemed so large and bright in his dark, shadowed face, and the change in her expression appeared to increase his anxiety as well as make the people closest to her fidget. Myra's gaze slid to his side and dropped; for some inexplicable reason, the boy who'd fetched the turtle for her had been pulled from his bed and now stood next to his uncle, one hand holding onto the side of the older man's pants pocket, too sleepy to be afraid. Seeing the direction of her eyes, Marcel swallowed, his Adam's apple jerking in his thin neck, and pushed his nephew forward; Myra thought she heard sharp intakes of breath in the crowd but couldn't be sure. The child looked up at her trustingly and stuck his thumb in his mouth—such an innocent gesture for the youngster who'd been entrusted with the first ingredient of his mother's life-saving medicine. At the sight of his small fingers, a memory, ugly with violence, roared to life in her mind—

"Your payment?"

The fee for removing the self-same dark spell she'd been paid to place on Lucius by a scorned and spiteful woman.

"The middle finger of your youngest daughter's hand."

She swayed slightly, but no one offered to help. She could understand why.

How would she repay this child's obedience? She reached a hand out and let her fingers smooth the nappy hair on the boy's head; how sweet the children always smelled! No matter how grubby, they always held the scent of sugar and swamp grass. She pulled away and curled her fingers into fists.

"I suppose," Myra said slowly, the unreadable pools of her eyes never leaving the boy's face, "I could use a cooking pit." She stepped off the porch and the group of men and women parted without comment, their faces creased in bewilderment as she turned and headed towards her shack, opening her chilled hands and welcoming the hot Louisiana darkness that enveloped her like an old lover. When she was just out of range of the flickering lights that ringed Janu's house, Myra stopped and spoke again, her words barely discernible above the renewed screaming of the night crickets.

"Mind you, line it with swamp stones, too."

✳   ✳   ✳

There was much talk in town, gossip and speculation as to why Myra seemed to have changed her ways from bad to good, dark to light. Still, no one risked approaching her to question her motives; to do so would have been disrespectful and might arouse the anger within her soul that the townspeople felt had gone to sleep—perhaps only temporarily. Myra didn't care what they thought, so long as they left her alone; while she had been lonely at first, the time had passed and she'd not only gotten used to her solitary existence, she found she actually preferred that other folks only bother her if they needed some small charm or illness treated. After she'd refused the third or fourth person who asked for a dark spell, it became clear that she'd turned a cold shoulder to the darker side of her faith, preferring white magic to the evil at which she'd ostensibly once been an expert.

The darkling's side, Myra knew, was nothing to scoff at. She could still feel its call within her, especially at night when the moon whispered and coaxed her to a special, temple-like place in the marshes where she would hum aloud and sway her body to a silent rhythm. On these nights a she-beast rose from some murky depth inside Myra, enticing others from the town who would join her and bring drums, their dark faces unrecognizable behind homemade masks under the starlight. Once she and her followers had sacrificed chickens and an occasional goat in this thirsty, sacred spot, but now she gave them small, powdered doses of a mildly hallucinogenic mushroom instead of the thick, foul-tasting animal blood. The change in the ritual seemed not to disturb them, and each apparently still found the spirits he or she sought.

But questions still plagued her, fragments of the same terrifying night still studded her dreams and sent her gasping awake under the morning's first rays of light. Myra and the townsfolk shared a platonic existence, but no more; although she no longer preyed upon their fears and hidden deviltry, they did not trust her, and while they warmed bit by bit to the changed woman she'd become, she—and they—never let down their guard.

Who?

Prime among the suspects was Lucius, father of small, defiant Sulu, the child whose finger Myra's iniquitous past had demanded as payment two years ago. While Myra knew herself to be different now, she could not go to the girl's father and try to explain why; even had she known the answer, no excuse on this earth could justify that monstrous mutilation. Likewise, no apology or show of regret would reverse the deed, though during the times she let herself think on it too long Myra's face burned with horrified shame. Perhaps the raw pink scar that spiraled across her belly and side like a gigantic spider was payback, though guilty as she was, murder was still a mighty high price to pay for a child's finger.

But there were others, too, dozens of people whom she'd wronged through the years that this town had been her home. Even Janu, the woman with the wise, wary eyes whose life Myra had saved, had reason to hate her, though Myra didn't know if Janu even knew the sordid truth or not: years ago, for the price of a suckling pig, Myra had worked a spell on Janu's husband that had caused him to go to another woman.

There was no chance for Myra to change her deeds now; the best she could hope for was to somehow atone. These people would never trust her because of what she'd been; she could never trust *anyone* until she knew who'd killed her.

✳   ✳   ✳

As each month went by, Myra grew more appreciative of the swamp and the creatures and growing things it sheltered; she also grew to know her body and remember the more private things that had at first remained just out of her mind's reach. She was not a virgin and the shadow–filled room that held her memories admitted a little more light with each sunrise; she could recall those special men—only a few—who had shared her bed over the short span of her life. In this small territory it was said she was the youngest mambo ever (she was in her late twenties), and folks knew no man in his right mind would marry a woman such as she, and God forbid she should bear a child. From her own perspective, Myra thought it was better, too, that there was no one so close to her whom others could use as a threat.

Still, she couldn't help the occasional longing for company and the touch of a male hand, and while she welcomed each returning memory eagerly, some only increased her hunger. Sitting on the front porch just after dawn one late summer morning, savoring the quiet and the damp, cool air that would turn hot and sticky in another few hours, her mind gave her the sudden picture of a man who had passed through these parts two years previous—a bible salesman of all things! Her mind's eye could see him now: tall and lanky with a head full of thick curls, black, black eyes and skin that glowed like rich mahogany wood. Myra could remember slipping her fingers into his hair and yanking his face to hers, their mouths colliding with a fierceness that would forever dull the memories of her two other lovers, could still feel his knowing fingers sliding across her hot skin. Remembering made her heart pound and her face flush, and she finally rose and headed into the swamp, scowling and thinking how damned silly it was for a grown woman to let an old memory bring herself right into hot flashes.

The swamp was her life. Myra's storehouse of herbs and medicines increased daily and the swamp held nothing she feared, not the cottonmouths or 'gators or poison sumac. She wandered where she would, collecting plants, salamanders and insects for drying, grinning at the sheer size of the bullfrogs and water bugs that called the swamp home. Almost everything that had been destroyed in the fire at her shack had been replaced; a few things—certain kinds of oils and candles—would have to wait until she scraped a little more cash from her charms and someone from town made a trip to New Orleans, but since most of what she once would have bought no longer needed replenishing, certain aspects of her supplies were not so critical. Myra felt happy and safe, though unconsciously she worried constantly about the more stealthy townsfolk and the people who had once come to her for dark practices; had they learned to live without their petty vengeances, or did they now go to someone else?

✳   ✳   ✳

"Miss Myra, I got me a problem."

"What's that?" she asked. It had been almost a week since the last person from town had come to ask for a favor and times were lean; with the decline of Myra's willingness to give out evil little jujus and such, so too had dwindled her popularity and livelihood. She still ate all right, but now her source of meat was mostly the rattlers that she caught in the swamp herself—the old saying about how they tasted pretty much like chicken was true—and she would have dearly loved to be able to fix up a nice plate of beans and pork for her supper. Few people seemed to need good luck charms in the small, isolated town, and while it was a frightening thought, Myra was starting to wonder if she shouldn't move on, maybe to New Orleans where folks would always be willing to pay for candles and oils blessed to bring them luck, protection, or just keep away the bill collectors. She remembered the city as a loud, wild place filled with men and women who were budding entrepreneurs, all itching to cash in on the stupid curiosity of endless wide-eyed tourists looking for that voodoo spell to make them rich or heal their ills, and in a place like that a person with her talents could make a killing right quick and not have to miss a meal for turning away a vicious man or bitchy mistress. Myra loved the swamp right down to her bones and she was a simple woman with few needs, but the bayou didn't seem able to support her unless she gave into the darker sides of the same people whom she'd rather were her friends. And here another youngster stood before her, a boy, and waited trustingly for her help; it seemed as though only the children would have anything to do with her anymore.

"It's my Mama. You 'member she's been sick, right?"

Myra nodded and could've slapped herself for not thinking to help before now. The child's name was Martin and his mother Alberta was the sickly woman who'd sent Myra a couple of cooking pots after the shack had been rebuilt; Myra was thoroughly ashamed when she realized she used one of those gifts nearly every day, yet had never thought to check on the woman's welfare. Had Alberta been ill all this time? Little good it did for Myra to turn away those wanting bad potions when good folk with children went untended.

"Well, she ain't getting no better." Martin looked at her worriedly and shoved his hands in his pockets; his mother had been sick for a long time and the boy was probably ten years old going on twenty. "I was hopin' you'd, you know, sort of come by all on your own. My Mama, she said not to bother you, but I thought I'd ask anyway. I could do a lot of stuff for you, Miss Myra, if Mama was better. You know, planting and hoeing, fetching things. We even got three baby chicks last week. You could have 'em all if you'd just take a look at her."

"Well, let's see if I can do some good before you go offering your chickens, Martin." Myra stood and went inside the shack to gather a few herbs; the thought of accepting one—just one—of the chicks was appealing. If she could get a hen, she'd cook the lazy, dull bird that pecked around the shack once the chick grew to laying. The thought of fried children—*real* chicken and not fried strips of snakemeat—made her mouth water.

Another minute and she and Martin were picking their way along the part of the dusty, disused path that connected her place to town. In places the grasses and reeds had narrowed the track to only a foot or so wide, and here more than anywhere it was plain to see the town didn't have much of a need for her services any longer.

She was concentrating so hard on her uncertain future that Martin made her jump when he suddenly spoke. "My Mama says someone put a bad charm on her, that's why she's sick," he said. Above the frayed collar of his T-shirt, his jaw jutted way out, as if just saying the words was a scary thing but he was bound to do it anyway. The stoic expression on his unlined young face, a strange, almost adult determination to deal with and conquer his own fear, reminded her of that long-ago conversation with tiny Sulu.

Myra glanced at him. "Why would someone do that?" she asked. The youngster shrugged and didn't answer; Myra guessed the boy's mother wouldn't have told him the reason anyway—even if she knew. It was an interesting idea, though: who besides Myra would have the knowledge to do such a successful bad spell on someone? They trudged another quarter mile in silence and the path started to widen where smaller trails led away from it to battered shacks here and there among the heavy green foliage; as the number of dwellings increased the path finally became more of a wide, dirt street beaten clean by countless feet over the decades, with the menfolk regularly scything back the willful greenery always creeping from its edges. Soon they were in the center of town, if the small collection of buildings could be called that: there was a dilapidated feed store with grimy windows that never carried more than fifty pounds of any one type of grain at a time, and the tiny general store that barely kept its doors open, so deeply were the residents in debt to it. Scattered on either side of the two structures were maybe another fifteen old houses, almost every one with a beat–up rocker or two out front or on a sagging front porch. At the end, finally, was the small Baptist church, its whitewashed sides better kept than the rest of the buildings. Of the seven or eight junky automobiles—vile–smelling machines that were so loud Myra thought she'd faint the first time she saw one—parked here and there by the houses, only the preacher's ran with any dependability, and most appeared to have simply been left on the road in favor of the more trustworthy transportation found in human legs. Occasionally she and Martin passed a house where the residents didn't mind the high heat of midday and watched the goings–on from the questionable shade of their front porches as they talked about World War II and the fighting that seemed about as close to them now as the concept of airplanes had once been to Myra; while a few men and women nodded politely, no one offered to start a conversation. As Myra and Martin passed the church, the preacher was dribbling water into a pot of listless flowers next to the church's entrance and he made no attempt to hide his frown as his gaze found Myra.

The house wasn't much farther. Stepping inside, Myra saw that Alberta's home was barely larger than her own, though in one dim corner there was a tiny woodstove for cooking and to help drive away the swamp chill at night. Two twin beds were placed head to head in one corner; the neatly made up one, Myra knew immediately, was Martin's. While the temperature had already soared into the eighties and the humidity was so high that sweat trickled down the back of Myra's neck, Alberta was huddled on the other bed beneath several frayed blankets. As Myra stepped to the bedside and drew the covers away from Alberta's face, the woman's attempt at a smile made her look more like a grimacing corpse.

Alberta had once been pretty, but whatever the sickness was that held her now had robbed her of any traces of beauty, perhaps permanently. Myra's memory told her that Alberta was not yet thirty, but Myra's recollections seemed to be off–duty today and she couldn't call back much else about the woman other than she wasn't married. Martin's father had been a drifter, a stranger with a silken tongue who'd stopped at the general store for a cold bottle of cola and wooed the then–teenaged Alberta with a suitcase full of lies. He'd disappeared a mere two weeks later; in spite of this, Alberta had wanted and kept the child she'd soon found filling her belly. Alberta's mother had died about five years ago and she and the boy had no other family, and as far as Myra could recall, no enemies either.

"'Berta?" Myra said softly, "can you hear me?" The woman's eyes fluttered weakly as she tried to focus on Myra, then they closed again. Myra touched her forehead, expecting to find a fever; instead, Alberta's breathing was faint and strained and her skin felt cold and dry—no wonder Martin had covered her with the blankets. Myra glanced at the child standing patiently beside her. "How long has she been like this?"

He frowned, the expression looking odd on so young a face. "I'm not sure—for a long time. A couple of months maybe, since before you was in that fire," he answered at length. "She finally seemed like she was getting on a little better not so long ago, then she got bad all over again—no, *worse*."

This was going to be hard, Myra realized as she gently pulled the covers down to just past the woman's collarbone. Alberta's skin was covered in dry, flaking scales, as if her body simply hadn't the energy to replace its own skin. The condition made Alberta look like a reverse image of a white ash tree, and try as she might Myra couldn't think of any ailment that would do this—at least nothing natural. But oh, there were *lots* of unnatural things to think about. She drew a finger along Alberta's shoulder and the dead skin powdered under her light touch. Alberta started shivering violently and Myra quickly pulled the blankets back up and tucked them beneath the sick woman's chin.

"Remember what you said about your mama thinking someone put a spell on her?" Myra asked. Martin nodded solemnly. "Did she say anything else, like maybe who? Or why?"

"No," he said. "We talked about it some, before she got so sick again she just couldn't speak no more—"

"When was that?"

"Two days ago." Martin shoved his hands into the pockets of his dirty tan–colored shorts as he concentrated. "It was right after I came home and found somebody'd been in the house here while mama was sleepin'."

"You mean someone broke in?" Myra asked with interest. She moved over a few steps and sat on the edge of Martin's bed, keeping an eye on Alberta.

"Can't really say they *broke* in," said the boy. "Just came in while she was sleeping and went through the chest of drawers. They sure had a lot of nerve, but I can't even say if they took anything."

"They went through your stuff, or your mother's?" Myra's eyes swept the dusky interior of the shack, noting a battered, paint–splattered chest at the end of Martin's bed. Piled on top of the chest were kitchen items: a small, mixed assortment of dishes and utensils, a worn–out dishrag beside a few wrinkled paper bags, and a couple of fire–blackened pots and pans.

"Mama's," he replied. He indicated the chest with a wave of his hand. "Only the top two drawers was gone through—the bottom two are mine. That's the second time it's happened, too."

Myra's eyebrows shot up. "Someone's come in twice?"

"Sure. The first time was before Mama got sick. We come home from church one Sunday and found just about everything in the house on the floor." His forehead creased. "That is kinda funny, ain't it? You think they left something here, some kinda potion? But how come it ain't made me sick, too?"

Myra waved off his question, stood and walked around the inside of the shack. On a shelf above Alberta's bed she found a brush with the woman's dark hair still tangled in its bristles; off to the side a hand–woven basket held dirty clothes. She guessed the boy did all the washing since his mother was so sick. "Was anything taken that first time?"

"Mama said she couldn't really tell—maybe an old pair of her underwear, though she couldn't figure why anyone would want her pants. Then again, she said they might've just floated away in the stream when she did the washing."

"Uh–huh," Myra murmured. Her feet carried her back to Alberta's bedside and she reached for a few strands of the dark hair that lay on the pillow; just the feel of the hair sent a faint sensation of the energy–sapping sickness that infected Martin's mother. Instinct told her fingers to shake away the hairs before their bitterness leached into her own skin; instead Myra forced herself to close her fist. Martin was chattering away, but his voice seemed to be oddly receding.

"We don't got no enemies, Miss Myra. Least none that we know about." He sounded much older than he was as he hesitated for a moment, then finally continued. "Used to be you was the one might do something like this, but folks say you've changed. That's why I thought maybe you could help. I hope I ain't made you mad."

"No, not at all." Her assurances sounded strained to her ears and even though it wasn't even meant for her own flesh, Myra could feel the sickness creeping through her slowly, radiating from the hand that held the hair from Alberta's head. It would be a simple but cowardly thing to drop the hairs and be done with it, to shy away from the charm hidden somewhere around here and causing this woman to be so ill. Myra clenched her jaw; she'd be damned before she'd give in to such a yellow impulse, and she'd search until she found it or dropped; from the way she was feeling; she'd have to get to it fast. "Stay with your mother, Martin," she said. Her voice was punctuated by small gasps of breath between every couple of words. "Don't come out of the house until I call, you hear?"

"Yes, ma'am." Myra tried but couldn't seem to get her vision to widen beyond a narrow strip a few feet directly in front of her. Thankfully the door was there; she couldn't really see the boy as he backed away from her, though she could hear the sudden fright in his voice.

Even in this sad cluster of shacks, there were clear divisions in the degree of poverty. Alberta's home was one of the few porchless dwellings, and there was only one step leading down from the wooden floor of the shack to the ground outside. Myra promptly tripped on it and went down on her knees; behind her Martin whimpered but did not come outside. She barely registered the feel of the dirt grinding into her knees and palms and the sting along the cap of her left knee as a sharp pebble slid across its width; there was an instant of wet warmth as a few droplets of blood seeped from the cut, then were greedily soaked up by the beaten earth. The world had become a dizzy place and staying on the ground seemed safest, so Myra rolled on one hip and forced herself into a sitting position. Now facing Alberta's shack, she aimed the narrow line that remained of her vision along the dirt and the step down which she had just fallen; she was having a terrible time making her fingers stay closed around the

DeadTimes

strands of hair and was concentrating on maintaining her hold when her gaze was drawn to a slight bulge in the ground under the step. Her fingers relaxed gratefully and Alberta's hair spilled out; the strength began rebuilding in her body almost immediately as she crawled on all fours and dug into the damp soil below the step with determination.

After a few minutes of effort, Myra brought up her find triumphantly. It was an old, gallon–sized mason jar, the kind the menfolk sometimes used to store their cherry moonshine. The lid had been badly battered and the jar buried upside down, so that the greenish liquid within—swamp water, most likely—seeped slowly into the soil pit that surrounded it. In the ugly depths of the jar floated a piece of cloth that might have once been light blue: Alberta's long–missing underpants. The heavy green growth which encircled the inside of the jar beneath the waterline proved that while the lichen had flourished on the glass while it held swamp water, when the jar's loathsome contents had depleted entirely it had been refilled, coinciding with the most recent ransacking of Alberta's shack and the woman's relapse into sickness.

Myra turned the jug upright and unscrewed the lid, then reached into the moss–filled water and pulled out the dripping wad of fabric. She wrung them out thoroughly and dropped them on the step, then pushed herself up and hauled the heavy jug around to the rear of the shack. Nearly all of her strength had returned and it didn't take long to find a tree branch a couple of inches around; two good whacks and the jar shattered, spilling its brackish moisture into a patch of the thirsty soil which led to the outhouse. Myra used the branch to push the pieces against the wall of the shack where the boy and Alberta wouldn't cut their feet, then returned to the front of the house. Just before she stepped inside, she saw the preacher watching her intently from outside his modest church down the street; as far away as she was, Myra could tell his face was still twisted into a fearsome look. Her mind made a few quick turns to try and link the man with Alberta and Martin but came up empty, as if it were too tired from tangling with this latest trick to worry about the town's cranky bible–thumper.

Alberta was already sitting up in bed; Martin was pacing around the small room excitedly as he waited for the small pot of water he'd set on the woodstove to come to a boil so he could make his mother a cup of tea. The sick woman's skin looked ravaged but her eyes were clear and bright, and she was thinking coherently for the first time in days. Studying her, Myra didn't know if Alberta would ever look quite the same as she had months ago—Myra vaguely recalled a young woman with beautiful skin and a fine, bright smile—but at least she was alive and from all appearances there would be no crippling after–effects. Anyway, Myra could recommend a dozen or more recipes that would help repair the damage done to Alberta's complexion. As Alberta looked at her from the bed, this time the woman's face came closer to showing the smile she'd intended when Myra had first walked in the door.

"I…don't know what to say," Alberta finally managed. "Thank you isn't near enough. This is the first time I've been able to speak in…a while." She glanced at her son and Myra could see that the nervousness of the old ways still remained. Perhaps it would never completely vanish. "We don't have much to pay you with, Miss Myra."

"I promised her the three chicks," Martin piped in. "I'll go find a sack to put 'em in."

He started for the door and Myra stopped him with a gentle hand. "One will be just fine," she said, then grinned impishly to hide her weariness. "But be sure it's the *best* one."

Martin nodded quickly and ducked outside as Myra turned to Alberta; already the woman's gray pallor had started to fade and no doubt a good washing would get rid of most of the scales of dead skin peppering her body. Myra held up the green–stained underwear that had been floating in the jar, then sorted through the small packets she had stuffed into the pockets of her shift until she had the three powders she wanted: hearts ease, lemon verbena, and ground salep, a good luck root. She picked the smallest rumpled paper bag from the jumble of kitchen things and carefully poured a bit of each inside it, then added a generous shake of the contents of another of her packets—cinders from the ruins of her own shack. "As soon as you can be up and about without Martin, wash these yourself, using plenty of lye soap, and let them dry with*out* rinsing. Then toss them and this little bag into the stove and burn them both until there's nothing left but ashes. Take the ashes out to the swamp—*you* do it, not Martin—at sunset on the same day you do the burning and throw them to the west." Myra smiled at Alberta. "And just to be safe, don't cook anything on the stove while you're burning your pants. You got all that?" Alberta nodded mutely.

Myra couldn't think of anything else. The lye would destroy all traces of Alberta from the garment before it was burned with the bag of herbs and cinders. Throwing the ashes into the sunset was really unnecessary, but it would symbolize the final end to the spell, and the woman had been sick for so long that Myra wanted to take every precaution. "Well," she said at last, "I'll be going now." Alberta opened her mouth to speak but Myra held up a hand. "No, really. You just rest up, and the chick'll do me fine."

She stepped outside and automatically glanced in the direction of the tiny town; to her relief the dour–faced preacher had moved along. Martin was waiting patiently by the walk with a small, threadbare burlap sack; Myra could hear faint *cheeps* coming from it and she smiled to herself and calculated how long it would be before the bird would being laying—*if* it was a hen. If not, she'd keep the one she had and fry this one—provided she could control her appetite until then. She took the bag happily, gave the boy's head an absent–minded pat, and headed for home.

Another half hour and Myra was back at her own place. It only took a few minutes to fight an old length of beat–up chicken wire into place so she'd have a place to put the chick where it'd stay separated from her crabby old hen. That done, she dusted her hands against her shift and pushed through the netting over the door; it would be good to get out of this dirty dress and away from the heat, and take a cooling sponge bath. But the instant her foot passed the door frame, Myra stopped cold.

Someone had been in her shack while she was gone.

*   *   *

They hadn't taken anything, at least as far as Myra could tell. She had an excellent knowledge of everything in her place, since she *had* to know immediately if she already had all the right ingredients to turn away a trick, like today, or make up a new charm. Myra hadn't paid much attention to regular personal possessions since the fire; as a result she didn't own much in the way of clothes: a couple of shifts made from donated fabric, a slip, a few pair of underwear. A quick search accounted for everything, including her towel and washcloth, and her one set of sheets. The only shoes she owned were the sandals on her feet. She knew better than to ever leave hair or nail clippings where someone else could get to them.

That left little besides Myra's storehouse of herbs, powders and mixes from the swamp, but even there nothing seemed amiss—and besides, all these roots and such were generally used on other folks, not herself. The whole thing was spooky, knowing someone had been here, *knowing* someone had gone through her things, but not understanding *why*. She couldn't begin to guess if one of the jujus of straw and herbs was missing, but again that didn't matter; they weren't personalized to anyone yet and they were all white magic anyway, nothing that could be twisted around.

What then? Myra went over her "inventory" again but still couldn't make a connection, and for the first time in weeks the troublesome question of her killer reared again in her mind. The attacker was still unknown and, presumably, lived in town. Was he—or she—finally getting ready to strike again? What would have happened had she been here for the person's visit? She shuddered.

After a third and final search, she shook her head in defeat. Her bag of rice was open and almost empty, and to be safe Myra tossed it in the corner to be disposed of later and opened a new one. As she fixed a light supper of seasoned rice and hot sauce—there had been no time to hunt in the swamp for turtle or frogs' legs today—she wondered if it had simply been one of the children from town, looking around inside her shack on a dare from friends, outright bold but too nervous to actually steal anything. That might explain why nothing seemed to be missing, but her sense of balance, of *self*, was disturbed and Myra knew she was not wrong. Someone *had* been inside her home and, more important, had done something.

But *what?*

*   *   *

Myra didn't feel well. Last night's supper of rice and hot sauce sat in her stomach like a ball of warm, sticky wax, and the niggling fear that she had been thinking in the wrong direction when she'd looked for something to be *missing* last night didn't help. Now it was pre-dawn and all she wanted to do was throw up and she couldn't; she had horrible stomach cramps and she was to go to the bathroom terribly, but nothing would come out that end either. At first Myra thought that maybe the heat had turned the hot sauce she'd poured all over the rice—she just *loved* the stuff—but then the thought occurred to her that something might have been *added* to it, though the only way would've been to use something long and skinny, like one of those fancy restaurant straws. If something *had* been added, she was in terrific trouble because she'd used up the last of the bottle and there wasn't even a drop left to try and turn the trick back on whomever had put it on her. An hour ago she'd groped her way across the shack and found her little beaded change purse; from it she'd pulled a shiny silver dime and shoved it under her pillow. Now, in the dim light just before sunrise she felt for it and pulled it out to see; Myra's stomach contracted painfully in either fear or sickness—she could no longer distinguish between the two—at the sight of the now blackened coin, proof positive that she had become someone's victim.

But *who?* That question was maddening enough, but another was much more crucial. *What on earth had she eaten?*

Her thoughts were bleary, unfocused mental impulses that faded in and out. So many people, so many reasons—valid ones, too. But she had tried to make good, to reverse at least some of the evil she had spread in the time before she "awoke." Obviously to someone her repentance had not been enough; as she doubled over for the second time in ten minutes, Myra realized that the spell she had removed from Alberta was slow and mild in comparison to this.

Gasping, she huddled on her bed and tried to think who would have the knowledge necessary to pull off a serious conjure like this one—not that the trick on Alberta wouldn't have killed the weakened woman had it been turned a third time. Myra had always been suspicious of Lucius, but with his wife and children he had little time to learn tricks, though there was always the possibility that he had paid someone else to do it. Yet that would bring him back full circle, wouldn't it? And what would have been the next conjurer's price? The finger from another child? Myra shuddered; she just couldn't accept that he would think revenge worthy of the cost.

There was still the question of the trickster's identity. Myra had started her own learning as far back as she could remember, and since it had been a family tendency the knowledge had come easier to her than it would to most others. That same education didn't come in books, and it would take time that a busy man like Lucius just didn't have—another reason she didn't believe it was him.

The preacher? She barely knew the man—had, in fact, dealt so little with him through the years that she didn't even know his first name. To her he was just the Reverend Pearl, though every time Myra thought of his glowering face and the way he'd watched her by Alberta's she had the feeling she was forgetting something. Now, racked by pain and with her concentration lagging on the simplest of tasks, was certainly not the most efficient time to try and bring up old facts. Her stomach and intestines seemed intent on tying themselves in knots, but what she *could* remember was that for as far back as anyone—and not only herself—could recall, tradition in this town had a woman providing the secrets—light and dark—not a man. Her mother had passed it to Myra, and her grandmother to her, and not a one had ever been married. The vague memory of that bible salesman flitted by and she smiled bitterly; she'd been so positive that union would bring a child, and had even used a charm or two at the time, but it was not to be. Thinking back now, Myra wished she'd gone beyond the simple charms and worked up a full-fledged trick to hide under the bed. Her gut quieted for a moment and she closed her eyes and dozed, exhaustion blacking out her thoughts and sending her quickly into the deeper realm of sleep.

When she woke up that evening, Myra finally remembered something of the history relating to Reverend Pearl, or at least his wife. She was gone—dead? The man had told everyone she'd gone to visit her parents in Atlanta—she'd always talked highly of her mother—and had died in a bus crash during her stay; her folks had arranged for Mrs. Pearl's body to be cremated and the ashes sent back to the town, where the preacher had held a small memorial service for her and displayed the urn. But something didn't set right with that tale, because Myra clearly remembered the woman—her first name was Louisa—coming to her for a spell sometime before she was supposed to have gone to Atlanta. The way Myra had been at the time, nothing had surprised her and she'd mixed up Louisa's trick quick enough, though right now, with her stomach cramping anew, Myra couldn't quite remember what it had been or why, or even what Louisa had paid—not that it mattered anymore. Turning it over in her thoughts now, Myra didn't believe the woman had died in any bus accident in Georgia; instead, Myra thought Louisa had gone somewhere. If Myra's mind was functioning the way it was supposed to—and who could tell *that* with the way she was feeling—Myra remembered Louisa as a pretty woman with a body built to drive a man crazy and an attitude that surely didn't seem fit for a reverend's wife.

As if to tease her, the pain in Myra's stomach waned a bit and she got up shakily, pulling off the sweat-stained dress and managing the sponge bath she'd forgotten the night before. Her stomach rumbled ominously as she slipped a clean shift over her head and waited dully for the cramps to start; instead she felt a mild pang of hunger, although the thought of actually putting food in her mouth made her nauseated all over again. She glanced over her food shelf and decided that maybe she could stomach some chicken broth but eyed the jar of bouillon cubes with suspicion. Still and all, she decided, it was a new jar and when she opened it the paper-wrapped cubes looked undisturbed. She made the liquid weak on purpose, afraid that a rich mixture might make her vomit. While the idea was tempting—like a hangover, she wondered if she might feel better if she went on and threw up—it was doubtful there was anything in her stomach to expel and if she didn't keep something down after all this time she was bound to dehydrate. But she still wished she could go to the bathroom.

But she was better, Myra decided, definitely better. Or so she thought until the cramps started again at midnight. By dawn of the second day her belly was swollen as though she were five months with child and she'd passed most of the night sitting on the rocker, slipping in and out of consciousness and too weak to travel the five feet to the bed. In one of her more lucid moments, Myra realized with a surge of frustration that she was dying…and there was absolutely nothing she could do about it.

※　　　　　※　　　　　※

Three days. Myra loved life above all things and had brazenly sold herself to prove it, but now all she wanted was for this hell to be over. Her guts twisted in agony and the blood in the veins beneath her skin crawled and itched all the time, growing worse with every hour that passed. She could feel the sickness, chart its progress as the stinging started in her neck and ran down her left arm, or perhaps began in the soft spot just to the inside of one of her hip bones to travel down her leg. If she could have found even the smallest bit of strength, she would have used it to claw at her arms and stomach to try and stop the insane prickling. Sometime during the past eternity of hours she had staggered to the bed and now curled between the sticky sheets, moaning and still wondering who'd done this to her. Despite winding in and out of delirium there was no need to wonder *what* anymore, not with the crawling sensation in her veins. Some type of snake blood, she realized, mixed in good and unrecognizable in that infernal bottle of hot sauce. Myra wondered if it were snakes or some other kind of creature that fed on her now within her own body. How foolish that she had never considered that someone else might put a spell on *her!*

"Myra? Myra, can you hear me?"

Myra opened pain-filled eyes at the sound of a vaguely familiar voice; the sunlight flowing through the single window of her shack told her that she'd managed to doze only for a moment.

"What?" she croaked. She wished the person would go away and leave her to die quietly and—hopefully—quickly. "Who's there?"

"It's Janu," the voice answered. When she tried, Myra could just make out the woman's face and someone else's, standing off to the side.

"Who else?" she whispered. "Who's with you?"

The question was met with silence for a moment, then a venom-laced male voice spoke. "Reverend Pearl."

Myra's tortured mind tried to connect the two but failed. "What do you want?" she managed. She was tired of having to ask these inane questions; people came calling to your house, she thought irritably, they should announce their business and not force a body to play guessing games. She wished she had the energy to tell them so.

She sensed rather than heard the preacher open his mouth to speak before Janu cut him off in a silky, deadly voice. "Why, Myra," she purred, "we've come to watch you die."

✳ ✳ ✳

"I remember now," Myra rasped. Where she had gotten the strength to do it she didn't know, but she'd managed to sit up and face her two tormentors. It might have been little besides sheer force of will. "It was your wife, preacherman, who came to me for a charm to take Janu's husband. You lied when you told the townsfolk she died in that bus crash in Georgia."

"Then you should remember the rest," Janu said, her face a study in dark shadows of hate. But Myra's mind wouldn't function and all she could do was stare at the couple blankly. "The night I stabbed you—the fire…no?" Janu laughed harshly. "Here you had no memory of it and all this time I was scared you might be coming after one of us at any time. Why, I could have just let the whole thing alone!"

Something slid across the inside of Myra's stomach, drawing a deep, knifing pain with it. Outwardly stoic, she set her jaw against the cry that tried to pass her lips; she'd be damned before she'd let these two killers enjoy the sight of her pain.

Janu wandered to the window and looked out at the swamp. Smelling blood just beyond their reach, horse flies batted enthusiastically against the netting Myra had tacked tightly over the opening. "The preacher here knew all along what you'd done—Lucius had told me *and* him before I told the man to shut up about it. Lucius had seen Louisa and my man leaving, but the Reverend here was too much a man of God to do anything 'cept try to save his face and the good name of his precious church. When I came to him that night and told him I'd killed you, then suggested he burn your shack down, he saw it as a way for him to get a taste of revenge without actually sinning—"

"Just doing God's work," Reverend Pearl broke in. Through her hazy vision, Myra could see the sheen of nervous sweat that covered his face. "Destroying the tools of evil that you'd used to wrong other folks through the years." The tremor in his voice smoothed out, and for a second Myra saw another preacher in her mind, all the more horrifying for the sudden resemblance.

"That's right," Janu said. "But I never did like butchering and getting my hands messy and I botched the job real bad, didn't I?" She smiled and raised her face to the sparse morning breeze that eased past the netting; Myra thought how different she looked from the woman that had almost died not very long ago.

"What about Alberta?" Myra rasped. "Why did you make her sick?"

Janu giggled before she spoke. "Alberta is nothing," she admitted. "At first she was only a test to see if my spells would work and if my learning was finally doing some good. Then, after you came back, I used her as a tool to get you out of here so's I could put the snake blood in your bottle of sauce. When I refilled that jug while she and the boy were off in the swamp and she got sick all over again, I knew the kid would get desperate and come to you. You done got yourself quite a fancy for doing good now." Her voice hardened. "Too bad you waited so long."

"But I saved your *life!*" In her amazement, Myra's voice was almost clear though the effort of speaking so loudly cost her plenty. "I *helped* you!"

"Anybody could have!" Janu spat. "Besides, you saved me from *what*? And *for* what? You took my life when you took my man and gave him to that whore—"

Myra saw the Reverend Pearl blink at Janu's words.

"—and left me with eight hungry kids and no way to feed 'em. All this time you've been turning folks away when they come to you for spells, I've been giving 'em what they want. Still, nothing you can do will bring back all those years I been on my own and lonely with nothing for company but crying children and worry over the next meal. I spent a long time thinking about it, a long time learning, and you ain't the only woman in this town who knows secrets. Your biggest mistake was in thinking you were." Janu's voice grew even fiercer as she leaned over Myra's shuddering body, though the fact that she saw no fear in Myra's eyes only enraged her further. "And let me tell you something else. I don't *owe* you nothing! A person don't owe someone who caused her that much misery, and keeping me alive only prolonged it and gave me the will to fight back and get even."

"I kept you alive because your brother asked me to!" Myra snapped, the fury in her voice startling both Janu and the reverend into taking backward steps. "And because of all those kids who needed their mother!" It was a good thing she'd come to the end of her sentence, because Myra had no breath left to utter another word; her chest felt like someone had dropped a blacksmith's anvil on top of it.

"Oh, spare me your retelling of attempts at saving your soul!" Janu cried. "They're all a little late now." She bent over the bed again and peered into Myra's pain–filled eyes. "You had me scared enough for a while, yes sir. Stabbed you myself, got so full of your blood that I had to slink through the swamp like a lizard so no one would see me that night." The woman reached down and grabbed Myra's hair angrily; behind her Myra heard the preacher choke slightly, but she barely felt the sting at her scalp. A lot of the room seemed to be fading away at the edges, like the final feet of the one silent film at a movie house in New Orleans she'd gone to years ago. "You must have had some strong magic, Myra. I felt the lifepulse go out of your body myself—when I pulled that knife out of you and pushed you on the floor, I sure did think you were dead." Janu released Myra's hair with a shove and Myra was dimly aware that the small bed bounced as her head was flung back.

"But it don't matter now anyway. The hot sauce was the biggest, but I've put so many tricks on your body that you couldn't save yourself even if you wasn't already sick—you'd never find them all in time to turn 'em back against me. You've had it," Janu finished contemptuously as she turned her back on her victim at last.

"You're nothing but a talking dead woman."

The door opened and Janu and the reverend stepped outside without bothering to look back; Myra didn't know about Janu, but perhaps the bible–thumper just couldn't stand to watch her die. She wondered how he would live with his conscience, knowing down deep that he really had helped kill her. But the bayou was a dark place and always had been so; the past few months of her life, with her feeble attempts to bring light and good into this swamp–surrounded town, had barely made a ripple in its shadows.

Soon the good Reverend Pearl would return with his matches and this shack which had been her home for such a pitifully short time would be consumed by his holy fire. She imagined that her body would burn but as she closed her eyes and felt the torture in her belly and the crushing weight inside her chest hurl her into unconsciousness, Myra knew she'd never feel the pain of the blaze.

CHAPTER IV
1585

She struggled up from sleep's seductive grasp, fighting to be free of the tight bedcovers as much as to escape the blackness that sucked at her with promises of unconcerned oblivion. Why, her foggy brain wondered, must I always awake to the sensation of pain? Why can I not open my mind and eyes to a normal morning and nothing more annoying than a missing blanket?

Her throat hurt fiercely; she couldn't prevent herself from groaning aloud and the startlingly loud echo of her own voice made her eyelids fly open. Where was she—*who*—was she? The sense of background was still vague; as always, it would take time—how much she didn't know—to bring enough things to the surface so that she could get her bearings. Struggling into a sitting position, she peered at her surroundings in the pre–dawn light.

Filmy curtains had been draped from thin beams around the bed. Beyond them, stone walls hung with heavy tapestries disappeared into shadows far above her head.

Stone walls?

Unnerved, she clutched at the bedcovers. She couldn't see much yet and it would be at least another half hour before any decent amount of light filled the room. Cold air touched her face and neck and she shivered; she was so *chilled*—and weak, too. Perhaps she had been the victim of yet another strength–sapping sickness.

Flexing her fingers and wiggling her toes, she tried to increase her circulation and warm up a little, but the effort was exhausting. A sense of self was slowly coming back—she thought her name might be Wendy or something similar, although the huge room slowly lightening around her made such a modern name seem out of place. She twisted on the bed and accidentally pulled her own hair, then examined the spill of heavy gold waves that fell, incredibly, to her hips. A thought from an old fairy tale filtered in and she smiled in spite of her discomfort; *maybe*, she thought, *I have become Rapunzel!*

Her hands were young and smooth, the fingernails clean and unblemished, clearly not prone to the hard work which she'd been accustomed to in by–gone times. Despite the chill, she lifted the coverings to see herself as soon as the light permitted and was pleased at what she found: the body was voluptuous and well–fed, and except for too–pale skin, seemed to be in perfect health. She ran her hands lightly down her stomach and thighs and the skin tingled in immediate response; obviously the girl had not been innocent.

There was enough light now to examine the room and she pushed through the gauzy curtains surrounding her mattress and climbed off the high bed. She found a gown hanging from a peg on the wall and slipped it on, then stumbled over small brocaded slippers on the floor beneath the gown; they fit her feet perfectly. While the walls were stone as she had first thought, much of the darkness she had mistaken for rock was actually the heavy tapestries placed there to help absorb the dampness. There wasn't much else to see: a few chests scattered around, a bench supporting double red cushions, a wooden table upon which rested a pitcher and bowl of water. Thick folds of a velvet–like fabric framed a heavy carved door which had been left open a crack; opposite that a massive fireplace, its contents long grown cold, dominated what she assumed to be the outside wall.

There was, however, a window on the same wall and it drew her. Sounds were starting to filter in, not only through the window but from beyond the door, footsteps, voices, the noise of a household rising. Not quite ready to step beyond this room and meet her new life, she slipped instead to the tiny window, wobbling a bit from the weakness that still pulled at her; since her last awakening had been such a shock, she would take advantage of this quiet opportunity to prepare herself.

The outside wall of stone was thick, and she had to stand unsteadily on her toes to see past the sill. A damp, spring breeze eased around the poorly made, mottled glass and the distorted sight that met her eyes caused her jaw to drop.

She'd never seen soldiers in full dress before.

✻   ✻   ✻

"Lady Gwendolyn! You're alive!"

The near–shriek of the maidservant startled her badly and she gave a little scream as she whirled away from the window. After searching the empty chests for better clothing, she'd wrapped herself in a blanket and had been staring outside for the better part of an hour, watching the sun climb and warm the rocks of the building—what she now realized was actually a castle. *What year is this?* she had wondered as she shivered in the meager rays that seeped into the room. *And where?* To enlarge the puzzle, the tiny girl's words had assaulted her ears in an arrangement of sounds and syllables that should have been utterly foreign to her.

"Of course I'm alive!" The scare jolted her sluggish mind a little and she snapped a reply at the girl's shocked face in the same unidentified language without the slightest pause, slipping easily into the role of authority. "Where the devil are my garments? All the chests are empty."

"Why, they're—I'll get them right now!" The girl rushed out of the room with skirts flying, almost yanking the ornamental curtains down in her haste. Knowing her own name gave Gwendolyn immense satisfaction and she edged to the doorway and peered after the maidservant. She could see little in either direction besides shadowed hallways and more entryways. The servant girl's voice floated back to her, its nearly hysterical tone borne on the castle drafts.

"Lady Gwendolyn is alive and calling for her clothes immediately!"

Cries of astonishment followed, then the sounds of scurrying people: thumping footsteps, a crash from far down a stairway as someone dropped something and another person cursed heartily. Apparently this was the way she would enter each new…what should she call them? Somehow the word *life* didn't seem quite right. Doubtless many in this castle expected only her cold corpse this morning, and it didn't take a scholar to realize that the simple linen bed gown she wore was the prelude to a burial shroud. Gwendolyn—*me*, she thought again—smiled and wondered of what ailment she was to have perished; she could hardly ask.

Within minutes the girl was back with an armload of long garments and odd underthings; she dropped them on the unmade bed and made for the door.

The girl's name flashed in Gwendolyn's mind. "Tell me, Maida, who is to assist me in my toilet?" she demanded of the girl's retreating back. "Would you leave me to fend for myself?"

The young woman froze. "No, uh—no, of course not." When she turned there was such a look of terror on her features that Gwendolyn felt her irritation soften. The little serving girl couldn't be more than thirteen or fourteen years old.

"What's the matter with you?" she chided gently, waving towards the bed. "Help me with these. You know I've never been able to do all the buttons." The maidservant returned reluctantly and began separating the raiments on the bed and straightening the bed linens. Gwendolyn waited patiently; her memory was still foggy and she had no idea which of the garments she should put on first. A few minutes passed and still Maida tucked and fussed about; Gwendolyn felt her patience growing thin. The girl's behavior was bordering on insolence.

"Maida, you've left me like this all morning and I'm going to catch a chill if I don't dress soon. Can we get on with it?"

Maida straightened and glanced at her fearfully, then gasped. "Why, you're standing in the sun, my lady!"

"Well, why shouldn't I? I *like* the sun—and it's hardly odd in the daylight, now is it?"

"But Lord Christopher…" Her voice trailed off.

"What about…his lordship?" Gwendolyn asked. The name meant nothing and her mind's inability to furnish the information made her testy. "Well? Answer me. I tire of this game you seem to be playing this morning."

"Ah, it's nothing, my lady." Maida gave her a relieved smile, the first genuine happiness Gwendolyn had seen the girl offer. "Look, I've brought you a new silk gown, completed only yesterday by the seamstress." She shook out the dress and held it up for Gwendolyn to see. "The green will complement your hair beautifully. Come, let's get you dressed before you take ill."

For all the aggravation Maida had caused, she was a capable and quick servant. While Gwendolyn scurried to the garderobe and back, the girl started a fire on the hearth and warmed water to wash. Within a half hour, Gwendolyn was fully dressed and admiring the fine material and workmanship of the long-sleeved gown inset with darker green ribbons, accompanied by at least a half dozen other pieces of clothing. When Gwendolyn looked down, she could see a heavily embroidered gold underskirt swelling from between a split in the deep green fabric; three strands of pearls and gold cascaded from her neckline to dangle a few inches above her waist. The gown's quilted, slightly puffy sleeves felt soft and warm on her skin and she smiled. She felt utterly pampered when a copper–colored feather–fan was tied around her waist and a dark green coat trimmed with fox fur almost completed the ensemble. What year was it that required her to dress like this? Gwendolyn fumbled for a moment when she discovered that the small jeweled knife usually kept in her pocket was missing, but Maida faltered only when she went to fasten a pearl brooch at Gwendolyn's throat.

"My l–lady," she stammered, "your n–neck—"

Gwendolyn touched her throat with searching fingers and the flesh was quick to respond with a surge of pain. "It does feel tender," she admitted. She had been too nervous to ask for it before now, but the situation offered no escape. "Hand me the mirror," she finally said. The girl obeyed and Gwendolyn not only glimpsed a huge, blue–black bruise on the side of her neck, but got her first view of her own face.

She stared at herself. The face, she decided, was a bit thin in comparison with the rest of the body's plumpness, and though the narrow cheekbones and slightly aquiline nose hinted at royal blood, the lips were a touch too full. She knew at once that her eyes were her best feature: a light and tawny brown, they glittered beneath naturally dark, arched eyebrows. Why, Gwendolyn decided before lowering the glass slightly, I suppose I'm actually... *pretty.*

Her gaze dropped to her neck once more. The bruise was another matter and she inspected it closely, trying to guess it origin. Clearly an attack—strangulation? She cursed silently as she envisioned herself watching her back for another lifetime.

"Maida, did anyone come to my bedchamber last night? Anyone at all?" Gwendolyn finally asked. It was hard to pull her eyes from the horrible discoloration.

The girl's answer was mildly accusing as she carefully drew Gwendolyn's hair into a knot and pinned it beneath a small, pearl–trimmed cap. "I don't know, lady. Forgive me for being bold, but you know I sleep in the servants' quarters." She sniffed and Gwendolyn smiled in spite of her oversight; apparently sleeping in the company of her own kind was not at all to the girl's liking.

"Of course—how could I have forgotten." She put the mirror face down on the table and motioned for the maidservant to complete her task. "I think we'll change that. From now on, you shall sleep at the foot of my bed."

✳   ✳   ✳

"I would like to take a stroll about the keep," Gwendolyn told the girl when the chore of dressing was finally done. "But I feel too faint to do so unchaperoned. Perhaps you can find someone—one of the men–at–arms—to assist me."

"Yes, my lady." Maida curtsied and was gone. While she waited, Gwendolyn circled her chamber again, glancing at the chests that someone had emptied last night, probably when she'd been thought dead. It wasn't long before Maida returned, prodding an unwilling soldier into the room. The man—overly tall boy was more accurate—stood before her, red–faced and uncertain in his ladyship's bedchamber. Sun freckles marched across his cheeks and Gwendolyn had a glimpse of bright blue eyes before the lad shyly fixed his gaze on the floor.

"This is Ferenc, my lady; he will make a fine escort for you. He is my *personal* choice."

Maida's emphasis was not lost on Gwendolyn. "I see," she said, inspecting the young man. "He certainly looks like a strong and capable escort. I'm sure I'll be quite safe." Ferenc blushed even more as Maida beamed at him. He offered his arm dutifully and they left the girl in the chamber to finish her work as he led Gwendolyn into the hall. Cautiously descending the narrow stone stairs, she tried to drink in her surroundings without gaping too much—the memories were there, but they were the worthless presumptions of another person when paralleled with the first *real* experiences in this new life.

As Ferenc guided her through the great hall, the sights and sounds were almost brutal to Gwendolyn's unprepared brain. People were everywhere. Men, women and children rushed about, each apparently having his or her own task yet never failing to bow or curtsy as she and Ferenc passed. Every one of her senses wanted to overload; even the toes of her feet curled involuntarily when they pressed against the rush–strewn floor.

Gwendolyn looked thankfully at the archway leading to the courtyard and motioned a doubtful Ferenc to lead her there, thinking the fresh air would clear her head and stabilize a stomach that seemed likely to embarrass her at any moment. As soon as they stepped out of the hall she realized her mistake, for if the hall and its occupants appeared frantic, the courtyard was nothing short of bedlam. Small boys beat at squealing pigs and bleating sheep, chickens squawked and floundered amid the boots of soldiers as they saddled and exercised their mounts and called out to passing maids leading cows and pullcarts. A little farther away she could see the outer walls and entrance as more people poured in from the countryside to set up booths and do the day's business—merchants, laborers, villagers—so many she couldn't put a name to them all. Her grip on Ferenc's arm grew desperate as the smells of animals and excrement filled her nose and pounded into her stomach, and he intuitively turned her back towards the castle and hall. Little sparkles of light were starting to dance in front of her eyes as they stepped back inside and Gwendolyn felt as if she'd finally arrived at some great sanctuary.

"I need to sit," she managed. The young man looked at her in dismay and glanced quickly around; she realized she was nearly hanging from his arm in her efforts to maintain control of her footing. His steadying grip was almost painful but she didn't complain, knowing it would be a thousand times more humiliating if it became necessary for him to carry her to a bench.

"Get up!" Ferenc snapped at a teenager sprawled lazily on the only bench he judged close enough. The sleepy boy failed to notice Gwendolyn and he returned an insolent glance; Ferenc's hand shot out and cuffed him viciously. "You dog—I said get up! Would you lose your ears for your disrespect?" The blow knocked the lad from the bench and sent him rolling to Gwendolyn's feet, where he gaped up at her in alarm.

"My lady—forgive me! I didn't see you—!" In his desire to escape, he half ran, half crawled away.

"No matter," she murmured, waving a weak hand. Ferenc eased her to the bench and bent over her, patting her wrists firmly, hoping to see the color return to her pallid face. The young soldier has a fierce side, she thought blearily, and was in fact quite capable—more so than his normal, boyish manner implied.

"Lady Gwendolyn," he said finally, "perhaps you would feel better if you broke your fast. I can take you back to your solar—"

"Yes," she interrupted. "That's an excellent idea—no wonder I feel so poorly! But I'd prefer to eat in the hall."

"The hall? With the servants? But Lord Christopher—"

"That is my wish, yes," she said firmly. "Please take me closer to the hearth. I'm cold and it will be quite warm there."

"But Lady, even now they prepare for the noon meal. They will be readying the butchered meat…"

"No matter," she said, rising. "It is hunger that saps my strength, not the sight of uncooked game. Surely they'll have some warm bread and ale." She glanced at the people scampering around the hall; away from the stench and uproar of the courtyard her stomach had quieted a bit and she offered her hand.

It wasn't just warm, it was *hot* by the massive fireplace. Quarters of venison and boar already turned on spits and the smells of stewing vegetables, chicken and fish filled the air. The room's clamor wavered at their appearance and nearly died altogether when Ferenc escorted Gwendolyn to a table and cleared a spot for her to sit. She looked around with interest at the heat–flushed and confused faces of the cooks and staff as they wiped at their smudged hands and looked stymied. Where before each had moved with purpose, they now milled about uncertainly. Ferenc stood rod–straight behind her as Gwendolyn settled herself at the rough table, waiting until she was comfortable before he spoke.

"Lady Gwendolyn wishes to dine," he said stiffly. "You will see to her immediately." His tone left no room for argument and a middle–aged woman—a gypsy, Gwendolyn's memory suddenly supplied—stepped forward without further prompting and gave an awkward curtsy. Gwendolyn could see the deep damage caused by heavy drinking in the veins about her nose and mouth, but her eyes this morning were clear and sharp. *Where the devil am I?* Gwendolyn wondered.

"What is my lady's wish?" she asked nervously in a thick but understandable accent, her hoarse voice confirming her beverage of choice.

"Something simple," Gwendolyn decided aloud, trying to put the woman at ease. "Bread, perhaps some ale. I will eat here where I can warm myself." The heat from the strong fire was finally making her feel better.

The serving woman bowed again and returned in just a few moments with thick slices of bread still steaming from the hearth and a slab of bright yellow cheese. Another maid spread a cloth of white linen before Gwendolyn and carefully placed a goblet of ale in front of her. Gwendolyn raised a piece of bread to her lips and the woman returned yet again, this time to offer a mazer of hot chicken broth. She bit into the crusty bread and her mouth watered obligingly; she was famished! Another bite and she stopped, realizing the staff still stared at her, frozen in the places.

"Please," she said and motioned with the bread still in her fingers. "Go on about your duties and don't mind me. I'll be out of your way within a quarter hour."

Confused by the implication that she troubled them, they watched her for a few more minutes before self-consciously returning to their tasks. Still, in five minutes it was as though Gwendolyn and Ferenc were in another part of the castle altogether and she tarried over her ale, enjoying the hustle and smells of the over-sized room—much the same as the bailey, she remembered, but without the rancid smell of refuse. A few minutes more and she felt gorged, physically and mentally, and in spite of the myriad of new things to be seen and experienced, she wanted nothing more than her bed and a good nap. One word could make it so and she realized how easily she could become spoiled in this strangely luxurious yet barbaric place where every command was instantly obeyed.

She rose and was shocked to find herself wobbling slightly; Ferenc was at her side in an instant to help her back to her chamber and bid his leave. In her absence Maida had once more filled the chests with her clothes: robes, gowns and coats again hung from the pegs along the wall. A smaller chest holding belts, jewels and her missing knife had been returned to its place at the side of the bed, yet Gwendolyn applauded Maida's most endearing touch—fresh flowers in a brass goblet.

Gwendolyn stood before the bed indecisively. It was nearing mid-morning; a few more hours and the horns would blow for the mid-day meal, for which she'd probably have little appetite. Yet if Lord Christopher—her mind gave her the startling word *betrothed* but stubbornly remained blank when she tried to recall his face—should require her presence…*Bah*, she thought abruptly. *He's been absent all morning; why should I care?*

The bed and freshly changed linens gleamed invitingly and she pulled off her shoes and cap and climbed beneath the top coverlet. Just a nap, she thought, a short one. Her head and neck—especially that—throbbed and her legs moved only weakly; she felt sure her body needed more rest to recover from her attack or illness of the previous night. Besides, Maida would probably call her in time to dress for her appearance at dinner.

*   *   *

Maida did call for her, but Gwendolyn was so exhausted that the serving girl was unable to rouse her and finally left a tray laden with food instead. It was two hours past mid-day when Gwendolyn finally awoke, once again ravenous and amazed anew at her surroundings until the morning's memories returned. The cold meal Maida had left was excellent, and Gwendolyn quickly devoured the trencher of mutton stew and pork slices with mustard, barely finding room for the custard of almonds and rice. She pushed the tray away and sighed; she could hear people calling to one another and dogs barking beyond the window—so much more to see and remember, yet sleep tempted her again.

No, Gwendolyn decided as she found her shoes and smoothed her hair back under her cap, she would not sleep away this first day, no matter how poorly she felt. If nothing else, there would be a spot before the fire in the great hall where she could sit and watch; there it would be easy to learn about the castle and its occupants. Each new face and task would sponsor a new memory.

A half hour later found Gwendolyn once again settled on a bench not far from the hearth where a different serving woman tended a roasting boar at regular intervals, periodically ripping off chunks of meat and passing them to the soldiers as they came in—obviously many besides her had missed the earlier meal. She studied each face intently and noted the dragon and wolves' teeth crest on the tapestries and capes, but her memory was an obstinate companion and refused her any detailed knowledge of the castle and its family name, much less her own surname. And something else—suspicion—pricked her senses. Just where *was* the elusive Lord Christopher? Most of the castle's inhabitants seemed to know she had been ill, and many had stopped with good wishes; why had Christopher himself not inquired after her health? Or had he counted on her death? Perhaps this betrothal was not to his liking…so many questions! Frustration made her fingers dance nervously in her lap and Gwendolyn realized a normal day would have seen her taking advantage of the waning afternoon light to sew on one of the many tapestries.

Finally dusk settled in and lighted candles and oil lamps began appearing, first in the dimmest parts of the great hall, then multiplying as the daylight rapidly began to fade. Though she was not at all hungry, Gwendolyn was looking forward to watching from her comfortable perch as the staff prepared and served the lighter evening meal, hoping to learn even more about the workings of this new home. But the atmosphere grew hushed and hurried and little attention was paid her way, and as each quarter hour ticked by, Gwendolyn grew more amazed; she'd expected the same flurry of activity, yet the servants and soldiers were rapidly disappearing! The main table and dais had been set with clean linens and goblets, and although the roasted boar in the hearth had nearly been consumed, no one arrived to replace it with fresh meat; only the remaining meat's considerable distance from the fire kept it from charring. Even the dogs appeared to have slunk away to secret sleeping places. Where earlier there had been at least two score people rushing about, a mere three-quarters of an hour after dark found Gwendolyn utterly alone in the great hall, with not even the stare of a gypsy woman for company.

✳   ✳   ✳

"Maida?" Gwendolyn climbed the stairs slowly, still feeling tired and a bit feeble; her legs threatened exhaustion but she forced herself to go on. Her call floated up, reminiscent of the echoing quality in the earlier hours of this morning—had the castle been empty then, too? Even the soft cork heels of her shoes created hollow echoes as she made her way to the bedchamber and yanked off her coat angrily. Where the devil was that serving girl? For that matter, where was *anyone*?

At least her instinct remained to lead her to the right chamber and she saw that while no servant was present, the bed had been straightened and turned down, a trio of candles lit and a goblet and decanter of wine made ready. But Gwendolyn longed for someone to talk to and while she knew Maida probably had other duties, she felt certain the girl should have spent the bulk of the day at her side. She looked around uncertainly. She would be freed of these day clothes, if only—

"Good evening, Gwendolyn."

She whirled and bit back a scream. A man dressed almost entirely in black stood in the darkness of her doorway, one shoulder still hidden behind the curve of the draped opening. Gwendolyn had the feeling of immense strength and her breath hitched as he stepped forward into the small circle of light cast by the candles.

"What?" he asked mockingly. "The brave Gwendolyn has no words of welcome for her dear betrothed?"

She looked at his shadowed face warily, wondering at this man who would first frighten her and then invite an argument. She desperately wanted to look at him, talk with him—get to *know* this stranger to whom she would, she knew, someday be married, yet a sharp response burst automatically from her lips.

"Indeed, Christopher. You look for words of welcome but try to frighten me into silence. Shall I still bid you good evening?" She had only a moment to feel bewildered by the bitterness in her own voice.

"Forgive me, my sweet." He bowed and her eyes narrowed; she knew his showy respect was not sincere. "I had thought this evening would find you pleasantly…surprised."

"Really?" she asked as she moved to the bench and sat carefully, arranging her gown to hide the shakiness in her legs. "And why should it? Another day, like all the rest." Gwendolyn waved a hand flippantly, stalling for time as memories, jarred by Christopher's presence, boiled into her mind. More than a few remained vague and tantalizingly out of reach—but most filled in the holes of her new life quite nicely, like restocking the larder.

No wonder the castle was empty—this fiend ruled by terror!

Anger exploded within her, familiar and energy–bringing even as it constricted her chest. She would *not* be cowed.

Gwendolyn was up in an instant and pacing the lighted area with furious steps, each increasing in fervor as Christopher watched with an amused grin. Regardless of her wrath, Gwendolyn's eyes still drank of him and studied each fine feature until it was locked away for future examination. He was gorgeous—tall and broad–shouldered under a short, circular cape edged with indigo ribbons, he boasted a head full of gleaming black curls that brushed his shoulders while a thick moustache graced wide, rugged features. He had forgone the ridiculous discomfort of a ruff and the annoyance of a hat, and his eyes were strange and glittery, and while her fear had been drowned by her fury, Gwendolyn found herself avoiding his gaze.

"Isn't it just like any other, my *dear* betrothed, who so conveniently manages to disappear for yet another day—this time while I lie so ill upon my bed that your servants thought me dead. Tell me what it is that you expected would bring me pleasure in this dreary, god-forsaken castle where you have nearly abandoned me? Perhaps," she continued in a cold voice, "you have become gracious enough to allow some piddling member of my family—perhaps a third or fourth cousin—to visit me after these many months. Or is it that you have finally gifted my father with a firm date for our marriage?"

Christopher threw back his head and laughed, teeth flashing strong and white. "You haven't changed, Gwendolyn! I had feared the worst—a simpering, terrified wench who would scream at the very sight of me." Three strides and he sat easily on the bed, as if accustomed to visiting her in her bedchamber. "Had that been so, I would have…missed your spirit."

"You speak in riddles and I have little patience for your games tonight," she snapped. "You may leave anytime."

He grinned again and something in her mind shifted—obscure recollection that filled her with dread. She clenched her teeth and stood her ground; she'd be damned if he would see her fear.

"Oh no, my *love*," he said in a voice dripping with sweetness. "I'll not leave—not at all." In the space of a heartbeat he was in front of her, crushing her against him, forcing her to meet the darkness of his eyes. She knew fighting would be useless, and she would not grant him the satisfaction of an embarrassing struggle; instead, she stood frozen in his embrace, an icicle just to spite him. He chuckled and Gwendolyn felt the cold skin of his lips against her ear. "Always the warrior, aren't you? But it ends now. *I* have no patience to replay the years I wooed you because of some devil's trick!"

Gwendolyn gasped despite herself—did he somehow know? She opened her mouth to demand an answer to her unspoken question and his mouth covered hers, rough at first, then lightening to a gentle insistence when her body betrayed her with response. One arm held her waist firmly as his other hand slipped up, lingered for a breathless moment on the curve of her breast, then began prying at the throat of her gown. Sweet fire blazed in her belly around the unspoken protests that whirled in her mind. *No!* she thought. She could not let this maniac touch her like this!

"My lady?" From the corridor, Maida's childish voice cut through the haze building in Gwendolyn's senses. Christopher's head jerked up with a growl and his grip slackened; in an instant Gwendolyn had squirmed away. The servant hurried into the room, a small pallet and bundle of belongings clasped in her arms.

"I'm sorry to be so la—*ah!*" Maida burst into the chamber, then gave a frightened squeak and threw herself backwards against the wall as Christopher whirled and snarled his wrath, snatching at the girl's arms with fingers curled into claws.

"Christopher, calm yourself!" Gwendolyn cried. She darted in front of him and yanked the girl sideways and out of his reach. "Have you gone mad?"

The bear-sized hand reaching for Maida paused, then drew back as the candlelight glittered on the beads pinned to the girl's bodice. He cursed and strode to the entryway, then stopped with his fingers gripping its handle as he fixed Maida with a black stare.

"Lady Gwendolyn will *not* be needing you tomorrow night, Maida. *Do you understand?*" Maida whimpered and turned her face against Gwendolyn's shoulder.

"Christopher, don't—"

"Be SILENT, Gwendolyn!" he roared. *"Did you hear me or NOT girl?"*

"Yes, Lord Christopher!" Maida's reply was more of a sob muffled into the silk fabric of Gwendolyn's gown, but Christopher seemed satisfied.

Then he was gone; neither footstep nor other sound filtered through the castle walls.

He was simply…gone.

✳   ✳   ✳

The girl was not to be calmed, and despite her unanswered questions about Christopher, Gwendolyn's exhausted body desperately craved still more sleep. The midnight hour was creeping past before Maida's tossing form finally quieted on her pallet, providing Gwendolyn with the stillness she needed to seek solace. Throughout the night, each time Maida turned restlessly or a log crackled in the fireplace, Gwendolyn's mind played tricks, imagining the stealthy sound of a footstep that might signal Christopher's return. Although she did not really believe he would visit her again tonight, her mind and body battled for control of her feelings, the mind recoiling, in terror from the dark promises in Christopher's black and bottomless eyes, her new and maddeningly traitorous body craving his touch upon her night–bared skin without regard for the damnation that might follow.

What was this hell into which she had been cast?

✳   ✳   ✳

Gwendolyn woke at first light but Maida was already gone about her chores; unlike yesterday, a fire had been started and the chamber barely held a trace of the spring dampness. Gwendolyn's thoughts were mercifully blank and she stayed in bed and stared at the fire, enjoying the warmth of the linens and a rare moment of contentment. It seemed only a few minutes before Maida came with warm water for washing and urged her to dress in the clothes that had already been chosen. Gwendolyn was still bleary and wanted nothing more than to take her time, and she watched the girl scurry around the room with growing irritation; when Maida tried to rush her to complete her toilet, she couldn't help grumbling.

"Maida, whatever is your hurry? I'd much prefer to dress leisurely—ouch! You're pulling too hard!"

"I'm sorry, my lady," Maida offered as she drew the comb through Gwendolyn's hair. "But we've many things to do before the Countess arrives, and she's expected by mid–day."

"The Countess?"

"Don't you remember?" Maida asked reproachfully. "Her squire brought the news only three days ago. And today's her birthday, besides. There's much to be done—Lord Christopher will want the best celebration arranged for his niece." Maida pulled a piece of red satin from her pocket and began twining it into the heavy plait she had made of Gwendolyn's hair.

"And how old will she be?" Gwendolyn asked.

"Well, let's see," said Maida. She brought the waist length braid up and began pinning it around the back of the circlet atop Gwendolyn's head, "I'm not very smart with my numbers but my kinsmen have been with the Báthory family for almost a hundred years, so at least I know the lineage. I believe Countess Elizabeth was born in the year of our Lord 1560; it's said today marks her twenty-fifth year."

1585! Gwendolyn's mouth dropped open. Christ—she was riding a swing back and forth through time!

✳   ✳   ✳

Gwendolyn waited for the Countess in the great hall, embarrassed by the fact that Christopher was, as usual, nowhere to be found. On the one hand she found it difficult to believe that his manners were so atrocious that he would not greet his own niece on the anniversary of her birth, *and* at the celebration presumably ordered by himself; on the other, and if last night was any indication, it seemed likely Christopher held no thought of today and Gwendolyn should have foreseen this. Already the first of the Countess's entourage was arriving, yet Gwendolyn's inquiries around the castle as to Lord Christopher's whereabouts were met with nothing but curt shakes of the head and a few strange looks. When four massive black steeds pulled an elegant palfrey bearing the Báthory crest into the courtyard, Gwendolyn reluctantly accepted the responsibility of making the Countess feel welcome.

As a lackey opened the palfrey door, Gwendolyn curtseyed deeply and bowed her head; a few seconds later she could see the hem of the woman's luxurious gown but the Countess gave no indication that Gwendolyn should rise. Impeccable court education guided her actions and Gwendolyn set her jaw and waited patiently, knowing that until her marriage Elizabeth thought of her as little better than a servant and humbled her purposely, but Gwendolyn was determined not to prejudge her aristocratic future niece before they had a decent chance to become acquainted, especially since few visitors came to this isolated castle. Staring at the ground and awaiting Elizabeth's leave, sudden realization cut into Gwendolyn's brain—how could the woman standing before her be Christopher's niece, when the man she had spoken to last night could hardly be more than his niece's age of twenty-five? Gwendolyn blinked; there must be some quirk in the lineage, perhaps a brother or sister, or even a half-sibling, nearly two decades Christopher's senior—it was probably to be expected in royal families.

"Lady Gwendolyn." Countess Báthory's voice was smooth and cold, and brought Gwendolyn the unwanted memory of the long and sometimes deadly icicles that hung from the castle archways in the winter. Gwendolyn took the woman's hand and rose gratefully; her legs were on the verge of cramping.

"I'm honored, Countess," Gwendolyn said formally. "Castle Báthory bids you welcome and entreats you to stay with us as long as you like. We celebrate with you the date of your birth and have prepared a feast in your honor. If you wish to rest before the festivities, I can show you to your chamber; I trust you will find it adequate."

"I'm sure," the woman replied absently as she glanced around the courtyard; still holding Gwendolyn's hand, she was rubbing the skin between her thumb and forefinger, as if testing some fine fabric.

Gwendolyn pulled away uneasily and motioned towards the hall. "This way, Countess."

Countess Báthory focused on her and smiled somewhat stiffly. "Please, call me Elizabeth. May I call you Gwendolyn?"

"Of course…Elizabeth." Gwendolyn studied her covertly as she led the way up the stairs to one of the larger guest chambers. Girlhood memories welled obligingly at her mental probing, tales of Countess Báthory's unsurpassed beauty—all obviously true. The resemblance between her and Christopher was unmistakable, though Elizabeth's features were feminine and softly rounded where Christopher's were strong and wolf–like. But both uncle and niece carried the same lustrous black hair, Elizabeth's piled atop her head and woven with gold filigree and pearls beneath a long, transparent veil. While Christopher's eyes were an undistinguishable color, Elizabeth's were a deep, doe–like brown, large and striking in a small face that showed clear, achingly beautiful skin that could have easily belonged to a girl Maida's age. Reaching the chamber, Gwendolyn couldn't resist complimenting her as the Countess inspected her quarters and warmed her hands before the hearth.

"The troubadours sing ballads about your beauty. I see they do not do you justice."

Elizabeth turned and gave Gwendolyn her first sincere smile since her arrival. "You are a most gracious hostess, Gwendolyn. I can see why my uncle speaks so highly of you—and of course, you are quite lovely yourself." A tiny frown flickered across her features. "But you should really put a poultice on that…bruise on your neck, or it may permanently discolor your skin."

Gwendolyn caught herself staring as Elizabeth's lip stretched wider to show the same strong teeth as Christopher's, then shook herself silently for her rudeness. "Forgive me, Countess—"

"Elizabeth," she corrected.

"Elizabeth. I'm sure you're tired from your journey, and the festivals won't begin for at least another two hours. At your leave, I'll see to the celebration and let you rest."

The Countess nodded, and Gwendolyn bowed out of the room and stood for a moment in the corridor, getting her bearings. There was something about the woman that spooked her, something…repugnant—though on her life she couldn't identify it. The Countess was washed and scented, and she was certainly polite; nothing had been said or implied that hinted at impropriety, yet Gwendolyn found nervous moisture beading on her forehead and in the valley of skin between her breasts. It was probably nothing more than the unpleasant feelings left over from the fright and the show of temper that Christopher had given her the night before. Nonetheless, his etiquette was growing more despicable by the hour and he would certainly get an earful from her as soon he was found; still, nothing could be done about him now. Torn between anger and resolution, Gwendolyn hurried down to check on the preparations.

✳   ✳   ✳

The height of the midday banquet, a few hours later than normal to allow the Countess time to rest, had been laid out and still Christopher's whereabouts were unknown. Gwendolyn fumed and took her place beside his empty chair at the high table with Elizabeth, watching as ladies–in–waiting and other companions from the Countess's entourage settled around the table with selected men–at–arms from the castle. *Perhaps that is what I need for company*, Gwendolyn mused, a few ladies whose idle gossip might help me pass the hours at this desolate place. Besides, she thought sullenly, Christopher could not in all decency avoid setting a date for their holy vows much longer—shocked, her mental calendar suddenly informed her that he had procrastinated nearly four years! Her small fists curled around each other; such a long time to be unchaperoned in this place—she would never understand how he had convinced her father to agree to such a thing. With a pang Gwendolyn realized too that she'd never known her mother and would need outside help preparing for the inevitable ceremony—a full range of servants and seamstresses would have to be procured. In spite of Lord Christopher's continued absence and the ever–present feeling of isolation, her spirits lifted at the possibility of a castle full of people—day *and* night! No more dark corridors and shadowed chambers empty of all but the sputtering of candle flame and the occasional chittering of fleeing rats. With a full staff, the castle would ring with life all the time; even the latest hours would hear the snores of menservants and the sleepy growls of their hounds, a cook or two keeping odd schedules to start meat roasting in time to feed the men before they left on the morning hunts.

"Have you no appetite, my dear–?" With a start, Gwendolyn realized that trenchers and meat had been set in front of her some time ago and were quickly cooling. The Countess leaned towards her with veiled eyes and motioned to the array of food being spread before them. "The repast is quite delicious."

"Forgive me. My thoughts were wandering." Gwendolyn cleansed her fingers with a square of linen and began to eat, occasionally casting pointed glances at the serving maids to make sure they didn't tarry. Once again, she felt the need to apologize for Christopher. "I beg your pardon for Christopher. I am at a loss to explain his absence."

To her surprise, the older woman laughed. "Oh, my dear! Don't apologize to *me*, of all people! I hardly expected to see Christopher before tonight."

"But," Gwendolyn sputtered, "I never anticipated he would be so rude—"

"Rude?" The Countess seemed delighted at Gwendolyn's words and laughed even more merrily. "Not at all—my, you are even more innocent than I thought! In fact," she looked at Gwendolyn conspiratorially, "it's an accomplishment that you've made it this far."

Gwendolyn frowned at her. "I don't understand."

Elizabeth sat back and wiped at her lips. "Never mind, dear. Sometimes I do prattle on, yet make no sense at all. Come now, they've brought the next course. If you don't eat properly, you'll never bring any decent color to your skin, and you're much too pale." She chuckled quietly and pushed a wooden bowl laden with hot dumplings towards her.

Gwendolyn tasted a bit—liver—and pushed the dish away, reaching instead for a platter of chicken from which drifted a familiar, mouth-watering aroma. She was just about to bite into a drumstick when Elizabeth slapped the meat from her hand. "Don't eat that!"

She stared at her future relation in astonishment. "Why not? It's one of my favorite dishes."

"But can't you smell the garlic? Christopher has a terrible aversion to the stuff—why, just the smell of it makes him ill."

"Really?" Gwendolyn sat back thoughtfully. "I don't believe he ever told me. I've always been fond of garlic and I'm sure he realizes I eat the seasoning quite often. One can hardly disguise the scent."

The Countess's eyes narrowed as she looked at Gwendolyn. "Perhaps that's one of the very reasons he…shall we say, *declines* your company?"

Gwendolyn felt her temper rise and slide dangerously on the edge of courtesy. True, the woman's words were snide and uncalled-for, but it still amazed Gwendolyn how quickly she angered—too rapidly to stall her response. "Don't be absurd," she snapped. "If it disturbed him overmuch, I feel certain he would have spoken of it."

Elizabeth patted her hand blithely, apparently unconcerned at Gwendolyn's disrespectful tone. "You're right, of course. There I go again—telling tales. Never mind."

The meal continued and although Gwendolyn was tempted to eat the garlic chicken just to spite her petty houseguest, she chose instead slices of hen breast flavored with ginger and marjoram, a dish that would surely not lend her breath an offensive odor. But curiosity nagged her; how could she have spent nearly four full years at Báthory castle and never known of Christopher's loathing of garlic? Had she in her present state simply forgotten?

More courses arrived—a seemingly endless array of meats, vegetables and desserts, until Gwendolyn vowed if she never tasted or saw another apple or fig she'd be a happy woman. There was no doubt that the Countess enjoyed the celebration immensely, alternately chewing and clapping her hands cheerily at the jesters and troubadours who wandered the hall during the desserts, flinging a steady supply of scraps to the beggars and dogs waiting patiently by the table legs.

The two women made sporadic conversation but Elizabeth seemed more inclined to pass the time listening to the troubadours' songs and Gwendolyn's attempts at entertaining the Countess finally died away. The meal weighed heavily in Gwendolyn's stomach and made her drowsy, and her face flamed when she jerked her head up and found that few servants remained in the hall and most of the guests had retired to their chambers to rest. All remnants of the food and dishes had been cleared and fresh linens set out, though it was unlikely that a full evening meal would be served given the late hour of the Countess's birthday banquet. Elizabeth, however, had chosen to remain and now leaned back against her chair and watched Gwendolyn with an amused expression, one lovely hand hanging lazily over the chair's arm.

"Have a nice nap, Gwendolyn?" she asked.

Gwendolyn quickly sat up straight and gazed around the nearly deserted hall. As before, most of the castle's daytime inhabitants appeared to have fled; an annoyance last night, it was a thousand times more embarrassing in the presence of Christopher's niece and her entourage.

"Forgive me, Countess," Gwendolyn answered as she smoothed her skirts. "I fear my recent illness still taxes me. I can't imagine where the servants have gone, but I'll be happy to escort you upstairs myself."

Elizabeth made a flitting motion with one white-skinned hand. "No matter about the servants—I find your company much more...ah, entertaining. The two of us shall retire to my chamber and talk. You've probably little opportunity for company in this isolated countryside, and I can bring you current on everything happening in Vienna. You should make that rake Christopher buy you a manor home in town, such as I have. Wintering in the family castle is terribly out of vogue, I'm afraid." A corner of her mouth pulled up in a little smile. "Bad for your health, too...as I'm sure you've realized." Countess Báthory turned away. "If we do happen to find a serving girl, I would be inclined to have a bath drawn before my uncle calls."

"Of course," Gwendolyn said demurely, then peered at her. "You seem so certain that Christopher will be here."

"But why wouldn't he?" she asked, looking at Gwendolyn as if the younger woman were some silly child. "No doubt other business occupies his time during the day, but dusk falls even as we speak. I fancy we'll enjoy his visit before the moon is fully risen."

✳   ✳   ✳

Upon seeing the woman to her chamber, Gwendolyn was spared the humiliation of having to search for a servant to attend the Countess's bath since two of Elizabeth's ladies had already seen to the task and a tub of steaming water awaited her. Heedless of modesty, the Countess immediately disrobed and stepped into the wooden tub with a contented sigh, motioning for Gwendolyn to sit and keep her company. Even with the full fire, the room quickly grew chilly with the onset of evening and Elizabeth didn't tarry long in the rapidly cooling water as her ladies lit candles to brighten the darkness; a short time later she stood and stepped into the warm robe offered by the youngest of her servants, a buxom blonde who despite her physical endorsements could hardly have been Maida's age. As the girl then brought a basin of fresh water and offered the Countess a small, corked bottle and a hand mirror, Gwendolyn smiled at the girl; what Gwendolyn had intended as a small offer of reassurance was met with a look of such stark terror that Gwendolyn nearly asked the child what was scaring her so. Before she could mouth the words, though, Elizabeth opened the container the servant had left and Gwendolyn watched with interest as the Countess poured something into her hand, then reached up and smeared it on her face. Thick, dark liquid dripped through the woman's fingers and ran down her wrist, staining her robe and filling the room with a vaguely familiar scent.

Gwendolyn could silence her curiosity no longer. "What is that?" she asked. "What does it do to your face?"

Countess Báthory turned towards her and Gwendolyn jerked when she realized the concoction spread upon the woman's skin was a deep, glistening red. Elizabeth's smile in the darkened oval of her face was truly startling and her tongue ran wetly over her lips, seeking stray droplets of the red liquid. "Why, it's a moisturizing potion, Gwendolyn. My own secret mixture. It makes the skin young again." She offered the bottle to Gwendolyn with scarlet fingers. "Would you like to try it?"

Gwendolyn squelched the urge to pull back and shook her head, unable to imagine that thick, viscid liquid covering her face. "Thank you, no. I have my own youth cream."

Elizabeth shrugged. "As you wish. My supply is running low anyway because of the journey—traveling makes procuring it difficult." She gave a low laugh. "Though I don't believe you'll ever find a potion such as mine." She lowered her face to the washbasin and began rinsing; instantly the water turned a muddy red.

"If you'll excuse me, Countess," Gwendolyn said, rising. "I would retire for a time. I've no appetite for further dining and feel the need for a short rest."

"A pity," said Elizabeth as she dried her face on a cloth, leaving a faint rust-colored shadow on the material. "Christopher will surely arrive at any time. But I'm certain he'll still be about later when you waken." She turned back to her mirror and inspected her face; the skin gleamed a gloriously healthy pink. "Rest well."

Gwendolyn curtseyed and fled to the corridor. The longer she was in the company of that woman, the more she was filled an unnamed dread; the thought of another hour in Elizabeth's chamber made her shudder. Her own chamber was still dark and silent except for a small fire but it provided an escape and she stretched out fully-clothed on the bed with relief; perhaps it was only her nerves and the last vestiges of the curious illness that had plagued her. An hour's nap would likely work a small miracle on her demeanor.

Gwendolyn awoke to full night and the sounds of Maida bustling around the room lighting candles and laying out evening dress for her mistress. A hearty fire burned and a small tray of food had been fetched should she find herself hungry later on. She noted with disappointment that Maida's pallet was no longer at the foot of her bed, clear indication that Christopher's warning was firm in the young girl's mind. Gwendolyn rose without comment and Maida came and took the comb, pulling it through Gwendolyn's thick hair thoughtfully with a gentle, regular stroke that almost put her back to sleep. She roused herself and Maida quickly helped her dress in what appeared to be one of her finest gowns, a deep blue brocade embroidered with sprigs of flowers and a white satin underskirt, then Maida slipped a ruby-colored knit cape trimmed in mink over Gwendolyn's shoulders to keep her from taking a chill. Beneath a veil as sheer as the one Elizabeth had worn earlier, Gwendolyn's over-abundance of hair was twisted into a long, ribboned tail around which Maida pinned glittering strands of small garnets and topazes. A matching golden necklace set with alternating garnets and topazes fastened around her neck. Gwendolyn noted with annoyance that once again she had misplaced her family dagger—perhaps she'd left it on the table at the midday meal. In a sudden, furtive movement, Maida leaned forward and dropped something cool and round in the cleavage of Gwendolyn's breasts— prayer beads? She arched her neck to try and see.

"What—"

Her servant cut her question short by reaching forward and briskly pinching Gwendolyn's cheeks to bring some color into her face. "There," Maida said with satisfaction as she eyed her fully dressed mistress. "I don't think I've ever seen you more beautiful—not that you don't look such every day," she added hastily.

"She does look stunning, doesn't she?" The Countess's confident voice rang clearly in the night-quiet of the chamber. "I can see why my uncle speaks of little else in his letters."

Gwendolyn found the idea that Christopher thought of her at all slightly ludicrous and she raised her eyebrows. "Indeed? I was unaware that he spoke of his...*charge* to anyone at all." Her mettle was already rising in preparation for Christopher's visit, which she felt sure would happen at any moment. If he had thought banishing Maida from her chamber would grant them a night alone, he should have checked the castle records—they would have verified his niece's arrival. Tonight it was *Christopher's* smug countenance that would be shaken, not hers.

"Oh, yes!" Elizabeth said, sweeping into the room with a shake of her satin-trimmed wool skirts and perching on the edge of Gwendolyn's bed. The vivid purple gown she wore deepened her eyes to black—or had they always been so?—and cast sensual bluish shadows along her neck and cheekbones. "His letters are rambling tributes of love—he moans like a lovesick soldier of the time when the two of you can be...joined." She smiled, full lips shining. "But enough—I'm sure he speaks of his love all the time." Her eyelids lowered slightly and Gwendolyn suddenly felt as if she were being examined by the castle surgeon. "The color of that cape is excellent on you, Gwendolyn. It's my favorite—red is so *rich*, don't you agree?"

Gwendolyn opened her mouth to reply but Maida's timid voice interrupted her. "My lady? I really must go. Lord Christopher..." Her voice faded away uncertainly.

"Of course," Gwendolyn said. "You may leave."

As if noticing the servant girl for the first time, Countess Báthory sat up. "Leave? But why—if your mistress has no further need of you, then you should stay and attend to me, child. I fear my ladies have retired for the night."

Warning bells began to ring—shriek, actually—in Gwendolyn's mind and she saw Maida swallow as the Countess's eyes traced the girl's sun-kissed cheeks, her neck, and finally lingered on the small swell of Maida's breasts showing above her bodice. Elizabeth's tongue flicked over her lips in the same manner as it had earlier when she'd sought the taste of that foul-looking youth potion smeared on her face, and Gwendolyn had the sudden, unshakable image of one of the huge and vicious castle cats cleaning the blood from its mouth after a kill.

Gwendolyn rose and took Maida's arm decisively. "I'm afraid that's impossible, Elizabeth," she said firmly as she steered Maida to the door. "Lord Christopher had a fit of temper last evening and banished the girl from the castle during the night hours. Besides, I'd given her my permission to visit her relatives and she's already past her appointed arrival. No doubt her family will come looking for her if she doesn't arrive within the half hour." Gwendolyn smiled sweetly, ignoring the Countess's black look. "A noblewoman must never break her promise—even to a servant." She nearly pushed Maida out, placing herself between the Countess and the door; her pulse was suddenly throbbing in fear and anticipation.

But the Countess made no attempt to follow Maida as she ducked out. Instead, she fixed her gaze on Gwendolyn and sighed plaintively. "Well then, perhaps you can help me with my evening ministrations." She rose and stepped to the hearth, stretching slender hands towards the flames. "I've never been good at performing those tasks alone, but I'd hate to wake one of my women. The hour grows late and I'm beginning to wonder if there isn't some validity in your belief that Christopher has utterly forgotten me tonight."

With Maida safely out of the room, Gwendolyn felt herself relaxing again. "I'm sure he'll not abandon us entirely. If he passes through the hall he cannot help but see there's been a celebration and remember your visit. If you prefer, we can wait there, where we might see him that much sooner."

"Actually, I like your chamber much better. It's much more...comfortable, don't you think?" The Countess smiled engagingly. "I've always been one to cherish private moments, especially when getting to know someone new."

Gwendolyn looked at her warily. What games did the Countess play now? "There's plenty of time to further our acquaintance, I'm sure. It might be more proper to greet my lord in someplace other than a bedchamber."

Delighted, Elizabeth laughed. "Oh, I'm sure he won't mind! That is— if he's coming at all." Elizabeth paced the room idly, poking a careless finger into Gwendolyn's jewel chest before stopping in front of Gwendolyn and gazing at her. "You really are quite beautiful," she breathed. "And so young and... healthy." The Countess's cool fingers brushed at a wisp of honey–colored hair that had already escaped the confines of Maida's weaving, then dropped to the skin of the younger woman's shoulder.

Gwendolyn flinched and stepped back involuntarily as Elizabeth eased closer, then suddenly pressed against her. Appalled, she turned to flee but found Elizabeth had trapped her—the bed blocked her path to the door. She hesitated and in that instant the older woman's ringed hand dropped to her breast and squeezed as her other hand motioned invitingly to the bed's soft coverlets.

"You act educated, but I wonder if you *really* know how to please your Lord Christopher," Countess Báthory purred. "Perhaps you'd like me to teach you." Incredibly, the older woman began to paw at Gwendolyn's skirts.

Bile rose in Gwendolyn's throat. "Countess, please—" She blocked the Countess's questing fingers with one hand while planting the other against Elizabeth's shoulder in an attempt to thrust her away. "You are mistaken, I have no such inclination!"

The woman's fist lashed across Gwendolyn's face and in her shock Gwendolyn tripped and fell atop the bed. Temper and angry words were one thing but an outright brawl something else again! Gwendolyn tried to scramble away, but the Countess grabbed her shoulders and wrenched her around, and in another moment she'd thrown herself forward and pinned Gwendolyn in place. Gwendolyn felt a sharp prick and the coldness of steel against her throat; a gilded dagger had appeared from a pocket in Elizabeth's cape and now dug sharply into the line of her jaw just beneath her chin.

"A shame, Lady Gwendolyn. I could have taught you things that would bring my uncle great pleasure—even in his poor state." Fear made Gwendolyn lurch under the woman's weight, then cry out as the dagger's edge pierced her skin. "Don't...move," Elizabeth panted. "Not yet—what a waste it would be to give you to Christopher, and simply to satisfy his appetite! I can think of a use far more fitting." She bent her head and for one nauseating moment Gwendolyn thought the Countess was going to kiss her; dagger or not, she vowed she would use her teeth to tear the woman's lips off.

But the Countess only shifted her position on Gwendolyn's fear–frozen body, sliding the blade threateningly down to a point just above the younger woman's pounding heart and staying the protest that would have spilled from her victim's mouth. She rubbed her cheek delicately against Gwendolyn's, then nuzzled her ear. Gwendolyn's pulse beat harshly and her lungs hitched, stealing her strength. "Shall I tell you what the secret ingredient is in my potion, my dear?" Elizabeth whispered. The woman's breath was warm on her cheek but smelled oddly of fresh meat, and Gwendolyn was afraid to move, afraid the dagger would slash the skin above her breast and permanently disfigure her.

I have saved Maida from this devilwoman, Gwendolyn thought in a panic. *Now who will save me?*

"Elizabeth, it's so good to see you!" Elizabeth's head whipped towards the door as Christopher's silken voice coiled around them and he strode into the room. "Though I fear you give my bride-to-be worse frights than I could have ever conceived. I must admit it disappoints me that you would treat my betrothed so poorly." In an instant he had plucked the gilded dagger from his niece's grip and buried it within the folds of his cloak. Then he pulled Elizabeth from the bed and set her on her feet, his fingers digging cruelly into the flesh of the Countess's arm. "I am ashamed to say that occupied as I was with other matters of...ah, business, the event of your arrival completely slipped my thoughts." He released her and bowed, then carried on as if nothing at all were amiss. "Today marks your birthday, does it not?" He smiled at them both and his eyes followed Gwendolyn as she sat up gratefully and retreated to the bench near the fire. "In spite of my anger at your misbehavior—or should I say to curb it?—I have brought you a gift." He brought a fair-sized bottle of glazed glass from the folds of his black cape and held it aloft; the firelight glimmered cheerfully on its red surface. "You realize, of course, that I have always known the 'secret' of your precious moisture potion. I have taken the liberty of procuring some solely for your birthday. I assure you it comes from only the finest of ingredients, the likes of which it is doubtful you would be able to obtain on your own."

Gwendolyn watched numbly as Countess Báthory gasped in pleasure and reached for the bottle with eager fingers. Christopher grinned darkly and held it higher, just out of her reach. She glanced at him impatiently, then froze as their gazes locked.

"I am sorely displeased with your treatment of Lady Gwendolyn, niece," he said in a low voice. Elizabeth hesitated, then clasped her hands nervously, unable to look away. "I had thought it was clear that Gwendolyn was mine and not to be...*touched*...by any other." His eyes were like pits of burned cinders that seemed to sear the Countess, and she shuddered and turned toward Gwendolyn. Incredibly, she dropped to her knees within the circle of her magnificent gown and inclined her head.

"Lady Gwendolyn, please forgive my loss of control," she said humbly. "My desires are...strong, and I fear at times they overcome my common sense. I beg your pardon most sincerely."

The sincerity Gwendolyn knew came from Elizabeth's dread of Christopher's punishment, and hearing the woman's honeyed words made her skin crawl almost as much as the memory of that bejewelled hand on her breast. Forgiveness on Gwendolyn's part was forced through clenched teeth and only to remove the woman from her presence. "Of course, Countess Báthory. It is of no consequence."

Elizabeth rose without further comment and returned to stand before her uncle. He held out his gift and she smiled like a beautiful young child and reached for it; as her fingers touched the glass, Christopher spoke again.

"Look at me, Elizabeth."

Her chin jerked up as though her uncle had pulled a puppet's string. Strange lights danced within his stare and Elizabeth's smile faded.

"You understand, of course, that this will not happen again."

The Countess nodded stiffly. Christopher pressed his gift into Elizabeth's palm and folded her hand around it.

"Then enjoy. But I think it would be best if you returned to Castle Csethje early tomorrow. You would find a repeat of tonight's little—what shall we call it? Sport, perhaps—most unpleasant." The last of his words came out in a hiss as he released her hand and propelled her towards the door. The Countess momentarily turned back to Gwendolyn and stared blankly at a point just above her head.

"Lady Gwendolyn, I assure you it was my good fortune to have made your acquaintance," Elizabeth said woodenly. "Pressing business bids me return to my home and makes it impossible to continue my visit. We will be gone at first light and I must therefore make my farewells now. I look forward to when we meet again, and wish you good eve." Thoroughly bemused, Gwendolyn watched as Countess Báthory curtseyed deeply and turned away. Life seemed to finally return to Elizabeth's pale form only as she brought the glazed bottle up and rubbed it against her cheek in a feline, epicurean movement; with a soft brush of fabric, she slipped out of the chamber and was gone.

"A narrow skirmish with death by the family dagger!" Christopher's low chuckle sounded in her ears and Gwendolyn smoothed the rumpled skirt of her gown and eyed him in irritation as he continued. "Does it not make your blood sing in praise of your rescuer?"

"Praise!" she flared. "Had you been with me in the great hall today, that dreadful scene most likely would never have occurred. You are a shoddy host indeed, Christopher Báthory, and have caused me no end of embarrassment in the eyes of your niece—speaking of whom, using the word 'mad' to describe that woman would be doing her a kindness. There are times I loathe the very sight of you!"

"Oh, really," Christopher said in amusement as he sat beside her on the bench. Gwendolyn balled her fists against the sudden urge to slap him. "I see you have yet to regain your full wits or you would surely remember that it is impossible for me to join you during the day. And 'mad' would truly be a kindness if used to describe Elizabeth—the word murderess would be far more correct. I should think that for once you'd be quite appreciative of my appearance."

"What!" Gwendolyn gasped. The ugly feeling of the Countess's cold blade pressing against her chest winked in her mind. "Murderess!"

Christopher slipped an arm about her shoulders, his cold fingers playing along her collarbone like little swirls of ice. "It's hard to believe you're so addle-brained you don't realize that her mysterious moisture potion is nothing but human blood which she obtains from scores of serving maids, virgins if those two women she employs can get their hands on any. As Elizabeth told you, her desires are strong—after forcing them to satisfy her lust, she tortures and slaughters them like so much cattle."

"Maida!" Gwendolyn cried and leaped to her feet.

"She's fine," Christopher assured her soothingly as he pulled her back down beside him. "I saw her fleeing the castle a few minutes before Elizabeth decided you were her next fountain of youth. Knowing how fond you are of the twit, I took the liberty of following her to assure she reached her home safely."

"You...followed her?" Gwendolyn regarded Christopher doubtfully and he threw up his hands.

"You have my word—I never touched her. She was not even aware of me behind her on the path. Besides," he said, settling back. "Her father is a crusty old sot. Had his daughter not returned by now, he would be beating at the castle doors, caring little for his own safety."

Gwendolyn relaxed a bit. She dared not think about Christopher's claims about his niece, but if memory served her correctly, he was telling the truth about Maida's sire; there was also the matter of her beau, the young Ferenc. Surely he too would keep an eye on the girl. *What is it*, she wondered, *that made her fear for the girl's life in this abominable castle?*

"Why me, of course," Christopher said softly.

Gwendolyn looked at him in confusion, then stiffened. Had she voiced her thoughts aloud?

Christopher drew her to him on the bench. "But why do you fear me, sweet Gwendolyn?" he breathed in her ear. "My only desire is to have you at my side for eternity. Yet you would slip from my grasp at the very moment I thought I had succeeded."

She tried to pull away but he pushed his fingers through the coil of her hair and cupped her head, lowering his lips to hers in a cold, sweet kiss. She shuddered under his touch but felt herself responding as his other hand slipped over the cloth covering her breast and rested on her hip; his touch left trails of frost yet his kiss and nearness fed a quickly building fire within her. She moaned and opened her mouth to admit his searching tongue; even as her arms slipped under his cape and around his back of their own will, she struggled to end this illicit meeting.

"Christopher," she pleaded in a small voice as his mouth moved from her lips to her neck, "you must stop—it's wrong to seduce me before vows bind us."

He brought his head up and caught her with his eyes; finally Gwendolyn understood her instinctive reluctance to meet his gaze. She felt instantly as if she were drowning, sinking with him into some cold, deep well filled with dark and irresistible promises of sexual ecstasy. Her eyes fluttered closed as all resistance fled.

"My sweet," he murmured. His voice was a soothing caress, a balm to her screaming senses. "It's a sad thing that the memory—our memory—still eludes you. Despite the vows that will never be, we have loved before and will yet again." Strength faded from her hands and they dropped from his back; she felt like a feather cradled in his strong embrace. His lips lingered on the skin of her neck as he leaned her against him and slid frigid fingers under the fabric of her gown to stroke her breast.

Pain suddenly blazed between her breasts and Christopher flung her away with a howl. Dazed and ripping frantically at the smoking fabric of her dress, Gwendolyn crumpled to the floor and finally succeeded in tearing the blackened shreds of cloth away from her singed chest. A star of pink, blistered skin fanned from her cleavage upwards, like a small, shattered sea shell.

"*Damnation!*" he screamed. Agony twisted the charred fingers of his hand as he whirled about the room, his wild eyes reflecting the flames from the fireplace as they flared momentarily. "*Where the devil did you get that—that THING? Tell me!*"

"Christopher, what's wrong? What thing?" Gwendolyn wailed. She snatched a wet cloth from the washstand and dabbed gingerly at the burn. "What are you *talking* about?"

"Those damnable *beads*—where did they come from?"

The candlelight was flickering wildly from his frenzied strides about the chamber. He gnashed his teeth and she realized with a start that they seemed overlong in the jumping shadows. She looked again at the burnt fabric and tender skin along the swell of her breasts in bewilderment; there, in charred bits, was the remains of Maida's prayer beads with its small, soot-covered crucifix.

"Well, I—"

"Never mind!" Still holding his injured fingers, Christopher stumbled heavily to the doorway. "No doubt they're a gift from that twittering serving girl. Dispose of them, and never bring such things into my presence again. Had I known about them, that cursed Maida would never have survived the night!"

"Don't you dare say such a thing!" Gwendolyn spat, gathering the ripped pieces of her clothes together and pulling herself straight. "Why would you threaten her? And why should a simple thing such as holy beads injure you so badly?"

"Do not tax me on this, Gwendolyn," he snarled. "I've lost the mood for chivalry and romance, and am sorely tempted to jar your lost memory in a most startling manner!"

Christopher's eyes blazed and Gwendolyn involuntarily stepped back; how quickly her passion for this strange nobleman turned to dread now that his hands were at his side instead of on her body. Inwardly she railed at herself for being such a coward; still, common sense made her keep silent and turn a stiff back to him, though doing so made her feel utterly defenseless. The hair at the nape of her neck raised eerily, as if an unseen evil touched her with its gaze.

"As you wish." Gwendolyn reply was cold and clipped.

She realized she was alone.

✳   ✳   ✳

It seemed to Gwendolyn that if she wasn't destined to wake in pain, her lot was cast to rise feeling as if not the least bit of rest had been given her weary body. Though she felt generally stronger since awakening to this strange castle three days ago, the nightly scenes with Lord Christopher—and especially Countess Báthory's presence—had done little to hasten her recovery. This morning had again found no fire on the heart,h or wash water and day clothes laid out for her morning toilet. Loathe to extinguish them the night before and seek sleep in the unrelieved blackness, the six tallow candles in her chamber had long burned themselves out. Full dawn was almost upon Castle Báthory, yet there was still no sign of Maida, and Gwendolyn felt her stomach twist in apprehension—had Christopher been lying when he'd claimed to have seen her safely home? Or had anger guided him last night and was the servant girl's poor body cold and covered with dew in some muddy gulch at this very hour?

"My lady?" Gwendolyn turned her head to see a young girl standing timidly in the entryway, washing cloths and a basin of fresh water balanced precariously in her thin arms. "May I enter and help you rise?"

"Of course." Gwendolyn sat on the edge of the bed and watched as the girl set the basin and clothing down, then searched through one of the chests for suitable attire in which to dress her mistress. "I don't remember seeing you before," Gwendolyn said at last. "What is your name?"

The girl, a tiny thing who couldn't be more than twelve years old, approached her shyly. "I am Klara, my lady." Klara's gaze dropped to the floor and Gwendolyn caught a desperate tone in her voice. "I hope you won't be offended that my mother has sent me to you without warning. I promise you I've been taught well in the ways in which to service you."

Gwendolyn sighed. If she sent Klara away and demanded Maida's return, it would be assumed the girl had either irritated her or performed poorly and Klara's back would probably be lashed—the same fate was likely even if she requested Maida to help train the child further. She was desperate to know Maida's whereabouts, but not at the cost of scars upon this child's back. "I'm sure you'll be fine," she said.

Klara smiled in relief and started combing Gwendolyn's hair, commenting in awe on the shining tresses. Although she was thorough, her inexperienced fingers lacked Maida's gentle touch; several times Gwendolyn bit back a sharp remark when her hair was tugged.

"Leave it loose," Gwendolyn said hastily when the girl approached with pins in hand. She couldn't bear the thought of Klara's clumsy fingers pushing hairpins against her unprotected scalp. "Tell me," Gwendolyn said as casually as she could, "where is Maida, the serving girl who usually assists me?"

"Have I displeased you?" Klara asked anxiously. Her fingers nearly lost their grip on the hairpins she was putting aside.

"No, of course not," Gwendolyn assured her. "Maida was to...run an errand—fetch something for me. That's why I expected her back this morning. Perhaps you could send someone to find her so that I might speak to her."

"Yes, Lady Gwendolyn." Klara curtseyed and turned away, but not fast enough to hide the mist of tears. Clearly the girl thought she was being dismissed.

"I will expect you back here within a quarter-hour to finish helping me dress," she said firmly. "It should take no longer than that for you to assign this task to a squire."

"Yes, my lady!" Klara said brightly and hurried out, most of the nervousness leaving her childish features. Gwendolyn nodded in satisfaction; it was highly unlikely the girl's mother would find time to have her whipped in so short a time, and the woman would dare not delay her daughter to mete out unjustified punishment. Besides, that she demanded Klara's immediate return should indicate well enough her acceptance of the girl.

A short while later Klara was back, Ferenc in tow. "Begging your leave, Lady Gwendolyn. I've brought Sir Ferenc to tell you of Maida's whereabouts." The young man stood uncertainly outside the bedchamber, painfully aware that his mistress was dressed only in her morning robe. After a few awkward seconds, he decided the ceiling was the best place for him to stare.

"Good morning, Ferenc," Gwendolyn said. "And where is Maida this morning? Is she well? Klara serves me capably, but I had expected no new maidservant."

"She is fine, my lady. I spoke with her father earlier; it seems Lord Christopher visited him last night and bade him send Maida and her brother to the village for supplies for the buttery." He risked a sly glance at Gwendolyn. "Maida's sire says he hinted at a wedding feast."

"Oh?" said Gwendolyn. She tried, but the thought of weddings and vows no longer held any joy for her. The change in attitude was inexplicable. "And when are they expected to return?"

"Not until mid–morrow," he replied. "It's doubtful they will reach their destination before noon today. They will need to stay overnight before making the trip back to Báthory."

"I see," she said. "I wasn't aware of Christopher's instructions." She turned away, then realized he was still waiting by the entry. "That will be all," she said in a voice sharper than she had intended. Ferenc inclined his head respectfully and made his exit.

Klara cleared her throat softly. "You mentioned an errand that Maida was to have run for you," she ventured. Her young face was expectant as she stepped forward with Gwendolyn's day clothes ready. "Perhaps I can perform this task?"

Gwendolyn pulled her gaze from the fireplace; on the fringe of the ashes she could see the ruins of Maida's prayer beads where she had tossed them last night. When Gwendolyn looked at the girl, her expression was thoughtful. "Yes," she said slowly. "I think you can at that."

Klara drew herself up, proud to be trusted with the task. "What is it you wish me to do, mistress?"

Gwendolyn drew a small purse from the jewel chest and dug out a coin. She handed it to the girl, who carefully tucked it into her bodice. "After I dress, I want you to find the friar and offer this coin as a donation from me. When he asks what he can do to repay my kindness, tell him I request that he send me a set of…prayer beads. *Blessed* prayer beads."

As Klara moved to help Gwendolyn don her ruff and jewelry, neither of them heard Sir Ferenc's quiet step take him away from his listening post outside the chamber.

✳   ✳   ✳

Gwendolyn inspected the modest gift the friar had sent back. She turned the string in her hands, watching the play of firelight reflect on the dark, oiled beads. Night came on quick steps, and as she had expected the castle was rapidly emptying; black memories of the time before her awareness turned like some huge, unspeakable creature in her mind, and Gwendolyn couldn't stop the tremors that crawled across her back. The beads she fingered offered not nearly the comfort she had hoped. What could they really do but anger the monster in man-form to whom she was betrothed? Today's thick sunshine had fled far too soon for Gwendolyn's liking and already Klara had helped Gwendolyn into evening dress and made her excuses for the night, lighting almost a dozen candles at Gwendolyn's request before departing. She would have lamented her disquiet—had there been another soul in the castle to hear.

Gwendolyn had no choice but to wait. Not even the option of flight was hers, for she was as ignorant of the Hungarian countryside around her as she was of the real reason behind the unease that gathered in her soul at the thought of Lord Christopher, and besides, there was no lackey or groom to saddle and guide a mount and venturing beyond the castle walls on foot was suicide. The wolves which roamed the wild countryside were as legendary and vicious as the tales the gypsies spun around their midnight campfires.

But, Gwendolyn wondered, what was the *true* difference if she surrendered to Christopher Báthory? She had already traded eternity for the privilege, however doubtful it might seem, of even existing here, now, in this very *space*. To follow Christopher's path might lead to damnation—but of what sort? The hours dragged as she pondered this mind-twisting question, the night growing older without the slightest indication that Christopher would come; at length Gwendolyn's lids grew heavy and she moved to the bed, folding the coverlet at its head and leaning back. Already the candles were half gone and sleepiness made Gwendolyn optimistic—perhaps Christopher had changed his mind, or found other business that needed his attention tonight. As the tallow burned ever lower, Gwendolyn's eyes finally closed and the prayer beads slipped from her fingers to form a small wooden puddle on the bedcovers as she slept.

※   ※   ※

In the corridor outside the chamber, a shadowed form motioned brusquely to his man-at-arms. In the space of a few breaths, Sir Ferenc eased silently to Gwendolyn's bedside and plucked the holy string from beside her skirt, offering a silent plea for forgiveness. In the hall, his lord turned his face away as the young soldier hurried past and made his way free of the castle, his breath a bitter mix of shame and relief.

※   ※   ※

"I've brought you a present." Christopher's deep voice jarred Gwendolyn awake and she sat up awkwardly, fingers making an alarmed and useless scramble for the friar's blessed beads. Her betrothed stood next to the bed, looking down at her with an unreadable expression in his fathomless black eyes. "You seem so taken with necklaces of late that I thought I would replace the one that was…ruined last evening." Gwendolyn could think of no good reason to refuse when he offered a hand to help her to her feet and lead her to the warmth of the fireplace.

"Forgive me. I meant to greet you properly when you arrived," Gwendolyn said hoarsely. Her eyes searched the dark floor frantically.

Christopher's gaze at her was knowing but his dark hair fell across his eyes before his dangerous stare could trap hers. "I'm sure you did, Gwendolyn. But see here—" He stepped behind her and something flashed in front of her vision momentarily, sweeping past her head and face to rest chilled and heavy along the crest of her collarbone above the rounded neckline of her evening gown. She felt Christopher's fingers—always so cold!—working at a clasp at the nape of her neck beneath the thick curtain of her unbound hair. Gwendolyn's trepidation grew when she heard the click of the latch as it caught and Christopher's hands dropped easily to her shoulders; to disguise her fear she pressed her chin awkwardly against her chest as she strained to see his gift. Even at this angle, she could view a wide necklace of woven gold and rubies spreading across her chest like a strange, intertwined metal ruff, the myriad chains glittering like sun-sparkled water dripping along a spider web. Every chain ultimately joined to a heavy circlet of gold in the center of the necklace in which three sharp ivory spears had been set.

"It's…lovely, Christopher." And indeed there *was* a deep and terrible beauty about the piece, all centering, she suddenly realized, in the ivory that represented wolves' teeth. "It's your family crest, isn't it?"

She sensed his toothy smile before he turned her to face him. "Yes, Gwendolyn. The Báthory family crest, and adorning your neck is my mother's own necklace—the same one that my father gave her on their wedding night." His arm encircled her waist and he pulled her close. "My wedding gift to you."

Gwendolyn leaned away, avoiding his eyes; when she found her voice it a had a faraway ringing quality, like weakening church bells. "A fine and generous wedding gift, but a little premature as we've yet to take our vows, don't you think?" She felt oddly numb; still, she managed to rearrange her mouth into a frown as she remembered something Christopher had said the night before. "But what was it you said last night—something about the vows will never be spoken? What did you mean?"

Undisturbed by her reluctance, Christopher pulled her back against the hard bones of his chest; Gwendolyn found she could no longer escape the hypnotism of his stare. "Vows? We need not voice our love with mere words in front of those who would turn to dust even as our youth shines eternal." The chill that continually seeped from his skin was a mockery as his body moved sinuously against her and coaxed a familiar heat from her depths, intensifying as his hips pressed against hers through the satin material of her gown; arguments were discarded as quickly as they flared in the whirling chaos of her thoughts and she had no voice with which to protest as he lowered her to the bed. Her skin was on fire and his ice-tipped hands were everywhere, cooling and making her tremble at the same time, igniting more flames than his glacial touch could extinguish.

Still Gwendolyn tried to resist, raining weak, futile slaps along his head and shoulders as he kissed the skin along her neck and collarbone. "No, Christopher! It's not right—"

"Who is to tell us what is right?" he murmured. An involuntary groan escaped as Christopher twined the fingers of one hand through her hair while the other pulled at her clothing and easily found its way past the buttons along her back and hips. His eyes raked her bared skin appreciatively, taking in the full breasts and gentle curves, lingering on the golden thatch of soft hair that guarded the entrance to her womanhood. She blushed and pulled at the covers but he stopped her with a deep kiss that sent forbidden promises reeling in her blood and made her reach instead to touch him, to feel the play of muscles beneath his shirt. In the next few moments he had shed his own attire and lain beside her, his chilly, rigid skin soaking up her precious warmth like a huge, thirsty sponge, his coloring so pale next to her healthy pinkness. His tongue trailed down her breasts and over a nipple, then snaked down her belly. To Gwendolyn's shame, her treacherous body arched to meet his searching mouth.

"Let me show you the *true* meaning of love, sweet Gwendolyn," Christopher whispered as he reached to cup her breasts. "The ultimate and *eternal* sharing of life between a man and woman." His teeth and tongue found a new area and pleasure exploded within her; Gwendolyn cried out and her fingers clutched at the dark mass of his hair on her stomach. Gasping for breath, she could only watch as he raised himself; her thighs opened with no resistance as he knelt between them. Terror bloomed suddenly, a huge and black abyss within her mind, and she whimpered and tried to pull away, but too late—his weight easily held her to the mattress.

"My love, why do you always fight me?" His white face floated above hers and his lips stretched to reveal strong, sharp teeth. "Have I not pleasured you, shown you more about your body in the last few moments than you ever dreamed?" He reached behind her back and lifted her shoulders with one massive hand. "You are *mine*, Gwendolyn," he hissed fiercely; the breath he drew to speak the words felt like a January wind against her ear. "Our vows will be sealed by blood, not some foolish, blithering priest. Nor will my desire for you be thwarted by another woman's bargain with the devil!"

In spite of the rolling fear that numbed her tongue and the horrible knowledge that he'd known who she was—*really* was, in her soul—Gwendolyn's body received Christopher's entering thrust with ease. His manhood was freezing inside her and as he began to move more quickly Gwendolyn felt as if she might be torn in two by some giant knife forged of ice.

"Cold," she whimpered. Still her arms crept around his thick chest to pull him closer, deeper. Would she ever be warm again?

"That's doubtful, dear one." Christopher's voice rumbled in her ear as he pushed aside the tangle of her hair and licked her neck where an artery pulsed just beneath the skin. "I fear it is not our destiny to be so."

Gwendolyn's eyes widened in shock as Christopher smiled at her, full and finally uninhibited, wolfen incisors glistening with pearly beauty. Before she could scream and with a viper's speed, his teeth sank deep. He drank at the same time a shared orgasm united them in sweet, shuddering agony.

The dark and freezing melody of an eternal winter chased away the mellow Hungarian spring night and Gwendolyn followed willingly into blackness.

CHAPTER V
1585

Awareness was instantaneous. There was none of the expected pain or any leftover sleepiness pulling at her with heavy, enticing arms, just an overwhelming feeling of disorientation and a slight brush of hunger deep within her belly. While she did not know *where* she was, she did take a little comfort in the spontaneous realization that she was still Gwendolyn of Báthory.

But the question of her location was more serious. A twist of her head showed nearly everything around her was steeped in a cold blackness that yawned nearly out of sight, yet despite the lack of illumination, Gwendolyn's eyes were able to pick out the closest details around her as she looked for an exit; a narrow rise of rough-hewn stairs at the far end of the cavernous room caught her attention.

She seemed to be lying on some sort of stone bench and she sat up, pulling away the coverings wrapped around her. Had she gone down here to sleep? Why would she do such a ridiculous thing? She couldn't recall and she frowned impatiently—another mind-taxing empty spot, one more in the thousands apparently fashioned just to infuriate her over the ages. She swung her legs down and shivered as her feet touched the floor; if a servant or one of Christopher's men-at-arms had thought it funny to place Gwendolyn in the castle dungeon while she slept, she'd see how amusing they found fifty lashes of the whip. Worst still would be Christopher's price for allowing such a travesty to occur in the first place. Rusted iron chains hung here and there along the rough stone walls, backed by sinister stains in shapes that seemed to move each time her gaze slid past to the huge devices of wood and iron and leather that squatted close by. The smell of the place was musty and thick, and vaguely…red. Something brushed her ankle and broke her train of thought; Gwendolyn looked down and even in the lightless room she could see the rat that rubbed her ankle like an affectionate, filth-encrusted cat. She grimaced and kicked it away without fear as she made for the staircase.

When Gwendolyn pushed through the door at the top of the stairs, she found herself in the rear of the buttery, a small room tucked off a corner of the tower which she seldom visited; there were few candles lit here and finding her way to the great hall in the dimness with her thoughts engaged on other matters was like wandering through a maze. When Gwendolyn finally stepped into the hall, it was to yet another evening-deserted room, though the high windows showed the last vestiges of daylight still lingering among the growing night echoes. It was odd that she could have slept for so long in such a brutally uncomfortable place as the horrible rooms below, but night was surely coming and as usual there was not a single servant to be found. Still, her ears picked up furtive sounds from the chambers above and she sought them, climbing the steep stairs with ease.

Gwendolyn's bedchamber was dark, but tidy and deserted, her clothes still hung neatly on pegs and the wash basin clean and dry. Unlit logs had been placed in the fireplace and Gwendolyn returned briefly to the corridor for a rushlight with which to start a fire—the chamber was damp and chilly, and the thought of warmth on her skin brought a smile to her lips. While the flames grew strong she found a half dozen candles and lit them around the room to further dispel the gloom.

When at last there was a semblance of light in the chamber Gwendolyn could finally see more than just a shadow of herself. Disbelieving, her throat closed as she looked down; the white gown that she wore was covered with filth and grime, and rat droppings clung stickily within its folds. The mass of yellow hair hanging over her shoulders was matted and dull, and when she reached to touch it, she realized with horror that dirt had caked under her fingernails. Shuddering, faintly nauseous, Gwendolyn hurried downstairs and drew water to wash, then returned to shed the filthy rags and throw them on the hot logs, watching in approval as they burst into flames. The water was frigid but Gwendolyn had no patience to warm it and she washed anyway, clenching her jaw against the temperature as the muck on her body peeled away like dead snake skin. She tried to remove the leaden weight of the Báthory necklace but found she couldn't work the clasp; the best she could do was wipe at it with a wet cloth.

That done, Gwendolyn found a clean but simple black gown and coat and dressed, then returned downstairs yet again to dump the filth-laden water. She brought more water upstairs and doused her head, feeling her body tremble as the frigid water soaked her hair and touched her scalp. The fire rapidly warmed the air around her but seemed unable to chase away the deep-bone chill Gwendolyn felt; as she sat before the fire and struggled to comb the tangles from her abundant hair with little success, she suddenly felt like crying.

Where *was* everyone—*any*one? She felt so bleak and hopeless, she would welcome even Christopher's presence. Though she could feel the heat of the fire on her face, still she couldn't stop herself from shivering violently.

There was a stealthy sound behind her and she jerked around.

Face drained of color, Maida poised in the doorway and stared at her with dumbstruck horror.

"Maida," Gwendolyn said plaintively and held the comb toward the girl, "would you help me with my hair? It's become so entangled I'm unable to draw the comb through." Maida gave no response and simply stared at her. "What's wrong?" Gwendolyn asked. "What ails you?"

"My lady, you're—you're alive!" she breathed.

The shocked statement brought no irritation to Gwendolyn; instead she merely looked at Maida with a serene expression. "Must we replay this conversation every three days?" she chided. "Come, attend to my hair."

Maida stepped into the chamber reluctantly and nearly snatched the comb from Gwendolyn's fingers. "But Lady Gwendolyn, it's almost full dark. I must be on my way home." The serving girl's voice was shaking so hard her words were barely comprehensible.

"It will take you but a moment or two—you didn't arrange it or help me dress." Having the girl near her made her feel warmer; hunger sharpened in her stomach. "Do you know if there's food still out in the bailey? I'm famished."

Maida finished her task with unusually clumsy fingers and set the comb on the table, then edged back as Gwendolyn reached for the hand mirror. "I imagine so, mistress. I—"

Gwendolyn's scream cut off the girl's words as the mirror fell from Gwendolyn's fingers and clattered on the table's surface. "I can't see myself!" she wailed. "Why can't I see myself?"

"Vampir!" Maida whispered in terror. She would have run to the door had not Gwendolyn's hand whipped forward to grasp the folds of her skirt.

"What did you say?" Gwendolyn demanded angrily. "Vampire? Why would you call me such an evil thing?" Her gaze fell on the hand mirror and she released Maida abruptly and touched the metal back of the looking glass with trembling fingers. "Is that why I can no longer see my own reflection? Can such a thing really be?"

The girl gave no answer but slid fearfully along the wall and out of her reach. If she could just reach the door—

"Please," Gwendolyn said without looking at her. "Stay for just a moment. I swear I won't hurt you—have I ever?" she entreated. Trembling, Maida stopped and shook her head nervously. Gwendolyn pushed the mirror away a little fearfully, then pulled her hair over her shoulder and began braiding it herself. It was easy to see that her gaze made Maida even more nervous and she turned her eyes to the table, hoping the servant would relax enough to explain. "Tell me of this…creature you speak, and why you would believe I have become one."

"Because you're dead!" Maida blurted. Her hands slapped at her own mouth as if to stop the words, but more flew between her fingers. "You died three nights ago and they placed your body in the family tomb. I saw you lifeless with my own eyes."

"But that cannot be," Gwendolyn said sharply. "Look!" She rose and held up her hands, then opened and closed her fingers. "How can you say I'm dead when even now I stand before you and speak?"

"I don't know!" Maida cried. She cringed as Gwendolyn stepped toward her. "Please—I must go! All who live here know it's not safe to be on the castle grounds after dark!"

"And why is that, Maida?"

The girl shrieked and stumbled back into the chamber as Lord Christopher's dark form appeared in the entryway, making her careen around the room like a child's toy as she tried to avoid moving within reach of Gwendolyn. He gave a low laugh. "I wonder what legend could cause such a belief among my countrymen and my serfs." A few steps put him in front of Maida and the serving girl cowered and backed against a tapestry–covered wall, looking frantically at the deepening night beyond the window as a tiny sob escaped her lips. Christopher's grin deepened. "If you believe so firmly in these tales, my child, then what of your presence here? Perhaps you are willing to be your mistress's first——"

"Stop it!" Gwendolyn's voice was strong and clear. "There is no cause but your usual cruelty to frighten the girl. Let her return to her home."

Christopher stepped back, indicating the door with a flourish of his arms. "By all means, dear Gwendolyn, whatever is your wish." He looked at Maida and gave a lean smile. "You are free to leave, child. I would suggest you do so most quickly." In an instant, Maida had gone.

Christopher stared at her expectantly, then finally paced the room as Gwendolyn finished attending to her hair in stony silence. At last, he spoke.

"I see you look quite fit—I was concerned you would be confused and perhaps wander the countryside dressed in rags like some crazed beggarwoman. You seem to have coped quite well."

"Indeed," Gwendolyn hissed and slammed the comb on the tabletop a final time. "And no thanks to you—you monster. What evil thing of the devil have you forced upon my unwilling body?" Dark red lights danced in her once tawny eyes as she glared at him.

His voice rang out in mirth and she ground her teeth—he seemed to be forever laughing at her. "My ears surely deceive me." His dark brows raised in mimed innocence. "I thought I heard the word *unwilling*. If I forced myself upon you, what of the kisses that met mine so warmly? And the body that opened so willingly to me? An easier battle was never fought," he ended smugly.

Gwendolyn's cheeks went scarlet. "Easy, perhaps—but still unholy."

Christopher guffawed. "Holy! If that word burns my lips, it should sear the very skin from yours." His rugged face darkened. "Your bargain with the devil has cost me eternity with the only woman I ever truly loved—and one whom I waited years to be with. Now her soul rests peacefully where I cannot reach and you are bound to take her place, whether it pleases you to do so or not. If I cannot possess her in spirit, I must be content with her in form—and that form, my *love*, is you."

Gwendolyn gaped at him. "What do you mean, take her place?" She pounded a small fist upon the table. "You do not *own* me, you conceited lout! Find another to satisfy your evil appetite. I will leave this place anytime I wish."

"Really?" Christopher's brows arched. "Then perhaps we should pack your things—we'll start with the mirror." He snatched it up and pushed it in front of her face. "You should really examine your smile—*if you can*. It's grown quite…strong." She yanked her face aside and he threw the mirror to the floor. It shattered and he kicked the pieces away. "A strange feeling, isn't it?" he demanded. "To look and be unable to see yourself. And if you find it to your liking to venture beyond the castle walls, you will find a host of other oddities—like the sun, the merest hint of which will blacken the skin from your fine and beautiful bones—or the villagers, who though pleased to find work and wages at the castle during the day, unlike your faithful Maida would be more than happy to pound a piece of sharpened oak through your breast should they catch you at one of your weaker moments.

"You have so much to learn, dear Gwendolyn." Christopher spread his hands. "And I must admit I cannot understand your reluctance—was it not your own fondest wish to live at all costs? In your foolishness, you have made a pact that would see you cheated at every turn. Yet I have given you that precious thing which you desired most: eternal life." Something out of place flickered in his deep, dark eyes: hurt. "Yet still you scorn me."

"Eternal life!" Gwendolyn cried. "What kind of life is this so-called gift of yours? Why, you have stolen from me not only the ability to do the simplest of humanly tasks, but the right to just sit peacefully among other men and women. No longer can I walk outside and feel the warmth of a summer sun on my face as I gather flowers—instead I must fear the sun's rays as an instrument of my death. For the rest of my existence I will see loathing and terror on the faces of those I would ask to serve me, even those upon whom I would never place a harmful hand. Of all the different days and times I have walked this earth, I have yet to be granted the joy of childbirth and the feel of my own baby in my arms, and now you wrench the same from me forever and make of me a hated and hunted thing in the eyes of mankind."

In her rage, her inexpert plait had fallen free and now her hair tumbled around her in the candlelight like a shimmering cloak. Like his niece Elizabeth, though he supposed for different reasons, Christopher had developed a fondness for the color red and found the newly-fired scarlet lights in Gwendolyn's eyes intoxicating as they flashed amidst skin so white it was almost transparent.

"Don't you see, Gwendolyn?" he said pleadingly. "The things of which you speak are only minor inconveniences, doorways to a world that you no longer need. In a short time you will learn to do things you never dreamed possible—we can even *fly*, for pity's sake! In its own way, the night is just as beautiful as day, the moon just as enticing as the sun was once warm. Given a little time, I promise—you'll learn to love your new existence, and I'll take you by the hand every step. Besides," he shed his cape and leaned back on the bed as his expression turned smug. "You have no choice."

※ ※ ※

"I don't want you to come here anymore."

In the months that had followed her second awakening in Castle Báthory, Gwendolyn had been incorrect in her assessment of only one thing: Maida had never looked at her with hate. Fear, yes—but never had there been even a hint of the loathing she knew was hidden so poorly among those few of the other villagers whom she actually saw scurrying away in the twilight minutes preceding full darkness. Her serving girl seemed to have either some warped sense of loyalty that drove her to see to Gwendolyn's comfort upon her awakening each evening, or Maida surely held some wretched, unfulfilled desire for the danger which increased with each sunset.

Despite Christopher's reasoning, pleading, and finally fury, Gwendolyn would not feed.

Last evening her "husband" had brought her a child, a living, breathing infant kidnapped from his mother's arms by some filthy and greedy servant of Christopher's during the daytime hours. In his anger Christopher had not even stayed to argue, simply thrust the naked and squalling baby into Gwendolyn's arms and quit the chamber. Gwendolyn's skin glowed paler each evening, until the veins in her body were nothing but empty blue trails under a fragile alabaster shell, yet even the agony of starvation would not end her miserable existence. The mind was willing, but the flesh far too strong.

The hour had been late and Maida was long gone; unable to bear the fire of the baby's skin against hers, Gwendolyn wrapped the boychild in a double thickness of blanket and rocked him until he slept. The woolen blanket was useless, little besides wrapping on an enticing, forbidden package; within a quarter–hour Gwendolyn had become nearly mesmerized by the pulse of life in his tiny pink body and she dropped his swaddled form on the bed and beat on the stone walls in frustration. Arms empty as she pressed against the opposite wall of the room, she could hear and smell the blood that pumped through the infant's small, strong heart.

In a panic Gwendolyn had snatched the boy from atop her bed and run from the castle, feet carrying her quickly along a path heretofore forgotten until she stood in front of a small hut almost a mile away. Though she'd fled full speed the entire way, she was not even winded when she beat frantically on the door.

"Who's there?"

Maida's timid voice sent a spasm of relief through Gwendolyn's feverish thoughts. She heard Maida's father bellow not to open the door but the girl had thrown the bolt before he could stop her. Warm, cheerful light spilled from the hut and Gwendolyn's servant stood just inside the door, terror and pity warring in her eyes. Her sire, an old man of nearly four score years, yanked his daughter aside and bravely placed his own body between Gwendolyn and his offspring.

"Begone! You are not welcome in our home!" he cried, crossing himself. "My daughter does not serve you during the night hours, evil one."

His genuflection burned Gwendolyn's eyes and she ducked her head, then pushed her burden into the arms of the astonished man.

"Tell your daughter to return the child to his parents, though I know not who they are," she hissed at the old man. "He was…given to me."

Gwendolyn had run then, back to the relative safety of the castle and away from those who would so love to part her head from the despicable form into which her spirit had been trapped…though even as she ran, Gwendolyn truly didn't understand why she should still want to continue this painful, empty existence.

And tonight Gwendolyn sat, head in her hands and staring at the rough woodgrain table, doing little besides following the swirls and gouges with her eyes and memorizing their patterns, her mind a blank, hungry horror. Each night her body whispered to her with black dreams of release that brought her closer to surrender and tested her vow not to feed upon some poor, helpless person. Deep within her mind, the shreds of what had once been her conscience asked insidiously who would be her first victim when she succumbed—how could it not be that same young girl who so faithfully tended her?

"Did you hear me, Maida?" Gwendolyn demanded, her voice hoarse. "You are to be gone from this bedeviled place each day well before the sun sinks below the horizon." Gwendolyn purposely kept her gaze on the table, knowing how easy it would be to trap the girl with her eyes and doubting her ability to release Maida if it happened. "I can no longer trust myself around you. You must leave immediately."

Gwendolyn heard the rustle of cloth and something clanged softly as Maida set it down on the chest. "The boychild has been returned to his mother," Maida said carefully. "The woman sends you a gift in gratitude for the safe return of her son."

"I want nothing but for you to LEAVE!" The last word was almost a scream as Gwendolyn's fingers yanked at her own hair in an attempt to keep her mind on something other than the scent of blood she imagined was filling every corner of the chamber. She turned dreamily to face the girl but Maida was gone, her footsteps already echoing in the hall below. Dark longing filled Gwendolyn and she had a sudden mental image of how easy it would be for her to catch the servant girl and bring her back. And then what? Gwendolyn's fingernails dug deeply into her arms, each opening a bloodless gash in her white skin. Distracted for the moment, she withdrew her fingers and watched with detached interest as the cuts closed and mended within the space of a few moments.

Would Christopher come to her tonight? And if so, what horrible offering would he tempt her with this time? Gwendolyn wondered if it was that question which was making her mouth water and her nerves sing until she wanted to spin off the walls like some child's top. Even now she still smelled blood and her eyes swept the chamber like a caged animal—then stopped abruptly at the jewel chest by the bed.

A large chalice of beaten brass sat upon a snow-white square of linen; the dark liquid within beckoned.

Dazedly, Gwendolyn's feet carried her forward until she stood above the goblet, staring down and into its crimson depths. It was blood—no, her mind corrected snidely, not blood: food. And she was so *very* hungry...Gwendolyn's tongue ran over her cold lips and along the edges of her teeth—so long and sharp now, and probably as white as the cloth upon which this tempting meal sat—but she would never see them. Was this the gift of which Maida had spoken? Surely no normal person would offer such a thing.

Her hands were shaking so badly it took both to grasp the chalice and bring it to her lips; juices filled her mouth in anticipation. The scent that drifted up was not what she expected and before she could stop herself the warm taste of salt and copper was in her mouth and pouring eagerly down her throat.

But it was all right, because the visions that filled her head were not of humans, but cattle—huge, gentle creatures with warm brown eyes and more than enough life to share with even a death-bringing creature of the night such as herself. Gwendolyn closed her eyes and drank, hearing the soft sounds of cattle lowing as the blood filled her stomach and chased away the ice in her veins. A short while later she was sick and fighting to keep the blood in her system as she staggered to the bed and collapsed; she felt as if she were human once again and ill because of tainted food or too much ale.

"Nauseating, isn't it?" Gwendolyn wearily raised her head from the pillow; her eyesight twisted and wobbled but still gave her a view of Christopher examining the empty chalice. His tongue darted out and he lapped a stray drop from the rim, then turned to her with glittering eyes. "You've waited so long, it will be a miracle if you can keep it down. Had you fed properly there would be no question, of course, but cow blood is not the chosen food of the *vampir*. I'll wager on the morrow you'll feel as if you've plied yourself with a full skin of cheap wine." He shrugged and sat beside her, smoothing her hair back tenderly from her forehead as she groaned and let her head fall to the pillow. His voice was infuriatingly sympathetic. "But it will fill your needs for awhile." He pulled her limp form against his chest, then leaned back and put an arm behind his head. "Myself, I prefer meals of a finer quality."

"You're evil, Christopher," she mumbled against his shirt. "And damned for all eternity."

He smiled cheerfully. "We both are, my dear. But at least we'll be together."

※　　　　※　　　　※

Gwendolyn had thought the problem of feeding solved with the discovery that she could consume animal blood, but though she gained strength daily, the sweet call of human blood tempted her more and more despite her now steady diet. It took flying into a false temper before Gwendolyn finally impressed upon little Maida that she had truly meant it when she ordered the girl to be out of the castle before sunset each evening. Maida had looked both hurt and relieved at the command and ultimately obeyed, though each night she now left a chalice of some type of animal blood in the hopes of soothing her mistress's unholy appetite. Christopher was spending more time with Gwendolyn each night, yet she had never known such loneliness. She yearned for companionship other than the handsome, sharp-tongued creature who stubbornly titled himself her husband, a man around whom she suspected she would never truly be comfortable. Comfort was something she had lost a lifetime ago, purloined with her ability to walk in the daylight without care.

As always, Christopher seemed to read her mind—she wondered if this was a skill she too might someday learn. In the meantime, he used his talents in the most maddening of ways.

"I've written Elizabeth," he announced one night. "She'll be here within a week. I've given instructions to the servants to prepare for guests at the castle. She's bringing ladies and men-at-arms and practically an army of servants; perhaps that will fill your need for company."

"I am not particularly fond of the woman," Gwendolyn said in exasperation.

"You should have spoken with me first."

"But why?" he asked in surprise. His face was a mask of innocence. "I would have invited her anyway. Whether you like her or not, she is still a blood relative. Besides—" he gave her a vulpine grin—"I thought you could *amuse* yourself with her entourage."

"You are disgusting," she snapped. "Why must you constantly strive to make me angry?"

"Because you are even more beautiful when your temper shows," he replied calmly, reaching to play with the fall of golden waves down her back. "One of these days, you'll have to admit your new existence to yourself and acknowledge that mortals are nothing more than prey to you now. You've become far superior to these fragile beings who cannot even venture into a harsh winter without the protection of dead animal skins."

Gwendolyn ignored his comments and pulled her hair smartly from his fingers.

"As for Elizabeth," he continued, unperturbed, "you should take your pick of those fools in her entourage. They certainly know the danger of serving her, Just as the villagers here are fully aware of the Báthory history. I would guess she'll probably avail herself with the choicest of your servants."

"What!" Gwendolyn jumped up with a snarl. "If she so much as touches Maida, I'll—"

"You'll what?" Christopher interrupted. "Even as a *vampir* you've not a violent bone in your body. Why, if we had such a thing as honor among us, you would be a disgrace!"

Gwendolyn stared at him in anger, knowing he was probably correct, then not caring. In a fit of temper she flung the chalice at him, hoping desperately to hear the sound of metal bouncing off his arrogant head. But though her aim was true, Christopher was much too quick and had ducked through the doorway before the goblet could find its mark. Gwendolyn gave the fallen cup a petulant kick and left it, making her way down to the disused dungeon and the small, secret pallet she had made for herself. *Such a lovely place to sleep*, she thought sarcastically.

Another visit from Countess Báthory. Was there to be no end to her torment?

✳   ✳   ✳

The Countess was already waiting in Gwendolyn's chamber when she climbed the stairs, but Gwendolyn had known that from the moment her eyelids had opened in the blackness of the lower dungeon. Even through the thick, ancient walls of the castle she could smell the woman. Elizabeth *bathed* in human blood—the secret moisture potion, Gwendolyn thought derisively—and spending time around Elizabeth would sorely tempt Gwendolyn. And Elizabeth had called Christopher's appetite a waste!

The beautiful Countess was reclining gracefully on Gwendolyn's bed and it nettled the younger woman that Elizabeth had the gall to feel so at home after threatening her hostess with a dagger on her previous visit. The last time Gwendolyn had been eager to impress the woman; she felt no such compulsion tonight.

"Gwendolyn!" Elizabeth said brightly as she sat up and stretched her mouth into in a wide smile. "I see you've fared well since my last visit. You look marvelous."

"Thank you, Elizabeth," Gwendolyn replied, not attempting to disguise the coldness in her voice. "There is something wrong with your chamber that makes it necessary for you to retire in mine?"

The Countess lifted her chin slightly. "Of course not, my dear. I simply realized that you would come here first when you awoke." She drew a sharp fingernail down the linen of the bedcover, leaving a faint trail of broken threads in the finely woven fabric. "Besides, Christopher bade me do as I wished in the castle. After all, we're family."

"I've no doubt he did," Gwendolyn said. Maida had built quite a fire and Gwendolyn stepped to the fireplace and prodded absently at the flames with an iron poker; the heavy logs turned easily at her touch. Though Gwendolyn still refused to feed upon human blood, Maida's nightly offering of animal blood sustained her fairly well and Gwendolyn could feel a barely constrained and almost brutal strength within the deceptively feminine lines of her arms and hands. "And by all means, you should do so." She turned her back on the fire and stared at Elizabeth; the glow of the flames behind her made Gwendolyn's figure little more than a black silhouette with glinting red–gold eyes. "But not in *my* chamber—nor with any of my personal possessions."

Elizabeth threw up her hands in feigned dismay. "My pardon, Gwendolyn! Had I known you felt so strongly about this…*little* intrusion, I would never have dared." The Countess swung her feet to the floor and stood, smoothing the skirt of her aqua–colored gown daintily. "Regrettably, Gwendolyn, we don't seem to be getting on as famously as Christopher—or I—had hoped. Perhaps it would be best if I, ah, *amused* myself in the daytime during the course of my visit rather than at night, lest another disagreement between the two of us cut short this visit as it did the last." She gave a spurious little grin. "I wouldn't want to upset you like I did the last time. Christopher would not be pleased."

If the Countess had thought to put Gwendolyn on edge by calling up the unpleasant memory, she failed miserably. To Gwendolyn the recollection of the dagger at her breast was hardly anything more then an old annoyance now, and the idea that this woman might be trying to intimidate her was blatantly ludicrous. That Gwendolyn suffered Elizabeth's presence was charity enough; she had no intention of bending to Elizabeth's will as well.

"I assure you, Elizabeth, there is little you can do now to frighten me. There will not be a repeat of the incident that occurred prior to the end of your previous visit, nor anything remotely resembling it."

"I never said there would be, dear Gwendolyn." The Countess was unruffled and her dark eyes found a sudden gleam as a thought occurred to her. "By the way, I thought I might have that serving girl—what was her name, Maida I believe—attend to me while I'm here. She seemed so capable and my own maidservant is young and has only been with my ladies for a few days; she could use Maida's tutoring." She gave a predatory smile as Gwendolyn's head jerked up.

"You do *not* have my permission to use Maida. I consider her my personal servant and she is forbidden to attend to anyone else." Something unspeakable and deadly stirred restlessly in Gwendolyn's mind at the thought of sweet little Maida being victimized by this perverted, murderous noblewomen.

"I see," Elizabeth said. "Then she is in the castle at night?" she asked innocently.

Gwendolyn felt her fingers curl into claws without her command. "That is of no consequence. Be warned, Countess. I see the girl as a serf and therefore one of my personal—and *favored*—possessions." For the first time since her unholy transition, Gwendolyn felt a hint of the power that she possessed struggle to take the form of anger. "Surely you have not already forgotten what I said about my personal possessions."

"Of course not," the Countess said with a toss of her head. Her expression turned sulky. "Although I'm sure Christopher will not approve of your treatment of me. Besides, as a member of royalty I should be able to have and do whatever I want—and with whomever I please. Christopher has always agreed with me in that respect."

"No doubt he has," Gwendolyn said through a sharp smile. "However, in this instance it is obvious that Christopher and I do not see eye to eye. And I should remind you, Elizabeth, that while Christopher may feel for you the bindings of family, I do not. I must insist that the servants of this castle and the village remain untouched and that you confine your entertainment and your ugly appetite to those poor, doomed souls who accompanied you on your trip." Gwendolyn glared at the other woman. "And I promise you I will not hesitate to vent my displeasure should I find that harm has befallen my serving girl."

The Countess blinked and backstepped unwillingly, and Gwendolyn finally saw a hint of fear in Elizabeth's eyes, though she still wouldn't trust the older woman to stay away from Maida. Maida would have to be told to stay elsewhere day *and* night until the Countess returned to Csethje three weeks hence.

"You may leave my chamber now, Elizabeth," Gwendolyn said in a soft, deadly voice.

From somewhere Elizabeth dredged up the courage to meet Gwendolyn's gaze for only a moment, then forcefully dragged her eyes away. "Yes," the Countess said, valiantly struggling to hide the shakiness of her voice. "I think that would be best."

*   *   *

"When is that woman going to leave, Christopher?" Gwendolyn demanded. "Her presence here is a curse to me every night!"

Christopher looked at her and laughed, and for an instant Gwendolyn could have sworn she saw merry lights in the blackness that was his gaze. "Well, well," he said mildly. "Aren't we in a temper tonight!"

"Damn you!" she hissed. "You're a curse to me besides!"

He watched as she paced angrily in front of the fire, then shook his head and spread his hands. "I thought you *wanted* the sounds of human voices in these halls at night."

"I did!"

"Well, here you have it. Sights, sounds, *people.*"

"And Elizabeth!" she snapped. "Always baiting me, in spite of her fear! Foolishly trusting that you will protect her."

"Alas, yes." Christopher sighed. "I must tell you she bent my ear well because of your threats."

"I never threatened her," Gwendolyn said scornfully. "I simply impressed upon her the importance of not trespassing in my chamber and leaving Maida and the rest of the villagers alone. She must satisfy herself with her own servants, not ours."

"That's hardly the way a normal hostess would behave." His back to her, Christopher grinned wolfishly as he waited for her response. He was not disappointed.

"What!" she said incredulously. *"Normal?* Elizabeth is hardly a *normal* guest, Christopher!"

He turned to face her and his expression grew serious. "Gwendolyn, you cannot go on like this. I know Elizabeth irritates you, but believe me when I say that I don't care a whit about the woman and she deceives herself when she claims I feel a family loyalty. I asked her here because I knew she would bring an entire entourage, an entourage of which you might pick without guilt any number of men or woman on which to satisfy your…need."

"No!" she railed at him. "I will not feed upon the blood of my fellow man like some…*leech!*"

"Fellow man!" Christopher's eyes widened in amazement. "You must be jesting!" He folded strong arms and smiled at her, purposely showing his pointed, beautiful fangs. "Fellow men, my sweet, walk hand–in–hand in the sun; they do not hide from another who hunts in the night. These puny folk are nothing but your *prey*—even cousin Elizabeth, if that is your wish." He reached for her, pulling her unresisting body towards the fire. Taking one of her hands, he held it close to the flames until she felt the heat against the surface of her skin.

"Do you feel that, Gwendolyn? The fire is warm on your hand but never penetrates inside, where you need it most." He thumped his chest for emphasis. "Trust me when I say that you will never, never feel warmth again unless you fill your appetite for human blood. The animal blood which you drink each night will never satisfy you, and while you refuse to admit it, you know I speak the truth when I say your need for real sustenance grows stronger each night."

"I cannot!" Gwendolyn cried, hiding her face in her hands. "It's wrong!"

"What is wrong?" Christopher demanded. "To prey upon those weaker than us? The mankind of which you speak so fondly has done so for a millennium, and will probably continue to do so even beyond our own perceived existence. Is it wrong to eat, Gwendolyn?"

"But they're *people*, Christopher." She looked at him pleadingly, desperate for him to understand. "They're alive and doing this terrible, terrible thing will unfairly rob them of that. What we do cannot be...*undone.*"

"Mankind does just that to all manner of living things, even to the animals that have thus far sustained you. Can't you see that?"

"To kill makes us monsters—I won't be that. I won't." Gwendolyn tried to turn away from him and flinched when his hands roughly pulled her back.

"You talk of monsters, Gwendolyn? Then let Elizabeth be your first meal. *There* is a monster; a woman who tortures and kills for no other reason than to fulfill her own sick sexual fantasies, then bathes in her victims' blood because her twisted mind believes it will keep her young. Our countryside is pitted with the graves of her victims, and the family name tarnished forever. Feed upon her—if anyone deserves to become prey instead of predator, it is surely Elizabeth!"

Christopher released her shoulders and Gwendolyn spun away from him. Damn him yet again, he almost had her convinced. Why did she listen to his words, so logical...so evil!

And yet...it was within her power to stop the Bloody Countess and save the lives of tens, perhaps hundreds of innocent maidens...

"No!" she cried. "You're as mad as she—just another cruel murderer!"

Christopher chuckled. The light of the flames highlighted his dark face and gleamed within the myriad curls of his hair. In spite of the hell of her existence and knowing what he—and she herself—was, Gwendolyn still found him attractive, still longed for the iciness of his touch.

"Murderer? Perhaps," he mused. He opened his arms and she could not resist stepping into his secure embrace. His cold lips caressed the golden strands of hair at her forehead. "Though I've never tortured anyone upon whom I've lain a hand." The skin at his eyes crinkled into smile lines as his fingers slipped the cape from her shoulders and tossed it on a chest. "Perhaps it's best if you leave her be. Unless you destroyed her beautiful body, we could well have the dubious pleasure of her company for the rest of eternity!"

Laughing at Gwendolyn's horrified expression, he swept her in his arms and carried her to the bed, never betraying his knowledge of Dorkó, the Countess's most trusted servant, listening just beyond the entrance to the chamber.

※　　　　※　　　　※

When Gwendolyn climbed the stairs to her chamber the next evening, Countess Elizabeth Báthory was gone, as was her entourage and every trace of her presence. In a way Gwendolyn was relieved; she detested the woman, more so because of the threat she had posed to Maida than as a result of the horror of her previous visit. Once again, however, the halls and chambers of the castle were silent and echoing, filled with nothing besides the squealing of inconsequential prey and predator: the chittering of an occasional mouse as it chased after a beetle, followed by the hiss of a hungry cat.

As usual, Gwendolyn's chamber was lit by the cheerful fire Maida had built. Also waiting was the full chalice of animal blood and she ignored the siren call that rose within her belly for the real thing—a need she could not bear to fill—and raised the goblet to her lips. The blood, strongly-scented and warm, filled her mouth and with a start she realized it wasn't the fire that warmed her meal, it was the weather. Maida faithfully built a fire for her mistress each night, yet it must surely be mid-summer now. Suddenly impatient, Gwendolyn gulped the rest of the red liquid and hurried down to the great hall. There she quickly threw the bolts on the main entry and stepped into the courtyard.

The night was beautiful. Gwendolyn had not ventured outside since she had run panic-stricken to thrust a stolen boychild into the arms of Maida's father months earlier. Now she craned her neck to see the stars that spilled heavily across the sky in every direction like the careless brush strokes of a celestial artist, the sparkling expanse interrupted only by a moon that might have been a huge dish of brilliant yellow paint. Warm summer air flowed around the bare flesh of her arms and along her neck and collarbone, tickling her skin and lifting her hair, bringing with it the faint sounds of crickets and owls from the woods outside the stone gates and the faraway bleating of a herd of sheep, sounds Gwendolyn knew a normal human could never have heard. She hugged herself happily as the smell of woodbark and wild grasses filled her nostrils.

"I see the fair lady has ventured from her prison at last," came Christopher's easy voice. "The night and all its charms await, my lady." He looked different as he stepped in front of her under the moonlight, more sinister and mysteriously attractive. A surge of desire filled Gwendolyn's senses and she reached eagerly to take the arm he offered; for once he did not wound her with a sharp comment. Instead, Christopher led her beyond the stone gate to a small clearing in the woods where the trees made a barrier of their own around a tiny, gurgling brook. Somewhere beyond the ring of trees she heard the soft croaks of frogs in an unseen pond.

"Let me show you how to make the night sing," Christopher murmured just before his lips covered hers and they knelt together in the soft grasses.

Cradled in his arms afterward, Gwendolyn willed her mind to stay blank. There were many things she needed to think about and plans to be made, but she dared not contemplate them in Christopher's presence. The seductive night air and the tryst with her lover had whetted the dangerous appetite within her treacherous body and made it seem as if her recent meal of deer blood had never existed. As each week passed Gwendolyn became more comfortable with her nightside existence, more *accepting*. More than anything else, she feared that one evening—perhaps soon—she would wake and the ability to resist the beast sleeping inside her soul would simply be…gone.

Then what would she do?

Despite her concentration, Christopher picked up that fleeting thought and although her eyes looked elsewhere she could feel his sharp-toothed smile at her side.

"Why, my dearest," he said quietly, "then you will feed."

DeadTimes

*   *   *

"My lady," Maida said softly.

"What are you doing here?" Gwendolyn demanded. Hot need, an almost sexual desire, had risen in her merely at the sound of the girl's voice. "I told you never to come into the castle at night!"

Maida's eyes sought the relative safety of the floor. "I…felt you wanted me." She risked a peek at Gwendolyn. "Didn't you?"

"I—yes, I did." Gwendolyn started to continue, then a faint sound drifted to her ears from the hallway and her eyes narrowed. Was Christopher there, seeking to spy on her? In two strides she was past the startled serving girl and yanking the entry curtains aside; discovered, a red–faced Ferenc stood uncertainly in the hall. "What is the meaning of this?" Gwendolyn challenged. "What are you doing skulking about like a dog?"

"He was afraid for me," Maida said from behind her. "I told him he could wait in the hall."

Gwendolyn felt her shoulders relax, but only a little. It was best to get this done quickly, before Christopher put in his nightly appearance, or…worse. Yet her curiosity was still piqued at the maidservant's appearance. "You say you came because you thought I wanted you?"

The girl twisted her fingers nervously, and glanced quickly at Ferenc. "Yes. I—we—"

"We plan to marry!" Ferenc blurted. If Gwendolyn had thought him blushing a few seconds ago, it was nothing compared to the scarlet cast that suffused his face now. She wanted to smile; instead, she found herself forcing away thoughts of the blood flowing just below the skin of this awkward young soldier.

"Congratulations," Gwendolyn said smoothly. Her mind raced ahead, trying to refigure the plan she had made. "When?"

"S–soon. We thought to elope," the girl answered.

"We came to say farewell," Ferenc added. "Maida thinks highly of you, in spite of…well. She wanted to see you before we left."

"So you plan to leave tonight?" Gwendolyn asked. This time she couldn't hide her surprise. "Already? Will you be returning?"

The young couple glanced at each other and Gwendolyn knew they wouldn't.

Gwendolyn sighed. "Well, that's probably best. You'll be so much better off far away from this place." She felt herself smile and in spite of the starvation that was slowly whittling away at her she felt a fierce, genuine happiness for Maida and Ferenc. "You'll have a wonderful life, with babies, and–and sunshine…" She turned away from them as a sudden sadness filled her, blotting out the momentary joy.

Ferenc cleared his throat. "Mistress, there's another reason I came here with Maida tonight. I came to ask your forgiveness."

Gwendolyn looked at him in bewilderment. "Whatever for?"

He raised his face and she saw shame and honesty battling in his eyes. "It was I who took your prayer beads the night that Lord Christopher…" His voice trailed off.

Gwendolyn's hand flew to her throat and closed over the place where scars would remain forever unseen. "You!" she gasped. "But why?"

Ferenc's head and shoulders seemed to slump together. "I was afraid, your ladyship. Lord Christopher commanded me to do so and I was terrified to disobey him."

"Oh," Gwendolyn said, and she could not disguise the hurt in her voice. Rage filled her, then despair, and for a dangerous instant she battled the urge to kill. Just as quickly she realized that it would change nothing and Christopher would have eventually found another way to claim her.

Ferenc took a few steps forward and dropped to his knees in humility. "I beg your pardon, mistress. I did not wish to cause you such pain."

Gwendolyn could not bear the sight of him like that; it brought to mind another on her knees in this very chamber, though that one had been out of fear rather than forgiveness. "Never mind," she said hoarsely. "Get up. I wish you both the best." An idea occurred to her, and she turned to rummage through one of the chests for parchment and quill. "In fact, I've a wedding present for the two of you, though outwardly it would seem more for Maida's benefit."

"Lady Gwendolyn," Maida asked gently, "there will be no one to…see to you now. May we…*do* anything for you before we go? Anything at all?"

Gwendolyn froze for a second, the quill still clenched in fingers momentarily paralyzed. Her dark nature would never allow her to accomplish this on her own, and if she truly meant to have it done, here was her only chance.

"Yes," Gwendolyn said slowly. "Yes, there is."

✵   ✵   ✵

Dawn.

Gwendolyn could feel the rays of the sun even through the thick walls of the castle, bidding her sleep and slowing her thoughts until each dragged and stopped like a heavy stone tossed into thick sludge.

A few minutes or perhaps hours later, and dimly Gwendolyn's subconscious perceived movement. She knew what and who it was—Maida and Ferenc, come to faithfully carry out her instructions. Such loyal servants! She wished she could have gifted them with wealth worth a hundred times more than the paper she had drawn up forever granting Maida her freedom and the simple purse of gold coins.

More movement now. Although she could neither open her eyes nor move, Gwendolyn still felt the sensation of being lifted, then turned and wrapped in something heavy. A thought surfaced thickly in the slow channels of her mind and she would have laughed if she could; perhaps Maida and Ferenc were at last covering her in her elusive burial shroud. Instinct made Gwendolyn want to struggle against those she knew would take her from her safe place of rest, but as she had expected, the sunrise had immobilized her and left her powerless. She felt like a baby, carried along with no control over its fate or destination, though she could summon none of the trust that an infant would feel within the warm circle of its mother's arms.

Gwendolyn wondered fleetingly where Christopher was and if, through the darkness of his own sleep, he realized what was happening to her and what she had done. She did not know where he slept and he had never volunteered the information. Once the idea that he did not trust her enough to know had hurt her, though she had supposed he certainly had his reasons; now she realized it had been a hidden gift. Had he insisted they rest together her friends—and truly they were more than servants—would not have been able to take her body. Even in sleep, Christopher was much too strong.

Climbing suddenly, her limp body at a angle that combined with her torpor and made her dizzy; she yearned for the simple relief of a moan, the small gift of opening her eyes to bring her balance back to normal. Was Maida at her feet? Surely it was the strong Ferenc who grasped her so firmly at the shoulders and bore her quickly up the stone steps. Even through the thick layers of her languor and the material wrapped so snugly about her flesh, Gwendolyn could feel and smell the hot blood pulsing beneath the skin of their hands.

Out of the darkness now, beyond the dungeon and buttery, then through the tower and into the gradually fading shadows of the great hall. Gwendolyn did moan then, an involuntary sound that escaped her lips as the couple moved her ever closer to the hated and yet longed-for light. At her shoulders and feet, the sweet warmth of their hands no longer felt good, meaning as it did that she was beyond the point of return. As Maida and Ferenc carried her from the castle, Gwendolyn felt a deep calm eclipse the darkness that had captured her soul.

An agonizing five minutes' journey and Gwendolyn felt Maida and Ferenc lower her gently to the ground. She knew instantly where she was as the planes and curves of her back molded against the bumpy earth: the clearing where she and Christopher had made love not so long ago and where she'd finally realized how close she was to losing her battle. The sun's rays painted her mind crimson and seared her eyes beneath her closed lids, but through her pain Gwendolyn could still hear the sound of the tiny brook somewhere to the left of her already spasming body and the cheerful twittering of sparrows. She tried desperately to remember what it might look like: bright green grass, perhaps the red and orange of field flowers growing along the weed-choked bank next to the silvery trickle of water. Above it all, the painfully bright sun.

Gwendolyn welcomed the feel of their fingers loosening her shroud and she knew a bittersweet joy as the black thing sheltered inside her deepest self twisted in horror and fear. She recognized the sound of Ferenc's sword as he unsheathed it, felt again the movement of her wrappings as he drew the sharp blade quickly down the length of fabric. Even before the split material fell to each side, he and Maida fled the clearing; neither wanted to watch.

Sweet, blazing agony. The sun took her and Gwendolyn felt as if she were a living meal being cooked upon a spit—perhaps her skin was even smoking. The pain was terrible yet cleansing, and when her muscles pulled into an involuntary fetal position, her body seemed a flaming mass of heat surrounded by an ever-growing blackness.

Gwendolyn offered a silent, fragmented thanks to Maida and Ferenc and hoped they would be safe. Somewhere in her fading consciousness she thought she heard a scream of fury from Christopher. She reached for it, but the broken voice spun abruptly away, and her only regret was that she would never be able to see the rage on his face when he realized that she had at last escaped him. It would have been amusing to tell him to spend eternity with niece Elizabeth.

The sun bore her to black oblivion on a great, spinning sphere of fire.

CHAPTER VI
1961

She was running, pushing through bushes and brambles and feeling thorns scratch bloody trenches into the exposed tender skin of her face and arms, letting instinct guide her through the blackness of an unknown night as the shrubbery and trees whipped by like flat, black paper cutouts. It was bitter cold and there was still snow on the ground, but they wouldn't track through here, it was too hard on the dogs' feet and too far away from the highway; the ice, sharp rocks and dried, broken thorns would easily cut skin—as she was finding out—and the animals were too valuable to take into such unwelcome territory. Much more valuable than the person they tracked.

She had no time to wonder about that strange, disconnected thought. She wanted desperately to stop, to crawl beneath the tangled branches of a dormant blackberry thicket and catch her breath, maybe sleep for just a half hour. She was tired and her throat hurt terribly, far worse than it ever had in times before, and for just a moment she believed she was simply hallucinating the pain, reliving the same injuries over and over. Panting and gasping, she might have been fleeing for hours; she just didn't know. Her body felt strange, heavier and ungainly, as though even the pretense of grace had disappeared from her form. The whiteness of the snow was shattered in all directions by the shadows of bushes, trees, and jagged rocks, and though her legs pushed on, she could make no mental connection as to her destination—she didn't even know if she was still being hunted.

An indeterminate time later, a house rose in front of her. Small and dark, but she knew this had been her goal all along; there was a tiny, safe glow from one window and her body automatically lurched toward that warmth, drawn to it like a lost ship to a lighthouse beacon. She stumbled up uneven wooden steps and fell, once, twice, then the door was flung open and welcome light spilled onto the shabby front porch, illuminating slowly decaying lawn furniture next to t.v. trays left to rust in the winter moisture. A woman wailed suddenly from the doorway and she opened her mouth to say something, to say *Be quiet for God's sake, before they hear,* but her throat felt like a mass of bloody hamburger and nothing would come out. The woman's hands were on her then, the touch a curious cross between rough anger and gentleness as they hastily pulled her inside and slammed the door, then released her; an instant later there was the metallically comforting sound of a bolt being shot firmly into place as the door was locked.

"Oh, my Lord! Look at you—what'd you get yourself into this time? Oh, Jesus—your *neck!*"

An ominous ringing began in her ears and telltale yellow sparkles teased the edges of her vision; if she wasn't careful, she was likely to pass out. She reached forward and her questing fingers found the worn plaster of a wall to steady herself as the woman came from behind her and into view. Her rescuer was an attractive, middle-aged black woman, her dark hair shot through by gray and pulled back into a conservative knot; her eyes were huge and sparkling with terror.

"Oh, Nathan," the woman moaned, one hand flying to her mouth. "They tried to lynch you!"

Nathan?

✳   ✳   ✳

The cracked and peeling mirror in the tiny bathroom showed him his new body. *I've never been a man before*, was his first thought as he looked into it. On the heels of that, *My name is Nathan Carter now*. His face was strong and broad, with a firm jawline and cheekbones, a wide nose above full lips. It was easy to see the shock that was still imprinted on his features, especially in the round eyes and the deep furrows along the ridge of his brow, although the woman in the other room—his wife Emily—attributed it to his near death the night before. He was a black man, big and well-muscled, used to hard work in the fields, and beneath the gleaming dark skin of his neck he could see scabbed-over wounds and the smudged color of *true* black: the bruises that ringed his neck from a rope he couldn't remember.

Wearing nothing besides a thin tee shirt and boxer shorts he watched the play of muscles in his arms and chest, feeling a pure physical power he'd never known in a woman's body. When he pulled his lips back, his teeth were large, a little crooked and startling white against the skin of his face; his fingers hooked around a plastic comb on the sink and he reached up and yanked it experimentally through the short but thick black hair covering his scalp.

Nathan cast a furtive, embarrassed glance at the closed bathroom door, then touched himself in wonder, cupping his balls and running his fingers along the length of his penis. His fingers were thick and hard, not at all gentle; even so his organ responded to the sensation immediately, lengthening into a semi-erection. He stopped and rinsed his face and trembling hands with cold water; he wanted to step outside this tiny bathroom and take his new wife to bed, experience the unsurpassable phenomenon of making love to a woman from a man's point of view, but there were other, more serious problems the two of them had to deal with right now, and his new mate would think Nathan and his sudden desire insane. It was a shame that for awhile Emily wouldn't be able to see past the ugly circle of bruises around his neck. His mouth stretched into a wry grin as he pulled on clean britches; women had been saying in one way or another for centuries that man was ruled by his dick instead of his head, and from the way he felt right now that just might be true.

The bathroom was off the kitchen and when Nathan opened the door he stepped directly into the room where Emily was setting breakfast on the table. Exhaustion and surprise had made him sleep almost twelve hours and when he'd awoke not long ago his mouth had already begun watering as he heard the sounds of cooking and caught the smells of sausage and potatoes. His wife—he still couldn't get over that—looked up at him with worry lines creasing her forehead as she moved from the sink to the table. Beneath a frayed yellow apron, she was wearing a cheap cotton dress a size too big with little daisies printed on it. In the morning light, Emily's eyes were not the deep black Nathan had expected; instead they were a clear light brown shot with flecks of gold and green—almost yellow in the sunlight. He thought she looked beautiful.

Nathan wondered fleetingly if the dress had always been a size large or if she'd lost weight—he didn't dare ask—before he stepped around the scarred wooden table to stand in front of her. She placed the last fork on the table and opened her mouth to say something when he lowered his face to hers and gently covered her mouth with his lips.

The sensation was incredible—like being a teenager all over again, discovering girls, boys, sex, life, all in an instant. Emily's lips tasted of honey and flour—she'd probably tested the biscuit dough as she cooked—and were soft and warm beneath his when she responded, like nothing he ever remembered putting against his mouth before.

Nathan forgot everything; breakfast, his jarring transition to manhood, even the rope and the grinding pain in his neck as his head tilted towards her. He was just *there*, with Emily, and no one else in the world counted now or ever. Another second and his hands were sliding over her shoulders instinctively, his heavy fingers working expertly at the plastic zipper at the back of the neck of her dress.

"Nathan!" Emily gasped. She pushed his hands away and he blinked, then felt himself blush. Thank God his skin was dark enough that she probably wouldn't notice. "What on earth's gotten into you?" Chair legs grated across the linoleum as she pulled a seat forward and motioned him towards it. "It's Sunday morning! And here I was, worried you'd be sick from last night. Sit and eat your breakfast."

A word flared in his memory and he snatched at it. "Come on babycakes, let's mess around a little before we leave."

The color along Emily's sharp cheekbones deepened slightly and she sat across from him and dipped a wooden spoon into the chunks of fried potatoes and sausage patties. "Why, Nathan," she giggled. "You haven't called me that since school!"

He leaned forward and grinned. "How about it?"

"No," Emily said firmly. She slapped a serving of food hard on his plate, like an army sergeant. "There's plenty of time for that later—right now you get to your meal. We have to leave in half an hour."

He thought briefly about suggesting a quickie, then shoved a forkful of potatoes in his mouth to stifle the word and reached instead for one of Emily's hot, homemade biscuits. A 'quickie' for his first time? Not a chance. He'd take his sweet time about this and learn to do it right.

✳   ✳   ✳

Harmony Baptist Church didn't have much going for it in the way of size; then again, Harmony, Georgia wasn't much in size, period. But it was a clean and well-kept clapboard building with a small, pointed tower to show its people the way to the Lord's house each Sunday morning, and despite the cold and the fresh snow that was starting to fall, Nathan thought it looked very comfortable and welcoming. The bitter weather served his purposes besides; on his back was a well-worn plaid coat and Emily had wrapped a wool scarf snugly around his neck. She hadn't said anything but he'd known it was so he wouldn't have to explain the scabs and bruises to anyone. Some things were safer left unsaid.

"Nathan! How've you been?" The pastor, an elderly man so thin his brown skin seemed stretched over his frame like ancient canvas, beamed at the two of them and reached to shake Nathan's hand as he and Emily climbed the steps toward him. "And Emily—now there's a fine women, for sure."

"We're just fine, Tate," Nathan said, smiling. He felt Emily's gloved hand tighten on his arm but she grinned.

"Why, if I hadn't already been married when Emily and her mama moved to Harmony, it might be her instead of Lana—"

"I heard that, Tate Williamson!" The threesome laughed as the pastor's wife peeked from the warmth of the church's doorway; Lana Williamson smiled at the Carters and waved them inside. "Come on, come on! No use standing out in the wind— services are already late." Nathan followed Emily inside and in another moment they'd found a place to sit about midway up the benches. Pastor Williamson made his way to the front of the small church using the aisle against the wall rather than strolling up the center.

Although he knew it wasn't so, Nathan felt as if this were the first time he'd attended these services and he looked around curiously, examining the church, the people, the modest display of objects at the altar that symbolized the faith of this small black community. He and Emily, he quickly realized, weren't the only ones without a lot of money here—most of the folks in the building wore clean but thoroughly used clothing; he could easily see where coats and caps that might have once been colorful had been handed down through several children in some of the families. There were faces he thought he recognized and names popped obligingly into his mind as his gaze ran up and down each pew; others he couldn't place, newcomers maybe, but more probably just those who kept within their own circle of friends. For all his looking around, Nathan didn't spot anyone with whom he thought he and Emily might not be on good terms. While that was in one way a comfort, Nathan fingered the wool scarf at his neck just enough to cause a twinge of pain in his misused flesh as a reminder that all was not as peaceful as it seemed in Harmony.

Nathan hadn't been paying attention to the service and around him people were picking up hymn books and he did likewise, glancing over to Emily's so he would know to what page he should turn. There was a hush in the room that grew longer and longer, and suddenly Nathan realized people were looking expectantly at him, as if he was supposed to do something. Even his wife was staring at him.

"What?" Nathan asked dumbly, making sure his voice was low enough so only Emily could hear.

"Stand up, dear. They're waiting for you to lead them." Emily's tone was patient, as if she were speaking to a confused child. "Third one." Her finger tapped a page in his book; at the top it was titled "When Jesus Comes to Call." He felt very conspicuous; he couldn't ever remember singing in public. To his relief his eyes founds the words and notes familiar and his voice carried clear and strong in the small chapel despite the throbs of pain the singing caused in his neck and throat. After the first verse, the rest of the parishioners joined in and in the joy of discovering his own rich voice, Nathan forgot his shyness.

✳   ✳   ✳

"Wonderful sermon, Pastor," a man in front of Nathan was saying as the man's wife, a chunky thing with a round, smiling face, nodded vigorously. The man turned and smiled widely at Nathan. "And Nathan's singing was glorious, as always."

"Thank you, Jacob," Nathan said smoothly. He muttered a silent word of thanks that he remembered the friendly man's name so quickly.

Beside him, Emily reached to grasp the woman's hand. "Ruby, how are you?"

"Well, you know how I never could take the cold," Jacob's wife complained good-naturedly. "It just seems like spring is never gonna come."

"I wouldn't stay out here and wait for it in the meantime," Emily said, "since it's only January."

Ruby laughed. "That's true enough."

"Where are the kids?" Nathan heard himself ask; it seemed the most natural thing to say next.

"Oh, you know," Ruby said again and rolled her eyes. "Out back with the rest of 'em, messing up their Sunday clothes. Speaking of," she looked around at her husband, "let's get the boys together and head home. I'm freezing."

Nathan and Emily watched and smiled as the couple descended the steps and Jacob waved good-bye. "I swear this woman is never warm!" As the two rounded the corner of the building, Ruby elbowed her husband and said something Nathan couldn't hear; Jacob laughed and called back, "Well, almost never!"

Nathan grinned and turned to his own wife; that last comment had brought to mind something else, left undone from earlier this morning. Emily was standing on the steps with a little smile on her face and Nathan was one step above her; he looked down and opened his mouth to suggest they go home and see about getting warm themselves when something over her shoulder and across the street caught his eye. Parked at the curb beneath the bare, limp branches of an overgrown willow tree was a black Ford pick-up truck, its dirty sides bettered and mottled with what looked like birdshot holes. Although their faces were indistinct from this distance, he could feel the malevolent gazes of the three men who sat watching him from the cab of the truck; still, the sight alone of that vehicle was enough to make Nathan's heart plummet into his gut.

"Let's go home," Nathan said. The thick silk that had been his voice a quarter of an hour earlier had hoarsened into burlap. He still couldn't recall their names but the men across the street, he suddenly knew, were the ones who had tried to kill him last night. Nathan's trepidation grew as he wondered what they would do while everyone was walking down the steps of the Harmony Baptist Church. He and Emily had to leave now, while there were still people walking on the street in the direction of their own house; at the same time he realized these men didn't know where he lived and he didn't want them to find out. sudden, sick terror for Emily filled him, overshadowing the thought of another rope about his neck and erasing entirely any leftover anger. "We'll walk this way." Nathan turned abruptly and pulled his wife down the street, following several couples as they made their way directly across from the truck but in a direction opposite Nathan's own house. A few folks looked resentfully at the truck and its occupants as they passed; most pointedly ignored it.

"Where are we going?" Emily asked in confusion. "I thought you wanted to go home." He was moving too fast and she stumbled slightly; he tore his gaze from the Ford only long enough to grab her elbow and keep her from falling, but when he looked up again the three men had already clambered out and were slamming the doors purposefully. At least, he thought through the hammering in his head, they hadn't pulled the two rifles from their slots in the gun rack above the seat. In response to the rocking of the truck bed, a ratty–looking tan and white hound jumped up and hung its front paws over the side of the truck's bed, baying at full lung power.

"Shaddup, Miller," one of the men said without much force.

The man's jaws worked and he spat a long stream of brown liquid onto the street, unmindful of the excess that dribbled onto the front of the checkered shirt that showed where his jacket couldn't be closed over his stomach. The way things looked, either the shirt hadn't been changed in a couple of days or the man had gone through an entire pouch of tobacco just this morning. The fellow leaned against the side of the truck and the dog tried to lick at his face; he smacked it without looking and the hound yelped and cringed away.

"Well, if it ain't nigger Carter and his wife," the man said nastily. Nathan felt Emily stiffen beside him and he put a restraining hand on her arm. The man's words had been clear enough to carry to Nathan and Emily, but at least they weren't intelligible to the people still standing on the church steps down the street.

"Leave us alone," Emily said coldly.

One of the men, the thinnest, laughed and poked at the man who'd belted the dog. "Look at that, T.J. His woman's gotta speak for him—you don't think there's something the matter with his speakin' voice, do ya?"

"Well, I don't know," the one called T.J. responded. "Maybe. Could be he talked hisself all out in that little conversation we had last night." He grinned and tipped his cap back; his teeth were brown with tobacco stains. "I'd be pretty surprised if he didn't understand yesterday's message, though." The speaker's deep southern drawl hardened until his tone was flat and emotionless. "In fact, I'm finding it damned peculiar he's able to say anything at all this morning."

"What's that supposed to mean?" Emily demanded. Back straight as a ruler, she took a step toward the truck, her slight weight tugging against Nathan's hand. "You men—"

"Let's go, Emily," Nathan said as firmly as he could in his sandpaper voice. His fingers locked onto the sleeve of her coat and he hauled her back unceremoniously. "Now is not the time."

"He speaks!" The thin one's expression twisted in mock amazement. He glanced quickly at the third man, who just stood there with a bored, mean look on his face and said nothing.

"So he does," agreed T.J. He glanced over his shoulder into the truck cab and said something to the dog; it was on its feet and snarling in an instant. "I've had this dog for a few years now," T.J. said, regaining his amiable tone. "Used to call him Joker. Then, a…while back I turned him loose on a nigger and he chewed the balls right offa him. For what he lost, I figured that ol' colored boy oughta be immortal, so I re-named the dog after him."

Emily gaped at the man in abrupt fright and Nathan felt his skin crawl as a memory flashed in his mind, a blurry newsprint photo showing the covered remains of a mutilated body found in the woods a few years back, a Negro drifter the daily paper had identified as Hiram Miller. He wondered if his wife remembered, then realized from her expression that yes, she sure did. "Getting mighty tired of hearing your words on the radio," said T.J. His eyes were little and a clear, cold blue; they glittered like wet steel in the overcast light of the gray morning. "Yapping about busing and equality and more shit than a person can shovel. Don't wanna hear it no more."

"Then don't turn on your radio," snapped Nathan, his anger spurting suddenly and momentarily blotting out reason. He'd put special effort into clearing his throat quietly so his voice would come out smooth when he did speak. Beside him, he heard Emily's sharp intake of breath as the trio's renewed attention focused on Nathan. "There's no call for you fellows to be listening to the Negro station anyway."

The third man finally spoke, and his tone was low and chilly, like the breeze that did its best to burrow through the worn places on Nathan's jacket. "Someone's got to keep an eye on you coloreds." He was cleaner and better dressed than his companions and now he pushed the rim of his cowboy hat back with a well-manicured forefinger. "That's us." He smiled grimly and his eyes bored into Nathan's. "And I think you know who we are."

For some reason this man frightened him much more than T.J., who Nathan was sure was nothing but a monster wearing human skin. But lightning would strike him twice where he stood before Nathan would let these three rednecks intimidate him in broad daylight, in front of his wife and almost on the very steps of his church.

"I don't care who you are," Nathan said in a stony voice. "You move along and let us be."

"You just watch your mouth," T.J. said angrily. "Don't be telling nobody to do nothing!" Nathan started to retort when a calm, low voice cut him off.

"Good morning, gentlemen," said Reverend Williamson. "Is there a problem here?" Several frowning couples had followed the elderly pastor over toward the truck, but the Reverend's expression was a mask of serenity as he looked at each man in turn, finally stopping on T.J.'s red face. "Ah, Sheriff Bennett, how nice of you to come by, though I hardly would have known you out of uniform." T.J. looked decidedly unhappy that the Reverend had recognized him and spoken his name out loud; Emily just looked shocked.

"Howdy," T.J. mumbled as his gazed flicked uneasily over the small but growing group.

"I don't believe I know you two," Williamson said as he turned to the sheriff's friends. "I'm Reverend Tate Williamson, pastor of the Harmony Baptist Church." Beneath lowered lids, Nathan saw that Tate casually kept his hands folded in front of his coat to deprive the visitors of their opportunity to refuse a handshake.

"Jerry," said the thin man in a curt voice.

"Jerry...?" The Reverend cocked his head and waited.

"Just Jerry."

Williamson nodded and glanced at the last of the three.

"And you are?"

He stared at Reverend Williamson, then one corner of his mouth turned up. "Adam Thayer." As the impact of the name settled in, no one in the crowd dared to breathe.

"Thayer?" the pastor finally repeated.

"That's right, Reverend Williamson. You might be familiar with my name." He motioned to his companions and they climbed into the truck without hesitating; the one called Jerry held the door for Thayer respectfully. "I'm Sheriff Bennett's brother–in–law. I also own most of this town."

✳   ✳   ✳

"Son, you just can't stay away from trouble, can you?" Tate's words were reproachful as Lana silently poured coffee into the round of cups set before the people in her kitchen. "And why won't you take off your coat? Lana's had the stove on for a half hour now baking, and it's hotter than Hades in here."

"Yes, Nathan," Emily said. "Why *don't* you take off your coat?" To make her point, she stood and tugged off her own jacket, then draped it on the back of her chair.

"As I was saying," the Reverend continued as he reached for the sugar, "you need to let things cool down a bit. Let that radio station find someone else to write its editorials. God knows there are plenty of other people in Harmony with something to say—mind you, it doesn't all have to come from Nathan Carter. Lots of folks are real unhappy about this busing business, and it's not just the whites. They're plenty of colored people who don't went to send their children all the way across town into some strange neighborhood where they won't be welcome anyway. It's a hard situation and it's going to take some time to work it out." He stirred his coffee, then added another lump of sugar for good measure.

"But that's not the only issue here," Nathan argued, leaning forward over his forgotten coffee. "That's only part of it, like a tiny fish in an ocean of bigger ones. Why, there're people in Harmony who are still afraid to go to the polls and vote! Separate stores, separate schools—they already treat us as though we barely exist. What will they think of next?"

"I have the answer to that one, Reverend," offered Emily. Before Nathan could think of what she might do, his wife reached over and yanked the woolen scarf from around his neck.

"Merciful Jesus!" Lana breathed. All the Reverend could do was stare speechlessly.

"You might as well take your coat off now, honey," said his wife in a sweet voice.

✳   ✳   ✳

"Why in heaven's name did you do that?" Nathan demanded as he followed his wife into their house. "Haven't we got enough problems without having to worry about Reverend Williamson?"

"That's *exactly* why I did it!" Emily exclaimed. "Because you need others to worry about *you*, someone who knows who's who in this town and can't be pushed around without a lot of folks screaming about it. Don't you see, Nathan? All those people out front of the church today, they all saw Bennett and Thayer threaten you!"

Nathan snorted as he put his coat away. "Nobody threatened me, Em. You're looking for a safety valve that just isn't there." He sighed. "Let's just drop it, Okay? I'm tired and my neck hurts. I could use a nap." He tried to grin at her. "The day of rest, right? What's for supper?"

"Sure, day of rest," she grumbled. "That's easy for you to say—you're not the one who's got to fix the fried chicken!"

"I'll help," he offered, following her into the kitchen.

"What!"

"I said I'll help. I can cook."

"Nathan Carter, we've been married for twelve years and I've never seen you so much as pick up a pot." She looked at him doubtfully. "And here you are suddenly claiming to know how to cook. I don't think I believe you."

"I *can*," he insisted.

Emily planted her fists on her hips. "Then why haven't you said anything about it before now?" she demanded.

He shrugged. "I don't know—maybe just to keep you surprised."

She opened the refrigerator door and reached for something, mumbling to herself.

"What?" he asked.

"I *said* my mama always told me never to trust a man. Here, mister know-it-all, this is our dinner. You can fix it while *I* take a bath."

With that final statement, Emily was out the kitchen door and Nathan was left holding cold chicken flesh.

* * *

A workingman's fingers, Nathan decided, were too thick and clumsy and not at all suited for kitchen implements; he'd cut at least three places in his left forefinger and narrowly missed adding another few dices to the middle one. Still and all, it wasn't a bad spread and when Emily peered around the doorjamb to check on him an hour later she was met with a host of good smells—southern fried chicken, mashed potatoes, homecooked mustard greens. He'd even come up with caramel pudding for dessert.

"Well, I'll be damned," she said in awe, even though she still wouldn't step over the line that divided the kitchen from the front room.

Nathan raised an eyebrow. "What kind of language is that for a Sunday afternoon?" he commented. "And you rested and clean too, while I'm slaving in this hot room and hungry to boot."

She rolled her eyes. "I'll just bet you're hungry—how much tasting have you done so far?"

Nathan grinned at her and decided not to answer that one.

"Supper's ready, babycakes. Sit down and let me show you how a man cooks a meal."

This time, before they served up the food, the two of the bowed their heads and said grace.

* * *

The meal was cooked just right and supper was a fine occasion; dessert was ruined when Emily looked up after the first spoonful of rich-tasting pudding and asked him to tell her exactly what had happened the night before. Suddenly the sweet flavor of caramel in Nathan's mouth went so thick he nearly couldn't swallow.

"I don't remember," he said shortly.

Emily put down her spoon and slowly pushed the bowl of pudding toward the center of the table. "In all this time you've never lied to me, Nathan. Leastways that I know of—which makes sense, of course, 'cause if I knew it I wouldn't be saying that, would I? Anyway, I don't think you have. Don't start now."

Nathan stared at her. The woman across the table—his wife and a stranger to him until last night (and still, his thoughts reminded him)—stared back, meeting his eyes without flinching. He didn't want to alienate her, not now and so soon, not ever, yet he was afraid that even when he told the truth, she wouldn't believe him anyway. But that was all he could tell, because that was all he knew.

"Someone tried to hang me."

She put her napkin down on the tabletop carefully, as if it were a thing made of old and brittle eggshells. Her eyes, such a wonderful, animal-like color, sparkled at him, but Nathan couldn't tell if it was a reflection from the soft kitchen light or tears. "I'm not blind, Nathan. I can see that. I want to know who, and while I think I know why, I want to hear the words from out of your own mouth."

He stared at his pudding for a long time, trying to out-wait the seemingly bottomless well of patience that sprung from Emily. When he was looking at a thin, drying skin across the top of his now-unwanted dessert, he finally spoke. "I can't tell you that. I don't know the answer myself."

When she spoke, he could hear the fear in her voice, the terror she was trying mightily to conceal. "Was it Sheriff Bennett? And Thayer?"

"I don't know," he answered, raising his eyes to hers. "I really don't know, Emily. Maybe. I think so. But I can't prove it. And even if I could, who could I go to?"

"You didn't see?" she questioned. Nathan noticed with almost childish irritation that her dessert, too, went uneaten; he had been so very proud of his pudding.

He shrugged and stood, reaching for the dirtied dishes and scraping the leftovers into the garbage pail without thinking. "You know how it goes, Em." For a second Nathan imagined how strange this must all be to Emily; for years his routine had probably been to sit idly by while she worked at the meal and the clean-up after. Now he had reversed the roles in one sitting.

"No," Emily said slowly. Her fingers laced and unlaced on the tabletop. "I don't know how it goes. I want you to *tell* me how it went, Nathan, put the words in my ears like you do everyone else's. I want to *know.*"

Nathan slowly turned to her, his eyes wide pools of nightmare memories in the slowly gathering shadows of late afternoon. They stared at each other for a few seconds, then he set the plate he'd been holding back on the countertop and sat back down.

"All right," he said. "You want to know, so I'll tell you. At least, what I can remember."

And he did.

* * *

They'd gotten him coming out of the WCTN radio station where Nathan did those on-the-air editorials. There'd been three, maybe four men including the driver, already wearing those hellish white pointed things as masks, not giving a damn that it was still full daylight and the whole neighborhood would see. But the timing had been right and there hadn't been many folks on the street just then; a few yelled and began running toward the struggle, most had simply stared in frightened indecision. Nathan hadn't even had a chance to see the vehicle, so quickly had he been given a good whack on the back of the head with something hard—a blackjack, or maybe something as simple as a roll of quarters rolled in a sock—and stuffed into the vehicle.

There wasn't a whole lot more to tell. They hadn't beaten or tortured him, or even dragged him around from the bumper on the end of a rope like he'd heard some of the Klansmen liked to do to troublesome Negro folk. By the time Nathan woke up, his head screaming with a headache the likes of which he'd never known, the truck had already been careening down a barely used side trail a good long way from any well-traveled blacktop. His kidnappers had merely strung him up from an old tree in Mills Field—quickly, as though they had better things to get to. He'd fought as they'd dragged the rope over his face, then forced him to stand on the hood of the truck. He remembered that much now, remembered thinking how high the hood of the truck was when they'd hoisted him up and shifted the truck into reverse. And yes, though he didn't say so now to Emily, he did believe it was that same battered black Ford.

Nathan remembered the inept grinding of the gears as the driver—Bennett, surely—whooped and slammed the clutch in, then out, and the furious, deadly revving of the engine right before the slick metal surface was jerked out from beneath his shuddering legs.

Above all, Nathan remembered the pain, hot and vicious, the grating *crunch* of his own neckbones twisting and snapping, the suffocating blackness that swallowed even the frantic and fading sound of his own bloodpulse in his ears; an agony that, while it was still vivid in his mind tonight, tried to melt into the remembrance of another such torment untold lifetimes ago.

Nathan shook his head to clear away the old images. Then—and yes, Emily had been right, he had never done this before—he lied to her.

He told her the rope broke.

Well, it had, really...

He'd broken it with his own hands.

*   *   *

Night and time to sleep. Oddly, the darkness inside seemed a little warmer now that the snow around the house was trying to melt into little frost-tipped puddles around the porch. Through the cracks of the tiny home, the spaces where the windows and sills didn't quite meet, Nathan could hear the wind soughing through the brittle uncut grasses surrounding the place, rustling and promising more cold after the slight relief of tonight.

Using the golden glow from a small lamp on the dresser, Emily undressed in front of him without shyness; Nathan watched her with his eyes alight until she noticed and her cheeks actually reddened for the second time that day. She started to shrug on a plain white nightgown but Nathan stopped her, leaving the warmth of the bed only long enough to wrap Emily in his arms and bring her back to the bed with him.

"The light," Emily protested, trying to get up again.

"Leave it on," he said huskily. "I want to see you." She blinked in surprise but forgot her argument when his mouth covered hers and his fingers began sliding over her cool, coffee and cream skin. His own flesh was dark, the contrast between them fascinating to his hungry sight as he pulled her with him to the surface of the comfortable, blanket-covered bed. His hands found patches of soft hair beneath her arms and across her legs and she giggled when he stroked it.

"Did you know that white women shave?" she whispered conspiratorially.

"I've seen pictures of them in magazines, wearing nothing but little bathing suits. They cut off all their body hair like a man does his beard."

"Mmmm," he said. "But if they do that, wouldn't it grow back all scratchy like a beard? It wouldn't stay soft, like here—" He touched her once, then again. "Or here either," he murmured. She sighed.

They didn't turn out the light for a long time.

    ✳   ✳   ✳

Working on a farm was damned hard, Nathan decided. Bad enough to shovel cow shit, worse to have to do it in the morning dark, since he wouldn't call that silly sixty-watt bulb hanging from twenty feet up at the hayloft's ceiling a light in any respect of the word. The thick, nearly overpowering stench of cattle manure surrounded him, filling every pore in his skin and sinking deep into Nathan's lungs every time he inhaled. Emily worked as a maid five days a week at the Holiday Inn by the interstate bypass and usually came home smelling of furniture polish and soap; he hoped to God *this* smell didn't settle so far into him that Emily smelled it on his breath when she kissed him at the door each evening.

Nathan grinned outright at the thought of his wife and the odd looks she'd shot his way as she handed him cold biscuits and sausage to munch on the way along with a bagged sandwich and apple before he'd left this morning, a glance that told him she wasn't at all adverse to the startling differences in the way her man had made love to her. The feel of her body floated back to him, doing a fine job of momentarily driving away the frigid air, if not the cow-smell. The sensation of having a woman's tightness surrounding a part of him was incredible, like nothing he'd ever experienced or tried to describe. He couldn't wait to get home.

"Nathan, you finished in there?" Mr. Davis, the owner of the farm, poked his head through the door. "It's almost light."

"Yes, sir," Nathan responded. He kicked the shovel hard a couple of times to knock loose the last of the cow dung, then leaned it in its place by the first stall. "What's next?"

"I want you to go up to Macon and pick up a part for the tractor. Here's the papers."

"Papers?" Nathan asked doubtfully as the old man handed him a rumpled brown envelope.

"Never you mind," Davis said. The hard old farmer dug a wad of cherry tobacco out of his pocket and tucked it into one weathered cheek. "They'll get you where I want you to be without trouble. You just do what you're told. Bus runs every hour in front of the town hall; you catch the seven o'clock going out and the nine o'clock coming back." He squinted at Nathan thoughtfully. "Say, you can tell time, can't you?"

Nathan could do a lot more than that, but he just nodded and bit back the sarcastic remark that rose to his lips.

"Good. Bus fare's in the envelope. I'll expect you back here by 9:30." Davis spat a stream of reddened tobacco water on the barn floor, then walked out, picking rudely at the back of his overalls.

Nathan pulled on the heavy work jacket he'd tossed aside when the shoveling had begun to build up bodyheat, then went outside, letting his feet guide him along the dirt road that connected the Davis Dairy Farm to two–lane blacktop and finally to Harmony itself. There wasn't much doing in the streets at this hour; most of the in–town residents were clerks and store–keepers eking out an existence only to support the farms in the community and the small paper mill just outside the other side of Harmony. With the exception of the grain store and coffee shop, most wouldn't open until nine.

The bus, a big silver and blue thing, was already idling loudly at the curb, belching black smoke while its driver sipped a thermos of coffee without opening his eyes. He jumped at Nathan's knock on the double doors and batted irritably at the lever that swung them open, then held out his hand for the fare as Nathan searched the envelope for the first half of the bus money Mr. Davis had tucked inside it. The driver closed the doors and shut out the cold once more as Nathan took his change and walked a few feet down the aisle before lowering himself to a seat across from the only other passenger. Nathan nodded politely, but the passenger frowned at him, his bony face sheened lightly with perspiration in the over–warm interior. Of the two, only Nathan flinched at the sound of the driver's voice.

"Hey, you can't sit there." The name tag across the driver's shirt said *Etheridge*.

Nathan looked at him, then glanced back at the other passenger. "Why not?" he asked in bewilderment.

"'Cause Negros got to sit in the back of the bus, that's why." Etheridge peered at him. "You one of them northern boys? Ain't you from around here?"

"What difference does it make where I sit?" Nathan protested. "The bus is almost empty."

"Because that's the way it is, nigger," the man across the aisle spoke. He was wearing a three–piece suit that would have cost a year of Nathan's salary. "Whites in the front, niggers in the back."

"There's no call for that kind of talk," Nathan said. "No reason for you to call me that."

The bus driver looked at Nathan with a strange expression, then the businessman answered him with a dismissive wave. "It's not poor language," he said. "It's just what you are."

"Either you go to the back or you don't ride," the driver interrupted impatiently. He looked at his watch pointedly. "We leave in two minutes. Your choice."

Nathan opened his mouth to retort, then shut it when he thought of Emily and his job at Mr. Davis's farm. What would happen if they kicked him off the bus and he couldn't get to Macon for old man Davis? Reluctantly, he rose and went to the back, settling himself just as the driver purposely lurched the vehicle into motion. As the Georgia countryside sped past, he thought about the words of the two men.

It's just what you are.

But what was he, really? Nathan Carter, a Negro man in 1961, not particularly well-educated but strong and willing to work hard. He could read and he could write, and he could tell time as well as anyone else with the same years of learning tucked into his mind. What was it that made one man think himself better because his skin was a different color? Nathan bled the same, hurt the same, and didn't feel any different at all.

And he should know.

*   *   *

"The Bible tells us that God made man in his own image." Nathan's voice rolled into the cheap microphone, still deep and clear as it fed through the low-budget amplifiers. "It does not say that God is a white man. It does not say that God is a black man. The Bible tells all men that their colors were created because of the Tower of Babel, and whether you believe that or not, believe this: *no* where in the Bible is it said that God created different races so that one man might be better than another!" Nathan carried on his carefully prepared editorial, still fueled by the memory of the ride to Macon on Monday. He could close his eyes and call it up as though it were happening all over again: the thick stink of exhaust, nearly suffocating in the over-heated rear of that bus, the stomach-sickening jolt as the rear axle magnified every bump and crack in the old two-lane road. Now he was nearly shouting into the microphone as he told anyone listening to the airwaves to believe in themselves and never lose hope.

"I am a Negro man!" he cried at last. "I feel the same pain as a white man, the same joy when I see a child, the same fear when I think of God's anger! We are all the same inside—never forget that!"

"Good speech," said Ben as he came out of the back room after hitting the OFF switch to cut the transmission. "Gonna fire up some folks, that's for sure." The sharp-faced younger man studied him. "I don't want to tell you your business," he said finally, "but I sure hope you ain't working up to a repeat of last Saturday night. To be honest, Nathan, I wasn't sure I'd be seeing you again after I heard what happened."

"Freedom's worth fighting for," Nathan told him firmly.

"Nothing free about being six feet under the hard ground," Ben shot back. "And I'll bet Emily's listening right now. You can count on an earful yourself when you get home."

Nathan couldn't argue with that; his wife had been angry with him for the last two days when she'd discovered there was no way of talking him into skipping the Saturday broadcast. Ben lifted a corner of the shabby paper shade that covered the room's small window and cautiously peered outside. "They've been out there the whole time, Nathan," he said softly. "Probably got the radio all tuned in, hanging on your every word. And you know they ain't cheering you on." Ben scowled. "They're just waiting for you, same as last time."

"I'll go out the back then," Nathan said grimly.

"You watch your silly ass, Nathan. You think they won't expect that? Maybe they got somebody hidden back there with a two-by-four, just waiting to carve the KKK initials into your skull, old man." Ben shook his head. "No, the two of us will leave together—now, while it's still light and there's plenty of folks on the street. There ain't but three of them in the truck. They won't try three against two." The younger man's lips stretched in a bitter smile as he shrugged on his jacket. "The odds ain't good enough for 'em." Nathan nodded.

The two men shivered beneath their coats as they stepped outside. The mild weather of earlier in the year had fled and although the snow was gone, the air today was icy and colder than normal for this part of the country. Yesterday it had drizzled all day and the rain had hardened into slender icicles along the drainpipes and eaves of the worn buildings; every now and then there was a muted *snap* as one of the fragile needles of frozen water fell and shattered. The eyes of the men in the truck followed them as they headed down the street and Nathan could feel adrenaline singing in his blood as he thought of what they might have done to him—*again*—if Ben hadn't accompanied him coming out of the station. Abruptly Nathan stopped, then veered towards the truck.

"Fool!" Ben hissed. He grabbed at Nathan's sleeve but missed. "Where are you going?"

"Mornin', gentlemen," Nathan said cheerfully as he stepped up to the passenger window, making sure to stand just behind the door so that Sheriff Bennett couldn't get enough momentum to swing the door open and smash him with it. 'Just Jerry' sat glowering behind the wheel while Adam Thayer, his face impervious as always, sat calmly in the middle. Nathan could see neat squares of white fabric beneath Thayer's serenely folded hands. He tipped his cap and nodded towards Thayer. "Hope you don't get your suit all mussed up, sitting in this here filthy truck, Mr. Thayer. I hardly recognized you fellows without your masks."

Bennett glanced over Nathan's head, noting the other man and several people who had stopped to stare openly at the truck now that Nathan and Ben were talking to its occupants. "You just be on your way, nigger," he growled. "Don't be bothering white folk."

"Why, I wouldn't dream of it." Nathan nodded and turned to go.

"Interesting broadcast, Mr. Carter." Thayer's words stopped Nathan before he could step away. The man's voice was as smooth as the uncoiling of a rattler, and suddenly Nathan couldn't wait to be gone, down the street and anyplace else but here with Ben and within a yard of these three ruthless killers. What had he been thinking to do something so stupid? "I found the part about feeling the same pain as a white man particularly amusing." Beside him, Just Jerry guffawed; the sound disintegrated into a choked cough at Thayer's cold glance.

"I don't think," Thayer said slowly as his head swiveled in Nathan's direction, "that you have any idea of the pain a white man experiences when he sees his land and schools and everything he's worked so hard for overrun by Negros."

"I've worked hard too!" The protest exploded from Nathan's mouth before he could stifle the words and he didn't care. "Harder than the likes of these two!"

Bennett's face went livid. "If I had Miller with me, he would've done chewed your face off, you fu—"

"I think it's time to go, Nathan." Ben's hand, surprisingly strong for its thinness, gripped his shoulder and forced him to backpeddle as far as the truck's front fender. Beneath the steel of his fingers, Nathan thought he detected a tremor in Ben's grasp.

Sheriff Bennett leaned out the window. "You liked swingin', didn't you, you tar-colored bastard?" he asked in a low voice, then spat in Nathan's direction. "Too bad you didn't learn from it the first time." Inside the cab, Thayer said something to Just Jerry and the man gunned the engine in response.

Nathan and Ben leaped out of the way as the truck dropped into first gear and the driver floored the accelerator. Still hanging through the window, one fist waving in rage, Bennett's parting snarl burned into Nathan's mind.

"Next time we'll do you up right!"

* * *

Friday night: a week of back-breaking work on the farm, with a half day of the same waiting for him tomorrow morning before he could get his pay and be off to the radio station. Last week Emily had finally started speaking to him in time for Sunday morning services, and though he'd had to listen to an hour's worth of Ben's ravings about his foolishness this past Saturday, at least his friend hadn't told his wife about the incident. Tomorrow, Nathan resolved, he'd be a little more calm on the radio. He planned to relay a story that Ben had told him about Julian Harris, a newspaperman in Columbus who'd won a Pulitzer prize for public service in 1925 for his outspokenness about the Klan. After that he was going to talk about the Negro homes being bombed in Cobb County and plead with everybody to be a little more patient and peaceful, then wrap the whole thing up with a few good hymns. Not cowardly, but a lot more sedate than the hellfire he usually tried to infuse into the airwaves.

"I don't want you going to that radio station tomorrow." Emily's voice interrupted his mental planning as Nathan struggled with the crust-covered pipe under the kitchen sink that kept wanting to leak. Since he didn't know what the hell he was doing, he would have welcomed her interruption if it had been on any other subject. He grunted a non-committal reply and kept trying to turn the pipe wrench, hoping he wouldn't end up just twisting the damned thing clear off.

The toe of her shoe caught him painfully in the knee and the wrench went flying off into the cans and jugs of cleaning supplies Emily kept under the sink.

"Hey!" he cried. "What're you doing, woman!" He kicked himself free of the cabinet and sat up, clutching at his knee and glaring up at her. "That's the only left knee I've got!"

"You're the only husband *I've* got!" she snapped back.

"But—"

"I don't want to hear it, Nathan Carter!" She was striding around the small kitchen now, her voice strong and furious. "If you keep doing this, I–I'll—" She sank onto a chair and buried her face in her hands. "I don't know what I'll do!" she sobbed.

He forgot about the throbbing in his knee and hurried to her side. "Em."

"Can't you just stop, Nathan? *Please?*" She lifted her face to him, the tears spilling from her tawny eyes cutting a wet grid across her smooth skin. "Let someone else do the crusading, all right? There are plenty of men like you out there, men with more money and more power, men with more *safety*. No one's going to make you a saint! Don't you get it, Nathan? You're the only one *I've* got!"

"But I can't up and quit, Emily. Not just like that—it wouldn't be…I don't know how to explain it." His eyes pleaded for her to understand. "It would be…cowardly, somehow. And all those people who listen to me every week, they'd know that. And then they'd be afraid because of it, and everything I've gone through would be wasted."

"All right, then." Her fingers found his and she clutched at his hands in desperation. "Then just this one last time. You can tell them, make up your reasons, say whatever you want, *but say goodbye!*"

"I—"

"I'll leave you, Nathan Carter. I swear I will. I'd rather go back to my mom's family in Mississippi then live with the fear that Reverend Williamson will knock on my door some morning and tell me they found your body hanging from some old dead oak tree." Emily shoved his hands away and stood, straight and tall.

"You make your own choice."

* * *

The fight for civil rights, Nathan decided, would have to go on without him, led by fine, strong men like Martin Luther King, Jr., and others such as him. A mostly sleepless Friday night and a solitary, back–breaking Saturday morning had given him plenty of time to think and, as Emily had demanded, "make his choice." Harmony, Georgia was a backwoods town with a no–account sheriff and a mayor as evil to his own kind as a man can be, but it was still his home and his life. And he meant to spend that life with Emily Carter and in as much peace as possible.

Lord, he was tired, and the unseasonably frigid wind did nothing to relieve the ache five hours of stacking feed bags had buried in his shoulder muscles. The sun was deceptively bright, bouncing over the ice–covered fields and making him squint and sigh with relief as he finally trudged along the street into Harmony and made his way towards the radio station. He had a new piece worked out, his goodbye editorial, mild but not at all apologetic, simply paving an easy way for someone else to pick up the microphone. Ben, he knew, would be disappointed; he also thought the younger man would think his decision the wisest one.

A block ahead was the radio station and Ben working to get his key to fit into the stubborn old lock. WCTN was poor, subsidized by voluntary, mostly anonymous donations from the Negro townsfolk and church pastors, with an occasional God-sent chunk of cash from northern white sympathizers; the building itself was little more than scrap lumber held together by hope.

"Hey, there!" Nathan called. "You need some help with that lock?"

Ben looked up, then glanced down again as the key finally turned. He waved as he pushed the door open. "I got it—"

The explosion painted Main Street in red and gold fire.

※   ※   ※

Nathan groaned. The ground was like a wet, gritty slab against his face, its cold already soaked through his clothes and into places on his body that he hadn't realized could actually feel this much pain.

"Get up, you hot-damned porch monkey."

Agony flared along his ribs as a heavy boot kicked at him and connected with bone. Nathan pushed himself to his elbows, then choked and spat a wad of blood onto the ground, his head dangling between his arms like a sadly out-of-shape kid trying to do too many push-ups in bootcamp. Every time he tried to draw a breath, there was a deep, sharp pain in chest. Must have busted a few ribs, he thought blearily. The explosion—

"Ben?" he croaked. Nathan brought one leg up, then the other, until he was in a kneeling position. There was a circle of people—men—around him, but no one extended a hand; he prayed they wouldn't see his raised rump as a target before he could gain his feet. His ears were feeding him a steady ringing sound, like church bells gone wild on Sunday. Between each note, he could hear the hungry sound of fire consuming the clapboard building that had housed the radio station. Nathan shook his head and tried to stand.

"He's too slow," a man's voice complained. In response, Nathan felt the back of his coat grabbed roughly; he gagged as someone hauled him to his feet and pulled the collar of his coat tight across the front of his neck in the process.

A different person laughed nastily. "I bet you remember that feeling, don'tcha Carter?"

Nathan wobbled and the harsh hand at his collar steadied him, then dropped away. He recognized Sheriff Bennett's voice and blinked, trying to bring the man into focus as he swiped at his eyes with a shaking hand. His fingers came away sheeted in blood and he stared at them stupidly.

Bennett laughed again. "Don't worry, nigger. Just a few scratches, that's all. 'Sides, you can't hardly see it 'cause of the color of your skin." Someone else—Just Jerry—chortled.

Dazed, Nathan squinted at the burning station, then his sight found the charred, unrecognizable mass sprawled across the curb that he knew had once been his friend. "Oh, God! Ben?" He lurched in that direction.

"Get rid of him."

That same cold voice that had complained about him not getting up fast enough. Nathan realized it was Adam Thayer, and he spun haphazardly in Thayer's direction. "You—"

"Shut up." Bennett grabbed Nathan's arm and yanked him back; Nathan squelched the scream that rose to his lips as Just Jerry wrapped a muscled arm around his back and squeezed Nathan's ribcage.

"Can we have a little fun first, boss?" Bennett whispered. Through the redness still dripping from his eyelashes, Nathan coughed and almost collapsed as he saw Just Jerry's expression light up.

"I don't care. I don't even want to know. Just do it quietly. And God help you both if you screw it up again."

Nathan's head lolled and his legs tried to give out; through the swollen slit of his left eye he saw Adam Thayer cross the street and keep going, not even sparing a curious glance at Ben's sad body at the curb or the folks beginning to knot around it. The ringing in his ears had changed to a hungry crackling sound cut by the noise of people running and yelling; thirty feet away a man was fumbling frantically at a fire hydrant with a wrench as someone else hollered that the fire was spreading. Far away, a siren's song filled the winter air.

"That's right," Sheriff Bennett called cheerily. "You folks just try and get some water on that fire. We're gonna see to it this man gets to a hospital. You all keep going, you're doing a fine job! Yes, sir, a fine one!"

Nathan tried to pull back. "No—"

It would have taken only half of Just Jerry's well-hidden gut punch to put Nathan out.

❋   ❋   ❋

"Wake up, boy."
Slap
"C'mon—
Slap
—git up."

"Uhhh." It was the best Nathan could manage. The pain, like a hundred bruises upon bruises, was unbelievable. He tried to suck in air and couldn't, almost blacked out again. For his trouble, he got another backhand blow across the face; whoever was smacking him didn't realize—or care—that they ran the risk of pushing Nathan back into the ignorant safety of unconsciousness.

Nathan shook his head instead, and instantly regretted it. The ache that settled in his brain was almost too much to bear. Bloodtaste filled his mouth and combined with the vicious, nausea-bringing stab of busted ribs; he leaned forward and vomited.

"Jee-zus, T.J.! He puked all over my shoes!"

Nathan felt his head jerked back as though he were outside himself and watching from a vantage point somewhere in the sun-laden trees far above. His hands, once so strong and powerful, couldn't obey his commands, and he could barely feel his legs. His nose was broken and closed; he let his mouth drop open—more pain—and drew in a spearing lungful of air as he waited for the next blow to fall.

It didn't. Instead, his chin thumped forward and hit hard on his own collarbone as his hair was released. Nathan sensed more than saw a man crouch next to him. "Carter? You hear me?" Sheriff's Bennett's voice was inquisitive. "I hope you ain't crapped out on me yet. We got things to do this afternoon, boy. And you are an *integral* part of my plans. Get it?" Bennett didn't wait for a reply. "Now, you best pull yourself together, and I don't mean tomorrow. Come on now, open those eyes and git yourself up."

Nathan would have thought it impossible, but he managed to find his balance and stagger to his feet, weaving between his two abductors as though he'd been on a three-day drunk. Nathan drew the back of his hand across his eyes and squinted at the results; still bloody, but not so bad. "Where are we?" His voice was raspy and barely audible.

"That ain't your concern." Sheriff Bennett spat a wad of ever-present tobacco juice towards Nathan's feet, smirking when it splattered Nathan's pants legs and shoes. In a more normal time, Nathan might have said something. As it was, his clothes were covered in mud and blood and vomit, and there were more pressing things to worry about. Top on the list was staying alive.

"Gonna give you a fightin' chance, nigger. A chance you sure as shit don't deserve. Here." Bennett pressed something cold and heavy into Nathan's left hand; he looked dumbly down at a battered old pistol with a cracked plastic handgrip.

"Have you gone crazy, T.S.?" Just Jerry demanded in a shrill voice as he stepped back nervously. "This nigger's gonna blow your fucking head off!"

Bennett snorted. "Aw, it ain't loaded, you fool. You think I'm stupid?" He poked Nathan hard in the shoulder as though he were trying to start a fist fight. "Now you listen up, shitface. That pistol ain't loaded, but there's bullets over there—" he swept an arm at a spot across the small, snow-spotted clearing in which they stood—"behind that rotted willow two trees back from the edge. Two bullets, Carter. One for me, and one for Jerry—"

"T.J.!"

"Shut the fuck up will ya?" Bennett hitched up the pants that were hanging below the beer belly spilling from beneath his jacket. "Like I was *saying,*" he glared at his companion, "two of 'em, in a little plastic bag. Two chances, nigger. That's all."

Nathan raised dull eyes. The words were hard to form but still understandable. "I'm no killer, Sheriff."

Bennett shoved his face close to Nathan's, his ice-chip eyes hard and mean. "Maybe you don't like to think so, Mr. Negro Radio Man. But I am, and you can bet your ass that Jerry is, too. Especially now that he knows you got a bullet that might have him in its sights." The sheriff stood back again, studying Nathan as he fought to stay upright. "You better hope you can stop dancing around long enough to aim, 'cause Jerry and me, well, we got plenty of bullets. And every one of 'em's got your colored face on it." Bennett reached a hand in his coat pocket and came out with his pouch of tobacco and a silver pocket watch.

"You got sixty seconds to run for the trees, Carter. Then we start shooting."

※　　　　※　　　　※

Four hundred feet had never seemed so far. Nathan didn't wait to be told again; he lurched towards the tree line not so much to find the ammunition but to gain the dubious safety that the trees offered. If he could just get there, he thought desperately, perhaps he could keep going, blend into the thickening forest long enough to get his bearings and get on out of this mess. He'd done it once before, hadn't he?

He knew it was a pipe dream from the start. With the frigid wind sweeping past his ears and the brittle crust of the thin snow cutting into his face and hands each time he fell, he had little time to regret his actions. Every instinct was focused on survival and the futile hope that he could somehow make it through this horrible, horrible nightmare.

A sharp *crack!* split the cold silence behind him. Nathan threw himself to the ground a half–second after a cruel rush of air tore past his left arm, taking a sliver of his battered jacket with it. There was no time left for wishful thinking as he crawled through the snow and wet, dead grass, his shoulders and rump rising and falling while Bennett and Just Jerry took half–hearted shots at him just for the hell of it. Incredibly, Bennett had been telling the truth, and he found the bag that the Sheriff had placed beneath the willow tree and tore it open, his split lips twisting in a bitter grimace to reveal broken teeth. Nathan wasn't even sure he could load the pistol and it was a miracle he didn't drop it. All he had as a guide was a vague memory of an old hunting rifle from a forgotten childhood in Alabama; his mind was far too frazzled to call up anything else.

His hands were numb, the blood frozen to a cold stickiness that slowed his shaking fingers even more as he tried to cram the two bullets into their chambers and force his scrambled thoughts to slow between the sick pounding of his heart. Peering through the gnarled branches and dried stalks of grass and weeds along the ground, Nathan felt bile threatening to back up his throat once more. He didn't want to aim this weapon, didn't want to shoot anybody. A vague part of him was amazed that the sweet, simple pleasure of holding Emily in his arms this morning had ever even existed.

Again there was the dull report of a gun; a millisecond later Nathan choked off a cry as a hole seemed to burst from his shoulder of its own accord, belching hot blood into the torn fabric surrounding it. He clapped a hand to it automatically, then dropped the gun at his feet in response to the agony he'd caused himself.

Another shot, this one missing the same shoulder by only a few inches, told Nathan the men were tired of their game. Bennett's voice boomed across the clearing.

"Time to die, Carter!" the Sheriff screamed. Nathan's pain–spasmed fingers searched frantically along the snow for the pistol he'd dropped as he kept the two men in his fragmenting field of vision. That was a hard task; they were weaving and bobbing across the clearing towards him as though they were the terrified ones with bruises and busted bones instead of him. His hand closed around the gun as Just Jerry popped up thirty feet on his right and fired. Nathan ducked and rolled, registering Bennett's words piece–meal in his ears through the crackling sounds of dead vegetation being crushed under his moving weight.

He came to a wobbling stop, pushed himself to his knees and pointed the gun in the direction of Sheriff Bennett's voice.

"You may be wantin' change, boy!" the man bellowed. The Sheriff's hands dropped into a deadly, practiced firing stance, his next words nearly drowned out by the thunder of gunfire. "But don't look for it in *your* lifetime!"

Nathan squeezed off a single, instinctive shot before Sheriff Bennett's bullet opened hellfire in his head.

CHAPTER VII
1961

Emily?" he whispered. His voice was thick and foreign to his own ears, faraway.

"What?" someone asked urgently. "What'd you say?"

He felt himself being pulled on, then propped against something cold and riddled with lumps, maybe the seat of an automobile.

Shit, he thought resentfully, pain *again*, and he could feel a wetness he knew already was his own blood, all over everything. The vehicle started with a jerk and sway much too pronounced to be anything but a truck, the exaggerated movement making it impossible to find a position that didn't cause excruciating pain. A ride that seemed endless, or was at least an hour long; then people yelling and screaming and pulling on him anew like he was in just fine shape, thank you very much, not a thing in the world wrong—God forbid these quarter-brained folks should treat him a little gently and him half hanging outta the cab of this truck with a bullet hole in his head.

"Bring him inside," a woman said. Her voice was tired and fraught with worry and fear, and he didn't recognize it. "I'll have to call the doctor—"

"No!" A man's snarl cut her off. "No one needs to know about this, you hear?"

"But he's hurt bad!" the woman cried in response. "He might be dying!"

"Don't be stupid," the man snapped. "Lookie here." A hand floated into his field of vision and prodded at his scalp; his head shifted and he groaned. "See?" the voice continued. "It ain't nothing but a flesh wound, that's all. Cuts on the head always bleed a lot. Your man'll have one hell of a headache in the morning, but that's all."

"But what if he has a concussion!"

"Just shut up and call the boy out here to help get him inside. He's been bounced around too much already. Hurry up!"

✳   ✳   ✳

He opened his eyes three hours later. The brain inside his skull was doing a sick dance of agony; still his gaze made a bleary course around the room, noting the unimaginative but clean wallpaper and fresh curtains, the matching floral bedspread that had been drawn up under his chin. Despite the obvious newness of the furnishings, there was pall over the room, an *oppressiveness* that permeated everything from the tasseled lamp shade to the green and gold fabric of the bedcoverings. He recognized it instantly: *fear*.

Every inch of movement brought a yard of pain, and bringing his hands up to where he could see his own flesh was an accomplishment of which he could be proud. His skin, he discovered through the haze of his headache, was as white as that of the sallow-faced woman who dozed in the rocking chair at the side of the bed.

He managed to turn his head to the side so he could study her in more detail and his eyes slid first across her thin, defeated expression then to the bedside table, finally coming to rest on the silver star and name tag which rested there.

When he realized who he was, he leaned over the side of the bed and vomited on the floor.

※   ※   ※

Why, I killed my own damned self, he marvelled the next morning. *Both ways. I killed Nathan Carter, just as he must have killed m—*

"I brought you some coffee, Thomas." Donna, his new wife of some twenty–odd years, stood just outside the bedroom door, her voice timid. "A–and some toast, with sweet orange marmalade, just the way you like it." She seemed absolutely terrified to actually step into the room.

"Not very hungry, but I'll see what I can eat." The best he wanted to try was a whisper; anything more strenuous, like breathing, made the headache worse. He didn't think he could stomach any more of the aspirins Donna dutifully offered him every four hours; his stomach had been roiling in protest half the day and was just starting to settle itself. A lot of that had to do with coming to grips with his new identity. For the first time, he didn't care to remember much about his new past, though there were some things he'd have no choice but to learn. But, he decided, only the basics; this time he was going to think of himself as New And Improved.

Donna came forward hesitantly, a gaudy plastic tray clutched between shaking hands, the spoon rattling within its mug of coffee. She looked lost as to where to set it, and for a moment he thought she might actually drop it.

"Donna, just put it down," he said irritably. "Stop shaking like I'm gonna smack you or something." She blanched and with a guilty twinge he realized that was probably exactly what she expected.

"I—I—" she stuttered, then pressed her lips together in fright.

"Put it over there." The "new" him waved at the dresser and the movement cost him immense effort. "All's I want right now is the coffee. Where's yours?"

She looked at him in surprise. "My coffee? Why, it's in the kitchen—"

"Well, why don't you get it and sit in here with me," he suggested. She opened her mouth to question him and he let himself glower at her just enough to give her the incentive to do what he'd asked. She scurried away obediently and a minute later she was back and sitting somewhat uncomfortably in the rocker with her cup of coffee clutched in nervous fingers.

Sheriff Thomas James Bennett—T.J. to his friends—settled himself gingerly against his pillows and got to the business of finding out about his life.

※   ※   ※

He didn't much like what he discovered. Learning all this stuff was a tricky business to begin with despite having an injury to the head on which he could blame his faulty memory, plus he had a hunch that the worst things were still to come. For instance, it hadn't taken Donna to tell him a few things—*important* things—that he already knew: one, he was a no-account murderer, and two, he was some kind of ranking member in the Ku Klux Klan. There were two murders that he knew of for sure: Nathan Carter and that drifter, Hiram Miller. It was hard to believe he'd been so cruel as to actually name his dog after a dead man.

And then, of course, there was the matter of that damned dog itself, Joker, Miller—whatever he wanted to call him. It was an easy bet that the animal would know in its guts that T.J. wasn't the same person he used to be. Then what?

And underlying it all, a bitter sense of resentment and a deep sense of disbelief. Had he really once been that greedy, naive old woman who'd left all those loose ends dangling like puppet strings just waiting to be yanked? T.J. would've gritted his teeth if it hadn't hurt so damned bad. Well, he'd just see how much he got slapped around this time.

Spending Sunday flat on his back in bed was just the ticket to fix up the nasty wound to his head, and he figured the dull-witted former sheriff hadn't had that much of a brain to lose to Nathan Carter's bullet anyway. No one from Harmony asked questions; besides, as the Sheriff of the town he wasn't expected to work on Sundays. That's why he had two deputies—bumbling jackasses, both of 'em—down at the station.

Adam Thayer was another matter though, and T.J. was disgusted at the fact that Thayer was an actual family member in his new existence. His brother-in-law came to see T.J. at mid-afternoon the day after T.J. nearly had the top of his head shot off, not long after Thayer had finished escorting his own wife back home after worship services. Looking at the lean man standing at the foot of his bed, T.J. found it incredible that Donna, his own timid, servile wife, could ever be related to Thayer. He was surprised to feel a whole mix of emotions whirling inside him for Thayer: admiration, envy, fear, even a basic, dark rage over their different classes. T.J. gave a bitter, secret smile at that thought.

"So," said Adam. T.J.'s new brother-in-law had dismissed Donna with a wave of his hand and now settled himself on the seat of the rocker with a decisive tug on the perfect pleat of one pants leg before folding his arms. "Jerry tells me you two took care of the Negro. I'm glad to hear it. Unfortunately, mostly due to your injury, it's unfinished business."

T.J. struggled to sit up amid the pillows and coverings Donna had tucked around him. He felt fat and unhealthy, as stuffed and plump as the feather-filled pillows. There was something else making him edgy and mean-spirited besides the beastly ache in his head, a siren scream in his blood that he realized with growing horror was the beginnings of alcoholism.

"What's unfinished about it?" T.J. asked. It was easy to push aside the thin admiration that was leftover from T.J.'s hazy past; now he downright disliked Adam Thayer and suddenly realized he didn't even want the man in his house. Bile backed up his throat and soured his saliva as T.J. realized something else, too; Adam Thayer was the only reason he *had* a house.

"Well," Thayer said, "we both know he had a wife. You remember we saw her on the street last Sunday when we were sitting out front of the coloreds' church. She is, of course, already asking after her husband. Seems she's already called down at the station four or five times this morning, according to Deputy Shelton."

"W–what should I do?" T.J. loathed asking, but knew it was expected.

"Why, you're going to have to 'find' the Negro's body, conduct an investigation, the whole thing. If you and Jerry hadn't been toying with Carter on Saturday, you all could've taken the body over the state line and dumped it in the swamp for the Highway Patrol to deal with—providing something was left after the 'gators got through with it. Now you'll have to make it look as though you're searching for some murderer." His brother–in–law raised an eyebrow. "Pin it on another colored, if you can. That would be best, in fact. In the meantime, go to the widow and bring her the bad news. And you're going to have to do it up right, no trouble–making." Thayer looked at him with hard eyes the color of dirty gravel.

"When you see that women, you're going to have to act like you're really, *truly* sorry that nigger is dead."

✳ ✳ ✳

Washed–out blue eyes stared back from the mirror, set in a puffy, over–fed face punctuated by patches of broken blood vessels and crowned by sandy hair that was too short and wanted to be greasy even when it was clean. T.J. straightened his collar and sighed, his hands patting his pockets and belt to make sure everything was there. All that weight—club, ammunition, service pistol—yet he still felt comfortable; after all these years, this overweight body had apparently grown used to the extra baggage.

God, how he wished someone else could do this.

T.J. stepped out of the bathroom and crossed the short hallway to the kitchen. Donna was at the sink, up to her elbows in suds and dirty dishes; six–thirty in the morning and already she looked tired. Their only child, John Howard, a thin thirteen–year–old with a face as pinched as his mother's, sat at the table and poked indifferently at a bowl of over–sweetened corn flakes without bothering to look up. T.J. started to cram his hat atop his head and barely stopped short of actually raking the brim across the ragged tear in the back of his scalp. Instead he rested it in a careful position along the surface of his hair.

He stared helplessly at his new family. Eating his own breakfast a half hour ago had been an ordeal and the thought of a future in this house was nearly unbearable. But it was all he had, and he would have to make do.

"Going to work," T.J. announced. He wasn't sure what response he'd expected, but whatever it had been, it wasn't coming. The boy kept playing with his food, and his wife merely gave a furtive glance in his direction then went back to concentrating on the mound of soap bubbles in the sink. T.J. sighed again and pulled open the back door, holding it wide on purpose and letting the cold wind sweep into the room and gain the attention of his listless wife and son.

"John Howard, you stop messing around and eat your food so's you can get to school and get out of your mother's hair. She looks tired enough to go back to bed and catch a few extra hours of sleep."

Confused, Donna finally lifted her head towards him. "But Thomas, you know I do the wash on Monday—"

"The wash'll wait," he said shortly.

He left Donna with her mouth dropped open in surprise while his son glared at him suspiciously.

✱   ✱   ✱

He'd been a lot of things—man, woman, even monster—and done a lot of things, had felt what he'd thought had been the whole imaginable range of human emotions. But, once again and not at all surprisingly, he was wrong: Never, ever had he experienced anything like the feeling of getting out of the police cruiser in front of Nathan and Emily Carter's beat–up little house. T.J. didn't think there was a word in the English language—or any language, for that matter—which could describe the combination of longing, regret and guilt he felt…and all of it so strangely intertwined with the fading remnants of the hate and brutality so carefully tended by T.J. Bennett during his not–so–long lifetime.

His few and precious memories of Emily were odd and softly focused, spiked with danger and romance, as though that existence had been the short reel of a silent movie seen through a gauze scarf. She opened the front door and stood there staring at him, her swollen eyes wide and frightened, but still unflinching. If she noticed the cold wind, she gave no sign.

For a few horrible seconds, as his throat tried to work the sounds out, T.J. Bennett wasn't sure whose voice might come from his mouth. Habit tried to make his chest work up a nasty wad of phlegm and he swallowed it back down and grimaced.

"Miz Carter," he finally managed. He remembered the hat on his head and hastily yanked it off, feeling the sharpness of the wind as it slid beneath his hair and bit at the lips of his wound.

"Sheriff Bennett." Emily lifted her chin, like a boxer asking to take a punch. "I expect you've got some news for me."

"I, uh—" T.J. swallowed again, then forced his tongue to work properly this time. "I'm afraid we've found your husband, ma'am. He's…what I mean is, I'm sorry to say it appears Nathan is, uh, dead." He hadn't the faintest idea how to blame Nathan's murder on some poor innocent, and wasn't going to try.

For a moment Emily Carter simply stood there, her deep–pool gaze locked onto his while her fingers dug viciously into the skin of her own arms; then she turned her back and walked inside. Before she shut the door, she stopped and spoke to him without looking around.

"You've never been sorry about a Negro man in your life, Sheriff Bennett." She couldn't have been more wrong.

✳   ✳   ✳

Next to telling the woman who'd once been his wife that he was now dead, bagging Nathan Carter's body had been one of the worse things T.J. ever had to do. It was utterly terrifying to see the corpse of someone he knew had been himself only the day before yesterday, and mind–twisting to think about the actual sequence of events that had taken place: him firing at Nathan Carter at the same instant that Carter must have fired at him. There was no doubt whatsoever in T.J.'s mind that his bullet had killed Carter at the same moment that Carter's bullet had struck pay dirt in his own skull. It was the most perplexing form of suicide. If he had to go through much more of this, he wouldn't know who the hell he was.

And the body…oh, Jesus. The sight was terrible, the smell worse, even though the weather had been cold and the temperature had dropped below freezing the last two nights. T.J. supposed he ought to be thankful that it wasn't summer and in the nineties. It was sad when the only thing good that could be said about a situation was that there were no flies or maggots or beetles to reckon with.

The corpse of Nathan Carter was barely recognizable. Not only had he been beaten so badly that his face had been swollen and tight when he died, the Sheriff's bullet, a .38 hollow point, had caught the man along the line of the left eyebrow, disintegrating most of that side of his head and exposing the red and gray pulp that was the inside of his skull to a hungry Mother Nature and her elements. In the daytime's cold and damp weather the bacteria and mold had already started to work, not to mention all the little scavengers in the woods that had come to enjoy a share of this fine, free meal. Only the thrashing of T.J. and his deputies through the grass and underbrush had frightened away the last of the hungry creatures.

"Shee–it," Shelton said. "Sure wish this was one of them big cities, where some lowboy from the morgue would have to come and shovel up this mess." He waved a hand in front of his face. "Course, they ain't much better when they're alive." He hawed aloud at his own joke.

"Think you'd smell any better if *you* was dead?" T.J. snapped. Shelton blinked and the sheriff motioned towards the ground. "Get over here and slide that end of the bag under his feet. Let's get this over with."

As the sheriff, T.J. could've ordered his men to do it all, and of course the old T.J. would've done exactly that. Now he felt a twisted sense of responsibility that made him pull on rubber gloves and help move the body himself. Even through the gloves he could feel the cold, stiffened flesh that had once been the living, breathing Nathan Carter, that had once been… But he couldn't allow himself to think about that anymore, couldn't let what was forever gone intrude on what was happening in the here and now. Nathan's previously ebony skin had turned gray and black and green, the remaining eye cloudy and covered with a slimy, whitish film that had originated at the wound and crept down the face and neck. Heart thundering in his chest, T.J. struggled to turn the body onto the bag while the still–open eye gazed at him in permanent, silent accusation; in some places the corpse was borderline soft and T.J. hoped to God his hands wouldn't sink right inside Carter's swollen body.

At last it was done, the dark green bag zipping away the sight of his crime as T.J. peeled off the gloves and wiped his face with a dirty bandanna. The gunshot wound on his head was bleeding again, seeping under his hair in a slow, uncomfortable dampness, and T.J. had one helluva headache. It was going to be a long time before he forgot this.

※　　　　　※　　　　　※

In a terrifyingly short time T.J. had come to realize that his was a very different existence than the one which the restless Nathan Carter had led. While it was not at all genteel, by Harmony standards he had it damned good: a house and a steady, easy job, a wife and son—though one seemed terrified of him and the other's affection was questionable—and most of all, a direct, irrevocable connection to Adam Thayer, the money behind nearly every worthwhile business in the town. But it was also a life filled with more hate and darkness than T.J. had ever realized was possible, and God knew he'd certainly seen some variety along the way.

This time, the hate came wearing robes of white and carrying crosses of fire.

"Now, here's what you do." Thayer pressed a heavy brown paper beg into T.J.'s hands. "Everything's in there but the switch. A friend of mine from Texas is sending me some radio–controlled switches, fancy stuff like you've never seen." His brother–in–law grinned, showing wide, perfect teeth, the kind that only the rich in a place like Harmony could afford. "They ought to be here by tomorrow afternoon, and Jerry'll hook them all up. He's very familiar with that type of thing."

"Then what?" T.J.'s hands were sweating, staining the paper bag where he held it.

"I'll call you sometime Saturday with the address. We're going to hit one of the houses in Mabelton, though the decision hasn't been made yet as to which one exactly. It'll belong to one of those big mouth political activists, though. You'll plant it while they're at church—"

"Me?" T.J interrupted. "Why me? Can't Jerry do it?"

Thayer looked at him strangely. "Why *not* you? Jerry'll be working at another location, anyway." He peered at T.J. "Say, you aren't getting cold feet, are you? Getting a little soft after digging up that body?" Adam's voice was sympathetic but his eyes were like cold marbles. "You should've let your boys handle that business, T.J. It's time you starting learning to delegate more."

All T.J. could manage was a nod, but this seemed enough to satisfy the other man. Thayer stood and dusted his hands together with finality, "Good, then we're all set. Don't worry about waiting for me to call Saturday. There's only a few places in this town you can be, and I can *always* find you."

* * *

"How would you take to the idea of moving?"

Fork poised in mid-air, Donna looked up from her plate in surprise as John Howard frowned. "Move to where?" she asked.

"Away from here," T.J. answered. "Up north, for instance. Remember—"

"I like it here," John Howard interrupted. "And besides, I just got old enough to be in the White Youth Alliance."

T.J. held up a hand to silence him. "I don't want to hear that," he snapped. He took the sharpness out of his voice with an effort and spoke more reasonably. "You don't need to be in the Alliance, John, and you don't need to be learning the stuff they teach either." From the corner of his eye, T.J. could see his wife watching him in fascination; Donna was looking better already, more rested and calm, less like the terrified fieldmouse she'd so resembled a few days ago. Changes, how well he knew, could come quick as a sunrise and be adapted to even quicker. Sometimes, though, adapting meant breaking, and he sure hoped to avoid that this time.

"Dad, what's the *matter* with you?" John Howard demanded. "The Alliance was all you talked about for years, now you don't want me in it? That doesn't make any sense!"

"Things…change," he muttered. He tore his gaze away from the furious glare of his son and studied the ragged edges of his slice of dry meatloaf instead.

"You want to go up *north*?" Donna asked.

"Yeah," T.J. said eagerly, looking up again. He leaned forward over the table, his dinner cold and forgotten. "It's been a long time since I talked to him—years, even—but I've got a cousin up there, remember? Robert, he lives in Des Moines, Iowa, and he owns a trucking company. The last time we talked he said he could probably get me a steady route running loads of corn feed to the western cattle states."

"Oh great," John Howard said scornfully. "A truck driver. Whyn't you ask him if you can work on the docks with his niggers?" The boy snickered.

"There ain't going to be no more talk like that in this house!" T.J. smacked an open palm on the table and his son flinched and stared at him. "I'm through with it—and so are you. Understand?" John Howard said nothing and T.J. kept talking. "There's going to be some changes around here, changes in attitude, changes in language, changes in a lot of things." He fixed his gaze sternly on the teenager. "And the first thing going is that word, you hear? Second, we're all going to do some real serious thinking about what exactly makes us believe someone's not as good as us because they look different."

John Howard dropped his fork on the table, the sound clattering over his hissed words.

"What did you say?" T.J. demanded.

"I *said*—" John Howard's voice rose to a near scream. "I never though my father would turn out to be a nigger lover!"

T.J. slapped the boy so quickly he had time only to wish he hadn't.

* * *

"You shouldn't have done that," Donna said timidly. She sighed, then climbed quickly into bed, pulling the blanket up high under her chin. "It'll only make things worse."

T.J. thought he could detect a slight tremor in her voice, and he wondered if it was the stress of the scene with John Howard or a spillover of the terror he had so effectively instilled in her life throughout the past two decades, the same fear that seemed to be quickly melting away in response to his changed treatment of her. He fought the scowl that wanted to take over his face, an expression so natural to him that it beckoned like breathing. He vowed he would not be that way any longer, not to Donna, not to John Howard, not to *anyone*.

"I know. I'll apologize tomorrow morning." Donna looked at him, speechless. He sat on the edge of the bed to take off his socks and heard the bed frame grown under his weight. After a moment he swung his legs up and under the covers, then rolled on his side to face her. "Look," he said, "let's not carry this to bed with us. There's time enough to fix it tomorrow, okay?"

Donna nodded mutely. Here and there the skin of her arms showing below the sleeves of her nightgown was still mottled by the shadows of bruises that he knew he had inflicted. Her flesh was pallid and doughy, not at all like the smooth and firm expanse of ebony he half–remembered, half–fantasized about. Still, there was a certain warmth, a certain *familiarity* that a part of T.J.'s mind also remembered and craved—even loved. His left hand slid beneath the blanket, then under the hem of her gown. His fingers eased along her hip, then tickled the warm space at the juncture of her thighs and she gasped a little, her body rigid.

"Come on, Donna," he whispered. "Loosen up some." He wanted to say something reassuring, maybe *Remember when we were kids?* or something equally silly. But the snide part of him that was the old T.J. snickered and reminded him that through everything, Donna had been little more than tits and a warm place to stick it; whether she enjoyed their lovemaking had never made a difference. *But it does now*, he thought grimly, though he felt a little desperate when he realized her reluctant, awkward responses were softening his erection.

Vague memories of a dark woman who had once slipped willing arms around him seared T.J.'s thoughts, and it was sadly easy to close his eyes and open his mind to that other life and that other woman.

* * *

"Don't know where those sumbitchin' switches got off to," Jerry complained. He was leaning over T.J.'s desk, his breath a noxious mini–cloud of old food and tobacco juice. "Never did come in. The fella said he sent the things by special delivery, but hell, that shit don't run to Harmony on the weekends. Bastard shoulda made the drive himself. Now we're gonna have to rig 'em up by hand."

"I'm sure you'll find a way," T.J. said sardonically.

Jerry ignored T.J.'s sarcasm. "Ran into Simmons at the tavern," he said conversationally. He turned and planted his hind end on the corner of the desk, crumpling a few yellowed sheets of paper in the process. T.J. started to say something, then decided against it; he didn't know or care what the papers had been for anyway. "Said you sold him Miller for fifty bucks." Jerry brought a hand up and jammed a toothpick between his lips; his next words came out rough and T.J. knew the toothpick was there only as a disguise for the grinding, generally pissed–off tone of the man's next statement. "I distinctly remember telling you I wanted that hound if you ever had a mind to get rid of him."

"Did you?" T.J. tried to look surprised and hoped he was doing a passable job. He'd known very well that Just Jerry had wanted that foul–tempered old dog; T.J. simply couldn't allow that animal—which would now chew *his* balls off in a second—to come into the hands of someone he didn't trust. And Just Jerry certainly fit that niche. "Well, I'm surely sorry, Jerry. It must've slipped my mind. Got some trouble with the boy at home, you know." The instant he said it, T.J. regretted the words.

Jerry's face lit up with interest. "John Howard? No shit. I always thought he was a model youngster."

T.J. tried to shrug it off. "Oh, he has his moments." Jerry nodded in understanding, as though they were comrades sharing some heavy secret. The truth, T.J. knew, was that Jerry didn't know crap about kids, wasn't even married for that matter. "Anyway," T.J. said, "I'm real sorry about Joker." He'd say anything to get the conversation away from his son and his personal life.

"You mean Miller," Jerry said with an amiable smile that fell far short of reaching his eyes. "Leastways, that's what you said you wanted to call him. Miller."

"Right," T.J. agreed. "Miller."

His mouth felt full of dirt.

✳   ✳   ✳

"I want to talk some more about moving," he told Donna in private Saturday night. John Howard had long since gone to bed—T.J. hoped—and he had some time alone with his wife. She looked sleepy but content; he didn't think it would take much to get her attentive.

He was right. Donna's face lit up immediately, and if she'd been a sad–looking puppy he was sure her ears would have perked. "You were really serious? When you said all those things?"

"I want us to actually pick a date," he continued. Her jaw dropped. "I'm going to call Robert next week, maybe Monday, and tell him that if he meant what he said, I'm ready to take him up on that job offer. If he's got an opening, we'll use that to plan when we leave. What do you think?"

"Are…are you sure?" Donna looked confused and pathetically hopeful, and T.J. wondered uneasily just how long this quiet woman had wanted to be free of this town—and maybe her once brutal husband. But what of her family?

"But what if he can't get you a job?"

"Then it might not be so easy," T.J. admitted. The bed sagged as he climbed in his side and pulled the covers up to his waist. He made no move to turn off the light. "I won't gloss things over, Donna. This is a big move. We've got a little saved, but it still means selling the house and finding somewhere to live in a strange town, pulling John Howard out of school and putting him in a new one…and what about Adam? You won't see him nearly as much. Maybe only once or twice a year, if that much."

She was silent long enough for a rope of worry to twist its way into T.J.'s gut. When she finally spoke, her words were a shock and a big lesson about how little T.J. had known about his own wife all these years.

"I never really *liked* my brother," she said.

✳   ✳   ✳

"Dammit, Thomas James," Thayer said in exasperation. "I thought you told me you knew something about explosives."

"No," T.J. said shortly. "You must have misunderstood me." Adam Thayer's eyes widened in surprise, then narrowed. T.J.'s nerves jangled; he'd rather have his brother–in–law shouting at him than staring at him like this. No telling what was going on in that viper's mind. "Well, then," Adam finally said in a purposely calm voice. "I'll just explain it…again." Now the man's eyes were nearly closed, no more than deep, horizontal slashes in his handsome face. "And you will pay attention, won't you?"

T.J. didn't dare do anything but agree.

"All right. Now look here at this diagram. It's simple." Thayer tapped the piece of paper with his forefinger. "Plastic explosives, eight sticks, more than enough to do the job. Set the cap in nice and snug, and spread out the fuse. The blueprints from the town hall say the gas furnace is in a utility room just inside the back porch; tuck the package below the back steps, pushed as far back as you can without actually crawling under. Be careful no one sees you—of course—and the only thing you can afford to be fussy about is making sure the fuse doesn't show. Bury it in the bushes, but make sure there's no break in the line." For a moment a heavy scowl crossed Thayer's features, making them ugly and weasel–like. "We were really counting on those switches coming in."

"So I have to light these by hand?" T.J. asked doubtfully. "Isn't that dangerous? And isn't it risky for the Sheriff of Harmony to be doing this? What if I get caught?"

Thayer stared at him in disgust. "I've never known you to act yellow, T.J. If someone stops you, just tell them you saw someone put something under there and send them to call the local law. Besides, you won't be in uniform, and you'll have plenty of time to get clear—a good thirty seconds per foot of fuse. Twenty feet and you'll have ten minutes to go back to your truck, and we're figuring thirty to forty feet of fuse to make it from the back porch to the alley." Thayer gave a derisive snort. "Some kind of change has come over you, boy. I can't believe a little scratch to the head's done all this." He looked at T.J. meaningfully.

T.J. gazed back without bothering to answer. What was there to say, anyway? He wanted only to take his wife and son away from this hate-filled, festering little town and go someplace where if you smiled at your neighbor and he happened to be a black man you didn't end up with a cross burning in your front yard. And T.J. sure didn't want to be the one lighting the matches anymore.

His brother-in-law sighed and turned his attention back to his plans for the bombings in Mableton. "You plant the bomb while the family is at church, then go around and park down the street from the house. When you see them get home—and this guy is regular as a bowel movement—drive around to the alley and park at the end, then walk on down and light the fuse. Then walk back to your truck and drive away. Be very, *very* careful not to do anything that'll draw attention to yourself—no speeding or getting into a scrape over the way someone's driving, you understand?" His face bland, T.J.'s mind was still spinning over the casual way Adam had used the word 'family' in reference to the people he planned to murder.

Thayer looked at his watch, pushed the bag over and handed T.J. a corner torn from a piece of note paper. "It's time for you to go. Here's the address. Don't screw this up, Thomas James. There's big eyes on this one, people from high up in the United Klans of America looking to see how we fare here in little pissant Harmony, how we run things internally and control things outside the town itself. You let me down and by Christ you'll wish you were never born."

Listening to the receding sound of Adam Thayer's boot heels on the worn floor, T.J. was already considering that.

✳ ✳ ✳

I'm not cut out for this, T.J. thought desperately. Just Jerry, T.J. knew, had followed him all the way to Mableton on the pretense that he had a few things to pick up that could only be gotten here, and wasn't that the biggest crock of bullshit? Having Jerry's rust-eaten old junker practically sitting on his back bumper during the entire trip from Harmony to Mableton had been enough to give T.J. a sick, pounding headache, probably from switching his eyes to the rear view mirror every ten seconds to see if the bastard was still there. Now T.J. grimaced and reached inside the bag Thayer had given him; his hand found the slick, cool surface of the explosives and he pulled them out, hating the way his fingers dug gently into the bricks. Crouched between this house and the one next door, he wished that someone would see him and call the Mableton police or come over and demand to know what he was doing, turn their dog loose on him, *anything*. But the afternoon was silent and cold; even the sidewalk beneath his numb feet was well-shoveled of the snow that might warn the man who lived here that someone had been screwing around the side of his house. T.J. had no doubt that Jerry, his half-brained sights set on the job of sheriff now that T.J. was losing favor with his brother-in-law, waited in the warmth of his own truck somewhere out of sight, checking to see that Thayer's instructions were followed. The bricks were wired tightly together and T.J.'s fingers were trembling as he pressed the detonating cap into the centermost one and made sure the fuse was securely attached before shoving the bomb underneath the steps and starting to string the fuse along the side of the house.

He stopped and peered around. The view of the street in front was blocked by a waist-high tangle of branches that in summer was a thick bush; the back gave him a clear view—and exit—to the street. From the deep shadows over-riding the walkway between the houses, T.J. was certain that not even Jerry could see him. On impulse he pulled out his pocket knife and flipped it open, then reached his arm as far underneath the porch as possible without crawling under or pulling the bomb back towards him. Frigid sweat beaded along his temples as T.J. found the fuse only inches from the blasting cap and severed it, looking around guiltily before putting away his blade.

At least a little relieved, T.J. strung the wire, hiding it carefully alongside the building and dormant greenery, feeding it to a point inside the back gate. A casual glance at the ground would never pick it up—you had to know it was there to spot it. He grinned and walked casually back to his truck where it was parked out front and a couple of houses down, settling himself inside as comfortably as he could in the icy temperature without actually starting the engine while he waited for the Negro folks to come home from church. *I can do this,* he thought triumphantly. *At least make it look like I tried, and give myself a reprieve for a short while.*

Fifteen minutes later—just when T.J. was on the verge of starting the truck anyway and be damned to the attention it might draw—there they came. There were five of them: the man and his wife, a middle-aged couple not much different from him and Donna except for the color of their skin, and three kids; a pretty girl John Howard's age, her skin like fused coal amid the layers of the light-colored scarf she wore, a boy a couple of years her junior with a bold, bright grin, and the youngest of all, a little girl no more five years old. Her heir stuck out in four or five of those thin, spiky braids with pink bows on the ends, and even from his perch across the street, T.J. could see the gap of a missing baby tooth in her smile. For a second his heart went cold, then he remembered the sweet feel of the fuse wire parting under his knife and felt his shoulder muscles unbunch as the family clambered up the front steps and let themselves in with a flurry of stomping feet and laughter. Ten more seconds and the street returned to silence.

Somewhere, T.J. knew, Just Jerry was watching and waiting.

T.J. gave them five more minutes to get settled inside the house, then gratefully started the truck, letting the engine warm momentarily before driving around and parking in the same spot at the mouth of the alley. He would have liked to leave the truck running so he could be sure of a safe and sure escape; now that he knew nothing would happen to the Negro man and his family, he no longer wanted to be caught and questioned. He simply wanted to get out and go home, make the arrangements that would take him and his own family as far as possible from the hellish little town of Harmony.

Pulse thumping sickly in his throat, T.J. walked down the alley and fingered the matches in his pocket. He had visions of lighting the fuse—harmless though it might be—and then hurriedly returning to his truck, only to have the old vehicle refuse to start, that fabled, foiled getaway of so many cop movies come to life. Sure, no bomb would explode—but church was over and many of this block's families had or were returning home from services even now. How would he explain his presence here, excuse his white face not only in a Negro neighborhood, but around the home of a prominent Negro community leader?

Still unseen, T.J. ducked through the open rear gate and hugged the garage wall, waiting to see if anyone had noticed him. His fingers felt chilled to the bone, and clumsy, too, as though he was trying to sew a tiny button on a shirt with all his fingers tied together. He crouched and found the end of the fuse wire, then fumbled with the matches; it took him three strikes to get a flame going, two more matchsticks before one would stay lit long enough to get the fuse wire burning. By the time he got back to his truck, his nerves had him gasping for breath as though he'd just run the length of the alley rather than taken it at a quick walk. He truly believed that the only thing that kept his unhealthy, overweight body from having a heart attack was the blessed relief he felt when the old truck started the first time he turned the key.

T.J. drove away, not quite believing he had actually pulled it off. Any second— as he turned the corner of the block, as he pulled smoothly into the traffic along the state highway leading back to Harmony—he kept expecting to hear, to *feel* the sound of an explosion. He was terrified something had gone wrong, even though he *knew*, at least as sure as he knew anything, that he had cut that fuse wire.

Yet he couldn't help the terror that made his knuckles white and bloodless where they curved around the cold steering wheel.

✳ ✳ ✳

"Morning, T.J. How's it going?"

T.J. swallowed before turning around, determined that he wouldn't show his fear of Adam Thayer, wouldn't think about what this man could and had already done to his life and his small family. Late yesterday afternoon he and Donna had talked more about moving, this time with a calendar and a red pen on the table in front of them. The conversation had been cut short when John Howard had come home early from some kind of practice—football, basketball, something— with a stab of shame, T.J. had realized he didn't even know. They had tried to talk to the boy again about moving, to include John Howard in at least some of the decisions that were going to redirect his life and his future, and it hadn't taken T.J. long to realize other things, too, such as the fact that his son was already hopelessly in love with the Klan and its twisted, dark ideals.

"Good morning, Adam," he managed now. "What can I do for you?" He tapped the pile of papers he held on the desk top, then pushed them aside; both of his deputies were out doing the morning donut dance, and he supposed it wouldn't have mattered anyway. One look from Thayer and they would have run like a couple of cowardly hounds.

His brother-in-law perched on the edge of the desk and T.J. thought wryly that it was a good thing he had cleared away the crumpled pile of forms; it would've been a shame to get any dust on Adam's fine suit. He guessed that corner seemed to be the sitting spot for people who were bound to give him a hard way to go. And oh, was he ever on the mark.

"Seems you and I ought to have a little talk," Thayer began in a congenial voice.

"Really." T.J. cocked one eyebrow and hardened his jaw. "What about?" The fear was still there, sure, but he figured it would only make a difference if he groveled and promised to mend his ways. Screw it; his days of kissing Thayer's ass were over.

Thayer's expression darkened a little at the interruption, then smoothed again. "My nephew stopped by the house yesterday afternoon, not long after you came back from Mabelton. The boy and I had a little—ah, chat."

Oh shit, T.J. thought. This was much, much worse than he'd expected. His excuses about the failed bombing were ready and waiting, but he wasn't prepared for a battle over his son. For a moment he almost rocked back in his chair at the nasty feeling of surprise in his gut, then he glowered and sat forward. "Is that so?" He tried to keep his tone from being outright belligerent, but was only partially successful.

Now his brother-in-law did frown. "Yes. He told me a lot of things, Thomas James. Like how you've been talking to my sister about moving up north and going to work for some trucking company. Taking the boy with you and teaching him a new way of thinking."

T.J. held his tongue and waited. More and more color had seemed to drain from Thayer's voice with each word, and a man would have to be blind not to realize that was an indication of how furious he was.

"Before you get the rash idea of moving, you should remember a few things," Thayer said. "Besides the fact that's my only sister and nephew whom you're planning to relocate, I've got a lot of time and money invested in *you*, and it goes way beyond just this crappy sheriff's job and that tidy little house you all live in. You and John Howard—remember how we planned it? Well, I haven't been lax on my end, Thomas James. You're this close—" Thayer made a motion with his thumb and forefinger. "—to being a Night Hawk. I think you know what comes with that: money, prestige, power—"

"I don't want it," T.J. cut in. He crossed his arms in a protective gesture and pushed his chin out.

"Excuse me?" Thayer slid to his feet, then leaned over and planted his hands on the desk, bending until his lean face was only inches away from T.J.'s own. "Did I hear you right? This certainly isn't the T.J. Bennett who came into my home three months ago and told me he wanted me to make sure his son got the best of the Brotherhood's education."

T.J. had just about reached his limit. He launched himself out of his chair and was pleased to see Thayer flinch at the movement, if only for a moment. "My son is exactly why we're moving, Adam. I see what your *education* is doing to him. He's just as mean and nasty as Jerry, and now he sneaks behind my back and goes whining to someone else about family matters that ought to be private. Is that something else you taught him?"

"I don't believe my ears are hearing this," Thayer said incredulously. "After all we've done—after all *I've* done for you—"

"You've done plenty all right, you murdering bastard!" Fear was trying to hammer little messages of caution into his mind, but rage pushed them aside. "Sure, most of the way things are for me and Donna and John Howard is my own fault. I know that. But even more than me, you took my son and taught him to hate—and for what? Because someone is a different race, or a different religion? Or just *different*." T.J. was shouting in his brother–in–law's face now, his own face red and streaming perspiration. "Well, we don't need that, do you hear? I *am* moving out of Harmony, and I *am* taking my wife and son with me! You can keep your ugly town and your ugly job—and your even uglier little secrets. We're going to make a new start where you dislike a man because he wronged you, not because his skin's a different color!"

Thayer stared at him in pointed silence for a minute, his complexion ashen except for two splotches of scarlet on his cheeks. When he finally tried to speak, it took him a few seconds to get the words past his lips. "That was quite a little speech. But I'm warning you, Thomas James. Other chapters of the Klan would hold a tribunal and banish someone...*undesirable*, but I don't like loose ends. And a man like you from the Inner Circle, and who knows as much as you do and then goes bad, that can be a real problem."

"Are you threatening me?" T.J. demanded. "Because if you are—"

"I had Jerry check on your work in Mabelton yesterday," Thayer continued as though T.J. hadn't spoken. "Had him check real close. Good thing, too; seems he found a big problem with the fuse wire on your set–up. Of course, if those damned switches had come in before this morning, it'd have been another story." Adam Thayer grinned suddenly, and T.J. wondered how it was he'd never noticed how predatory Thayer's teeth looked. "But not to worry. Jerry fixed it right up. He's always been a good man on the explosives; turns out he's a helluva lot better than you are, as a matter of fact."

T.J. gasped; he couldn't help it. "He...fixed it?"

"Blew pieces of that nigger and his family right to the clouds," Thayer hissed at him.

"God," T.J. croaked. He groped behind him for the chair and sat heavily.

"Well," Thayer's voice was light again. "Seems like you got some thinking to do, Thomas James. Maybe you ought to re–evaluate your priorities, reconsider moving up north, throwing your career and everything away. Like I said, I don't like loose ends—but I don't like wasted effort, either. Especially when the effort is on family." Thayer moved towards the door. "I reckon I'll give you a call at the house later this evening and see how things are going." He pulled the door open and started to step outside.

"Adam," T.J. said.

Thayer paused and looked expectantly over his shoulder to where T.J. sat rod-straight on his wooden chair. He smiled a little. "Yes?"

T.J. stood and planted his feet apart; his hands hung in tight fists at his sides but his words were calm and cold.

"Don't. Bother. Calling."

Lips pressed tightly together and nostrils flared, Adam Thayer's expression was thunderous as he slammed the door behind him.

✳   ✳   ✳

Hard work, T.J. thought, is a true balm for the soul, especially when it accomplishes something a man can *really* see, right then. Where once he might have thought them funny, especially if he'd been throwing a Negro man into the cell, T.J. now found the graffiti scrawled across the walls of the cell blocks disgusting and hateful. Amid crude, uneducated drawings of men and women with over-size genitalia, twenty years and hundreds of prisoners had built up the words "Niggers Die!" and "Whites Rule Now!" to a nearly palpable layer. Too many times the same deputies who were out cruising the town right now had thought it amusing to give a marker to a would-be artist and watch them "paint." T.J. now found it entirely satisfying to watch all the words, black or white, run into one smeary color under a sponge soaked in ammonia water.

Eyes burning from the fumes, T.J. dumped the last bucket full of dirty water down one of the toilets and flushed it, then tossed the sponge and bucket into the supply closet and washed his hands. The office clock ticked its way toward the noon hour, and through the front window he could hear the occasional sound of a passing car and the muffled conversation of people hurrying past, though the glass itself was so covered in frost that passers-by were only shadows gliding on the ice. His stomach, spoiled as it had been, was demanding food in spite of his nervousness over the argument with Thayer and his feeling of defeat and guilt at learning his plans to avoid the bombing in Mabelton had failed. If he didn't eat soon, he'd end up with another headache on top of everything else, but he was determined that at least the quantity of food that he ate was going to decrease.

T.J. shrugged on his jacket and hat, pulled the door behind him until he heard the lock catch, then stepped outside, blinking in the winter sunlight that bounced savagely off the snow of the roofs and unshoveled sidewalks. His patrol car was parked in its usual spot at the front curb and he settled himself behind the wheel and started it, listening to the powerful hum of the motor as he waited for the engine to warm up while he glanced around. Someone was leaning back in the shadows of the doorway of the five-and-dime across the street; he squinted and thought it might be Jerry.

T.J. grimaced, thinking about the house in Mabelton again. *Maybe,* he thought, *I'll drive home and have lunch with Donna.* In the old days he would've headed for the same coffee shop that the other guys visited each morning for brew and donuts, flirting cruelly with the lunchtime waitress, a overly–made–up woman unfortunately built like a cow, stringing her along for a half-price lunch (and never a tip) with the promise that he'd call her some night and they'd go out for drinks. No more though; today the best thought he had was of a homemade bowl of soup and a nice, logical discussion with Donna about moving, this time, as much as he loved his son—and he really did—without the boy around to throw his version of a terrible teenaged tantrum.

T.J. slipped the car in drive and glanced across the street again, trying to see through the glare and the frost obscuring the windshield, wishing the heater would work a little faster and clear the glass. He leaned closer to the window and finally rolled it down in frustration. It *was* Jerry, standing just inside the edge of the doorway's shadow, and this time, Jerry had seen him, too.

Still in the shade cast by the building, Just Jerry lifted an arm in greeting, letting his glove–free hand pass into the sun. As T.J. stared, Jerry waved again, rocking his hand back and forth at first, then stopping to hold something up as though he thought T.J. ought to see it. From the driver's seat, T.J. felt his belly tighten as he scarcely made out the evil grin that spanned Jerry's dimly–lit face from ear to ear.

T.J.'s eyesight had always been pretty good, and to prove it, he was one of the best marksmen in Harmony. Strangely, thinking about that made him remember Nathan Carter, and for an instant he fiercely regretted ever having learned to shoot.

Sunlight winked on metal in Jerry's hand, making T.J.'s eyes water when he strained to focus on the object.

T.J.'s gut seemed to shrink in on itself until his stomach was surely no larger than a baseball. He settled his hands tightly on the steering wheel as he realized exactly what it was that Just Jerry held.

Amid the memories of Harmony and the cruel sparkle of sun–washed steel, T.J. recalled Thayer saying this morning that those son–of–a–bitching radio controls had finally been delivered. Somewhere below the low, well–tuned throb of the car's engine, he thought he detected the tiniest of clicks.

The last thing Sheriff Thomas James Bennett heard was the sound of his own eardrums exploding.

CHAPTER VIII
1986

He woke to the sound of singing: sweet, sappy and piercing as only a soprano on morning radio could be—Olivia Newton John twittering about something that might have been love but registered only as agony in his abused brain. Groaning, he made the mistake of rolling over beneath a mountainous pile of bedcoverings; the movement sent a surge of nausea through his stomach and up his throat. He suppressed the stream of vomit only long enough to stumble his way uncertainly to the bathroom.

He felt better then, despite the fact that he was sitting on his rump in silk pajamas on cold ceramic tiles in the bathroom and trying to spit away the taste of bile. He tried to stand but his legs were weak and uncooperative, the chill floor soaking through his pants legs like a gigantic, freezing leech. He managed at last to crawl across the threshold of the bathroom and back onto the plush carpeting of the bedroom floor, leaning his head against the wall and panting, resting atop the carpet's warmth as his gaze explored the room and his fingers dug into the carpeting up to the middle knuckles of his fingers.

There were a lot of strange things in here, far more complicated–looking than anything he'd ever experienced. A curved telephone with square buttons and a twenty foot coiled cord, unlike any telephone he'd ever seen, something else with blinking red numbers he assumed was a clock, the strangest artwork on the walls. Although he sat at chin–level next to a huge bed, he could see windows on the other side of it that extended from nearly one end of the room to the other and disappeared out of his line of sight on beyond the bed. Could this be his home, his apartment? While a row of heavy draperies had been pulled open, from this angle he could see only the blue of clear sky. Somewhere outside, he felt sure the sun was shining.

He looked down and ran slender fingers across the nap of the gray carpet, its surface so thick and rich that his lean body, dressed in the deep maroon pajamas, seemed like some accidental bloody spill across its surface. A few feet away was a six–foot–long lacquered dresser a deeper shade of gray trimmed with chrome; beside it was a luxuriously over–stuffed chair covered in a fabric with gray strips exactly matching the color of the furniture. He'd never been in such an expensively decorated room.

Some time later he sat forward with a start, realizing that he had fallen asleep, propped against the wall like some discarded doll. He managed to push to his feet and take a few shambling steps to the edge of the bed before sitting again; he felt better, though feeling *good* seemed about as far away as the moon itself. A sliver of sunlight had worked its way around the edge of the farthest window and he studied it for awhile, then found the energy to go the window and look out.

He almost threw up again.

The windows were floor to ceiling; hundreds of feet below, water shimmered and spread dizzily across the horizon. How high was this building? For a second he couldn't make his mind comprehend its automatic answer of "thirty stories"––stories were something that in his experience had always come in twos and threes, apartments above general stores in small country towns. Then his brain kicked into over-drive and supplied another fragment or two of memory: Apartment—condominium, really—No. 3003, Lake Point Tower. He swallowed his shock and forced himself to look down again, down down down to the people and vehicles moving along Lake Shore Drive and the lakefront of Chicago, grateful for the sealed and unbreakable glass between himself and oblivion.

If it hadn't been for that…

* * *

His driver's license told him he was Wilmot—Will, for short—Keefe, a twenty-seven-year-old white male with light blue eyes and hair so black it was shocking against the pale, fragile skin of his face and body. He was young, fairly handsome, and, as an engraved business card in another fold of his wallet advised him, an attorney in what he remembered to be a very large law firm in downtown Chicago. Each item in the leather wallet he'd found on the nightstand jogged neatly into its slot in his mind and contributed to his gradually growing sense of hopeful disbelief.

He was young and unmarried. By all appearances, he was financially stable, perhaps somewhat wealthy. The only uncertainty in his future rested in the unremembered reason he had swallowed a thirty-count bottle of fifteen milligram Valium the night before, washing the whole mess down with half a liter of Bailey's Irish Cream. But why?

Whatever the reason, Will felt certain he could work it out. He concentrated on probing his memory for things that might have made a man sink into a depression that deep—embezzlement, murder, blackmail—yet nothing clicked. A few vague problems, difficulties with his parents, the fuzzy recollection of a quarrel with a faceless lover, but suicide?

Will couldn't help smiling, though the movement in his face only made his head ache more fiercely. There had been so many failures, so much misery…hardly a fair trade for the price Mae Johnson would ultimately pay. But at last, for the first time, he thought he might have a chance at a normal life.

* * *

The dose of pills Will had swallowed would not be so quickly flushed from his system. By mid-afternoon he felt better, but not so improved that he actually wanted to go outside. He settled instead for opening his briefcase and removing the office file inside; after a moment's indecision, he spread its contents on the glass table in the dining area of the huge room that doubled as the living and dining room. He hadn't felt well enough to face the task of dressing, though he had managed to figure out the coffee system and brew a strong pot. As far as work was concerned, Will's mind was a badly jumbled puzzle that needed study, and he hoped that reviewing a case file could push a few more of the pieces back into line.

A half hour later he sat back and frowned. An interesting case, but nothing pressing enough to warrant bringing home. In fact, this file wasn't tagged for action for another month, as though he'd known it would be awhile before he returned to the office...something that in itself explained why he felt no compulsion to telephone a vaguely remembered secretary and explain his whereabouts on what he believed was a Tuesday afternoon.

Restless and sickly, Will prowled the condominium, searching through the closets and drawers until he found a cache of old photographs in a Florsheim shoebox. He carried the box to the living room and settled onto a cream–colored leather sectional sofa that was one of the most comfortable things upon which he'd ever sat, then went through the photos slowly, like a voyeur taking a leisurely look at someone else's life. It helped only a little; some of the snapshots brought information instantly: his now dead parents, three sisters long since migrated to warmer or more fashionable parts of the States, the oldest of whom had made millions investing in high–risk stocks and now spent half of each year "resting" on the French Riviera. Other things were not so clear; a parade of people whom Will assumed to be schoolmates and past and present friends dotted the pictures, yet their names eluded him, the place and meaning each had held within his life a blank page and more than anything else an indication of how little those people had actually meant to him. Once in a great while shots of different women appeared, their ages marking the passage of time in his life, but these, too, remained a mystery. Had there been no one about whom he cared? Or who cared about *him*?

Will sighed and put the photographs aside. The most recent photograph, identified by the processing stamp on its back, had been of himself and another guy, both smiling and waving at the camera from what Will realized was Six Flags Amusement Park in Gurnee, Illinois. Yet all he could bring to mind was that he and this man had spent a holiday—Memorial Day—enjoying the rides, a weekend of unseasonably warm weather, a day full of sweet and fatty foods. Nothing else.

I should eat, he decided. The vague recollections of junk food made Will realize that something on his stomach would probably make him feel better. Standing uncertainly in the small but efficient kitchen, he studied the microwave oven fiercely, as though by concentrating he could force the forgotten skills back into his brain. He'd just about decided he might be able to operate the thing when the telephone hanging just inside the kitchen doorway rang.

He stared at it in indecision. Should he answer it? What if it was his secretary—what was her name, Angelique—calling to ask him to handle something? Suppose he wasn't able to answer her question, what then?

Ringgggggg

Each time, the bell seemed to get louder and more insistent, until it sounded as though it might be *screaming*—

Ringgggg

Seven rings, eight—

Will snatched the handset from its cradle.

"Yes?" His voice was nearly a shout.

Silence for a moment, then: "You don't have to bite my head off, Willie." The words were petulant.

"Don't call me Willie," he said automatically. "Who is this?" Something turned over in Will's memory, a sluggish thought that rippled away before he could grasp it.

"What do you mean *who is this?*" the faceless caller demanded indignantly. "Don't play games with me. I tried to reach you all last night, dammit! I even came over, but that damned doorman said you'd left instructions saying no one was to disturb you. I was terrified you'd done something rash—"

"What do you want, Arden?" The man's name, at least, had finally pushed its way through the rusty places in Will's mind. There was another shocked, dramatic pause; Will was about to suggest only half-jokingly that they stop this soap opera act and get on with it when Arden finally spoke. This time, his tone was more hushed, uncertain.

"Will, I—I only wanted to make sure you were all right, you know that. Look, I'm sorry about the way I've been acting. I realize how it must seem, how unfeeling. I'm not that way at all, inside, when it counts. Can't I see you? Can't we talk things out?"

Dread suddenly filled Will, along with the instant, absolute knowledge that he didn't want to talk to this man, didn't want to hear what had to be said. He opened his mouth to say so, but Arden's next words ground everything to a halt.

"Hell, Will. You know me. I never expected to live *this* long, much less forever. But I guess you did."

✳   ✳   ✳

The soda can was cool as Will rolled it across his skin, feeling the tickle of moisture transfer itself from the aluminum to his forehead. He'd never been in Illinois before—at least as far as he could remember in the convoluted paths of his past—and now that he was, Will found it a little hard to believe. He'd always thought the northern part of the central United States to be cold and forbidding, a climate much like a long-ago Salem Village's except that in the cities the snow fell from dirty, overcast skies in great clots upon miasmic, filthy tenement houses that barely sheltered their freezing occupants. A place where a five dollar bill could bring you the drug of false utopia and ten could buy your neighbor's death.

But Grant Park in the summer was exquisite, Buckingham Fountain itself defying description as its arches of water created shimmering rainbows in the bright afternoon sunlight. People whizzed by on streamlined versions of roller skates and twelve-speed bicycles in eye-blistering colors, their faces pink with exertion and tanned by the sun. The park, the city—even what little he'd seen of it so far—was nothing like the gray industrial wasteland he'd always pictured. It was *beautiful*.

"Hi."

Will didn't look up as Arden dropped onto the bench beside him. He couldn't bear to look Arden in the eyes just yet; denial and embarrassment warred against the sense of self-acceptance that this body had spent a lifetime cultivating. Will had thought he'd seen it all, experienced it all—even the things that all the people populating Grant Park today would swear didn't exist. His mouth twisted bitterly. But there was always something fresh to be thrown at him, wasn't there?

Arden touched his hand tentatively and Will jerked away. "Don't do that!" Will's voice was louder than intended and sharp, too much so. Involuntarily, he glanced up; Arden's hazel eyes were wide with pain.

"Why are you being this way?" Arden asked urgently, "Why won't you let me comfort you? All we have now is each other."

"I—I don't want—" Will started to say *you*, but the claim choked in his throat. That wasn't true, was it? He wanted Arden very much, didn't he? "I don't want to be like *that* anymore," he managed instead.

Arden leaned back, his expression puzzled. "Like *that*? You mean gay? Is that what this is all about?" He brushed a spill of fine, light brown hair off his brow and shook his head. "I don't understand. What you're saying...it's what a boy goes through in puberty, not an adult man who accepted what he is years ago. Is it remorse? Repentance? Because it won't change anything, Will, you *know* that.

"Going straight now won't take the AIDS virus from your body."

Will couldn't help it. He covered his face with his hands and sobbed.

* * *

When the afternoon light had dimmed, he and Arden went back to Will's condo, where Will sat and watched as Arden moved comfortably around the kitchen, mixing this, pouring that, measuring something else, all of which finally coalesced into a plate of food that smelled good—like some sort of pasta with a French seafood sauce—but was still tasteless in Will's mouth. The meal was awkward and nearly silent, and after the dishes were cleared and stacked in the dishwasher, Will moved to the living room and sat, staring at the darkened screen of the television and lost in unwelcome contemplation of his new future. A few minutes later, Arden sat quietly next to him on the couch, then slipped an arm around his shoulders.

Will shrugged it off. "Don't," he said. How many times today had he used that word?

Arden stood abruptly. "I realize you're hurt, and you're afraid," he said grimly. "But so am I. And sooner or later I'm going to need some support too. I have a right to expect that support to come from you, Will." Arden's eyes were dark and angry, yet never quite lost their look of...*longing*. "I need you, damn it! And it's only right, it's only *fair*, that you be there for me."

Will looked up doubtfully.

"I became HIV positive because of you, remember? *You did this to me.*"

Seconds later the front door slammed, leaving Will to sit alone in his darkened condominium, overwhelmed with guilt and his own impending death.

✳   ✳   ✳

The blankness of his memory had fled, and with it had gone the cushion of ignorance that had led Will to believe on that first, beautiful day of his new life that he might have a chance at a fulfilling existence. A virtual library of information awaited him in the mind of this young, gay attorney. Some of that information had come too late to its owner; by the time AIDS had made its first deadly appearance in the streets half a decade earlier, then built to common knowledge several years later, Wilmot Keefe had been a player on the gay circuit far too long to save his own life or that of his chosen lifelong companion, Arden.

It took Will nearly three weeks before he could force himself to call Arden. In all that time, Will's telephone hadn't rung once, and he came to realize that with the diagnosis of his disease had also come his separation from society. Not one of his former lovers or friends called to check on him—not that a former lover would want to do anything but kill him now—nor had a single person from work called to ask his advice, schedule a conference with clients, or messenger him a document to be reviewed. None of his sisters knew of his illness; in fact, they had no idea—as far as he remembered—that he was even gay. And what good would it do to tell them anyway? A whole regiment of diseases awaited him, each more debilitating than the last as his body lost more and more of its defensive capabilities. Better he should divide his estate among them and Arden—provided his lover outlived him—and let them find out after he was dead.

Arden.

It was an impulse thing, instantaneous.

"Hello?"

"Hi," Will said. His voice sounded hoarse and disused, and he had to clear his throat before he could speak again. Had it actually been that long since he'd spoken to another person? He supposed it had.

There was another of the silences that Arden favored so much, but this one had an air of indecision rather than drama. When Arden finally spoke, he sounded bitter and lonely. "What do you want?"

I've done this. It was a thought comprised of equal parts marvel and horror—marvel that Will could have had such a profound impact on the attitude, the *life*, of another person, and horror that his abuse of this influence had metamorphosed a man who had once been a trusted friend and cherished lover into a sad and brittle human being.

"I'm sorry, Arden," Will blurted. "Can I—can I make it up to you somehow? What can I do?"

Silence again, the seconds ticking by, stretching to almost a full minute before the answer came.

"Just... *be* there."

"I will," he promised.

"If I disgust you," Arden continued quietly, "then you don't have to do anything. Just be my friend, my companion, like we have for years. And I'll be yours." He paused again, as though unsure whether to finish the sentence. In the end, it spilled from his lips anyway.

"We got into this together. We shouldn't have to die alone."

✳ ✳ ✳

There were, surprisingly, two good years before the horror began. Each time Will tore a new month off the calendar in the second bedroom, which he turned into a home office shortly after his suicide attempt, he experienced something trembling between happiness that he and Arden had made it through another little slice of the calendar and dread at the thought of what awaited them both. Skulking along the edge of everything, fed by the fact that both he and Arden still felt as healthy as they had before the ugly results of their attempt to donate at a long-ago neighborhood blood drive, was the ridiculous hope that nothing would ever happen; neither would begin that vicious descent into death and they would live happily ever after.

His firm, Will soon discovered, was not nearly as accepting of his disease as it had been of his sexual preferences, which had at least become more discreet as he had grown older. The reason Will had felt no compulsion to go into the office or even call in had been because, tactfully put, the firm had put him on a "voluntary" sabbatical, a discreetly paid leave of absence that would eventually transfer itself to permanent disability. In the meantime, his supervising partner had packets messengered to him at the condo about every six weeks or so: leases to be reviewed and redrafted substantially in advance of the termination dates, other things such as research memoranda that could be done using his computer at home and which required substantial work but had no immediate deadline; still, even those dwindled as time went by. To keep himself from stagnating, Will began taking pro bono cases from the local gay activist groups, small matters that didn't require extensive court appearances or long hours. The difficult items he left for the liberalists who were still disease-free. God willing, they would someday find acceptance for AIDS victims in the community.

He and Arden spent a lot of time together, and Will treasured it. The only dark spot in their relationship was sex: though he had been determined to keep an open mind, Will simply...froze when Arden tried to touch him. A part of him yearned for the affection, the intimacy he knew Arden wanted so desperately to give, yet no matter how Will tried, he could not be what he no longer was. It was an emotional and physical roller coaster that periodically kept him awake for hours as Arden stayed over at the condo more and more. Lying next to his former lover at night and listening to Arden's soft, even breathing, Will fantasized about waking Arden and taking him gently into his arms, dreamed of loving Arden in the physical ways that he once had. But he could not; sometimes he cursed his own soul and the straight–laced old schoolmarm who would not let him be what he should in this life. Ultimately, Arden accepted that, deciding that the emotional side of their relationship would have to suffice, proving to a shamed Will that Arden's love was truly unselfish.

✳ ✳ ✳

Twenty–six months to the day after Will had tried to kill himself, Arden sat across from him at the dining room table.

"I have cancer, Will." Arden's voice was calm and quiet, his face the color of thin milk atop a body growing leaner by the day. "The doctor says its Hodgkin's disease."

Will swallowed. Over the past two years he'd come to cherish this man the best way he could—like a brother, a best–of–all–possible friend, a soulmate. Death for both of them had always been parked just behind every new sunrise; still, he'd let himself be so easily lulled by the passing of each day.

"What now?" he finally managed.

Arden looked at him, his face a picture of stoicism. His words were brutally clear. *"I die within six months."*

✳ ✳ ✳

In all the twisted, see–sawing years, nearly half a millennium, Will couldn't remember willingly watching someone he loved die. Forgetting such a thing was unthinkable, though Will admitted to himself that his memory was faded and spotty in places, especially when he tried to push his thoughts back to the much earlier time of what he'd come to think of as his Real Life. Watching this horror, however, he sometimes thought that if he *had* been through it, his own spirit would block it from his memory forever.

In the best of times, Will wished it was him instead, anything to ease Arden's suffering. Sequestered in his bedroom in the darkest hours, those just following his visits with Arden at the hospital, he raved aloud at God, at the Devil, at the Wilmot Keefe who had escaped this fate by swallowing a bottle of medicinal freedom two–and–a–half years ago and doomed a foolish old woman to take his place. At other times, looking down at his former lover's nearly skeletal features, his heart twisting in pity and fear, Will dreamed selfishly that *he* had been the one to die first. What, he wondered in uncontrollable bouts of self–pity, was worse? Dying yourself, or staring helplessly as AIDS ravaged the one person in the world you loved, then left you to drown alone in an uncaring and cold existence?

And through it all was Arden, grim and uncomplaining, his mouth a vivid slash of continual pain as the cancer hammered swiftly through his deteriorating body, forever ahead of whatever medication the unflappable doctors administered.

Will was there at the end. It was a hot, clear night at the end of July, and he was standing at the window staring out and across the black expanse of the lake, his mind as blank and black and empty as the world seemed beyond the glass. He had come to hate the ringing of the telephone and the myriad possibilities that waited at the other end of an open line: a platoon of doctors with their ongoing tests and maintenance programs, laboratories, hospitals, the hospice in which he had prearranged to spend his own final months.

And, of course, Arden…

The voice on the telephone was soft and cool, professionally distant. Will made it to the hospital in time to hold Arden's shrunken form for a heartbreaking five minutes, then Arden opened his eyes, still such a spectacular hazel even though they were clouded with pain.

"Will…" Arden stared at him and hesitated.

Then died in his arms.

Arden's final, dying pause was his most dramatic of all.

※   ※   ※

Will's own dying, it seemed, would not be nearly so merciful or quick. The disease progressed at its slowest and the years plodded by, each one a curse that tormented him further with every jab of a nurse's needle, each new test ordered by a curious young doctor. After Arden died and the torture of a funeral attended by dozens of hostile, accusing relatives, Will reevaluated his plans for the future. Originally Will had believed he would precede Arden by several years; now that the nasty, lonely truth was evident, he was faced with the emptiness of his life and the regret that came with the foreknowledge of his own death—so many things he wished he'd done! He thought of his sisters, wondered what they would be like after all the years of his being incommunicado. How did they look, how did they act? Perhaps he had nieces and nephews by now, brothers-in-law, whole families. Will hadn't stayed in contact beyond the obligatory Christmas cards, and he fingered the last three now, touching the silk embossing on one, chuckling again at the inane joke on another. In the end he put them away, pleased with his decision not to inflict his illness upon their lives in the interest of self-pity and the selfish desire not to be alone during a well-furnished but sickly life that did not seem inclined to end within a month or two.

※   ※   ※

Four years into his disease, Will's immune system surrendered the last of its paltry efforts on his behalf, and racked by the worst-yet case of pneumonia, he stumbled into the emergency room on a Sunday morning.

Will still did not want to die. Hang in there a little longer, he told himself, listening eagerly to the doctors tell him to keep fighting while the FDA worked through the red tape and approved this drug for human testing, or that one, all with unpronounceable names that fled Will's brain as soon as the last syllable was mouthed. At the bottom of it all, the unspoken truth glittered in the too–cheerful smiles of the nurses who fed him and washed him and lifted his shriveled, twiglike hips onto the bedpan.

After six bouts of pneumonia, each worse than the last, Will's scarred lungs were far too weak to work on their own. The research facility to which he'd offered himself as a test subject placed him on a respirator that did the hard work for him and wore a bloody, constantly throbbing spot in the corner of his mouth where the tube ran from his throat to the machine. His protests, little but breathy mewls by now, went unheeded as they shot him up with morphine and threaded the tube down his windpipe; after all, this was a research hospital and the bringers of sparse comfort, controllers of the painkillers, his doctors— couldn't very well give up a test subject at the height of his illness and attempted treatment program. The ability to speak was eliminated entirely by the respirator, and with horror, Will realized the error of his choice; *they* would put him through as many more months of experimentation as could be wrung from his wasted body, and then more, if there was any way possible.

Eleven more months. He didn't know how they managed it.

*   *   *

He knew instantly the day they came to kill him.

It was early morning, before seven o'clock. Most of Will's days and nights were spent drifting in and out of consciousness; for every hour he was awake, and a sixty–minute stretch became more and more a rarity, he was out for two or three. Strangely, this morning Will was not just awake, but really awake—eyes alert and opened wide, mouth and nostrils dry around the various tubes that ran up and beyond his sight. His face was always cold, and had been since the day they hooked him to the respirator and the chilly oxygen began its continuous journey into his chest, but this morning a new kind of cold washed over him, something much more pronounced than the normal shivering of his rail–thin form buried under the mound of blankets the nurses had piled atop him.

Three doctors, one head nurse, and one balding man stuffed into a stiff black suit and bearing an official–looking black notebook. With a sudden certainty, Will knew that his killers had come this early so that they cold hustle his remains from this bed and this room as quickly as possible, rush the pathetic debris of his corpse off to the morgue and out of their world, all by eight o'clock at the latest, and thank you so much for your kind cooperation.

The man with the notebook bothered him. Who was he? The county coroner? Or perhaps some lower echelon clerk, just doing his grub work and putting in his time before he could move up the promotional ladder towards Chief Coroner. What gave this uncaring man the right to watch Will die?

"Mr. Keefe?" Will's gaze jerked towards the speaker, a middle–aged doctor with hair graying in a perfect *GQ* style. Will wanted to be frantic, wanted to run as fast as he could from this latest and most deadly physician who gazed down at him with dark, empty eyes, but his own emaciated body simply would–

n't let him. In spite of all his suffering and his often–repeated prayers for death, now that he was faced irrevocably with it, he wanted–again—very much to live.

But wasn't that always the way?

"Mr. Keefe?" The doctor's tolerant voice again, recalling, *demanding*, Will's attention. He blinked at the white–robed figure, no longer able to utter anything more than vague groans.

"Mr. Keefe?" The doctor—his name, Will suddenly remembered, was Gideon—tried a third time, then continued when he saw that Will was finally listening. "The administrative board has come to the conclusion that it is no longer beneficial or economical, to either you or the facility, to continue your treatment." Though he'd known for months that these words were coming, Will's eyes still widened and he felt his laboring heart stutter a bit. There had always been that *hope*, hadn't there? That hope that *they* might someday march into his room and announce that *Yes! We've found that elusive miracle! The cure!*

But not today.

Not for him, ever.

The balding man in the suit stepped forward. "You may recall, Mr. Keefe, that the documents which you signed upon admitting yourself for research purposes give us the right to discontinue treatment at such time as it is deemed advisable in our reasonable discretion." His voice was prim.

So that's what he is, Will marveled. *A lawyer, of all things.* For a fleeting moment he wished, more than anything, that he could laugh.

"After a careful review of your case history and its progress—" He glanced at Dr. Gideon and the other man nodded. "Or rather, its *lack* of progress for some time now, the facility's administrative board has come to the, uh, *unfortunate* decision that such time has arrived."

Will tried to shake his head but managed only a small quiver. Another of the doctors stepped forward, this one an elderly woman who was obviously in charge of the others. "Mr. Keefe," she said gently, "my name is Dr. Nahum. As the hospital's chief administrator, it is my responsibility to carry out the board of directors' instructions." Her voice was soothing, her eyes, a faded robin's egg blue, compassionate. "I'm so very sorry, Mr. Keefe." She reached a cool, lined hand forward and stroked his freezing forehead; Will felt oddly comforted. "But there's nothing more we can do for you, and we feel it is unspeakably...*cruel* to prolong your illness. Do you understand?"

Unable to talk, incapable of telling her that he didn't care if it was cruel, he didn't care how much pain there was to come in his future, he just wanted to keep on *living*—the best Will could do was an almost imperceptible twitch...

And watch as this woman, who believed to her soul that she was doing him a great kindness, turned off the machine that furnished the reliable, steady breeze of life into his lungs. For one utterly ludicrous moment, Will wondered hysterically if this was how a once–loved pet felt as the euthanasia needle made its deadly plunge.

This time, death was like a huge black pillow that descended with terrifying speed.

CHAPTER IX
Now

It took two seconds—
One
Two
—to realize the screams were her own. Then she began to fight.

✳   ✳   ✳

"Say, man! Get the fuck away from her! You stupid, fucking dickhead—you're fucking up my best whore! Yo, whatsa matter? You gotcha dick in your ear, asshole? I said, get the fuck away from my merchandise!"

"Damned bitch! She—"

Someone punched her, but it was just one more dull thud against the battered shell her skull had become. She hissed and grabbed at the blow, but too late. She wanted to stand, yet her head felt too heavy, like a bowling ball mounted on a spring and swinging uncontrollably to and fro. The best she could accomplish was to drag her legs back together, lead-like fingers twisting through the dirty sheets in search of her skirt, or better, her switchblade.

"Oh, you fucking whoreson, what'd you make her take? 'Ludes? A hit of acid? What? I've had just too much patience with you, Jackson. I find out you fed this bitch Ice and you a dead man, you hear?" Tyrone's voice rocked through the room, warped in her ears, the words only marginally understandable. She wanted to vomit, but felt too sick to manage even that.

"Woman, git your ass outta that bed and find your clothes. You better pull it together, right now." Her pimp's voice was nearly shrill with rage. "We—"

"Give me my money back!" the john demanded. "The bitch bit me!"

"Fuck you!" Tyrone spat. "You shouldn't pumped her fulla shit—I told you not to. You got what you deserved!"

"She wanted it!"

"I don't give a flying *FUCK* what she wanted, I TOLD you not to give her *nothing*!" Tyrone was screaming now, almost jumping up and down. "Why the fuck couldn't you just get a blow job without doing shit? Huh? Why not?"

Someone pounded on the door. "You assholes take it outside or I'm calling the cops!"

The banging cut through some of the fog in her head and she scrubbed at her face, trying to wipe away the nasty sense of vertigo, then blinked stupidly as her trick strode to the door and yanked it open. Skinny fist still raised, the desk clerk stood there, his mouth dropping in surprise at the still-naked man, a six-foot bruiser topping two-thirty. The clerk squeaked and tried to jump out of range, but the john's reach was too quick. The guy yanked the smaller man forward by the collar, nearly lifting him off the floor. "Another fucking wise guy, right?" he snarled. The john's eyes were red and wild and hungry. "You got something to say, ass–licker?" He shook the clerk hard. "*Do* you?"

"Nnn–no," the desk clerk stammered.

"Good," the trick snapped. "Then get the fuck outta my life!" He shoved the clerk backwards and let go, smirking as the thin man stumbled and fell on his butt in the hallway right before the door slammed.

A loud, metallic click rose above the sound of the door closing. "Speaking of getting the fuck outta someone's life, I'm tired of you being in mine." Tyrone's voice was cold. "No no— don't turn around." The john froze, still facing the door, and Tyrone kicked the man's clothes to him. "Now you pick 'em up real slow, get 'em on, then you just get the fuck out. Don't wanna see you round here no more. You got it?"

Somewhere between the desk clerk and the slam of the door her head had stopped spinning. At least now she could sit up without having to press against the walls with her hands to stop them from undulating. More fumbling; finally she found the rest of her clothes and began pulling them over her cold flesh far more slowly than her would–be customer. "It's about time, you dumb cunt," Tyrone said through clenched teeth.

"I'm gonna call the cops," the trick said softly. "I'll swear you two rolled me."

It was a useless threat and they all knew it. Tyrone sneered. "Sure you will, fuckface. And Perdita and I'll walk you to the station house. Won't we, baby?"

She managed a nod, then cursed herself for moving too fast.

The guy twisted his head slightly, until she could see a sliver of his thick, boxer–like profile; the blue of one eye glinted like a dirty sapphire.

Perdita, she thought. *That's me.*

The translation came instantly,

The lost.

God help me.

*   *   *

"What the hell did you think you were doing? And what the fuck made you bite him? Are you fucking crazy?"

"I don't know." Perdita was in far too much pain to think about anything, everything. She groaned and leaned against the door as the shocks under the car made it bump and rock, wishing the door would open and simply let her fall out. She hated Tyrone's Cadillac; although it was only six months old, the thing stank of cigarette smoke, old booze, and used condoms. "He was an asshole."

"Shit!"

Perdita hit the dashboard hard as Tyrone jammed on the brakes and cut over to the curb. She tried to twist away as he shoved the gearshift into PARK but the younger man was too fast to elude and she cried out as his sharp–nailed fingers dug into her left ear and hauled her across the front seat. "Now you listen to me," he yelled as she flailed at him. "No—cut it the fuck *out!*" He shoved her back against the door hard enough for Perdita to lose the breath in her lungs for a few seconds.

"Okay!" she gasped. "Okay!"

Tyrone was nearly on top of her, his dark face almost indistinguishable in the murky gold light from the dashboard; only his eyes were clear, the whites shockingly bright, the black pupils deep pits of anger. When he spoke, Perdita could feel the moist heat of his breath bathe the skin of her face.

"Now you listen up, Perdie. I'm sick of you, you hear? I took you in when you was on hard times—"

"I know—"

"Shut *up*, damn you!" He punctuated the command with a smart slap on her bruised cheek and she whined. "As I was *saying*, I did you some good turns, pulled your ass right outta the fucking garbage. And I see you been fucking me over at every chance, using the trick money on blow—"

"No!"

"—or maybe a bottle of reds here, half an ounce of Columbian there. *And I am pure–D fuckin' TIRED of you spending MY money, do you hear me, BITCH?*"

"But—"

The second slap was a lot harder, and filled with a lot more knuckle. Blood laced between her teeth and leaked from splits in the fuller parts of her lips. She ground her jaw against the cry that would have escaped and probably made Tyrone angrier.

"Now," Tyrone released her and leaned back against his seat, his tone almost conversational. "You go on back to your place, and you get yourself mended and cleaned up—and brush those stinking teeth of yours, too—and then go out and earn me some money. The way you're *supposed* to." Her pimp's head swiveled in her direction, and his eyes were very, very cold.

"Or you're gonna hit the streets in a way you never counted on."

✳   ✳   ✳

Perdita's apartment was barely more than a rathole. Called a garden apartment, it was really part of a former basement that some enterprising (otherwise known as greedy) slumlord had thought to divide with walls and a few pipes so that down–on–their–luck hookers like herself had a place to sleep besides behind the alley trash containers. The two–room, one–windowed apartment was damp and dark, and hardly had a cleared spot of floor anywhere. Fat and fearless cockroaches crawled among the grease–encrusted dishes in the kitchenette, larger waterbugs skittered amid the piles of dirty clothes thrown everywhere. Cleanliness, it seemed, had certainly not been a high priority.

Perdita sighed and dropped her purse on the beat–up formica table that separated the kitchenette from the living room, the larger, darker part of the apartment that boasted a lopsided foldout couch that smelled like animal piss—obviously dragged out of an alley somewhere. From the corner of her eye she saw a roach scramble over the table's edge and make for the uncharted territory of her purse; reflexively she smashed it with the side of her fist, then grimaced at the gooey mess plastered on her skin. She shook the mangled body onto the floor, where it was lost in the accumulation of old candy wrappers, clothes, and Christ knew what else.

Perdita examined her face in the bathroom, a closet that had somehow grown a gurgling toilet, leaky sink and a cheap and filthy shower. She didn't much like what she found, but nothing short of plastic surgery could help her now, so it would have to do. She felt bruised and battered and at least forty years old—almost too old to be tricking—and she looked every bit of fifty. Her dark, dirty hair showed gray streaks here and there, and beneath the bruises and blood smeared across her face she saw dry lines etched around the corners of her mouth and across her forehead. Too much make–up around the eyes made her look like a fucking raccoon. Her hands and fingernails were thick with dirt and her mouth twisted in disgust; she figured a shower alone would take ten years off her appearance. She didn't know what kind of miracle would make her look her true age of thirty.

It took ridiculously long for the running water to get hot enough for a shower, but the wait was worth it. While the water was still lukewarm, Perdie discovered a dusty bottle of spray cleaner under the kitchen sink, and now the shower stall was, if not quite sanitary, at least usable without her thinking she'd end up with something horrible on the bottoms of her feet. Standing under the hot spray and feeling the filth rinse away as she scrubbed at her skin with a piece of cheap soap was revitalizing, nearly euphoric. Her mind was a jumble of thoughts and, for a change, readily available memories: Jackson, the deadly trick of this morning who'd meant nothing before he'd beaten her, and even less now; Tyrone, the pimp who'd pulled her from drug addiction and near–death four years ago; a past as ugly and mottled as the bruises that covered her face— a drunken mother, a sexually abusive stepfather, quitting a school filled with classes that were far too complex for her to understand anyway and going to work as a waitress in a sleazy all–night pancake dive. Too many years, too little money, and too much hunger—the private kind that couldn't be filled by a plate full of food—as she weaseled her way through her twenties, always looking for a better way and a bigger high. The crash had come on an extended roadtrip with a scummy biker who'd discovered he could make a fortune by shooting her up with horse and selling her to his buddies. When he'd blown all the money and couldn't afford the H anymore, he'd dumped her, wasted and nearly dead of malnutrition, on a side street in L.A. She'd come all the way from Nashville to the west coast just to die screaming in her own addiction.

But Tyrone had been there with his businessman's eye, to pick her up and clean her out, then to lock her in an empty basement with nothing but water, waiting it out as Perdita pummeled the door and the walls until her fists were bloody and her voice was raw from wailing promises of anything if only he'd give her Just one more fix. For the first three days, two of his friends held her down while he force fed her; after that he left a plate on the steps and she fed herself with her fingers, feeling the heroin's call filter away a little more each day. At the end of a week, he brought her out; dazed, weak, but sensible enough to speak and be spoken to.

But that had been four years ago, and now was now, and in her endless search for a way to mask her life, Perdie'd sunk almost all the way back down again. The hot water ran out and she shut off the shower and stepped out, shaking the towel to make sure it was roach–free before drying herself. Jackson had given her something this morning all right, not heroin but something almost as potent and enough to reawaken an almost four–years–stifled yearning. Ice? If so, she was in serious trouble; that shit was addictive from the first use. Even now her hands were shaking from need, her teeth grinding as she stared at her woman's face in the pitted mirror above the sink. *I won't*, she thought grimly. *I won't go back to that. This is the new me, and I won't be that again. Not ever.*

She found a greasy comb on the sink, washed it and pulled it through her tangled hair. She could use a haircut, she decided, a trim to even up the ragged ends—but later, after her hands stopped twitching. Whatever Jackson had given her had only been one hit, and all she could do was hope that fool didn't know how to make it; there were dozens of other drugs besides Ice that could be ass–kickers, and if she could make it through that hell four years ago, the new Perdita could survive this one. Just being clean and thinking clearly made her feel better and she peered at her face and thought that maybe, after all these bruises faded—especially the huge black one across her right eye and temple—she might not be such a bad–looking broad after all. She was nicely built, though fucked–up eating habits—cheap, fatty fast foods—showed in the flab that was starting to settle around her waistline and thighs. But her breasts were large—always a plus for a whore—and not too saggy, and she had nice long legs with only a few dimples in her ass. Yeah, she thought, if I clean up my shit, I could do okay. But only if I *stay* clean. If her head hadn't hurt so bad, she would've laughed at the difference between this time and the dreamlike luxury of her last life.

Perdita found a limp robe that didn't look too grimy and put it on to ward off a little of the chilliness that pervaded the basement apartment. The place was a shambles, and looking at it made an old and familiar lethargy try to settle in. What good would it do to clean it—who gave a shit, anyway? She blinked and pushed the thoughts away, forcing herself to move around, picking up clothes and piling them in one corner, collecting garbage—rotting, uneaten food, empty beer and soda cans, you name it—anything to occupy her mind and help stave off the seductive call bubbling in her bloodstream. There was nothing in the refrigerator but a nearly empty bottle of cheap vodka and a crumpled package of bologna; that went in the garbage when the smell of it almost made her vomit.

She did the dishes, clenching her jaw and smacking at cockroaches with a rolled up newspaper as they fled the intrusion of her hands in the mold–encrusted sink. Getting the cracked dishes washed and into the drainer didn't help much in the overall picture of the place, but combined with Perdie's other efforts it was a start. Scrubbing was too strenuous for her head to take and would have to wait for another time. Right now Perdie was starving and each step was turning into a nasty throb across her abused eye, a lingering gift from this morning's beating. She searched her purse and was rewarded with a crumpled five dollar bill; there was a Latino market around the corner and the money was enough to get her sandwich makings and a diet soda. She would eat and take a short nap—somewhere in this place was a beat-up alarm clock—and later find some passable clothes and maybe turn a couple tricks if she could find a few customers who didn't mind beat-up goods. Ironically, she found the idea of hooking bland and not at all frightening or disgusting. Better yet, she figured that her actually working ought to make Tyrone a little happier. Maybe he'd give her some money for groceries.

Outside, it was stifling and nothing like the coolness she'd left in the basement apartment, the hazy air filled with the characteristic mixture of smog, garbage and neighborhood cooking smells. Perdita made her way hesitantly down the street, a little overwhelmed by all the noise and people, mostly dangerous-looking young men who lounged along the sidewalk or sprawled against buildings, some sitting on steps, others listening to boom boxes while half-in and half-out of cars despite the terrible heat. The store itself was dark but not cool; stepping inside was like entering a closet filled with the scent of old dust and meat gone bad. Still, the visit was good for a cold Diet Pepsi, a small package of bologna and a loaf of bread. She paid and left quickly, preferring the smog to spoiled air.

Shambling back to her apartment, all Perdita could think of was her shabby little couch and the comfort it offered. She wished for a tub so she could soak her screaming muscles in a hot bath; better yet, a couple of aspirins—now *that* would be just the ticket. Too bad she had less than fifty cents left, not even enough to buy a travel tin of the no-name stuff. But eating would make her feel better—

"Hey, you! Perdita Malsueno! *Hey!*"

At the sound of her name, Perdie paused and looked up warily. All she wanted to do was go home and mind her own business on the way there, thank you very much. When she saw the cop car at the curb, she could've spit in frustration. Now the sidewalk was empty; all the kids who'd been proudly displaying their gang colors had instantly melted away. Shit, she thought, just what I need. Some two-bit copper looking for a little afternoon amusement. And I'm *it*.

"Get over here."

Shit, Perdita thought again. And this bastard knows my name; why bother to run? Then, and more important, *Christ, I hope my hands aren't shaking too badly*. She licked her lips and stepped cautiously up to the passenger side of the squad; now her heart was thundering in time to the throbs and pings of pain shooting through the rest of her body. "What can I do for you?"

The cop on the passenger side, a fat guy with silver blond curls and cold blue eyes, roared with laughter. "You hear that, Neil? What can she *do* for us!" he gasped. "Jesus, that's rich! That's gotta be the best line I've heard all day!"

Perdita stood and clutched her bag tighter, unsure of what to do or say. Instinct made the words *Fuck off!* skitter on the edge of her tongue, but she was about done in and just wanted to get this over with as quickly as possible; mouthing off would only make things worse. The cop was still chuckling and wiping at his eyes, pounding the dashboard every now and then for emphasis, each blow making the name tag on his chest that said *Miles* jiggle.

"Can I go now?" she asked finally.

Miles abruptly stopped laughing. "What's in the bag?" he demanded. "Give it here."

She hesitated, suddenly afraid this pig of a man would look at the contents, then toss everything on the ground.

The cop grabbed for the door handle. "You stupid whore—"

"Okay! Here!" Perdita thrust the bag at him and stumbled back a few steps, then stopped. He ripped into it, then cursed as his hand dug through the contents.

"Shit! What's this? Your fucking lunch?" He snorted and started to crumple it up.

"Hey, don't!" Perdita protested. "Come on—"

"Cut it out," his partner said. "She's miserable enough."

"Fine."

The other cop, a slimmer version of the first, snatched the bag from Miles, leaned past his partner and offered it to her. "Come a little closer," he commanded. "Over to my side." Perdita reluctantly obeyed; she knew this one from somewhere, but that was certainly no surprise. The last couple of months had been bad, with a run-in every couple of days. It was a bad sign that despite her nervousness and her headache, she could even remember that his name was Gallagher, and now he was staring at her, his gaze a hundred times sharper than his dumb partner's.

"You take a little something today, Perdita?" he asked softly.

"N-no," she stammered. She couldn't help it; just being questioned by dicks had always pissed her off, and she wasn't feeling so hot right now anyway. "Nothing." She tried to sound a little more convincing, but her bravado disintegrated when the patrol car's door swung open and Gallagher got out and stood in front of her. She was a pretty lanky woman—at a not-too-heavy five-nine it was a point in her favor—but he was a good six inches taller.

He pushed his face close to hers. "You're lying to me," he said softly. "I hate liars worse than anything."

She opened her mouth, then swallowed back the smartass remark that would have spilled out. *What the fuck,* she thought tiredly. *The new me, right?*

"I had some trouble with a—a guy earlier. He, uh, made me take something." Gallagher raised an eyebrow and she shook her head, trying not to jar her skull. "I don't know what. But it don't matter." She looked at him pleadingly and held out a hand. "I'm straight right now, okay? I just wanted to, you know, get something to eat and go home. That's all. Okay? Please, can I go?"

He hooked a finger under her jaw and carefully lifted her chin. "Is that what happened to your face?"

She nodded and pulled her head back reflexively, ignoring the resulting stab of pain across her eye and forehead. The cop leaned even closer, then sniffed in surprise. "You take a bath this morning or something?"

"A little while ago," she answered in a small voice. She could feel her face turning a dark, shameful red.

Gallagher looked at her thoughtfully, then waved a hand. "Yeah, okay. Go on." He stopped at the driver's side, then shot her a warning glance. "But stay off the shit, Perdita. Don't let me catch you on *anything*, you hear?"

She looked at him numbly, not believing that he was actually *leaving* and she was still standing here, a free woman, when the simplest of blood tests could probably throw her ass in the tank for at least a three-day stretch. His partner glanced at her resentfully, then shrugged and turned his attention to a sudden jumble of words from the police band, dismissing her. Another two seconds and the patrol car pulled away.

Stumbling back to her apartment, Perdita couldn't help grinning a little, in spite of the sickness that wanted to twist her guts and the trembling deep in her muscles.

✳   ✳   ✳

Perdie was brushing her teeth carefully when Tyrone pounded on the door the next afternoon. She had cavities—six of 'em, one a deceptively small thing on a front bottom tooth that hurt like a son–of–a–bitch if something cold hit it. She was dressed and clean, and a carefully applied layer of make–up hid as much of the bruising as she could manage. Her face, though, still looked pretty bad, and no powder in the world was going to disguise the massive swelling along her cheekbone.

"Perdie, you bitch, you open this fucking door or I'll break it down!"

"I'm coming," she called. "Just a second." Tyrone's fist was raised for another barrage when she pulled the door open. "Hi."

He scowled and lowered his hand, then peered first at her, then at the apartment as he pushed past. Dressed in a ridiculous red leather suit with scrolled red cowboy boots on his over–sized feet and a wide–brimmed cowboy hat, he looked like a curious, feminine clown. Perdita stifled the urge to tell him so; that surely wasn't the way to get her beaten–to–hell face to heal. Tyrone scanned the room suspiciously, then turned back to her. "Where've you been?" he demanded.

"Right here," she said. "You told me to clean up, remember?"

"Yeah, well I ain't running no charity, baby." He scowled again. "It's great to see you straighten up and all, but that don't mean dipshit in my wallet, you get my meaning?"

"I worked last night," she said defensively. "Twice. Wasn't easy with my face all messed up."

"Lemme see." Tyrone studied her for a few moments, frowning a little over the egg–sized black and purple knot on her right temple. "I've seen worse. You'll heal." He folded his arms. "All things considering, you look real good. Better than in a long time. So where's the money, baby? Since you workin' and all."

"Right here." She handed him a small fold of bills and watched as he counted it. "I know it ain't much, but I wasn't feeling good enough to go down to the strip. And this," she touched her forehead self-consciously, "you know, it kind of takes away a little." Tyrone counted the money again, his eyes dark. "But it'll be better," she said hurriedly. "In a day or so I'll be just like before—"

"You know this is your last chance," he interrupted as he folded the money around a huge wad of bills. "I've been fucking around with you for four years now. Stay away from the drugs, Perdie. I don't even want you doing blow. You just can't handle it." He strode to the kitchen and opened the refrigerator, then shut it and glanced at the cleared table and empty sink. "You got any money, any at all?" She shook her head and Tyrone peeled three twenties from the roll and tossed them on the table. "Get you some food."

Her pimp pulled open the front door, then stopped to glare at her. "You're doing better. I wouldn't have thought it, but you are. Just don't fuck it up." He glanced around again, taking in the swept floor and the bag of trash waiting to go out. "You go ahead and turn your neighborhood tricks and make a little money, but you make sure that money—all of it—comes back to me. And I wanna see you back on the strip in three days."

Perdie nodded her agreement, then locked the door behind him and listened to his footsteps as he clomped up the stairs in those silly red boots. On the kitchen table, dull green beneath the buzzing, fluorescent light, the sixty dollars beckoned, tempting her with hot possibilities.

Sixty bucks. A lot could be had for that—crack, blow, horse. Even Ice, if she wanted a fast track to hell.

All she had to do was choose.

✳ ✳ ✳

The supermarket was huge, noisy, and crammed with people. Most of them—though she didn't think these fleshy stay-at-home bitches with their squalling, runny-nosed brats were any better than her—stared at her in distaste and got the hell out of her way. It was just as well; Perdita couldn't remember the last time she'd been anyplace this clean and with this much food, and a couple of times she'd run her cart smack into someone else's.

She'd come here because she figured it would be cheaper and she could get more for her money then from the rip-off market on the corner. It'd been a hike, too—a good fifteen blocks—but she figured on saving enough for bus fare that would take her back and drop her off within a couple blocks of the apartment.

It took a long time, one decision after another to make about prices and what to buy that wouldn't take too much in the skills department to fix— Perdita had never been a fancy cook and she had other things to think about right now. What didn't take long was realizing that sixty bucks in a grocery store, even a real one, wouldn't go far. Perdita had lived on bread, lunch meat and cheap fast food for longer than she could remember; that and not having the kitchen utensils needed to fix any of this stuff made her end up buying a lot of macaroni and cheese and canned goods. But food was food and the thought of having supplies in the apartment gave her a definite sense of security—something, at least, stood between her and starvation.

At the end of the checkout line, she couldn't believe it. Over fifty-five dollars and all she had was four bags! Still and all, enough to make it impossible to walk home, and at least her math, yet another of her shortfalls, hadn't been too bad; she'd been afraid she'd get up there and not have enough money to pay for everything, end up stuck with the humiliating choice of what to put back while some gum-chewing teenager rolled her eyes and waited. But the bags, plastic things that kept trying to spill everything if she set them down, were heavy, and by the time Perdita made it to the bus stop she was heat-sticky and bitchy; her head, at the point where she'd taken the hit, was doing a drumbeat of pain that made her vision shimmy with each pulse of her blood. The bus was nowhere to be seen, but the wait would give her a chance to rest—if only she could get these damned bags to sit upright without dumping everything on the sidewalk.

Something screamed pitiably behind her. Perdita whirled and saw an alley leading into shadows between the two buildings at her back. Forms moved within the semi-darkness—a couple of teenagers using a stick to poke at something that cried miserably behind a trash bin. She frowned; what was it? Jesus Christ, it sounded like a baby yowling. But that was impossible—

Another cry, this one more frenzied. One of the boys laughed harshly. His words, beneath the guffaws of his companion, floated back on the sludgy summer air: "Look at that, Bennie! Got it that time—I think the fucker's bleeding!"

Oughta keep my mouth shut, Perdita thought. *Mind my own damned business.* Instead, "Hey, what the hell are you guys doing?" came out without so much as a pause for a breath. Her voice was challenging, comfortable in its aggressive tone.

"Fuck off, slut," one of them snarled back.

Those damned bags finally balanced, Perdita glanced around. She could see the bus at last, a vague shape shimmering through the waves of smoggy heat wavering above the street, but it was still a good six blocks off. Behind her another wail came from the alley; she realized the bastards were beating on a cat. "Leave it alone," she commanded. "It's mine."

They stopped and looked at her in disbelief, then took a couple steps towards her. "Say what?" one finally asked.

"Shove it, bitch," the other interrupted. "If it's yours, *come and get it.*" He was close enough now for her to see his small, mean eyes, like dull brown marbles floating in a skinny face marred by purple acne scars. He grinned. "Come on. Whatcha waiting for?"

Perdita hesitated and farther down the alley the cat mewled again, the sound lonely and in pain. She knew how it felt to be both, yet facing off with these two—

"You come and get it or I'll nail *your* pussy right to the wall," brown-eyes said.

"Damn you," she hissed. Old habits never quite disappeared and her fingers closed around steel in the pocket of her jeans. The blade was warm, heated through the denim by her flesh.

"Kill it, Bennie," the first one said flatly.

His friend moved obediently back towards the trash bin, a two–by–four dangling carelessly from one hand. "Never liked cats myself," the guy said agreeably.

"Don't," Perdita warned. She eased inside the alleyway, almost crouching. "Just leave it alone and get lost."

"Hey man, look! The broad's got herself a blade!" Brown–eyes laughed, then held up his hands and backed away from her with a dead smile. "Who gives a flyin' fuck about some mangy cat anyway? You want it that bad? Hey, go for it."

Behind her, the bus rolled by, spreading exhaust fumes over the grocery bags piled at the curb. The two kids sauntered away, neither in any big hurry. Fifty feet down, they turned into a gangway and disappeared briefly, then the leader's head appeared briefly and he leered at her.

"Gonna be looking for you, baby. I promise." Then he was gone.

Glancing quickly to the street to make sure the bags were still in place, Perdita folded the switchblade away and squatted next to the trash container so she could peer underneath. Far in the back, amid the garbage scraps and broken boards, was a yellow stray, green eyes glittering with mistrust and pain. "Here, kitty, kitty," she coaxed. "Come on, now, you're okay. That's right, you're—"

The sound of glass breaking made her head whip around. At the mouth of the alley, the two teenagers were kicking at her grocery bags, scattering cans and toilet paper in every direction. "Stop it!" she yelled, scrambling to her feet and running towards the bus stop. "Damn you, you little sons–a–bitches, cut it *out!*" They laughed uproariously and took off around the side of the building and out of sight.

Momentum carried her to the curb, then sent her sprawling as one of them stepped forward and thrust a foot in front of her. When she went down, Perdita felt the glass from a broken bottle of apple juice slice into her palms, followed quickly by a sharp kick in her ribs.

"Cunt." Brown–eyes was hovering over her. "Where's your fucking knife now, huh?" He kicked her again and she rolled away, feeling liquid from the shattered remains of a couple bottles soak into her clothes. The pavement scraped against her elbows, but Perdita hardly felt it as she jammed a hand into the pocket of her jeans, searching for the switchblade. "You're not so—"

His friend yanked on her attacker's jacket. "Come on, Rico. Forget her, man— there's a cop car coming!"

"What?" The one named Rico froze, then spat on her. "You lucked out this time, whore. But I ain't finished with you yet. I don't like bitches trying to fuck with me. Remember that— and remember that I'm coming for you."

Silence then, and Perdita prayed they were gone for good as she struggled to get up and began to crawl around on the sidewalk, trying to pull some of her stuff back into those stupid, plastic bags. Furious tears threatened and she ground her teeth against them; crying wouldn't do any fucking good. Footsteps crunched in the debris and she tensed and looked up.

"Trouble's always finding you, isn't it?" Gallagher stood over her, frowning.

"What happened, you drop your groceries?"

"Something like that," she muttered as she grabbed for a crushed roll of tissue.

He bent and began picking up cans and stuffing them into one of the bags. "Funniest thing I ever saw," he said casually. "A blouse with a boot pattern across its side."

"Yeah, it's real funny," Perdie said under her breath. Face flushed, she ripped open the roll of tissue so she could wipe her bloodied palms on a length of it. She was a mess again, clothes dirty and soaked with apple juice, and more pain—always—this time in her ribs. Not too bad, though, just another more nasty bruise. At least it wasn't broken.

"I'll take you home." The cop grabbed two of the bags. "Get the rest of your stuff and let's go."

"Hey, don't bother," Perdita protested. She was loathe to admit that the thought of a free ride, even from a cop, was tempting. It would also put her out of range of those teenaged assassins.

"No problem." Gallagher waved at the squad and it rolled smoothly to the curb, an unsmiling Miles behind the wheel. Dour-faced or not, at least when she looked at Gallagher's partner she didn't see any indication that the man held any kind of personal grudge against her.

Reluctantly Perdie got in the back when Gallagher held open the door and handed her the other two bags, then winced as it shut and locked automatically. She'd never been in a cop car except when she'd been pinched, and it was a frightening, claustrophobic feeling.

Gallagher turned and rested his arm on the back of his seat. His lean face was divided into neat triangles on the other side of the steel screen. "So what was that all about?" he asked again.

"A little trouble with a couple of guys, that's all."

"I seen those two taking off down the street," Miles interjected. "Looked like Crips jackets—bastards. You better watch out for them."

"Trouble over what?" Gallagher waited expectantly.

Perdita looked at her hands and tried to scrub off a little of the street grit and blood against her legs. Her palms were an odd mix of sweet stickiness from the apple juice and red from the grazed wounds in her skin. Outside the squad's windows the city rolled by, its occupants each doing a slow cook in the brutal summer sun.

"A...cat," she admitted at last.

"What?"

"I said, a *cat*."

Gallagher looked momentarily confused. "You'd fight a couple of guys who are probably killers over a stray cat? Are you nuts?" He shook his head. "That's a stupid thing to die for, lady."

"I didn't see it coming to that," she snapped.

"Here you go," Miles said suddenly. The car slowed to a stop. "This is it, right?"

"Yeah," Perdie answered, her voice grim. "Thanks for the ride." She pulled her bags along the seat and waited nervously at the door closest to the curb until

Gallagher got out and opened it. It felt good to get out of that back seat; just being around these two was making her queasy.

She bent to get her groceries, but Gallagher reached past her. "Here, I'll get those." He hefted two of the tattered bags, then moved toward her building.

"Hey, wait," Perdita protested. "I can—"

"No problem." He motioned to her to catch up. "Which door?"

She glared at him. "What's it to you? Aren't you taking this 'good deed' bullshit a little far?"

"You got something to hide?" he challenged.

"Fine." Perdita pulled irritably on the knob to the entry door. "Come on in if you want to so bad." She stomped inside, briefly considered dropping the front door on him, then changed her mind. After all, he *was* carrying her groceries. "Watch your step here," she said sullenly. "It's dark."

Gallagher followed her down the short flight of steps and watched as she unlocked first the deadbolt, then the knob lock. Inside the apartment she flicked on the light, more aware of the apartment's dark shabbiness than she had been in years. For all his confidence, the young policeman—with his starched uniform and perfectly pressed slacks—looked terribly out of place here. He was, she thought, just too fucking *blonde*.

"Where do you want these?" he asked. She pointed wordlessly to the kitchen table, hoping a cockroach wouldn't crawl out from under its edge.

"Nice place."

Perdita's head jerked up. Was that derision in his voice? "It keeps me off the street." She had to fight against the urge to raise her voice. "So now you've seen it. You gonna leave or gonna move in?"

"You can do better than this, Perdita." The cop picked up a small, cracked lamp from an end table, peered at it for a moment then set it back down. He didn't flinch when she looked at him incredulously, just nodded. "Sure, you can."

"There's nothing wrong with it." Too late, she realized pride—and what did she have to be *proud* about anyway?—was making her words strident.

"Oh, give me a break. You got roaches crawling everywhere, mice—probably rats too, only they're too crafty for you to spot 'em. You want to live in a hole like this for the rest of your life?"

"I think you should leave now." Perdita's voice was cold, her jaw rigid. "I didn't invite you in here to begin with, and I certainly don't need your insults."

Gallagher shrugged and walked back to the front door. "Yeah, okay. I'm sorry—maybe I come on a little too strong sometimes. But you think about it. You could get a job—"

"As what? A fucking hash slinger?"

"Waitressing is an honest living," he said patiently. "My mother was a waitress."

"I don't believe my ears." She covered her eyes with her fingers for a moment, trying to push away the headache left over from the fight in the alley, then threw her hands up. "What is this? Save-A-Soul, Incorporated? How'd I get to be your personal case? Could you just tell me that?"

Gallagher shrugged again, then stepped out the door and into the hallway. "You just seem like you could use a hand, that's all."

"I don't—"

He closed her own door in her face.

* * *

"So, baby, you ready to work the strip tonight or what?" Tyrone was waiting at the door, his skin a fine mahogany above a cream–colored silk shirt. "Come on, let's go. I ain't waiting all night." He glanced around the room, small and finally clean enough to satisfy Perdita. He seemed uncomfortable in the absence of the former clutter and dirt. "How you making out with the neighborhood johns?"

"Okay," she called from the bathroom as she plastered another coat of peach lipstick—her new color—across her mouth. "Not as good as the strip, of course."

"Of course," he mimicked. He didn't say anything for a second and she heard him move something, then curse.

"What?" she asked.

Silence for a second, then, "I said, how's your face doing?"

"It's almost healed." She picked up her small purse, a red thing that matched the tight leather skirt she'd found on the closet floor when she'd gone through it. She stepped out of the bathroom and was smiling when he grabbed a handful of her carefully trimmed hair and yanked her nose–to–nose with him.

"That's real *good*, you fucking bitch!"

"What's the matter?" she cried. The stinging in her scalp made tears spring to her eyes. "Hey, come on! Let go!"

"I'll tell you what's the matter! What the fuck is *this*?" He shoved his fist under her nose; in it was a wad of crushed bills. "You said you gave me all the money, and here I'm thinking about forking over funds so you can get some new clothes! You lying, sneaking, little cunt!"

"I did!" Perdita pushed against him. "I gave you all of it, I swear it!"

"Then where did this come from?" he screamed. "What the fuck is a hundred bucks doing under this lamp! Huh?" Before she could avoid him, Tyrone back–handed her hard across one cheek.

"Don't hit me!" she shrieked, trying to back–peddle with her hands in front of her face. "I'm just getting to where I can work again!" Tyrone shoved her away and she stumbled, nearly tripping over the worn couch. "I don't know where it came from! I swear it!" The pimp's face was furious, his hard–knuckled fists itching to split her skin. "Listen," she entreated, "maybe I hid it there awhile ago and forgot it, you know, back when I wasn't doing so great, when I was into the crack. If I'd have found it, you know I would've given it to you!"

"Is that so?" Tyrone's voice was a sneer. "Damn you, Perdie. I'm getting just too tired of your shit, girl." He crammed the money in his pocket, and his voice was frigid. "The next time I catch you skimming, I ain't gonna mess up that pretty face. I'll have a friend of mine work you over where it won't show."

Tyrone's mean eyes glittered. "That way you can still work, and every time a john puts a dick to you, you'll scream. All your tricks'll think they're making you come." He threw back his head and laughed delightedly.

Abruptly the pimp stopped and stared at her.

"Maybe," he whispered with a grin, "I'll have it done anyway. Just for the fun of it."

He slammed out of the apartment and Perdie resisted the urge to yank open the door and throw that damned living room lamp at his back. *Asshole,* she fumed. He was supposed to give her a ride downtown; now she'd have to walk it, since she sure didn't have the dough for a cab. And where the hell *had* that money come from? She hadn't—

The thought died in mid-conception, splintered by another that was far more amazing.

Gallagher!

Perdita scowled and snatched up her purse, then stopped to check her reflection in the bathroom mirror to make sure Tyrone hadn't split her lip. She was okay there, just a little too pink along the cheekbone, but that would fade in a half hour. Why would that stupid cop leave her a hundred bucks? If it'd been pity or thoughtfulness, it'd almost gotten the hell beat out of her—what an idiotic thing for him to do! And now, on top of everything else, she had a three-mile walk. Perdita brightened a little, though; at least she looked pretty good tonight. Now that her face was almost healed and she was clean besides, it'd be easy for her to pick up four or five hundred, maybe more, and whether or not he was still pissed about that hundred bucks, Tyrone wouldn't mind her taking a cab home after that.

She stepped outside, automatically closing her nose against the stench of garbage from the trash barrels along the side of her building. It was hot—no hotter than normal, she supposed—but the prospect of the hike ahead made the heat seem immediately unbearable. Her heels slipped on an unidentifiable piece of muck on the sidewalk, no doubt spilled from someone's lop-sided toss at the cans. Grimacing as she came out of the gangway, Perdita raised her head at the sound of an idling engine.

Gallagher's squad car waited at the curb.

* * *

"What the hell'd you do that for?" she demanded. Perdita's face was furious as they stood outside a snack shop just beyond the area where the strip officially began.

"Don't tell me you couldn't use the money." Gallagher's slender features had a stubborn set.

"I never even had a chance to count it! You fucking idiot, he threatened to have me worked over for holding out on him! You could've gotten me killed with your damned good intentions."

"Are you sure you don't want a donut?" Gallagher asked mildly. "The frosted ones are the best."

"Are you listening to me, you bastard?" she yelled. Inside the car, Miles glanced up from his newspaper, then dipped his attention back to the sports page. "I said you could've gotten me killed!" She balled her fists in frustration, aching to give him just one good punch on the side of the head, see how he'd like it. "What's so interesting about me anyway? Why don't you just leave me alone? Why *me*?"

Gallagher shrugged, a habit that was quickly beginning to infuriate her further. "Why not? Everyone needs a hobby."

Perdita stared at him, open-mouthed. The air temperature had to be at least ninety and this jerk-off was making her so angry it felt like a hundred and ten. "Hey, don't do me any favors, *officer*. Take up needlepoint." She turned away in disgust and started walking the last few blocks to her spot.

"It's not my fault you were stupid enough to get caught," he called. "Next time use your brains and make sure you don't leave the money where he can find it."

Perdita stopped and glared back at him. "There won't *be* a next time, copper, you hear me? Now you go on home to your nice little house in the suburbs and your nice little wife, or girlfriend, or whatever. Just get out of my life!"

Even as she stalked off, Perdita could feel him smiling behind her.

✳   ✳   ✳

Jesus, she was tired! That last bastard had been one peg short of a psycho—not physically, but emotionally. Uncontrollable, unpredictable, *frightening*. One minute he was simultaneously humping her and talking animatedly about his printing business and how things were going so good, the next he was limp and crying, red-faced snot and all, about his old lady and what she'd do if she ever found out he had to come to a hooker so he had shit to fantasize about when he fucked her. Being soothing was not her strong point—there'd been damned little sympathy in her own life—and Perdita had a hard time talking soft to some blubbering, overweight wanna-be-exec still clad in a polyester tee shirt and socks. But she'd managed, oh yeah, though what she wanted to do was push his tear-and sweat-stained face off her shoulder and tell him to look in the Yellow Pages under therapy. Still and all, he'd been good for seventy-five bucks—a quarter C-note more than her asking price over the last week or so, so maybe all the sniffling had been worth it.

Five a.m. was a great time of the day, she thought. She could enjoy the almost smog-free air rushing through the cab's open back window even through her tired senses. A smudge of pink—dirty but pink nonetheless—showed above the tops of the passing buildings. What was that old saying? *Red sky in the morning...hooker take warning?* Now there was an interesting variation on a worn-out quote. Perdie giggled aloud, then looked purposely away from the driver as he glanced quizzically at her in his rear view mirror. Another block and the taxi was cruising the dark street next to her building, the driver none too happy to be in this less-than-favorable neighborhood.

"Pull over here," Perdie instructed. She thrust a ten and two singles at him and got out, making sure she had her purse before she closed the door and he pulled away. As a teenaged runaway a million years ago, she had forgotten her purse in the back seat of a cab just like that one; thirty seconds later the car, and all her money and identification, was nothing but a memory in the bright headlights of Saturday night L.A. traffic. To be honest, the money, a couple hundred dollars, would have only stalled the inevitable by a few days.

The smell inside the hallway was worse than usual, so fetid and heavy that Perdita nearly gagged. *Good God, what the hell died in here?* she thought. The overhead bulb, a pathetic, dirt-covered attempt at illumination to begin with, was burned out and thin glass crunched under her high heels as she groped her way to her front door. The closer she got, the worse the stench, and Perdita gritted her teeth at the thought that some wretched drunk had crawled in and died in front of her step. Still, nothing stopped the toe of her shoe as she felt her way tentatively forward and finally hated when her toot thumped against the bottom of her door.

Blind in the darkness, Perdita reached forward to feel for the keyhole. Her questioning fingers sunk deep into something cool and wet and viscous, like a congealed mass of lumpy gelatin clinging to her door.

She absolutely refused to scream.

※　　　　　※　　　　　※

"Pigs! Assholes!" She was ranting, her voice rising to a crescendo, yet she was powerless to control it. And why should she? The memory of the disgusting mass of skinned, stretched fur and bloody flesh that had been nailed across the lock to her apartment this morning returned, providing visual back-up to the still-pungent scent Perdita seemed unable to scrub away. To make matters worse, she swore she could still smell the feline's guts on her fingers.

Gallagher stood in the hallway, frowning at her but not *at* her, and sure, she knew the difference. They both understood the reasoning behind the grisly little memento, and she even knew—at least by sight—the rotten punks who'd done it. None of that fooled Gallagher, or even herself; Perdita was raving out of the helpless fear borne of the realization that the two gang members had discovered where she lived.

"We ought to get you out of here," Gallagher said. "It's not safe."

"Oh, that's rich," she snorted. "And just where am I supposed to go? The Hilton? Or maybe home with you."

"Sure, why not," he said promptly.

She stared at him; he really *was* out of his mind. "Fuck you," she said finally. "I like it here just fine, and I ain't leaving."

His shoulders lifted a little self-consciously, as though someone had called the habit to his attention. "Suit yourself. But you'd better watch your back, Perdita. Those guys've got it out for you in a big way."

"Well, thank you Sherlock," she said sarcastically. "I guess I could've figured out that one without your help. And say, what are you doing here again anyway?

Don't you have better things to do with your time? And where's your uniform?"

"I'm off duty."

"Don't you ever sleep?" she demanded. "Surely to Christ you've got a life somewhere."

Gallagher ignored her and glanced at the dried brown smear running down the outside of the front door. "I could get you a dog," he suggested. "Something big, with a lot of teeth."

"Forget it. No way am I gonna pay to feed some bigass watchdog that'll probably drag me down the sidewalk and crap all over the apartment besides. Besides, I never liked dogs."

He folded his arms. "Okay. How about a cat?"

She couldn't help laughing. "And what good's that supposed to do? Will it claw them to death when they bust in the front door?"

He grinned. "Won't do any good, I guess. But your face sure lit up when I said it."

Perdita averted her eyes. "I don't need no litter box stinking up the place," she grumbled. "There's nothing worse than cat smell—"

"Oh, baloney. Mix half a box of baking soda with the litter and change everything once a week, no one'll ever know you even have one unless it shows itself. How about it? There's some nice little tabbies over at the pound."

"No," she said firmly. "Besides, those cats at the pound are doing fine. They're warm and dry, and getting those three squares a day. Life couldn't be better."

"Sure," Gallagher said agreeably. "Until they overstay their welcome and the docs euthanize them."

"Well," Perdita swung back and fixed him with a dark stare. "We all get put out of our misery sooner or later."

*   *   *

She couldn't believe it. There he stood in his snappy cop's uniform, a big, shit-eating grin on his face and a basket in his arms with a stupid pink bow on the handle and a solemn-eyed yellow cat inside.

"Oh, fuck," Perdie moaned. "What are you doing, Gallagher? I don't want any damned cat." She rubbed her eyes and tried to push her sleep-wrinkled hair out of her face. What time was it—*Christ*—seven a.m.! She'd gotten to sleep less than two hours ago, and last night had been a shitcase, too. Didn't this guy realize everyone else in the world wasn't following his schedule? Coming home for the last two weeks had become its own special slice of hell, each night waiting for another bloody treat or worse, a confrontation that had to happen sometime. Those boys, she knew, would never forget.

"Come on, Perdie. Let me come in, huh? I figured this was one present I could give you and not get in trouble for." Gallagher inclined his head toward the basket. "Look at her. You two were meant for each other." On cue, the cat meowed, a sweet, inquisitive sound.

Perdita turned her back on him and took a few steps, then dropped onto the couch and yawned. "Take her back where you got her. I'm allergic."

"Bullshit," Gallagher said mildly. He stepped inside and toed the door closed behind him, then set the basket on the couch next to her. "Besides, 'back where I found her' is an alley a couple blocks away." He raised an eyebrow. "We all know how life is for the alleycats around here."

"Life is hard on a lot of things," Perdita retorted. "I don't have time for no fucking animal." Even so, she couldn't resist a glance at the fat female cat—an odd thing for a stray to look so well–fed. She just missed being gold; instead the animal looked as though someone had dumped stripes of tacky yellow paint over a background of dirty tan. Still and all, the feline's eyes, were large and pale…and tired.

Perdie certainly knew what it felt like to be on the street and tired, all right.

The cat got up and stretched, it's wide torso lengthening momentarily, then climbed out of the basket and onto her lap. It curled up and rubbed its chin along her forearm as a slow purr began to vibrate along Perdie's stomach. Her hand moved of its own accord to stroke the cat's head.

"Shit," she muttered.

"Come on," Gallagher said. "Give it a try for a few days. Look," he pointed to the basket. "I even bought a box of cat food. That and a bowl of water and you're all set. What could be easier?"

She fell asleep on the couch with the cat purring contentedly on her lap, and never even heard Gallagher close the front door securely behind him.

✳   ✳   ✳

"Shee–it, where the fuck did you get this mangy thing?" Tyrone's shoulders hunched in disgust and he backed away from Alma. The newly named cat watched him with an expression that seemed almost distasteful, then slipped into the bathroom and curled around Perdita's ankles as she applied the final touches to her make–up.

"She doesn't have mange. Besides, I like cats. And this place needed something to liven it up."

"I woulda thought you'd had enough of 'em with that dead–assed animal that got hung on your door." Suddenly the pimp gave a wet, hearty sneeze. "Fuck it all, man. I gotta get outta here—always was allergic to the little sons–a–bitches."

Perdita poked her head out of the bathroom, afraid of losing her ride downtown. "Hey, don't leave without me, I'm almost ready."

Tyrone sneezed again, this time harder, then shook his head. "I'll be waiting in the Caddy. Shee–it," he said again. He sent Alma a nasty scowl, then hastily retreated from the allergy zone.

Perdita laughed and reached down to ruffle the warm fur along the cat's spine. "Good girl. Guess he won't be spending much time in here anymore, will he?" She grinned to herself; that suited her just fine. The yellow cat had been here for only three days, and Perdita found she much preferred its company to anyone else's.

Alma gave a little mewl and rubbed the hefty length of her body along

Perdita's hand. Petting absently, a faint trace of movement beneath her fingers brought Perdita up short. "Hey," she said softly, "what's this?" Muffled through the bricks of the building, she heard the dim sound of Tyrone's car horn as he pushed it impatiently. "Yeah, yeah, I'm coming." She slipped a hand under Alma's belly again, then abruptly stood, snatched up her purse and stormed out of the apartment. If this was any indication of how her night was going to be, it was gonna be an ass–kicker.

That fucking cop had given her a pregnant cat.

✳   ✳   ✳

"Well, this is just great!" Perdie raged. "You take her back." Gallagher said nothing and she pounded the table with the side of her fist; Alma wisely decided to duck under the couch. "What am I saying? What am I *doing*?" Perdita glared at him. "Why don't you get the hell out of my life? And take that damned, knocked–up cat with you!"

"It's no big deal—" he began but she cut him off with a sharp wave of her hand.

"*No big deal?* Oh no, of course not! You don't have to fuck around with it, you don't have to think about it. *I* do. Don't you get that?"

"Oh, calm down," Gallagher said in exasperation. "So she's going to have kittens, so what? She has 'em, they get a little mother's milk for a few weeks, and we them take to the pound. Simple."

"Boy, aren't you the one to jump at the suggestion of the pound *now*," she sneered, "when a week ago you spent a shitload of effort trying to convince me how I shouldn't let a certain old yellow stray end up there."

"That was different," he pointed out. "Alma is exactly that—an *old* cat. Older animals have a very poor chance of getting adopted and besides, the minute they found out she was pregnant they would've given her a good–night shot, babies and all." She stared at him, appalled, and he spread his hands. "I never said it was right, just that this is the way it is. You think you don't have time for a cat and a few kittens? They've already got two hundred of the things, and they certainly don't want five or six more."

Perdita sat heavily on one of kitchen chairs. Alma peered from beneath the couch, her barely–tan eyes reflecting the light like flickering twin beacons. It'd only been a few days, yet already Perdita had come to relish the cat's company, enjoying the sorely–missed warmth of another living creature that demanded little in return besides food and attention. It'd been so very long since she'd had a pet, but...add five or six more? God.

"I don't know why I let you talk me into these things," she said helplessly. "I can barely afford to feed Alma, let alone a bunch of babies. And I don't know *anybody* to give them to—"

"I'm willing to bet," he said firmly, "that a lot of the other working girls would appreciate a little company just like you did."

"You're willing to bet, huh?" Eyes sharp, Perdie tapped a fingernail on the scarred surface of the table and leaned towards him. "But just how much, Mister Policeman? How about we bet the number of kittens I still have when they're weaned, how about that? What I can't move, you take. That's the deal."

The bastard, he didn't even hesitate.

※ ※ ※

A mini–symphony of plaintive mewls greeted Perdita when she opened the door at five–thirty in the morning a week later. She snapped on the light as soon as she got all the way inside, knowing that Tyrone was waiting at the curb to see it before he would leave. Because of the cat—and especially when she'd lightly mentioned that Alma was going to have kittens any day—the pimp wouldn't even come in the apartment anymore. But Tyrone still drove her home and waited for the light, as he had every night since the dead cat had been nailed to her door, making sure his merchandise was safe and sound for the night. She knew, though, that he was getting tired of it; at five in the morning, good ol' Tyrone liked to be in his crib and surrounded by the latest two or three of the teenaged girls he was always picking up at the bus station and priming to turn onto the streets. All prettied up and healthy, Perdie was bringing in a grand each night, but she wasn't worth losing sleep over for too long.

She locked the door behind her and glanced around the small front room. Next to the couch was Alma, lying on the dingy but clean towel Perdita had spread for her. Perdie smiled in spite of herself and in spite of the pains–in–the–ass she knew the new additions would eventually be. Surrounding the new mama, suckling tentatively, were eight fragile kittens, and not a yellow one in the bunch. Every last one of 'em was either black or white—not even one had the smallest splotch of another color anywhere on its fur. Perdita would've thought at least two would be yellow, like their mother.

She crouched next to the little family and studied the tiny kittens. While it was far too early to determine sex, it was odd that the patterns seemed to match—at least to her admittedly faulty memory—the litter from another cat, the memory still blasted in the recesses of her mind from lifetimes ago. A bewildered frown crossed Perdita's forehead; she found the idea that, even though separated by so many switchbacked years, this litter of newborn cats might mirror that other litter frightening in a bone–wrenching way that even the neighborhood gang bangers couldn't evoke. What did it mean? Something, she was certain—seldom did anything of significance just 'happen' to her. Everything in every existence had revealed itself to be cause and effect; no wasted moments, no useless actions, not even any impulse emotion. Cause and effect, pure and simple.

Gallagher, she realized nervously, had caused these cats to make their way into her life.

Question of the day: What would the effect be?

※ ※ ※

"Here you go, kitty. Come and get it." Perdita set the bowl of dry food next to the water bowl and watched as Alma strolled nonchalantly into the kitchen and began to eat. The kittens, all eight of them, began to yowl immediately, missing the warmth of their mother in the early morning coolness of the apartment. Perdita slid to the floor gingerly, always on the look-out for cockroaches although their numbers had dropped drastically in the last month, then stroked her yellow cat's fur, now shiny from the occasional brushing. She ignored the spoiled meowing from the other room, knowing the kittens would find their way to mom and the food soon enough. They were eating more and more solid food, and while they were cute little buggers, one more week and she could start giving them away. Gallagher had a definite home for four of them, and she'd found a couple girls on the strip who were willing to take two more; only two left, and that wasn't bad at all. Besides, and here Perdita grinned to herself, if she couldn't give them to anyone else, Gallagher won the prize.

Still, she'd prefer to find real homes for the last two, places where they were truly wanted instead of the last-minute "Oh, I'll give it a try" situations that they'd surely end up with otherwise. There were a couple more working girls she knew over on Sunset—

The knob on her front door rattled.

Her face jerked toward the door in time with the mother cat's. It'd been a little noise, barely noticeable...but enough to make Perdita's heart begin a heavy thudding within her ribcage as her pulse rate jumped.

Gallagher? No way; he'd knock politely, call out in that cajoling voice of his to let him in. Tyrone, of course, would simply pound on the door, all the while yelling at the top of his lungs about ungrateful bitches who should've expected him to be there—except Tyrone and his allergies wanted nothing to do with Perdie's apartment now that all these cats had made it their home.

Who then? Perdita stood cautiously, cocking her head and trying to listen over the thunderous, interruptive beat of fear in her body. She thought she heard a high-pitched, childish giggle, barely perceptible, perhaps more her terrified imagination than anything else. Standing now, she did a silent sidestep to the kitchen drawer and managed to slide it noiselessly open; in another second she'd lifted a flimsy steak knife, her only one besides the switchblade in her purse, which was too close to the front door for Perdita to risk going for it.

She stared hard at the apartment door and its row of locks. Had she locked the deadbolt? She must have, she always did. Why, then, did she feel so vulnerable? You idiot, Perdita thought grimly, because any braindead youngster over a hundred pounds could kick in that fucking door without breathing hard. She glanced around automatically, but the only other way out was the back door with its own deadbolt, the key to which was also in her purse in the living room. The one tiny window wasn't an option; shielding it were rusted burglar bars.

A few feet away, the kittens were suddenly quiet. Crouched in front of her ankles, tail now twitching violently, Alma shocked Perdita by hissing outright, the only such noise Perdita had ever heard her make.

Perdita ground her teeth and clutched the cheap knife, praying it wouldn't slip from her sweaty hand. *I'm in trouble now*, she thought clearly.

The front door exploded open.

* * *

Heart pounding, Perdita stepped forward and faced the two teenagers she'd confronted in the alley. After that fight, she had expected this, and waited, and waited some more, stupidly falling into the eventual trap of believing that each passing day increased the odds in her favor that the young men had forgotten her and gone on to torment some other victim who would provide them with more interesting sport. The carcass on her door should have warned her better, should have told her that their anger was alive and serious, and undeniably calculating. Now she was trapped in her apartment, and this silly–ass steak knife wasn't worth anything against the switchblades that were gleaming in their hands.

A fragment of memory flashed in her thoughts—a television show, a book, maybe just a gritty piece of street advice; she couldn't recall which: *Denial of Privacy*. A women should never, ever let herself be taken anywhere alone with an abductor; fight, scream, do whatever you had to—including taking a few blows—but *don't let them get you alone.*

Which was exactly what she was—and with *two* attackers.

She tried taking the offensive. "Get out!" Perdita yelled. "Just get out right now and no one will get hurt!" She kept the steak knife tucked behind her, not ready to show her only hand.

The one with the bad skin and nasty brown eyes—Rico, his friend had called him back in the alley—ignored her and hopped lithely over a chunk of the wrecked wooden door. "Sorry about the mess, babe," he said. He grinned, showing a mouthful of surprisingly beautiful teeth. "Me and Bennie came to visit. We figured you wouldn't invite us in, so we just took the lib–er–tee."

Bennie followed his partner inside and stood next to him, the pair effectively blocking any escape. He said nothing, only looked around the shabby little room with a repulsed expression. For one reckless moment Perdita felt like asking Bennie if his own place looked any better, then lost the impulse when he spotted her purse and grabbed it. She didn't bother protesting when he up–ended its contents on the floor and searched her wallet for cash—very little—since she knew it wouldn't do any good. She had to clench her jaw to keep quiet when his dirty fingers found her switchblade and held it up.

"Hey," Bennie said conversationally. "Nice piece." The battered knife he held in his other hand clicked shut and he shoved it in his pocket, then hit the button on hers. The blade sprang free, a clean sweep of deadly silver. His smile was a dark pit across his face.

"What do you want?" she asked. It was an instinctive, incredibly ridiculous question.

"Oh...this and...that," said Rico. His gaze darted around the small room, touched briefly on the bathroom door then came to rest where she stood pressed against the kitchen sink.

"You've got all my money, now go."

"It ain't enough," Bennie said flatly. "I need something more, something to make me feel better. You shouldn't have fucked with us."

"Look," Perdita said desperately, "why don't we just forget that." She tried to think of a way to make herself look small and not so threatening, but came up empty. "Anyway, that was a long time ago." Reasoning with them was a tactic destined to fail, but she couldn't help herself. "Besides, you got your revenge. You wrecked my groceries, nailed that dead cat on my door—"

Rico laughed loudly and elbowed his friend. "Yeah. Man, wasn't that just the greatest fucking idea or what?"

"But it ain't enough," Bennie repeated. Perdita swallowed; in the alley, Bennie had seemed the milder of the two, a foolish underestimation on her part.

"There's nothing else, so just get out of my place now!" She let her voice rise until it was almost a scream. Surely to God someone would hear through the wreckage of the door—then again, this was L.A. Like every other overpopulated city, no one would be willing to get involved.

"Shut up, you bitch!" Rico yelled right back. Something moved near the couch and his head whipped towards it, fast as a snake. "What the hell was that?"

Bennie laughed. "This is too good! Check it out!" One hand darted down, then held up a squalling kitten. "Toys, man!" Alma appeared from beside the couch and hissed viciously, saliva spraying from her barred fangs.

"Put it down, you asshole!" Perdita screeched. She followed the demand with a old porcelain plate from the dish drainer, bunching her fist in victory as it connected firmly with the side of Bennie's head and shattered. He dropped the kitten as he jerked and grabbed for his head, then looked at his fingers, now smeared with blood; with a lightning spring, Alma snatched the kitten from under his feet and dashed across the room with it.

"Oh man," Bennie growled, "you fucked up big time, sugar. We were only playing before, but now—"

"What's going on in here?" a deep voice demanded. Rico and Bennie whirled nearly in unison. "Can't you Puerto Ricans keep your arguments to yourselves? And what the hell happened to this door?" Perdita couldn't believe her luck. It was the superintendent, a large, greasy man of questionable age who hardly ever showed his face. Right now he looked pissed as hell, as though all the shouting had drowned out the voices on his late late movie.

Perdie saw her chance. "Call the cops!" she cried. "Quick!"

Rico bounded to the doorway, his speed rivaling the cat's rescue trip. "Get the fuck out!" he screamed into the man's face. Surprised, the man gaped and backpeddled. "Get the fuck out or I'll *do* you! You hear me, fat motherfucker?" Perdita's small hope died when the hefty man turned and stumbled from sight, the fleshy rolls beneath his stained tee shirt bouncing vigorously as he retreated. *Dear God*, Perdita thought, *please let him call the cops. Please.*

Bennie was still stunned by the sight of his bloody fingers when the two hoodlums returned their attention to her. While the wound on his head was hardly a scratch, it had served to tick him off royally. Now he lifted red-rimmed eyes to her and Perdie wondered couldn't help wondering what these two were flying high on. "Ready to party, whore?"

Rico giggled, then squatted and peered around the floor. "Hey Bennie, let's find us some party favors first, whaddya say? Here—got one!" He grabbed at something, then held up a kitten triumphantly, waving it at Perdita as it mewled. "Come on, slut. Wanna throw something? I'll use pussy here as a baseball bat and go for a fucking home run." He swiped at the air and the kitten screeched.

"You chickenshit bastard," Perdita's voice turned taunting. "What's the matter? Am I too *big* to take on? You only got the balls to fuck with a cat? Come on, *big* man."

Rico scowled, but didn't drop the kitten. "This is all just too bad, you know? We only came to fuck around a little, get a little free ass, maybe mess up your place for the hell of it." He twisted his wrist and stared at the tiny cat dangling from his hand as though mentally dismembering it; its round blue eyes blinked back in fear. "But now I think we have to get serious; now I think you're just a used-up old hooker with a too-fucking-big mouth that we need to shut for good. Whaddya say, Bennie-boy?"

Bennie wiped his hand on his jeans and smiled, a deadly stretching of his lips that was deceptively placid. "Fucking-A." Perdita flinched when another kitten, attracted by its sibling's cries, wobbled out from, under the sofa and sniffed curiously around Bennies boots. He bent and picked it up, then stroked its head gently before glancing at Rico. "We should've brought some lighter fluid."

"Hell, yeah! Now *that* would've been a sonofabitch to see, huh? Flaming party favors!"

"Why don't you guys just get the hell out," Perdita suggested. Her right hand still clutched the steak knife, while the other found and wrapped around a heavy apple juice bottle that had been drying on the counter. A quick glance across the undersized kitchen told her she didn't have much else to throw: the drainer itself, a bottle of dish detergent, the beat-up old toaster. She wasn't much for clutter anymore and kept her stuff stored away. "Let's face it. I'm not worth taking heat over, and you know the cops are on their way by now."

"*I* don't know that." Rico looked at his partner in mock innocence. "Do *you* know that?"

"Nah," answered Bennie. "That old dickwad's too scared to do anything but hide in his apartment and clean the shit out of his pants. Ain't no blue knights gonna come and save your worn-out ass this time." Anticipation made his face brighten. "Come on, Rico. Let's do it. I'm tired of waiting."

"Hell, yeah," Rico said again. He held up the kitten and wrapped cruel fingers around its neck. "Let's start with the fucking cats. I hate these things." He squeezed suddenly and the kitten gasped and began to claw frantically at his hand.

A streak of off-color tan launched itself at his chest at the same moment that Perdita threw the juice bottle with all her strength.

And the battle began.

∗ ∗ ∗

Color, chaos, and a riot of noise—overturned furniture and flying lamps shot by Perdita's disjointed vision. Reflex made Bennie drop the kitten he held when Rico screamed as Alma buried a full set of claws deep into his stomach and ripped at his shirt with her teeth, trying to claw her way up to his throat. He flung the blue-eyed kitten in Perdie's direction just before the juice bottle collided with his nose, giving a satisfying *crack!* Rico howled and spun away, crashing first into the lamp table then the wall. The instant her kittens were freed, Alma let go and dropped to the floor, easily dodging Bennie's enraged kick.

Rico's hands flew to his nose, trying to press it back into shape as a spray of blood leaked through his fingers. "She broke my fucking nosth!" he bellowed. For all its loudness, his voice sounded like he had a bad head cold. Perdita almost laughed as Bennie turned towards his friend; instead she decided to dash out of the box-like kitchen and into the living room, try to circle around. If she could get to the bathroom, she might be able to lock herself in until the cops got here. But that would leave the cats unprotected—

Bennie caught her movement from the corner of his eye and lunged for her, knocking aside the beat-up wooden rocker that stood in his way. Perdita screamed and jerked back as she swiped at him with the kitchen knife, opening a red line across the inside of one of his palms that parted the small web of skin between his middle and ring fingers.

"You slut!" he screamed and yanked his hand out of her reach. "I'll carve you up for that!"

"Fucking bith," snarled Rico as he spat blood. He spun and went for her from the left, the cats forgotten. Already out of the kitchen and with Bennie on her right, Perdita realized her mistake: she was trapped between them, pinned against the short wall between the bathroom and kitchen. All she could do was crouch there, knife ready, and pray she'd hurt them enough so that they'd be too leery to attack. Somehow she didn't think so.

"Stop it!" Perdita said desperately as she swung the knife back and forth. "Or one of you is going to get hurt. Who wants to be the volunteer?"

"No pain, no gain," Rico declared as his gaze flicked to Bennie. He grabbed for Perdita with one hand and jabbed out with the other, the tip of his switchblade grazing her ribcage, opening her blouse and spewing a line of fire across her side. She pulled out of reach, then darted forward on his backswing, shoving the steak knife nearly to the hilt in the flesh of his left side and twisting it savagely before yanking it out. His shocked face went a satisfying shade of gray as he gasped and stumbled back, clamping his hands over the wound; his shirt was soaked with blood almost instantly.

But Perdita's victory was short-lived. Too late she realized she'd taken her eyes from Bennie for longer than she should have, and only the fluke of her spinning around and backwards kept the skin of her throat from splitting under Bennie's high swing at her with her own switchblade. Instead, his powerful, arcing strike caught her across the upper chest, starting at the top of her shoulder and scraping down her collarbone and across her upper ribs. The pain was immense, nearly blotting out everything else as her vision sparkled and she struggled to keep her grip on the steak knife. She lashed out instinctively with the knife and felt an instant of resistance as it met, then sank into something soft before she pulled it back again, determined to hang onto it. Bennie hissed in pain and she tripped backwards, hugging the wall as her other hand tried to feel her way along the wall. Beyond the golden spots dancing in her vision, she saw Rico drop to his knees.

"I'm hurt, Bennie!" He seemed to have forgotten the pain of his broken nose. "The bitch cut me bad!" He coughed as he struggled up on one knee, then sank back with a gasp; both his hands were dripping as he tried to press them against his side.

"Oh, you're gonna pay now," Bennie said softly. His left arm, blood seeping through a hole in its sleeve, came up and slapped at her in a harmless gesture, but reflex made her lash out with her knife hand, vaguely aware of the feel of the skin along her chest puckering open like a ripped hem. On the downward motion of Perdita's useless jab, Bennie kicked hard at her ankles, and she wailed as new pain, fierce competition for the napalm–like agony across her chest, hammered through her legs when her feet were jerked out from under her and she hit the floor. The knife, her only defense, skittered from her numbing fingers and slid out of sight. Her senses were blurring, but…was that a siren she heard, or just the singing of her own blood as it pounded in her ears? She rolled on her side and drew her legs up and against her bloody chest protectively, wishing for unconsciousness but fighting against it. Through her slitted eyes, she could see Rico coughing little bits of blood onto the floor, still trying to get to his feet.

"Hang on, man," Bennie said grimly. "I'm gonna finish off this little problem and get you out of here." He bent over Perdie without wasting any more time and she tried to push him away with one weak hand, then moaned as his blade—*her* blade—cut a deep, excruciating stripe down her forearm. Even so, her hands came up again and again in defense, twitching as he batted them aside with the switchblade, leaving streaks of hot pain each time. One of his hands found her hair and he buried his fingers deep, ignoring her pathetic punches at his chest; another second and he used her hair to haul her, screaming anew, to a sitting position. She hung there, throat exposed as she clawed at his hand ineffectively.

Bennie glanced quickly at his friend, then looked back at her, his eyes dark and feral. "Don't have time to do you right," he hissed. "But I ain't gonna do you easy."

"No—" The word bubbled into a harsh shriek as Bennie slid the tip of his switchblade neatly between two ribs just below her right breast, then angled the blade and pushed upward quickly. Rigid, pressed against the wall at her back and with nowhere to go, she thought she might never stop screaming, just as she thought the blade might never stop going in and in and in…

The room slipped out of focus as the handle of the switchblade rammed against her ribcage; all she could see was Bennie's huge face only an inch away from hers as he grinned and pulled sideways as hard and far as he could, opening her up like a butcher working on a side of beef before he yanked the switchblade free. She lost her scream abruptly as blood bubbled up her windpipe and gushed from her mouth. Perdita's hands fell and Bennie let go of her hair and watched as she slid back down the wall, the front of her clothes a wet, scarlet sheet.

"Fixed you good." He sounded pleased. "That'll teach—"

"Police—freeze!"

Somehow, amazingly, Perdita managed to open her eyes. Standing in the doorway was Gallagher, gun drawn and swinging back and forth between Rico's still slumped position on the floor and Bennie. Bennie snarled and reached for Perdita again.

"Touch her and I'll shoot," Gallagher said coldly. "Just get up and move away, and do it *very* carefully. And leave the weapon behind." Gallagher stepped carefully over the rubble and stepped to Perdita's side as Bennie dropped her switchblade and backed away, his face a blood–streaked scowl as he tracked the muzzle's aim. Miles edged in from behind Gallagher and slipped around to the other side, his sharp eyes on both of the young men.

"I'm hurt," Rico whined from the floor.

"Yeah, man," Bennie said. "She cut him up, see. We was just acting in self–defense. He needs an ambulance."

"I don't give a shit about your friend," Gallagher said matter–of–factly. He nodded at his partner, and Miles holstered his own gun and crossed the room; before Bennie could protest, he spun the younger man and slammed him face–first against the wall, yanked his right wrist back and snapped one end of a pair of handcuffs around it, then jerked the other down to finish the job. Miles pulled him around and pushed him forward.

"Hey, you don't gotta be so rough!"

"Shut up, jagoff," Miles barked. He hauled Bennie across the room and shoved him down next to Rico, then held him as he reached to catch the set of handcuffs Gallagher tossed him from his own belt. A quick, hard fist to the side of the head made Rico gasp and drop the switchblade he'd been concealing and Miles kicked it across the room, then looped the other set of handcuffs through Bennies and fastened Rico's wrists. Finally, the sturdy cop pulled them both to their feet, ignoring Rico's gasping objections. "You ain't hurt that bad, you wuss," he growled. "You'll walk out on your own or I'll drag both your asses. Which'll it be?"

"Can you handle them both?" Gallagher looked at him worriedly.

"No problem." Miles glanced at Perdita's crumpled form. "I got it covered. I'll call an ambulance for your friend there." He shook his head doubtfully. "She don't look so good, buddy." He pulled his prisoners through the wreckage of the living room and out the door.

Gallagher squatted next to her. "Perdita? Perdie, can you hear me?"

Her eyes had closed again and she forced them back open; they felt gummy and reluctant, as though even they were bleeding. "What are you doing here?" she whispered. Her voice was a soft gurgle and he winced. "Don't you ever sleep?"

"Rotation," he answered automatically. "They changed our shifts." Perdie felt as though someone had unzipped her and her insides, her lungs, might spill out as his fingers moved cautiously under her arms where she hugged herself. He pulled her hand back and stared at its crimson coating. "Oh, Jesus," he breathed. "What the hell happened here?"

"Fight." She choked, then coughed weakly, blood and froth leaking from her mouth.

"I can see that." Gallagher kneeled next to her. "I'm gonna try to pull you up so you can breathe better. It's gonna hurt—"

"Don't...bother," she gasped. "Too late anyway."

He shook his head stubbornly. "Don't say that. You'll be fine." She made a wheezing sound that was supposed to be a laugh and he decided that maybe it wasn't a good idea to move her after all. "What's this?" He leaned out of her line of sight and came back with the bloodied steak knife. "Did you use this?" She nodded slightly and closed her eyes. "Why?" he demanded. "Shit, they might've only roughed you up, trashed the apartment and split if you hadn't starting cutting!"

"I...had to." She was fighting for air and the policeman leaned closer to her mouth, straining to hear. "They were going to kill the...kittens."

Gallagher sucked in his breath in disbelief. "You went through this for a bunch of cats? What is it with you?"

"An old...debt," she managed. "Time to repay." She coughed violently, then moaned as a huge gout of blood spilled down her chin.

"What?"

"Doesn't matter." Her voice was low but surprisingly clear. Suddenly Perdita smiled at him, her face bathed in her own blood like some hideous Halloween mask. "Thanks for everything, Gallagher. Thanks for *trying*."

"Hey, come on," he said softly. He stroked her forehead gently. "Hang in there. The ambulance'll be here in a minute."

Perdita didn't answer. A great, sparkling mist had settled over everything she could see, making Gallagher's face slowly recede behind its thin veil. At its edges, the gold began to deepen as darkness crawled towards its center.

She sucked in air, feeling it sting and bubble in her chest as her heart kept up its stuttering attempt to beat and simply pushed more blood from the gaping hole in her right lung. Somehow she found the strength to touch his cheek. Eyes filled with pain, Gallagher bent so close her crimson-covered lips were nearly touching his ear.

"Thanks again," Perdita tried to whisper. "Time to pay the final bill." But he couldn't understand her words.

And the mist swirled into a smoke-filled cloud.

EPILOGUE
The End of It

EPILOGUE
The End of It

The Dark One sat at the battered formica table, surrounded by the pathetic remains of the woman's last life. This dingy, shabbily-furnished apartment that she had struggled to clean and turn into a home—already the cockroaches had returned, as though they could sense the fact that its occupant was gone for good. Dozens of them gathered in the sink and within the small, forgotten bag of garbage in the far corner of the kitchen. Better still, another hundred or so skittered in hungry circles around the rich stains of blood on the floor, puddles so thick that some were still tacky to the touch beneath the dried outer crusts.

The coroner had removed her body yesterday, and that cop friend of hers, Gallagher, was seeing to it that the county gave her a decent, if inexpensive, burial and had even ordered flowers to be put on her unmarked grave. How touching—Mr. Good Samaritan himself. Plus the cop had taken the whole scrawny bunch of mewling cats home with him. Too bad; the demon could've used a little fun right now. Still, the smell of death and the woman's blood, mingled with the younger, drug-infused blood of the two young men who had so industriously worked at killing her, hung aromatically in the air and he breathed of it deeply.

Abruptly, the creature sitting on the kitchen chair scowled, his eyes sparking sudden red beneath the heavy brows of his V-shaped face while his mouth curved down in an ugly, tooth-rimmed snarl. Damn her! *He* was the one who cheated others, not the reverse! How could this have happened?

He studied his sharp-clawed fingers pensively; he was much the same today as he had been in 1825 when, for recreation alone, he had assumed the shape of a lesser demon and answered her stupid, awkward call. Wallowing in the spilled blood of the old woman's cats had been nothing beyond showy indulgence. How triumphant he had felt at the time—he would have another soul in only a few short years! Nine lives? Not really—only eight, because he had counted the life that Mae Johnson had already lived as the first in the bargain. Admittedly, that had been stretching the deal on his part. And how many years per life? Only one or two at his most generous...except, of course, the one in Chicago that he had let drag out for simple amusement. Each life its own horrible lesson to keep him entertained while he waited—and he so loved to be entertained—and the years passed. Long or short—the time didn't bother him anyway. What was a year, or a decade, or a century? He had eternity.

But the Dark One had miscalculated. He had thought that the proverbial hells-on-earth through which he had put Mae Johnson were simply sport for himself and that he had fulfilled his duty of warning her of the eternity that waited—fair payment for so foolishly selling her so-precious soul. He'd never considered that a higher Power would eventually look with pity upon the woman (or man, as the case had happened to be) as she struggled with each problem that the demon threw her, always trying to do the "right" thing. How stupidly *touching*. Now the creature spat on the floor in disgust, his saliva smoking and sizzling before it abruptly melted away. Why was he the only one who figured the stupid broad was getting what she deserved for bargaining with him to begin with?

He drummed his blackened nails on the table for a moment, then slammed his hand on its top in frustration. The same deceptively delicate–looking fingers that had painted his own face in blood so many years before now cracked the grey formica and caused the metal frame to heave inward with a squeal, leaving the table wobbling on uneven legs. After all that effort, here he sat in this damned, empty apartment with only the leftover smells and creeping cockroaches to ease his appetite.

And she'd told him not to cheat *her*—what a crock. He sighed and decided it was time to leave, move on to a fresher victim.

If you couldn't win the game, why bother to play anymore?

A black idea suddenly spun into his mind and he couldn't help wonder if he might pay dearly for suggesting it. But after a few moments the Dark One realized that yes, it would be allowed, and he let a diabolical grin spread across his angular face. So the spreadsheet was balanced after all! He would be allowed to punish the woman one more time before she escaped into that boring, eternal peace that he himself so loathed and which should have been denied her except for the sappy, forgiving disposition of another more powerful than himself.

Because wasn't it true that despite his assurances to the contrary, he had cheated Mae Johnson way back in the beginning? It really wasn't fair that he'd counted the original life of the old woman as the first of her installments. That life had been done with, lived *before* their deal, and therefore wasn't really…*applicable*. Thus, she deserved that one more life still owed her, had it *coming*, so to speak. Although with her unhealed injuries it would be a short one, he could still give it in return for the life she'd offered for that oldest cat nearly two centuries ago. The Dark One still remembered her last words and that made him grin even wider. One must *always* pay old debts. And the demon would pay his.

Right *NOW!*

If The Dark One could not take the woman's soul with him on his return ride to hell, he could at least cherish for eternity the memory of her terrified, though regrettably short–lived, screams from deep within her cheap coffin.

THE END

Welcome to the DarkTales Community...

DarkTales is more than just a publisher of dark fiction, it's also a web–based community of professional writers, editors, publishers, artists, critics, and fans of outré art and vision.

At the heart of the DarkTales community is an active e–list hosted by Topica at http://www.topica.com. Sign on and prepare yourself for a barrage of emails on a wide range of subjects. With few rules, the DarkTales e–list is recommended for mature subscribers.

Visit the DarkTales website at http://www.darktales.com to learn more about the e–list, upcoming titles, and new DarkTales anthologies currently open to submissions.

...we're bringing horror to the world.

www.darktales.com

Support Your Local Independent Bookseller!

One of our West Coast retail outlets slapped us upside the head a while back, complaining we spread a lot of ink about how to purchase DarkTales titles from our website, while ignoring the existence of the independent bookstores that carry and sell DarkTales titles, lending their support to the whole endeavor. The last thing anyone at DarkTales wants to see is a world completely overrun by the monster booksellers so, given the opportunity, please purchase your DarkTales titles through the independent outlets who have shown us such good support. We'll make a little less money per title, but we'll sleep better at night.

For a current list of DarkTales booksellers, stop by our website at www.darktales.com. If you're a retailer and presently not carrying DarkTales titles, get hip and stop by the website for details and contact information. Dave's ready to take care of you.

As always, the website stands ready to serve customers who can't find a local outlet. Stop by for a list of current titles and order on the spot with your credit card.

DarkTales Novels
$17.99—$19.99

DarkTales brings you the finest novels from established writers like Yvonne Navarro and J. Michael Straczynski, as well as new voices on the scene like Steven Lee Climer and Sephera Giron.

Currently Available
A Darkness Inbred by Victor Heck . . $17.99
Clickers by J.F. Gonzalez
& Mark Williams 19.99
DeadTimes by Yvonne Navarro 19.99
Eternal Sunset by Sephera Giron 17.99
Secret Life of Colors by Steve Savile . .17.99
Tribulations by J. Michael Straczynski . .19.99
Soul Temple by Steven Lee Climer 17.99
Demonesque by Steven Lee Climer . . .17.99

Coming in 2001
Faust: the screenplay by David Quinn
The Shaman Cycle Series by Adam Niswander
A Flock of Crows is Called a Murder
 by Jim Viscosi
Harlan by David Whitman
and more...

Coming in 2002
Eternal Nightmare by Sephera Giron
Dream Thieves by Steven Lee Climer
The Harmony Society by Tim Waggoner
and more...

For a Current List of Titles and Prices visit...

DarkTales Collections and Anthologies
$17.99 each

Currently Available
Moon on the Water by Mort Castle... $17.99
Scary Rednecks by David Whitman
  & Weston Ochse 17.99
The Asylum Vol. 1 ed. by Victor Heck... 17.99

Coming in 2001
The Asylum Vol. 2 ed. by Victor Heck
Six-Inch Spikes by Edo van Belkom
Cold Comfort by Nancy Kilpatrick
Dial Your Dreams by Robert Weinberg
and more...

DarkTales Deluxe Chapbooks—$8.99 each

Currently Available
Holy Rollers by J. Newman
Filthy Death, the Leering Clown
  by Brett A. Savory & Joseph Moore
In Memoriam by Mort Castle
Lifetimes of Blood by Adam Johnson

Coming in 2001
Natural Selection by Weston Ochse
Deadfellas by David Whitman
The Compleat Levesque
  by Richard Levesque
and more...

...www.darktales.com

Order by mail or via the web at:
www.darktales.com

DarkTales Publications
P.O. Box 675
Grandview, MO 64030

Shipping Charges:
$4.95 U.S.; $6.90 Canada; $10.00 overseas
(plus $1.00 per each additional book)

SINISTER ELEMENT

A personal invitation from Alister James:

Sinister Element Online is the best dark zine on the web, published the first of the month, every month, free to all that possess the courage to venture within. Merely partake of the folklore, philosophy, esoterica, and fiction, or participate in its creation—the choice is yours to make.

We're waiting for you. So what the hell are *you* waiting for?

http://www.sinisterelement.com

DeadTimes was initially printed by DarkTales Publications in March, 2000, using Garamond type on 60# offset white. The cover is 10 pt. stock with glossy finish. The book was designed and typeset by Keith Herber, cover design by Kim Thornton. Editorial by Butch Miller. Proofing by Angela Owen and Robert Mingee.